RICK DALTON—Once he had his own TV series, but now Rick's a washed-up villain-of-the-week drowning his sorrows in whiskey sours. Will a phone call from Rome save his fate or seal it?

CLIFF BOOTH—Rick's stunt double, and the most infamous man on any movie set because he's the only one there who might have gotten away with murder. . . .

SHARON TATE—She left Texas to chase a movie-star dream and found it. Sharon's salad days are now spent on Cielo Drive, high in the Hollywood Hills.

CHARLES MANSON—The ex-con's got a bunch of zonked-out hippies thinking he's their spiritual leader, but he'd trade it all to be a rock 'n' roll star.

HOLLYWOOD 1969—

YOU SHOULDA BEEN THERE

Once Upon a Time in Hollywood

COLUMBIA PICTURES PRESENTS

A FILM BY QUENTIN TARANTINO

LEONARDO DICAPRIO   BRAD PITT
MARGOT ROBBIE

IN

ONCE UPON A TIME
IN HOLLYWOOD

MARGARET QUALLEY   TIMOTHY OLYPHANT
JULIA BUTTERS   DAKOTA FANNING   BRUCE DERN

AND

AL PACINO

TECHNICOLOR ®

PRODUCED BY

DAVID HEYMAN   SHANNON MCINTOSH
QUENTIN TARANTINO

WRITTEN AND DIRECTED BY

QUENTIN TARANTINO

Once Upon a Time in Hollywood

A Novel

by Quentin Tarantino

HARPER PERENNIAL PAPERBACK

NEW YORK • LONDON • TORONTO • SYDNEY • NEW DELHI • AUCKLAND

Cover art © Visiona Romantica, Inc. Cover photographs by
Andrew Cooper © L. Driver Productions, Inc.

See permissions to reprint previously published material on page 401.

HarperCollins books may be purchased for educational, business, or sales promotional use. For information, please email
the Special Markets Department at SPsales@harpercollins.com.

FIRST EDITION

Book design by Jen Overstreet

Cover design by Joanne O'Neill

LIBRARY OF CONGRESS CATALOGING-IN-PUBLICATION DATA HAS
BEEN APPLIED FOR.

ISBN 978-0-06-311252-0

21 22 23 24 25 BVGM 10 9 8 7 6 5 4 3 2

This book is dedicated to

My Wife
DANIELLA

and My Son
LEO

Thanks for creating a happy home
from which to write in.

ALSO

To all the actor *Old Timers* who told me
tremendous stories about Hollywood in this period.

And it's because of them that you hold
this book in your hands now.

Bruce Dern * David Carradine * Burt Reynolds
Robert Blake * Michael Parks * Robert Forster
and
especially
Kurt Russell

Once Upon a Time in Hollywood

Chapter One

"Call Me Marvin"

The buzzer on Marvin Schwarz's desk Dictaphone makes a noise. The William Morris agent's finger holds the lever down on the box. "Is that my ten-thirty you're buzzing me about, Miss Himmelsteen?"

"Yes it is, Mr. Schwarz," his secretary's voice pipes out of the tiny speaker. "Mr. Dalton is waiting outside."

Marvin pushes down the lever again. "I'm ready when you are, Miss Himmelsteen."

When the door to Marvin's office opens, his young secretary, Miss Himmelsteen, steps in first. She's a twenty-one-year-old woman of the hippie persuasion. She sports a white miniskirt that shows off her long tan legs and wears her long brown hair in Pocahontas-style pigtails that hang down each side of her head. The handsome forty-two-year-old actor Rick Dalton, and his de rigueur glistening wet brown pompadour, follow behind her.

Marvin's smile grows wide as he stands up from the chair behind his desk. Miss Himmelsteen tries to do the introductions, but Marvin cuts her off. "Miss Himmelsteen, since I just finished watching a Rick Dalton fuckin' film festival, no need to introduce this man to me." Marvin crosses the distance between them, sticking out his hand for the cowboy actor to shake. "Put 'er there, Rick."

Rick smiles and gives the agent's hand a big pumping shake. "Rick Dalton. Thank you very much, Mr. Schwartz, for taking the time to meet me."

Marvin corrects him. "It's *Schwarz*, not Schwartz."

Jesus Christ, I'm fuckin' this whole thing up already, Rick thinks.

"Goddammit to hell . . . I'm sorry about that . . . *Mr. Sch-WARZ.*"

As Mr. Schwarz does a final shake of the hand, he says, "Call me Marvin."

"Marvin, call me Rick."

"Rick . . ."

They let go of each other's hand.

"Can Miss Himmelsteen get you a tasty beverage?"

Rick waves the offer away. "No, I'm fine."

Marvin insists. "Are you sure, nothing? Coffee, Coke, Pepsi, Simba?"

"Alright," Rick says. "Maybe a cup of coffee."

"Good." Clapping the actor on his shoulder, Marvin turns to his young girl Friday. "Miss Himmelsteen, would you be so kind as to get my friend Rick here a cup of coffee, and I'll have one myself."

The young lady nods her head in the affirmative and crosses the length of the office. As she starts to close the door behind her, Marvin yells after her, "Oh, and none of that Maxwell House rotgut they got in the break room. Go

2

to Rex's office," Marvin instructs. "He's always got the class-iest coffee—but none of that Turkish shit," Marvin warns.

"Yes, sir," Miss Himmelsteen answers, then turns to Rick. "How do you take your coffee, Mr. Dalton?"

Rick turns to her and says, "Haven't you heard? Black is beautiful."

Marvin lets out a Klaxon-like guffaw, while Miss Himmelsteen covers her mouth with her hand as she giggles. Before his secretary can close the door behind her, Marvin yells out, "Oh, and Miss Himmelsteen, short of my wife and kids dead on the highway, hold all my calls. In fact, if my wife and kids are dead, well, they'll all be just as dead thirty minutes from now, so hold all my calls."

The agent gestures for the actor to sit on one of two leather sofas that face each other, a glass-top coffee table in between, and Rick makes himself comfortable.

"First things first," the agent says. "I send you greetings from my wife, Mary Alice Schwarz! We had a Rick Dalton double feature in our screening room last night."

"Wow. That's both flattering and embarrassing," Rick says. "What did ya see?"

"Film prints of *Tanner* and *The Fourteen Fists of McCluskey*."

"Well, them are two of the good ones," Rick says. "*McCluskey* was directed by Paul Wendkos. He's my favorite of all my directors. He made *Gidget*. I was supposed to be in that. Tommy Laughlin got my part." But then he magnani-mously waves it away. "But that's okay, I like Tommy. He got me in the first big play I ever did."

"Really?" Marvin asks. "You've done a lot of theater?"

"Not much," he says. "I get bored doing the same shit again and again."

"So Paul Wendkos is your favorite director, huh?" Marvin asks.

"Yeah, I started out with him in my early days. I'm in his Cliff Robertson picture, *Battle of the Coral Sea*. You can see me and Tommy Laughlin hangin' out in the back of the submarine the whole damn picture."

Marvin makes one of his declarative industry statements: "Paul-fuckin'-Wendkos. *Underrated action specialist*."

"Very true," Rick agrees. "And when I landed *Bounty Law*, he came on and directed about seven or eight episodes."

"So," Rick asks, fishing for a compliment, "I hope the Rick Dalton double feature wasn't too painful for you and the Mrs.?"

Marvin laughs. "Painful? Stop. Wonderful, wonderful, wonderful." Marvin continues, "So Mary Alice and I watched *Tanner*. Mary Alice doesn't like the violence in modern movies these days, so I saved *McCluskey* to watch by myself after she went to bed."

Then there's a small tap on the office door, just before the miniskirt-wearing Miss Himmelsteen enters the office, carrying two cups of steaming coffee for Rick and Marvin. She carefully hands the hot beverages to the two gentlemen.

"This is from Rex's office, right?"

"Rex said you owe him one of your cigars."

The agent snorts. "That cheap Jew bastard, the only thing I owe him is a hard time."

Everybody laughs.

"Thank you, Miss Himmelsteen; that will be all for now."

4

She exits, leaving the two men alone to discuss the entertainment business, Rick Dalton's career, and, more important, his future.

"Where was I?" Marvin asks. "Oh yeah—violence in modern movies. Mary Alice doesn't like it. But she loves westerns. Always has. We saw westerns all through our courtship. Watching westerns together is one of our favorite things to do, and we thoroughly enjoyed *Tanner.*"

"Awww, that's nice," Rick says.

"Now when we do these double features," Marvin explains, "by the last three reels of the first film, Mary Alice is asleep in my lap. But for *Tanner,* she made it to just before the last reel—which was nine-thirty—which is pretty good for Mary Alice."

As Marvin explains to Rick the movie-viewing habits of the happy couple, Rick takes a sip of the hot coffee.

Hey, that's good, the actor thinks. *This Rex fella does have classy coffee.*

Marvin continues, "Movie's over, she goes to bed. I open up a box of Havana's, pour myself a cognac, and watch the second movie by myself."

Rick takes another sip of Rex's delicious coffee.

Marvin points at the coffee cup. "Good stuff, huh?"

"What," Rick asks, "the coffee?"

"No, the pastrami. Of course the coffee," Marvin says, with Catskill timing.

"It's fuckin' sensational," Rick agrees. "Where does he get it?"

"One of these delicatessens here in Beverly Hills, but he won't say which one," Marvin says, then continues with

5

Mary Alice's viewing habits. "This morning after breakfast and after I leave for the office, the projectionist, Greg, comes back and screens the last reel so she can see how the picture ends. And that's our movie-watching routine. We're very happy about it. And she was very much looking forward to seeing how *Tanner* ends."

Then Marvin adds, "However, she's already figured out you're gonna hafta kill your father, Ralph Meeker, before it's all over."

"Well, yeah, that's the problem with the movie," Rick says. "It ain't *if* I kill the domineering patriarch, it's *when*. And it ain't *if* Michael Callan, the sensitive brother, kills me—it's *when*."

Marvin agrees. "True. But both of us thought you and Ralph Meeker matched up pretty well together."

"Yeah, me too," Rick replies. "We *did* make a good father-and-son team. That fuckin' Michael Callan looked like he was adopted. But with me, you could believe Ralph was my old man."

"Well, the reason you matched up so well together was you two shared a similar dialect."

Rick laughs. "Especially when compared to fuckin' Michael Callan, who sounded like he should be surfing in Malibu."

Okay, Marvin thinks, that's the second time Rick has put down his *Tanner* co-star Michael Callan. That's not a good sign. It suggests stinginess in spirit. It suggests a blamer. But Marvin keeps these thoughts to himself.

"I thought Ralph Meeker was sensational," Rick tells the agent. "The best damn actor I ever worked with, and I've worked with Edward G. Robinson! He was also in two of the best *Bounty Law*'s."

Marvin continues recounting his Rick Dalton double feature from the night before. "Which brings us to *The Fourteen Fists of McCluskey*! What a picture! So much fun." He pantomimes shooting a machine gun. "All the shooting! All the killing!" Marvin asks, "How many Nazi bastards you kill in that picture? A hundred? A hundred and fifty?"

Rick laughs. "I never counted, but a hundred and fifty sounds right."

Marvin curses them to himself. "Fuckin' Nazi bastards . . . That's you operating the flamethrower, ain't it?"

"You bet your sweet ass it is," Rick says. "And that's one shit-fuck crazy weapon you do not want to be on the wrong side of, boy oh boy, let me tell you. I practiced with that dragon three hours a day for two weeks. Not just so I'd look good in the picture, but because I was shit scared of the damn thing, to tell you the truth."

"Extraordinary," says the impressed agent.

"You know, it was just sheer luck I got my role," Rick tells Marvin. "Originally, Fabian had my part. Then eight days before shootin' he breaks his shoulder doin' a *Virginian*. Mr. Wendkos remembered me, talked the brass over at Columbia into getting Universal to loan me out to do *McCluskey*." Rick concludes the story the way he always does: "So I do five movies during my contract with Universal. My most successful film? My Columbia loan-out."

Marvin removes a gold cigarette case from his inside jacket pocket, pops it open with a *ping*. Offers one to Rick. "Care for a Kent?"

Rick takes one.

"Do you like this cigarette case?"

"It's very nice."

"It's a gift. From Joseph Cotten. One of my most cherished clients."

Rick gives Marvin the impressed expression the agent is demanding.

"I recently got him both a Sergio Corbucci picture and an Ishirō Honda picture, and this was a token of his gratitude."

Those names mean nothing to Rick.

As Mr. Schwarz slips the gold cigarette case back in the inside pocket of his jacket, Rick quickly digs his cigarette lighter out of his pants pocket. Snaps open the lid of the silver Zippo and lights both smokes in his cool-guy way. When he's done lighting both cigarettes, he snaps the lid of the Zippo closed with loud panache. Marvin chuckles at the show of bravado, then inhales the nicotine.

"What do you smoke?" Marvin asks Rick.

"Capitol W Lights," Rick says. "But also Chesterfields, Red Apples, and, don't laugh, Virginia Slims."

Marvin laughs anyway.

"Hey, I like the taste," is Rick's defense.

"I'm laughing at you smoking Red Apples," Marvin explains. "That cigarette is a sin against nicotine."

"They were the sponsor of *Bounty Law*, so I got used to them. Also, I thought it was smart to be seen smoking them in public."

"Very wise," Marvin says. "Now, Rick, Sid's your regular agent. And he asked me would I meet you."

Rick nods his head.

"Do you know why he asked me to get together with you?"

"To see if you wanted to work with me?" Rick answers.

Marvin laughs. "Well, ultimately, yes. But what I'm getting at is, do you know what I do here at William Morris?"

"Yeah," Rick says. "You're an agent."

"Yeah, but you already got Sid as your agent. If I was *just* an agent, you wouldn't be here," Marvin says.

"Yeah, you're a special agent," Rick says.

"Indeed I am," Marvin says. Then, pointing at Rick with his smoking cigarette, "But I want *you* to tell *me* what it is you think I do."

"Well," Rick says, "the way it was explained to me is you put famous American talent in foreign films."

"Not bad," Marvin says.

Now that the two gentlemen are on the same page, both take big drags off their Kents. Marvin exhales a long stream of cigarette smoke and goes into his spiel: "Now, Rick, if we get to know one another, one of the first things about me you'll learn is *nothing* . . . and I mean *nothing*, is as important to me as my client list. The reason I have the contacts I have in the Italian film industry, and the German film industry, and the Japanese film industry, and the Filipino film industry, is both because of the clients I represent and what my client list represents. Unlike others, I am not in the *has-been business.* I am in the *Hollywood-royalty business.* Van Johnson—Joseph Cotten—Farley Granger—Russ Tamblyn—Mel Ferrer."

The agent says each name as if he's reciting the names of the faces carved on Hollywood's Mount Rushmore.

"Hollywood royalty with a filmography peppered with all-time classics!"

The agent gives a legendary example: "When a drunk Lee Marvin dropped out of the role of Colonel Mortimer in *For a Few Dollars More*—three weeks before filming—it was *me* who got Sergio Leone to take his fat ass to the Sportsmen's Lodge and have coffee with a newly clean-and-sober Lee Van Cleef."

The agent lets the magnitude of that story settle in the room. Then, taking a nonchalant drag off his Kent, he blows out the smoke and adds another one of his declarative industry statements: "And the rest, as they say, is *new world western mythology*."

Marvin zeroes in on the cowboy actor across the glass table. "Now, Rick, *Bounty Law* was a good show, and you were good on it. A lot of folks come to town and get famous for doing shit. Ask Gardner McKay."

Rick laughs at the Gardner McKay dig. Marvin continues, "But *Bounty Law* was a totally decent cowboy show. And you have that and you can be proud of that. But now, on to the future. . . . But before the future, let's get a little history straight."

As the two men smoke cigarettes, Marvin begins quizzing Rick as if he's either on a game show or being interrogated by the FBI.

"So, *Bounty Law*—that was NBC, right?"

"Yep. NBC."

"How long?"

"How long what?"

"How long was the show?"

"Well, it was a half-hour show, so twenty-three minutes with commercials."

"And how long did it last?"

"We started in the fall schedule of the '59–'60 television season."

"And when did you go off the air?"

"The middle of the '63–'64 season."

"Didja ever go to color?"

"Didn't make color."

"How'd you get the show? You come in off the street, or did the network groom you?"

"I had guested on a *Tales of Wells Fargo*. I played Jesse James."

"So that's what got their attention?"

"Yes. I still had to screen test. And I had better be fucking good. But yes."

"Go through the details of the movies you did during your hiatus?"

"Well, the first one," Rick says, "was *Comanche Uprising*, starring a very old, very ugly Robert Taylor. But that became a theme in almost all my motion pictures," Rick explains. "Old guy paired with a young guy. Me and Robert Taylor. Me and Stewart Granger. Me and Glenn Ford. There was never just *me* on my own," says the actor, frustrated. "It was always me and some old fuck."

Marvin asks, "Who directed *Comanche Uprising*?"

"Bud Springsteen."

Marvin makes an observation: "I noticed on your résumé

you worked with a helluva lot of those old Republic Pictures cowboy directors—Springsteen, William Witney, Harmon Jones, John English?"

Rick laughs. "The get-it-done guys." Then he clarifies, "But Bud Springsteen wasn't just a get-it-done guy. Bud didn't *just* get it done. Bud was different than those others."

That interests Marvin. "What was the difference?"

"Huh?" Rick asks.

"Bud and the other get-it-done guys," Marvin asks. "What was the difference?"

Rick doesn't have to think about his answer, because he figured this out years ago when guesting on *Whirlybirds* with Craig Hill, helmed by Bud.

"Bud had the same amount of time as all the rest of those goddamn directors," Rick says with authority. "Not one day, not one hour, not one sunset more than anybody else. But it was what he *did* with that time that made Bud good." Rick says sincerely, "You were proud to work for Bud."

Marvin likes that.

"And goddamn Wild Bill Witney gave me my start," Rick says. "He gave me my first real part. You know, a character with a name. Then he gave me my first lead."

"What film?" Marvin asks.

"Oh, just one of those juvenile-delinquent hot rod flicks for Republic," Rick says.

Marvin asks, "What was the title?"

"*Drag Race, No Stop*," says Rick. "And I did a goddamn Ron Ely *Tarzan* for him just this last year."

Marvin laughs. "So you two go back a long way?"

"Me and Bill?" Rick says. "You bet."

Rick's getting into his reminiscing and he sees it's going over well too, so he leans into it. "Let me tell ya 'bout goddamn Bill Witney. The single most underrated action director in this goddamn town. Bill Witney didn't just direct action, he *invented* directing action. You said you like westerns—you know that whole Yakima Canutt action gag where he jumps from horse to horse, then falls and goes under the hooves, in John Ford's fuckin' *Stagecoach*?"

Marvin nods his head yes.

"William *fuckin'* Witney did it *fuckin'* first, and did it one year before John Ford, *with* Yakima Canutt!"

"I didn't know that," Marvin says. "What picture?"

"He hadn't even made a feature yet," Rick tells him. "He did that gag for some fuckin' serial. Let me tell you what it is like being directed by William Witney. Bill Witney works under the assumption that there was no scene ever written that couldn't be improved by the addition of a fistfight."

Marvin laughs.

Rick continues, "So I'm doing a *Riverboat*, with Bill directing. Me and Burt Reynolds in the scene. So me and Burt are doing the scene, sayin' the dialogue. Then Bill goes, 'Cut, cut, cut! You guys are puttin' me to sleep. Burt, when he says that to you, you punch him. And, Rick, when he punches you, that makes you mad, so you punch him back. Got it? Okay, action!' And so we do it. And when we get done, he yells, 'Cut! That's it, boys, now we got a scene!'"

The two men laugh inside the cloud of cigarette smoke that's filling up the office. Marvin's starting to warm up to Rick's sense of hard-earned Hollywood experience. "So tell

13

me about this Stewart Granger film you mentioned?" Marvin asks.

"*Big Game*," Rick says. "An African-great-white-hunter piece of crap. They were walking out of it on airplanes."

Marvin guffaws.

Rick informs the agent, "Stewart Granger was the single biggest prick I ever worked with. And I've worked with Jack Lord!"

After the two men chuckle over the Jack Lord dig, Marvin asks the actor, "And you did a picture with George Cukor?"

"Yeah," Rick says, "a real dog called *The Chapman Report*. Great director, terrible picture."

The agent asks, "How did you get along with Cukor?"

"Are you kidding," Rick asks, "George fucking loved me!" Then he leans a bit over the coffee table and says insinuatingly, in a lower voice, "I mean, *really loved me*."

The agent smiles, letting the actor know he gets the insinuation.

"I think that's a thing George does," Rick speculates, "He picks a boy on each movie to go ga-ga over. And on that picture it was between me and Efrem Zimbalist Jr., so I guess I won." He goes on to illustrate, "So in that picture all my scenes are with Glynis Johns. And we go to a pool. So Glynis is in a one-piece swimsuit. All you can see is legs and arms, everything else is covered up. But me, I'm in the teeny-tiniest pair of swim trunks the censors will allow. Tan swim trunks. On black-and-white film, it looks like I'm fucking naked! And it's not just a shot of me jumping in the pool. I'm in these tiny trunks, doing big dialogue scenes with my ass

14

hanging out, for ten minutes of the fuckin' movie. I mean, what the fuck—am I Betty Grable over here?"

Again the two men laugh, as Marvin removes a small leather notebook from the opposite inside jacket pocket of the one containing Joseph Cotten's gold cigarette case.

"I had a few of my satellites look up your statistics in Europe. And as they say, so far so good." Searching for the notes in the little book, he asks out loud, "Did *Bounty Law* air in Europe?" He finds the page he's looking for, then looks from the page to Rick. "Yes, it did. Good."

Rick smiles.

Marvin looks back down at the book and says, "Where?" searching the page and finding the data he's looking for. "Italy, good. England, good. Germany, good. No France." But then he looks up at Rick and says as consolation, "But, yes, Belgium. So they know who you are in Italy, England, Germany, and Belgium." Marvin concludes, "So that's your TV show. But you've done a few flicks, so how did they do?"

Marvin looks back down at the little book in his hands, flipping through the little pages, searching its contents. "Actually"—finding what he's looking for—"All three of your westerns, *Comanche Uprising*, *Hellfire*, *Texas*, and *Tanner*, did relatively well in Italy, France, and Germany." Looking back up to Rick: "With *Tanner* doing even better than that in France. Can you read French?" Marvin asks Rick.

"No," Rick answers.

"Too bad," Marvin says as he removes a folded-up Xerox page stuck in the little notebook and hands it across the coffee table to Rick. "This is the *Cahiers du Cinéma* review of

Tanner. It's a good review, very well written. You should get it translated."

Rick takes the Xerox from Marvin, nodding at the agent's suggestion, though the actor knows full well he'll never do that.

But then Marvin raises his head to meet Rick's eyes and says, suddenly enthusiastic, "But the best news in this whole fuckin' book: *The Fourteen Fists of McCluskey*!"

Rick's face lights up as Marvin continues, "Now, in America, that did okay for Columbia when it was released. But in Europe, *Fuck me!*" He lowers his head to read the information in front of him. "Says here *The Fourteen Fists of McCluskey* was a fuckin' smash all over Europe. Played everywhere and played for fuckin' ever!"

Marvin looks up, closes his little book, and concludes, "So in Europe, they know who you are. They know your TV show. But even more than the guy from *Bounty Law*, in Europe, you're the cool guy with the eye patch and the flamethrower that kills a hundred and fifty Nazis in *The Fourteen Fists of McCluskey*."

After making that huge statement, Marvin grinds his Kent out in the ashtray. "What was your last theatrical feature?"

Now it's Rick's turn to grind out his cigarette in the ashtray, as he grunts, "A horrible children's movie made for the kiddie matinee crowd, called *Salty, the Talking Sea Otter*."

Marvin smiles. "I take it you are not the title character?"

Rick smiles grimly at the agent's joke, but nothing about that movie does he find funny.

"That was the film Universal dumped me in to finish

my four-picture contract," Rick explains. "Which just goes to show how much Universal gave a fuck about me. I remember that prick, Jennings Lang, selling me a whole bill of goods. Luring me over to Universal with a four-picture deal. I had Avco Embassy offering me a deal. National General Pictures offering me a deal. Irving Allen Productions offered me a deal. I turned them all down and went with Universal because they were the major. And because Jennings Lang told me, 'Universal wants to be in the Rick Dalton business.' After I signed up, I never saw that prick again." Referring to the time *Invasion of the Body Snatchers* producer Walter Wanger shot Jennings Lang in the groin for fucking his wife, Joan Bennett, "If anybody deserved to get their balls shot off, it's that prick Jennings Lang." Adding bitterly, "Universal was *never* in the Rick Dalton business."

Rick picks up his coffee cup and takes a sip. It's gone cold. He puts it back down on the table with a sigh.

Marvin continues, "So for the last two years you've been doing guest shots on episodic TV shows?"

Rick nods his head in the affirmative. "Yeah, I'm doing a pilot for CBS right now, *Lancer*. I'm the heavy. I did a *Green Hornet*. A *Land of the Giants*. A Ron Ely *Tarzan*, the one I mentioned I did with William Witney. I did that show *Bingo Martin* with that kid Scott Brown."

Rick doesn't like Scott Brown, so when he mentions his name, he subconsciously gives a dismissive look. "And I just finished an *FBI* for Quinn Martin."

Marvin sips his coffee, even though it's gone a little cool. "So you've been doing pretty good?"

"I been working," Rick says as if to clarify.

17

"Did you play the bad guy in all these shows?" Marvin asks.

"Not *Land of the Giants*, but the rest, yeah."

"Did they all end in fight scenes?"

"Again, not *Land of the Giants* or *The FBI*, but the rest, yeah."

"Now the sixty-four-thousand-dollar question." Marvin asks, "Did you lose the fight?"

"Of course," Rick says. "I'm the heavy."

Marvin lets out a big "ahhhhh" to make his point. "That's an old trick pulled by the networks. Take *Bingo Martin*, for example. So you got a new guy like Scott Brown and you wanna build up his bona fides. So you hire a guy from a canceled show to play the heavy. Then at the end of the show, when they fight, it's *hero* besting *heavy*."

But then Marvin goes on to explain, "But what the audience sees is *Bingo Martin* whippin' the guy from *Bounty Law's* ass."

Ouch, thinks Rick. *That fuckin' smarted.*

But Marvin's not done. "Then next week, it's Ron Ely in his loincloth. And the week after that, it's Bob Conrad in his tight pants kickin' your ass." Marvin drives his right fist into the palm of his left hand for effect. "Another coupla years playin' punchin' bag to every swingin' dick new to the network," Marvin explains, "is going to have a psychological effect on how the audience perceives you."

The masculine humiliation of what Marvin's suggesting, even though he's only referring to playacting, is making Rick's brow perspire. *I'm a punching bag? Is this my career now? Losing fights to this season's new swingin' dick? Is that how*

18

Tris Coffin, star of 26 Men, felt when he lost his fight to me on Bounty Law? Or Kent Taylor?

While Rick dwells on this, Marvin moves on to another subject.

"Now, I've had at least four people tell me a story about you," Schwarz starts, "but none of them know the whole story, so I want you to tell me." Marvin asks, "What's this about you *almost* playing the McQueen role in *The Great Escape*?"

Oh Christ, not this fucking story again, thinks Rick. Though completely unamused, he laughs it off for Marvin's benefit. "It's only a good story for the Sportsmen's Lodge crowd." Rick chuckles, "You know, the part you almost got. The fish that got away."

"Those are my favorite stories," the agent says. "Tell me."

Rick has had to tell this shaggy-dog story so much, he's reduced it down to its basic elements. Swallowing his resentment, Rick plays the part that's a little out of his range: a humble actor.

"Well," Rick begins, "apparently, at the same time that John Sturges offered McQueen the title role of Hilts, the Cooler King, in *The Great Escape*, Carl Foreman"—referencing the powerhouse writer-producer of *The Guns of Navarone* and *The Bridge on the River Kwai*—"was making his directorial debut with a film called *The Victors*, and he offered McQueen one of the lead roles, and, apparently, McQueen vacillated so much, Sturges was forced to draw up a list of possible replacements for the character. And, *apparently*, I was on the list."

Marvin asks, "Who else was on the list?"

"Four names on the list," Rick says. "Me and the three Georges: Peppard, Maharis, and Chakiris."

"Well," Marvin enthusiastically insists, "outta that list, I can totally see you getting it. I mean, if Paul Newman was on the list, maybe not, but the fucking Georges?"

"Well, McQueen did it." Rick shrugs. "So what does it matter?"

"No," Marvin insists, "it's a good story. We can see you in the role. The Italians will love it!" Marvin Schwarz then explains to Rick Dalton how the genre film industry in Italy operates.

"McQueen won't work with the Italians, no matter what. *Fuck the fucking wops*, that's what Steve says. *Tell 'em to get Bobby Darin*, that's what fucking Steve says. He'll work for nine months in Indochina with Robert Wise but won't work two months at Cinecittà with Guido DeFatso for any amount of money."

If I were in Steve's position, I wouldn't waste my time in a shitty wop western either, Rick thinks to himself.

Marvin continues, "Dino De Laurentiis offered to buy him a villa in Florence. Italian producers offered him a half a million dollars and a new Ferrari for ten days' work on a Gina Lollobrigida picture." Then Marvin adds as an aside, "Not to mention the pretty-much-for-sure Lollobrigida pussy to go along with it."

Rick and Marvin laugh. *Well, that's a different story*, Rick thinks. *I'd make any movie ever made if I thought I could fuck Anita Ekberg.*

"But," Marvin says, "that just makes the Italians want him more. So even though Steve always says no, and Brando

20

always says no, and Warren Beatty always says no, the Italians keep trying. And when they can't get 'em, they settle."

"They *settle*?" Rick repeats.

Marvin illustrates further: "They *want* Marlon Brando; they *get* Burt Reynolds. They *want* Warren Beatty; they *get* George Hamilton."

As Rick endures Marvin's career postmortem, he can feel the burning, stinging sensation of tears starting to build behind his eyeballs.

Marvin, oblivious to Rick's anguish, finishes, "I'm not saying the Italians don't *want* you. I'm saying the Italians *will* want you. But the reason they *want* you is they *want* McQueen but they can't *get* McQueen. And when they finally realize they're not going to *get* McQueen, they're gonna *want* a McQueen they can *get*. And that's you."

The glaring, brutal honesty of the agent's words shock Rick Dalton as much as if Marvin had slapped him across the face as hard as he could with a dripping-wet hand.

However, from Marvin's perspective, this is all good news. If Rick Dalton was a popular leading man in studio features, he wouldn't be having a meeting with Marvin Schwarz.

Besides, it was Rick who asked to meet Marvin. It's Rick who wants to extend his leading-man career in feature films rather than playing bad guy du jour on television. And it's Marvin's job to explain to him the realities and the possible opportunities of a film industry he doesn't know shit about. An industry that Marvin is an acknowledged expert in. And in Marvin's expert opinion, Rick Dalton being *like* one of the biggest movie stars in the whole wide world is a wonderful opportunity for an agent who places name American talent in Italian motion pictures. So he's understandably puzzled when he notices tears running down Rick Dalton's cheeks.

"Whatsamatter, kid?" the startled agent asks. "You cryin'?"

An upset and embarrassed Rick Dalton wipes at his eyes with the back of his hand and says, "I'm sorry, Mr. Schwarz, I apologize."

Marvin grabs a box of tissues off his desk and offers it to Rick, consoling the weepy thespian. "Sorry nothing. We all get upset every once in a while. Life is hard."

Rick yanks out two Kleenexes from the box, with a harsh ripping sound. As macho as he can muster under the circumstances, he wipes his eyes with the tissue paper. "I'm okay now, just embarrassed. Sorry about this humiliating display."

"Display?" Marvin snorts. "What are you talking about? We're human people; human people cry. It's a good thing."

Rick finishes wiping away the wetness and puts a phony smile on his face. "See, all better. Sorry 'bout that."

"Sorry about nothing," Marvin admonishes. "You are an actor. Actors have to be able to access their emotions. We need our actors to cry. Sometimes that facility comes at a cost. Now tell me, what's the matter?"

Rick composes himself and then says after a gulp of oxygen, "It's just I've been doing this over ten years, Mr. Schwarz. And it's a little hard to sit here after all that time and come face-to-face with what a failure I've become. Coming face-to-face with how I ran my career in the ground."

Marvin doesn't understand. "What do you mean, failure?"

Rick looks across the coffee table and tells the agent sincerely, "You know, Mr. Schwarz, once upon a time, I *had* potential. I did. You can see it in some of my work. You can see it on *Bounty Law*. Especially when I had solid guest stars. When it's me and Bronson, and me and Coburn, and me and Meeker, or me and Vic Morrow. I had something! But the studio kept puttin' me in flicks with faded old fucks. But me and Chuck Heston? That'd been different. Me and Richard Widmark, me and Mitchum, me and Hank Fonda, that'd been different! And in some of the movies, it's there. Me and Meeker in *Tanner*. Me and Rod Taylor in *McCluskey*. Shit, even me and Glenn Ford in *Hellfire, Texas*. By that time Ford didn't give a fuck no more, but he still *looked* strong as hell, and *we* looked good together. So yeah, I *had* potential. But whatever potential I *had*, that prick Jennings Lang at Universal pissed it away."

Then the actor exhales a defeated, dramatic breath and says to the floor, "Hell, even I pissed it away."

He looks up and meets the eyes of the agent. "I totally pissed away a fourth season of *Bounty Law*. 'Cause I was done with TV. I wanted to be a movie star. I wanted to catch Steve McQueen. If he could do it, I could do it. If during the entire third season I hadn't been an uncooperative pain in the ass, we would've sailed into a fourth season. And we coulda all done well and all parted friends. Now Screen Gems hates me. Those goddamn *Bounty Law* producers are gonna hold a grudge against me for the rest of their lives. And I deserve it! I was a prick on that last season. I let everybody goddamn know I had better places to be than this fuckin' pipsqueak TV show." Rick's starting to get teary-eyed again. "Doin' that

23

show *Bingo Martin*, I hated that prick Scott Brown. Now, I was never as bad as him. You can ask the actors I worked with, you can ask the directors I worked with, I was never as bad as him. And I've worked with pricks before. But the reason *this* prick got to me? I saw how ungrateful he was. And when I saw that, I saw myself."

He looks at the floor again and says with sincere self-pity, "Maybe gittin' the snot wiped outta me by this season's new swingin' dick is what I got comin'."

Marvin listens to the whole explosion that bursts forth from Rick Dalton with his mouth closed and his ears open. After a moment, the agent says, "Mr. Dalton, you're not the first young actor to land a series and fall under the spell of hubris. In fact, it's a common ailment out here. And—look at me—"

Rick raises his eyes to the agent's eyes.

Marvin finishes, "It's forgivable."

Then Marvin smiles at the actor. The actor smiles back.

"But," the agent adds, "it does require a bit of reinvention."

"What do I hafta reinvent myself as?" Rick asks.

Marvin answers, "Somebody humble."

Chapter Two

"I Am Curious (Cliff)"

Rick Dalton's stunt double, forty-six-year-old Cliff Booth, sits in the waiting room of Marvin Schwarz's office on the third floor of the William Morris Agency building, leafing through an oversized copy of *Life* magazine that the agent provides those who wait.

Cliff wears tight Levi's blue jeans and a matching Levi's blue jeans jacket over a black T-shirt. This outfit is a leftover costume from a low-budget biker flick that Cliff worked on three years earlier. Actor-director Tom Laughlin, an old buddy of Rick's and a friend of Cliff's (they all did *The Fourteen Fists of McCluskey* together), had hired Cliff to stunt-double a couple of biker characters in a motorcycle movie he was starring in and directing, *The Born Losers*, for American International Pictures (it would end up being AIP's biggest hit of the year). In the film, Laughlin would play, for the first time, the character that would make him one of the most popular pop-culture movie characters of the seventies, Billy Jack. Billy Jack was a half-breed American Indian–Vietnam veteran–hapkido expert who didn't mind demonstrating it on the violent biker gang known in the movie as the Born Losers (a stand-in for the Hells Angels).

Cliff's job was to double one of the gang members known as Gangrene, played by David Carradine's old buddy Jeff Cooper, who Cliff kind of looked like. However, during the last week of the shoot, Tom's stunt double dislocated his elbow (not performing a gag but skateboarding on his day off). So Cliff filled in doubling for Tom that whole last week of the shoot.

At the end of the shoestring production, when given a choice between seventy-five dollars or keeping the Billy Jack wardrobe—leather boots included—Cliff opted for the outfit.

Four years later Tom Laughlin would star in and direct the movie *Billy Jack* for Warner Bros. Laughlin would be disappointed by how the studio marketed the picture. He would buy back the rights himself, then sell it state by state, market by market, like an old carny promoter. Laughlin four-walled movie theaters and flooded the local TV stations with enticingly cut TV spots aimed at kids watching television in the afternoon after school. Laughlin's maverick distribution innovations, along with his having made a pretty terrific movie, made *Billy Jack* one of the biggest sleeper success stories in the history of Hollywood. And once that happened, Cliff's blue-jeans wardrobe became so identified with the high-kicking hero that he had to stop wearing it.

While Miss Himmelsteen sits behind her desk in the outer office answering the telephone ("Mr. Schwarz's office," pause, "I'm sorry, he's with a client right now, can I ask who's calling?"), Cliff sits on the colorful uncomfortable couch by her desk, huge *Life* magazine laid out on his lap, leafing through the pages. He's just finished reading Richard Schickel's review of the new Swedish film that has all of America's puritans and many of their newspaper-based opinion makers in a tizzy. This new movie has both Johnny Carson *and* Joey Bishop, as well as every comedian from Jerry Lewis to Moms Mabley, making puns out of its catchy title.

From the couch, Cliff calls to Miss Himmelsteen behind her desk, "Have you heard of this flick from Sweden, *I Am Curious (Yellow)?*"

"Yeah, I think I have," Miss Himmelsteen says. "It's supposed to be dirty, isn't it?"

"Not according to the U.S. Court of Appeals it ain't," Cliff informs her.

Reading directly from the magazine, Cliff recites, "'Pornography is a work lacking in redeeming social value.' And according to Judge Paul R. Hays, 'Whether or not we ourselves consider the ideas of the picture particularly interesting or the production artistically successful, it is quite certain that *I Am Curious* does present ideas and does strive to present those ideas artistically.'"

He lowers the huge magazine and meets eyes with the pigtailed young thing sitting behind her desk.

Miss Himmelsteen asks, "What does that mean, exactly?"

"*Exactly,*" Cliff repeats, "it means the Swedish guy who made it wasn't just making a fuck film. He was *trying* to make art. And it doesn't matter if you think he was a total failure. And it doesn't matter if you think it's the biggest piece of shit you've ever seen in your life. What *matters* is he tried to make art. He didn't try and make smut." Then, smiling and shrugging his shoulders: "At least that's what I get out of this review."

"Sounds provocative," the young pigtailed lass remarks.

"I agree," Cliff agrees. "Wanna go see it with me?"

A sarcastic smirk spreads across Miss Himmelsteen's face, as she asks with just the right touch of Jewish comic timing, "You wanna take me to a dirty movie?"

"No," Cliff corrects. "According to Judge Paul-something-Hays, I just want to take you to a Swedish film. Where do you live?"

Before she can stop herself, she instinctively answers, "Brentwood."

"Well, I'm pretty familiar with the cinemas around the Los Angeles area," Cliff informs her. "Will you allow me to choose the theater?"

Janet Himmelsteen is well aware she hasn't even agreed to go on a date with Cliff yet. But both she and Cliff know she's going to say yes. Now, William Morris has a rule against miniskirt-wearing secretaries dating their clients. But this guy ain't a client. Rick Dalton's the client. This guy is just one of Rick's buddies.

"You choose," says the young lady.

"Wise choice," says the older man.

They both share a laugh as Marvin's office door swings open and Rick Dalton in his tan leather jacket emerges from the agent's office.

Cliff quickly stands up from Marvin's uncomfortable couch and throws his eyes toward his boss, to read the demeanor of the meeting he just completed. And since Rick looks a little sweaty and a little distraught, Cliff figures the meeting didn't go so hot.

"You okay?" Cliff softly asks.

"Yeah, I'm fine," Rick says briskly. "Let's just get out of here."

"Sure thing," Cliff says. Then the stuntman Cliff spins on his back heel, till he's facing Janet Himmelsteen, his movement so quick it startles her. She doesn't make a noise, but she does instinctively flinch. Now that Cliff is standing directly in front of her (over her, actually), smiling like a blond Levi-clad Huck Finn, Miss Himmelsteen sees how truly handsome this guy really is. "Opens this Wednesday," Cliff informs the young lady. "When do you want to go?"

Now that he's fully engaging her, goose pimples break out all over the fatty part of her arms. Under the desk, her sandaled right foot rises off the ground and runs down the back of her bare left calf.

"How about Saturday night?" she asks.

"How about Sunday afternoon?" Cliff negotiates. "I'll take you to Baskin-Robbins afterward."

That reaches beyond the Himmelsteen giggle to her actual laugh. The woman has a lovely actual laugh. He tells her so and discovers she has a lovely actual blush.

He reaches down and plucks out one of her business cards, sitting in what looks like a clear-plastic bus stop for business cards, and brings it up to his eyes to read.

"'Janet Himmelsteen,'" he reads out loud.

"That's me," she giggles self-consciously.

The stuntman removes his brown leather wallet from

the back pocket of his blue jeans, opens it up, and makes a show of sliding the white William Morris business card inside. Then the blond fella starts walking down the hall backward to catch up with his boss. But he still continues his comedic patter with the young secretary: "Now, remember, if your mother asks, I'm not taking you to see a dirty movie. I'm taking you to see a foreign film. With subtitles."

He gives her a wave just before he disappears around the corner and says, "I'll call you next Friday."

When Cliff and Miss Himmelsteen saw *I Am Curious (Yellow)* at the Royal Cinema in West L.A. that Sunday afternoon, they both liked it. When it comes to cinema, Cliff is far more adventurous than his boss. To Rick, movies are what Hollywood made, and with the exception of England, all other countries' film industries are simply the best they can do, since they're not Hollywood. But after all the blood and violence Cliff experienced during World War Two, once Cliff returned home, he was surprised at how juvenile he found most Hollywood movies. There were some exceptions—*The Ox-Bow Incident, Body and Soul, White Heat, The Third Man, The Brothers Rico, Riot in Cell Block 11*—but they were irregularities in a fake normalcy.

After the devastation that the countries of Europe and Asia experienced during the Second World War, once those countries slowly started making movies again, oftentimes surrounded by the bombed-out rubble remnants of the war (*Rome, Open City; Big Deal on Madonna Street*), they discovered they were making them for a far more adult audience.

While in America—and when I say "America" I mean

"Hollywood"—a country where its home-front civilians were shielded from the gruesome details of the conflict, *their* movies remained stubbornly immature and frustratingly committed to the concept of entertainment for the whole family.

To Cliff, who had borne witness to the stark extremities of humanity (like the heads of his Filipino guerrilla brothers stuck on spikes by the occupying Japanese), even the most entertaining actors of his era—Brando, Paul Newman, Ralph Meeker, John Garfield, Robert Mitchum, George C. Scott—always sounded like actors and reacted to events the way only characters in movies did. There was always a level of artifice to the character that stopped it from being convincing. After he got back to the States, Cliff's favorite Hollywood actor was Alan Ladd. He liked the way the diminutive Ladd would practically swim in the modern forties' and fifties' fashions he wore. He didn't care for him in westerns or war films. He disappeared in cowboy attire and military uniforms. Ladd needed to be in a suit and tie and preferably a snap-brim fedora. Cliff liked his look. He was handsome without being movie-star handsome. Since Cliff was so damn handsome, he appreciated other men who weren't but didn't need to be. Alan Ladd looked like a few guys he served with. He also liked that Ladd looked like an American. But he loved the way the little guy fought fistfights in his movies. He loved how he socked the shit outta the character actors who specialized in playing gangsters. He loved that droopy lock of hair that hung in his face during the fight. And he loved how Ladd used to roll around on the floor with the heavies. But his absolute favorite thing about Ladd? His voice. He had a no-nonsense way of delivering his lines. When Ladd acted opposite William Bendix, Robert Preston, Brian Donlevy, or Ernest Borgnine, they all seemed like hambone actors when compared to him. When Ladd got mad in a movie, he didn't *act* mad. He just got sore, like a real fella. As far as Cliff was concerned, Alan Ladd was the only guy in movies who knew how to comb his hair, wear a hat, or smoke a cigarette (okay, Mitchum knew how to smoke a cigarette too).

But that just goes to show how unrealistic Cliff found Hollywood films. When he saw Otto Preminger's *Anatomy of a Murder*, he laughed at what the newspapers referred to as the film's "shockingly adult language." He joked with Rick, "Only in a Hollywood movie would 'spermicide' be considered 'shockingly adult.'"

However, when he saw foreign movies, the actors had a level of authenticity that just wasn't there in Hollywood movies. Hands down, no question about it, Cliff's favorite actor was Toshiro Mifune. He'd get so into watching Mifune's face, he'd sometimes forget to read the subtitles. The other foreign actor Cliff dug was Jean-Paul Belmondo. When Cliff saw Belmondo in *Breathless*, he thought, *That guy looks like a fucking monkey. But a monkey I like.*

Like Paul Newman, who Cliff liked, Belmondo had movie-star charm.

But when Paul Newman played a bastard, like in *Hud*, he was still an enjoyable bastard. But the guy in *Breathless* wasn't just a sexy stud prick. He was a little creep, petty thief, piece of shit. And unlike in a Hollywood movie, they didn't sentimentalize him. They always sentimentalized these pieces of shit in Hollywood movies, and it was the phoniest thing Hollywood did. In the real world, these mercenary fuck faces didn't have a sentimental bone in their body.

That's why Cliff appreciated Belmondo not doing that with his little shitheel in *Breathless*. Foreign films, Cliff thought, were more like novels. They didn't care if you liked the lead characters or not. And Cliff found that intriguing.

So starting in the fifties Cliff started driving to Beverly Hills and Santa Monica and West Los Angeles and Little Tokyo to see black-and-white foreign films with English subtitles.

La Strada, Yojimbo, Ikiru, The Bridge, Rififi, Bicycle Thieves, Rocco and His Brothers, Open City, Seven Samurai, Le Doulos, Bitter Rice (which Cliff thought was sexy as hell).

"I don't go to movies to read," Rick would tease Cliff about his cinephilia. Cliff would just smile at his boss's teasing, but he always felt proud of himself for reading subtitles. He felt smarter. He liked expanding his mind. He liked the task of grappling with difficult concepts that didn't present themselves at first. After the first twenty minutes, there was nothing more to learn about a new Rock Hudson or Kirk Douglas movie. But these foreign movies, sometimes you had to watch the whole movie just to know what it was you saw. But he wasn't buffaloed by them either. They still (one way or another) had to work as *a movie*, or what was the point? Cliff didn't know enough to write critical pieces for *Films in Review,* but he knew enough to know *Hiroshima Mon Amour* was a piece of crap. He knew enough to know Antonioni was a fraud.

He also liked looking at events from different perspectives. *Ballad of a Soldier* gave him a respect for his Soviet allies that he never had before. *Kanal* taught him maybe his wartime experience, compared to some, wasn't so bad. Bernhard Wicki's *The Bridge* made him do something he would have thought was impossible: cry for Germans. He usually didn't share these Sunday afternoons with anybody (Sunday afternoon was his foreign-film day). Nobody else in his circle was interested (it was almost comical how little the stunt community cared about film itself). But Cliff even liked going to these movies by himself. This was his private time with Mifune, Belmondo, Bob the Gambler, and Jean Gabin (both handsome Gabin and shock-white Gabin); this was his time with Akira Kurosawa.

Yojimbo wasn't the first time Cliff saw a Mifune or a Kurosawa film, having seen *Seven Samurai* a few years earlier. Cliff thought *Seven Samurai* was magnificent. He also figured it was a one-off. But the newspaper critics convinced the stuntman to investigate Mifune and Kurosawa's newest effort. After walking out of the tiny shoebox-sized cinema in an indoor shopping center in Downtown L.A.'s Little Tokyo, having just seen *Yojimbo*, Cliff was sold on Mifune but not yet on Kurosawa. It wasn't in Cliff's nature to follow the work of a movie director. He didn't really hold movies in that high regard. Film directors were guys who shot a schedule. And he ought to know—he worked with enough of them. This idea that they were like some tortured painter who agonized over which shade of blue to put on their canvas was a far-fetched fantasy of what moviemaking was. William Witney busted his ass to get his day done and have good footage at the end of it. But he was hardly a sculptor turning a piece of rock into a woman's buttocks that you wanted to fondle.

But something about *Yojimbo*, beyond Mifune, beyond the story, spoke to Cliff. And he thought that extra element *might* be Kurosawa. His third Kurosawa film proved the first two weren't a fluke. *Throne of Blood* knocked his socks off. He was a little concerned when he heard it was based on Shakespeare's *Macbeth*. Cliff never responded to Shakespeare (though he wished he did). Now, Cliff was usually a little bored when he watched a movie. If he wanted excitement, he'd drive laps at a track or he'd run a dirt bike through a motocross course. But with *Throne of Blood*, he was fully absorbed. Once he saw the image of Mifune, filmed in charcoal black and white, in full military armor, covered in a hundred arrows, it was official: Cliff Booth was an Akira Kurosawa fan.

After the violence the world was subjected to during the forties, the fifties were all about emotional melodrama. Tennessee Williams, Marlon Brando, Elia Kazan, the Actors Studio, *Playhouse 90*. And in every way, Akira Kurosawa was a perfect director for the turgid fifties, the era his most renowned string of films appeared in. American film critics embalmed Kurosawa in praise early, elevating his melodramas into high art, partly because they didn't understand them. Cliff felt that after fighting the Japanese as long as he did, and being their captive during a time of war, he understood Kurosawa's films far better than any critic he ever read. Cliff felt Kurosawa had an innate gift for staging drama, melodrama, and pulp, as well as a comic-book

35

illustrator's talent (Cliff was a big Marvel comics fan) for framing and composition. As far as Cliff was concerned, no director he'd ever seen had composed shots with more dynamic wit than "the Old Man" (what Cliff called the filmmaker). But Cliff felt where the American critics got it wrong was referring to the director as a "fine artist." Kurosawa didn't start out as a fine artist. Originally, he worked for a living. He was a working man, who made movies for other working men. He wasn't a *fine artist*, but he had a sensational talent for staging drama and pulp *artistically*.

But even the Old Man was susceptible to falling for his own notices. By the mid-sixties, with *Red Beard*, the Old Man would change from Kurosawa the movie director to Kurosawa the Russian novelist.

Cliff didn't walk out of *Red Beard*, out of respect for his *once-favorite* movie director. But later, when he learned that it was how darn ponderous the Old Man became on *Red Beard* that prompted Toshiro Mifune to vow to stop working with Kurosawa, Cliff took Mifune's side.

CLIFF'S TOP KUROSAWA FILMS
1. (tie) *Seven Samurai* and *Ikiru*
2. *Yojimbo*
3. *Throne of Blood*
4. *Stray Dog*
5. *The Bad Sleep Well* (for the opening scene alone)

Cliff's connection and devotion (though *he* would never call it that) to Japanese cinema wasn't limited to just Kurosawa and Mifune.

While he didn't know the names of other directors, he really liked *Three Outlaw Samurai*, *The Sword of Doom*, *Hara-Kiri*, and *Goyokin*. And later, in the seventies, he adored Shintaro Katsu's *Blind Swordsman* character, Zatoichi. So much so that, for a while, Katsu replaced Mifune as Cliff's favorite actor. And Cliff went fucking gaga over Katsu's brother's film series *Baby Cart from Hell*, especially the second one, *Baby Cart at the River Styx*. In the seventies, he also saw that wild, sexy Japanese movie where the chick cuts the guy's dick off, *In the Realm of the Senses* (he took a couple of different dates to that movie). He also dug the first of Sonny Chiba's *Street Fighter* movies (the one where he rips the black guy's cock off). But when he went to the Vista to see Mifune's *Samurai Trilogy* (all three on one Sunday afternoon), he was so bored that he didn't see another Japanese film for two years.

But there were a lot of foreign filmmaking heavyweights of the fifties and sixties Cliff *wasn't* enamored with. He tried Bergman but wasn't interested (too boring). He tried Fellini and really responded at first. He could have done without all his wife's Chaplin bullshit. In fact, he could have done without his wife altogether. But he liked the early black-and-white films a lot. But once Fellini decided *life was a circus*, Cliff said *arrivederci*.

He tried Truffaut twice, but he didn't respond to him. Not because the films were boring (they were), but that wasn't the only reason Cliff didn't respond. The two films he watched (in a Truffaut double feature) just didn't grab him. The first film, *The 400 Blows*, left him cold. He really didn't understand why that little boy did half the shit he did. Now,

Cliff never spoke to anybody about it, but if he did, his first case in point would be when the kid prays to *Balzac*. Is that something French kids do? Is the point that that's normal or is the point he's a little weirdo? Yes, he knows it *could* be meant to be the same as an American kid putting a picture of Willie Mays on his wall. But he doesn't think it's *supposed* to be that simple. Also, it seems absurd. A ten-year-old little boy loves Balzac that much? No, he doesn't. Since the little boy is supposed to be Truffaut, it's Truffaut telling us how impressive *he* is. And frankly, the kid on-screen wasn't impressive in the slightest. And he definitely didn't deserve a movie made about him.

And he thought the mopey dopes in *Jules and Jim* were a fucking drag. Cliff didn't dig *Jules and Jim*, because he didn't dig the chick. And it's the kind of movie, if you don't dig the chick, you ain't gonna dig the flick. Cliff thought the movie would have been better all the way around if they just let that bitch drown.

Since Cliff was a big fan of provocation, he dug *I Am Curious (Yellow)*, and not just the sex shit. Once he got used to it, he liked the political discourse as well. He loved the film's black-and-white photography. *Breathless* looked as artful as combat footage. But this was so monochromatic and luminous that Cliff wanted to lick the screen, especially whenever the girl Lena was on it. The (sorta) story of *I Am Curious (Yellow)* is about a twenty-two-year-old college student named Lena, played by twenty-two-year-old actress Lena Nyman, who is dating a forty-four-year-old filmmaker named Vilgot, played by the film's forty-four-year-old director, Vilgot Sjöman.

Both Lena's (the real Lena and the screen Lena) are starring in Vilgot's new movie. At first, the movie goes back and forth between Lena and Vilgot and footage of the pseudo-political provocation documentary that they're making together. Miss Himmelsteen was a little confused by that at first, and so was Cliff. But pretty soon he got the hang of it, and Cliff found it challenging in a way that made him feel clever for getting on the film's wavelength. Cliff assumed the filmmaker was using his randy college-student girlfriend as his on-screen pretty face and puppet. Yet right off the bat, Vilgot tosses her in the middle of some very stimulating political discussions and debates. Early footage of Vilgot's movie consists of Lena, armed with a microphone and a handheld camera, practically assaulting Swedish bourgeois citizens on the street with her accusatory questions ("What are you personally doing to end the class system in Sweden?"). Cliff thought some of it was monotonous, and some of it went over his head, but overall he found the film engaging.

He especially got involved with a discussion about the role and the *necessity* of the Swedish military in today's society. The debate is conducted on the street, with a group of young Swedish military cadets and a group of other young Swedish people, who feel all Swedish citizens should refuse military service and work a mandatory four-year service for peace. Cliff thought both sides made good points and was glad to see neither side get mad at the other.

Also, because the debate was allowed to grow, it led to more pertinent and practical questions. Like *exactly* what would the military do if Sweden was occupied by a foreign adversary? And what *should* they do?

Cliff never wondered what Americans would do if the Russians, or the Nazis, or the Japanese, or the Mexicans, or the Vikings, or Alexander the Great ever occupied America by force. He knew what Americans would do. They'd shit their pants and call the fucking cops. And when they realized the police not only couldn't help them but were working on behalf of the occupation, after a brief period of despair, they'd fall in line.

But the more the film unspooled, the more confusing it became. Cliff could see a lot of that was on purpose and some of it was just that it's a weird movie.

But the more he watched it, the more intrigued he was by the film's gamesmanship. What is the real Lena story and what is Vilgot's film?

At one point, he wondered why the movie is getting so damn melodramatic. Then he realized, it's Vilgot's movie that's getting melodramatic. The *movie Vilgot* isn't as good a filmmaker as the *real Vilgot*.

The implications of what's real and what's a movie interested Cliff. Especially when Cliff thought about it later and realized the implications of Lena's father's involvement in the movie. *Wait a minute, so the whole story of Lena's father isn't real? Is he her father, or is he just an actor playing the role of her father?* And that's acknowledging that in real life *he is* an actor playing her father. But is he the *movie Lena's* father, or is he an actor playing her father in *Vilgot's movie*?

All these cinematic questions intrigued Cliff far more than they did Miss Himmelsteen. He felt her leaning back from the screen, while she felt him lean forward. At some point, he heard her say under her breath, "I am bored yellow."

That's cool, he thought. *It's a weird movie.*

Okay, all this cinema verité stuff is all well and good, but what about the movie's claim to fame, the fucking? That's why Cliff came to see the movie (not entirely), but he was *curious*. And it's most definitely the reason he took Miss Himmelsteen. The man who engages Lena in the sex scenes that originally got the film seized by customs when it was first sent over from Stockholm is not Vilgot (Cliff was glad he didn't have to see that tub of shit fuck). It's a shady married guy (played by Börje Ahlstedt) who Lena meets through her father.

While watching the first real sex scene ever projected in American cinemas, between Lena and Börje in the young woman's apartment, Cliff had the sensation he was watching something new. Recently, other mainstream films had played patty-cake with these types of scenes. The nipple-suckle lesbian seduction between Susannah York and Coral Browne in *The Killing of Sister George*. Anne Heywood's masturbation scene in *The Fox*. Oliver Reed and Alan Bates's nude wrestling match by the fireplace in *Women in Love* (Cliff never saw that flick, but the trailer for it made his jaw drop). But Sjöman's nude sex scene broke new ground for mainstream theatrical distribution. The film was originally seized by U.S. Customs on the grounds of obscenity. The movie's American distributor, Grove Press, went to court to fight for it, lost the first battle when a federal district court upheld the customs ban. But that was Grove Press's strategy. They wanted to appeal and have the judgment overturned. That way, a judgment would be passed down that didn't just apply to *this film* but to *all films* with this type of provocative sexual material. And that's exactly what happened when the U.S. Court of Appeals reversed the findings of the federal court, turning Vilgot Sjöman's film *I Am Curious (Yellow)* into the cause célèbre film of the moment. And ushered in a new wave of sexuality into modern mainstream cinema. It became the first and by far the most profitable of a small wave of artistically minded erotic films that would prosper for a few years, while both the film industry and audiences decided how far down this road they were willing to go—with the pornographers momentarily sidelined, wondering how much ground the mainstream was willing to cede.

As Cliff and Miss Himmelsteen watched the sex scene in Lena's apartment, they were both gripped by the exciting sensation of seeing something new for the first time, and they intertwined fingers once the scene got going.

Cliff thought back to what Richard Schickel wrote in that *Life* magazine in Marvin Schwarz's outer office:

> Ten—even five—years ago, this would have been
> dreadfully shocking aesthetically and culturally,
> not to mention morally. But we have in every area
> of thought and art been brought so teasingly close
> to this level of explicitness that it's a relief to arrive
> there and finally be done with it.

The first sex scene in *I Am Curious (Yellow)*, and for all intents and purposes modern cinema, wasn't exactly erotic (Cliff didn't get an erection), but the first flash of explicit nudity was for sure titillating. But what really made it memorable was how witty it was. Director Vilgot Sjöman filmed the first real sex scene to hit these shores like the comedy of errors most quickie trysts turn out to be. Sjöman strives to stress the realistic awkwardness involved in coupling. The couple wants to get it on; we the audience, who have been waiting for this the whole movie, want them to get it on; but the director throws one realistic obstacle after another in the way of their midday quickie. After many attempts, Börje can't get Lena's pants unbuttoned, and she slightly bitches him out for his fumbling ("Can't you do it?"), till she's forced to stop kissing and take matters in her own hands, removing her pants herself. He tries to fuck her standing up; she stops him ("I can't do that"), a statement obviously based on past experience. When they have to go to another room to retrieve a mattress, they shuffle like little toy soldiers with their pants binding their ankles together. They practically destroy a room retrieving the mattress, yank it into the living room, then realize Lena's recording equipment is stacked all over everything (reel-to-reel tape recorders, loose tapes, microphones), so they need to pile all that shit up if they want to lay the mattress on the floor and fuck.

Cliff thought it was one of the best scenes in a movie he'd ever seen. It's definitely the most realistic. He's been in apartments like that, fucked a girl like that on a mattress like that on a floor like that. Cliff has quickly stacked up magazines, comic books, paperbacks, and record albums to fuck girls on floors, couches, beds, and the backseats of cars. Cliff has also been known to travel great distances with his pants tight around his ankles with only his fully erect penis to guide the way.

And Cliff thought the fucking-on-the-bridge scene was

even sexier. Cliff loves fucking in public. He loves making out in public, getting his cock sucked in public, and being jerked off in public. After those two scenes, Cliff thinks he's seen the film's two big moments. But neither he nor Miss Himmelsteen were prepared for the *pubic hair* scene. It's the scene where Lena and Börje lie naked together and talk as they fondle each other, her face right next to his flaccid penis, her fingers moving in and out of his generous bush of pubic hair, planting light kisses on his cock. Sitting in the cinema in Westwood, holding hands with Miss Himmelsteen, watching a scene like that in a *real* movie, starring a *real actress*, Cliff felt that he was watching the dawn of a new day in cinema.

Later, Rick asked Cliff, did he fuck Miss Himmelsteen?

"Naw," was Cliff's reply.

But he did tell Rick she sucked his cock in his Karmann Ghia on the drive back to her home in Brentwood, but that was their only date.

By 1972, Janet Himmelsteen would become a full-fledged agent at the William Morris Agency, and by 1975 she would become one of their top talent agents.

From that point on, she kept her blow jobs above the line.

Chapter Three

Cielo Drive

Rick Dalton's 1964 Cadillac Coupe de Ville, with his driver Cliff Booth behind the wheel, pulls out of the underground parking lot of the William Morris building onto Charleville, then turns one block down onto Wilshire Boulevard.

As the vintage Cadillac and the two vintage guys drive down the busy street, the hippie subculture that has invaded the town in a locust-like swarm proceeds to parade down the sidewalk in their blankets and frocks and dirty bare feet. Troubled Rick Dalton, who still hasn't shared the reason for his anxiety with his buddy Cliff, glances out the car-door window and comments on the hippie passersby with disgust. "Just look at all these fuckin' weirdos. You know, this town useta be a nice fuckin' place to live in. Now look at it." Then he remarks with fascistic disdain, "I swear they oughta line 'em up against a wall and shoot 'em all."

They turn off of busy Wilshire and make their way back to Rick's home on Cielo Drive, taking calmer residential streets. Rick rips a cigarette out of his pack of Capitol W's, tosses it in his mouth, and lights it up with his Zippo, then snaps the silver lid closed in his tough-guy way. As he sucks the smoke a quarter down, he says to his driver, "Well, it's official, ol' buddy." His nose does a loud snot sniffle. "I'm a has-been."

Cliff tries to console his boss. "C'mon, partner, what are you talkin' about? What did that guy tell ya?"

Rick spits out, "He told me the goddamn truth, that's what he told me!"

Cliff asks, "What's got you so upset?"

Rick spins his head in his buddy's direction. "Comin' face-to-face with how I threw my whole goddamn career in the toilet, that's what's got me so fuckin' upset!"

"So what happened?" Cliff asks. "That guy in there turn you down?"

Rick takes another deep drag off his cigarette. "No, he wants to help me get into Italian movies."

Quick comeback from Cliff: "Then what's the problem?"

Rick screams, "I gotta do fuckin' Italian movies, that's the goddamn fuckin' problem!"

Cliff decides to keep driving and let Rick blow off steam. The actor sucks down another lungful of smoke while simultaneously feeling sorry for himself. As he exhales, he chronicles, "Five years of ascent. Ten years of treading water. And now a race to the bottom."

While negotiating Los Angeles traffic, Cliff offers up some perspective. "Look, I ain't never had much of a career to speak of, so I can't rightly say I know how you feel—"

Rick interrupts, "Whaddaya mean? You're my stunt double."

Cliff tells it like it is: "Rick, I'm your driver. Since *Green Hornet* and since your driver's license got taken away, *that's* what I am. I'm your gofer. I'm not complaining. I like driving you around. To the set and back. To auditions. To meetings and shit. I like house-sitting in the Hollywood Hills when you're gone. But I ain't been a full-time stuntman for a while now. So from where I'm standing, goin' to Rome to star in movies doesn't sound like the fate worse than death that you seem to think it is."

Rick counters quickly, "Have you ever seen an Italian western?" Then, answering his own question, "They're awful! It's a fuckin' farce."

"Oh yeah?" Cliff counters back. "How many you seen? One? Two?"

Rick says with authority, "I've seen enough! Nobody likes spaghetti westerns."

Under his breath, Cliff says, "I bet some Italians kinda like 'em."

"Look," Rick says, "I grew up watchin' Hopalong Cassidy and Hoot Gibson. Watchin' a wop western, directed by Guido DeFatso, starring Mario Bananano, ain't gonna ring my fuckin' bell." Finishing his Italian tirade as he flicks his cigarette out of the car-door window, "Understand, I'm still pissed that spaghetti bender Dean Martin's in *Rio Bravo*. Forget about fuckin' Frankie Avalon dying at the fuckin' Alamo."

"Again," Cliff ventures, "I ain't you. But it seems to me like a pretty nifty life experience."

"What do you mean?" a genuinely curious Rick inquires.

"Photographers takin' pictures of you all the time. Sippin' cocktails at little tables lookin' at the Colosseum. Eating the best pasta and pizza in the world. Fuckin' Italian chicks."

Cliff deduces, "If you ask me, that beats hangin' 'round Burbank, losin' fights to Bingo Martin."

Rick guffaws, "Well, ya got a point there."

Then the two men start snickering, and pretty soon a smile creeps up on Rick's face. Cliff putting out fires for Rick has been an essential part of their dynamic since the two became a team. Sometimes those fires are figurative, like right now. But the first fire that forged their partnership was a *literal fire*.

It was during the third season of *Bounty Law* (the '61–'62 season). Cliff Booth was brought in to double the series lead. Rick didn't take to Cliff right off. For one really good reason: Cliff was way too handsome to be a stuntman. *Bounty Law* was Rick's pussy party. He didn't need a swingin' dick, who looked better in Rick's costume than Rick did, horning in on all that ample tail. But he started hearing about Cliff's exploits in World War Two. He learned Cliff wasn't *just* a hero. He was one of the biggest heroes of World War Two. He won the Medal of Valor, twice. The first time for killing Italians in Sicily. There were a lot of reasons why he was given that distinguished honor the second time. But the main reason was, except for the fellas that dropped the bomb on Hiroshima, no other American soldier had more confirmed kills of Japanese enemy soldiers than Sergeant Clifford Booth.

Rick, on the other hand, would have spent months jumping off of kitchen chairs to get flat feet if he thought it would keep him out of the Army (especially during wartime). Nevertheless, he admired men who served and served with distinction.

But the fire that forged the bond between the two men

happened about a month into Cliff's time on *Bounty Law*. One of the episodic directors on the show, Virgil Vogel, had an idea that the series' main character, Jake Cahill, would wear a big winter jacket and the jacket would be dyed nurse-shoe-polish white. Now, in real life it would look ridiculous. But on black-and-white film it would look kind of neat. However, wardrobe took so long preparing the jacket, it wasn't ready for Vogel's episode. So the producers just earmarked it for the following episode. And on the following episode, at the end, Jake Cahill gets set on fire. Everybody thought that would be a good way to utilize this big winter coat they spent so much time prepping.

Cliff was ready, willing, and able to do the fire gag. But after it was explained to Rick what was entailed and what to expect, the actor decided he'd give it a whirl. So fire accelerant was placed on the back of Jake's big white winter coat, far away from his face and hair.

However, what nobody on the crew knew—not even the wardrobe department, because they had sent the jacket out to get dyed—was the white dye they used was 65 percent alcohol-based. They didn't know and nobody told them because there wasn't a fire gag in the episode that the white garment was originally planned for. So with Rick inside, when they touched a flame to the back of Jake's jacket, it burst into a blazing Roman candle.

When Rick heard the rush of his jacket going up in flames, his panic accelerated as much as the flammable costume. Immediately, he felt the flames going past his shoulders and licking and popping around his head. At that moment he was ready to do the very worst thing he could have done in that situation: take off running in a blind panic. But just before Rick could go apeshit, he heard Cliff Booth calmly say, "Rick, you're standing in a puddle of water. Just fall down."

Rick did just that, and shortly the flames were put out, before they had a chance to do any real damage. And that was when Rick and Cliff became *the team of Rick and Cliff.*

The other real cool cachet that Cliff Booth brought to the party: As well as being a good friend, a good stuntman, and a war hero, in this world of make-believe, Cliff was a *real killer.* Just on his television show alone, Rick killed something like two hundred and forty-two people. That's not counting how many Indians and owl hoots he killed in his western movies or those hundred and fifty Nazis he killed in *The Fourteen Fists of McCluskey.* And, when he played the twisted black-leather-gloved psycho killer in *Jigsaw Jane,* he dispatched most of his victims with a shiny silver stiletto.

Rick remembers drinking booze and discussing his *Jigsaw Jane* character with his stunt double at the bar located inside the Smoke House, off of Riverside Drive. As they talked and drank, Rick asked Cliff, had he ever killed an enemy soldier with a knife?

"Plenty," answered Cliff.

"*Plenty*?" Rick repeated, surprised. "How many is *plenty*?"

"What?" Cliff asked. "You want me to sit here and count?"

"Well, yeah," Rick said.

"Well, let's see . . ." Cliff thought. He started counting silently to himself on his fingers, until he ran out of fingers and had to take another lap around the track, then he stopped and said, "Sixteen."

If Rick's whiskey sour had been in his mouth at the time, he'd have come close to doing a comedic spit take. "You've killed *sixteen* fuckin' guys with a knife?" he asked incredulously.

"Japs in the war," Cliff clarified. "Yeah."

Rick got quiet, leaning forward and asking his buddy, "How'd you do it?"

"Do you mean how *could I* do it, mentally and emotionally?" Cliff asked. "Or how *did I* do it, physically and practically?"

Wow, good question, Rick thought.

"Well, I guess first, how did ya do it?"

"Well, not every time, but most of those times was me coming up behind some joker and taking them by surprise. A rock gets in some guy's shoe. He straggles behind his company to take off the shoe, git rid of the rock. I come up behind him, stick a knife in his ribs, hold my hand over his mouth, and twist the knife till I feel him give up the ghost."

FUCK, Rick thought.

"But," Cliff said, holding up his index finger, "now I fer sure killed him. But did he die because of *me*, or did he die because he got a rock in his shoe?" Cliff philosophized.

"So let me get this straight," Rick clarified. "You stick a blade in some Jap's ribs, then you cup a hand over his mouth, squashing the scream, then hold him through the whole damn death rattle till he dies in your arms?"

Cliff took a swig from his highball glass filled with room-temperature Wild Turkey and said, "Yep."

"Wow!" Rick exclaimed, as he knocked back some of his cold whiskey sour.

Cliff Booth smiled to himself as he watched his boss wrestle with this idea, then asked provocatively, "Wanna know what it feels like?"

Rick's eyes moved up to Cliff's face. "Whaddaya mean?"

Cliff repeated low, slow, and deliberate, "I said, would you like to know what it feels like?" Then added with a shoulder shrug, "You know, for your character."

Rick didn't say anything for a while. The bar seemed to get real quiet, then Rick Dalton let escape a very soft "Yeah."

Cliff smiled at his friend and employer, took a big gulp of booze, laid the heavy glass down hard on the bar, and said with another shoulder shrug, "Kill a pig."

What? Rick thought.

"What?" Rick said.

"Kill. A. Pig," Cliff repeated sinisterly. After a beat of silence, where the words "kill a pig" hung in the air, Cliff continued to explain.

"Buy yourself some big fat hog. Take her home to your backyard. Then get on your knees next to her. Hold her, feel her, feel her life, smell her, hear her grunt and snort. Then, with the other arm, stick a butcher knife right into her side and hold on, brother."

Rick on his barstool listened to Cliff, mesmerized.

"Now, she's gonna scream like a son of a bitch and bleed like a bastard. And she's gonna fight you. But you keep holding with one hand, while you keep sticking that blade inside of her with the other. And even though it'll seem like an eternity, somewhere in the first minute you'll feel her die in your arms. And that will be the moment you truly feel *death*. *Life* is a bleeding, screaming, violently jerking pig in your arms. And *death* is you holding a bunch of heavy un-moving meat."

As Cliff described the entire step-by-step murder of the imaginary pig, Rick grew paler and paler, imagining himself acting out that scenario in his backyard.

Cliff realized he had his audience by the throat, so he swooped in for the kill. "So if you wanna *experience* what it's like to kill a *man*, killing a pig is as *legally* close as you can get."

Rick swallowed hard, as he grappled with whether he could do that.

Cliff added, "Then take that pig to a butcher and have him cut 'er up for ya. Bacon . . . pork chops . . . sausages . . . pork shoulder . . . pig's feet. You consume that entire animal. And that will be you showing respect for the death of that beast."

Rick swallowed down some more whiskey sour. "I don't know if I can do that."

"Oh, you can do it," Cliff assured him. "You might not *want* to do it, but you *can* do it. In fact, a case could be made, if you *can't* do it, you don't deserve to eat pork."

After a moment Rick slapped his hand on the bar and said, "Okay, goddammit, I'll do it. Let's get a pig."

Now, of course, Rick never did it. There were enough moving parts to this experiment that it was easy for Rick to lose momentum. *Where do I buy a pig? How do I clean up all that blood on my pool patio? How do I get that dead pig outta my backyard—she probably weighs a ton? What if the fucking thing bites me?* But even though Rick never actually *did* it, he absolutely *contemplated* doing it. Which was its own form of calculated cold-blooded murder, similar to *Jigsaw Jane*'s black-gloved killer.

Cliff drives Rick's Cadillac up into its spot in Rick's driveway in front of his house on Cielo Drive. Directly outside of the windshield, looming huge, is a giant oil painting of Rick wearing a cavalry uniform, grimacing, with a foot on his face. This is one section of a six-section outdoor billboard that advertised *Comanche Uprising*, the first feature film he headlined once *Bounty Law* made him a television star. The full billboard consisted of Rick Dalton as his character, Lieutenant Taylor Sullivan of the U.S. Cavalry, on the ground surrounded by (apparently) Comanches, with the chief placing a moccasined boot on the side of Sullivan's face in a victory pose, pinning the angry, helpless Cavalry officer to the ground. An old friend of Rick's found the section of billboard in an antiques store in Dallas, Texas. The friend bought it and sent it to Rick. Rick, however, never really cared for that poster, except for the fact it featured *him* and not top-billed Robert Taylor. Nor did he harbor any illusions that *Comanche Uprising* was anything other than what it was—a routine fifties' Cavalry vs. Indians potboiler. Its virtues included working with salty-dog western-helmer R. G. Springsteen and how damn fancy Rick looked in his blue Cavalry officer's uniform. But, other than that, the motion picture was unmemorable.

So when Rick received the billboard section featuring him, he initially thought, *What the fuck am I gonna do with this*? His answer was to just leave it outside in the driveway.

That was five years ago.

As Cliff switches off the ignition, Rick goes into one of his passive-aggressive tantrums. He's upset about something, so he makes himself upset about something else. In this case, the billboard in the driveway.

"Can we *finally*"—gesturing broadly toward the oil painting—"get this fucking thing outta the driveway?"

"Where do you want me to put it?"

"Throw it away for all I care!"

Cliff makes the disappointed face of a child. "Awww, Felix found that for you." He prods, "Don't be jaded, that's a cool gift."

"Just because I don't want to spend every morning and evening staring face-to-face with an oil painting of my mouth, like I've done for the last five years, shouldn't insinuate I'm jaded." Rick clarifies, "I'm just tired of fuckin' lookin' at it, alright? Can't ya just put it in the garage?"

Cliff chuckles, "Your garage? It's a mess."

Rick instructs, "Well, can you clean it out enough to stick the billboard in?"

Cliff removes his sunglasses and says, "Yes, I can." Then clarifies, "But that's not a this-afternoon thing; that's a weekend kind of thing."

An exasperated Rick vents his frustration in a less bossy way: "It's just I don't need a big picture of myself in front of my house. It looks like I'm advertising the Rick Dalton Museum."

Then, all of a sudden, the *whoosh* of a motor and the sound of Beatles harmony invades their driver's side ear. Both men turn to their left and spy, for the very first time, Rick's new next-door neighbors, *Roman and Sharon Polanski*, in their vintage 1920s English Roadster. The Beatles song *A Day in the Life* emanates from the car radio, tuned to 93 KHJ. The car containing the handsome Hollywood couple sits at the bottom of a hill that constitutes their driveway, waiting for their electronic gate to open. Roman is behind the wheel, his wife in the passenger seat, clunky plastic clicker in Sharon's hand. The two lovebirds are carrying on a lively conversation neither Rick nor Cliff can hear above the rumbling of the Roadster's engine and the Beatles' pretentious sound design. Cliff sees only the stunning blonde in the passenger seat, while Rick looks right through her to the diminutive Polish auteur in the driver's seat.

Apart from Mike Nichols, no other young director at the time was more successful or more famous than Roman Polanski. But the Polish megaphone-wielder had a level of popularity that eluded his stage and screen colleague Nichols. In 1969, Roman Polanski was a *rock star*!

He had made a name for himself when he directed his first feature, the Polish language *Knife in the Water*. The film was a hit on the foreign-film circuit and was even nominated for best foreign film at the Academy Awards. After the success of his first film, Polanski moved to London and started making movies in the English language.

Two of the films, *Cul-de-sac* and *The Fearless Vampire Killers* (where he met his wife, Sharon), were admired but didn't make much of a mark financially. But his psychological thriller *Repulsion* was a sleeper hit that broke out of the art-house ghetto into mainstream success. After a slew of bad *Psycho* copies from Hammer Studios and the thrill-less thrillers coming out of France, like the pulse-devoid *romans de gare* of Claude Chabrol or the amateur-night-in-Paris fumblings of the so-called Truffaut–Hitchcock films, along came Polanski's London-set *Psycho*-ish thriller *Repulsion*. When it came to how to do a modern-day Hitchcockian thriller for a with-it audience, that pulsed to a swinging London beat, with *Repulsion* Roman cracked the code.

Polanski's character study of twisted paranoia, starring the beautiful but damned Catherine Deneuve, *worked*. But where a Hitchcock thriller *worked* to entertain, Polanski's movie *worked* to disturb. Hitchcock could and did disturb too—*Suspicion*, *Strangers on a Train*, *Shadow of a Doubt*, and of course *Psycho*. But only up to a point. With Polanski, audience disturbance *was* the point.

Polanski's Hitchcockian thriller by way of Buñuel struck a chord with audiences.

After Polanski showed he had a penchant for getting under an audience's skin with *Repulsion*, head honcho of Paramount Studios Robert Evans invited him to come out to Hollywood and make a movie. He lured Roman, an expert skier, into his office by sending him a script for an upcoming movie on their slate about competitive skiing called *Downhill Racer*.

And then, in a decision that would later make Paramount's stock price go up three points, Evans handed him the novel of Ira Levin's *Rosemary's Baby* and said, "Read this." The rest, as Marvin Schwarz would say, is *horror-movie history*.

Levin's slim novel, essentially a novella, tells the story of Rosemary Woodhouse (Mia Farrow), a young newlywed who's married to an ambitious actor named Guy Woodhouse (John Cassavetes). They move into a classic New York loft and start a relationship with an eccentric elderly couple that live in the building, Minnie and Roman Castevet (Ruth Gordon and Sidney Blackmer). Little does poor Rosemary know, the couple are a pair of Satanists looking for a vessel to birth the long-prophesied Antichrist. Evans's prescient vision that Polanski was the one to bring this product to the screen has to go down as one of the all-time inspired decisions ever made by a studio executive.

After reading the material, Polanski only had one qualm. But it was a big one. Polanski was an atheist. And if you don't believe in God, you must equally reject the idea of the devil. Now, many directors could and would say, *So what? It's just a movie. You don't have to believe in giant monkeys to direct King Kong.* And they wouldn't be wrong. But Roman didn't feel comfortable making a movie that reinforced the belief in religion, a philosophy he thoroughly rejected. Yet the filmmaker could see what a good movie this could be. So how did he reconcile his personal beliefs with the material? He staged the material as written but added an almost imperceptible perspective change.

Nothing, until the film's final moment, confirms Rosemary's sinister suspicions. Polanski never gives the audience a glimpse of anything that can be labeled supernatural. All of Rosemary's "evidence" of the sinister conspiracy she feels is taking place against her is anecdotal and circumstantial. Since we care for Rosemary and we're watching a horror movie, most audiences take her investigative gaze at face value.

But instead of the elderly couple down the hall being the leaders of a coven of sinister Satanists, and instead of her husband selling his soul and the soul of his unborn child to the devil, *maybe* it would be equally likely, and frankly more probable, that Rosemary is suffering from acute paranoia brought on by postpartum depression?

Now, true, at the climax it is revealed that, yes indeed, the Castevets and their friends have perpetrated a conspiracy against Rosemary. But the actual existence of Satan himself is still ambiguous. Who's to say the Castevets and company aren't just a bunch of fucking lunatics? If at the end they all yelled, *Hail, Pan!* as opposed to *Hail, Satan!* would you question the validity of their belief?

Among any of the other filmmakers who Evans could have hired to direct that book, it's almost unimaginable that they wouldn't have made it a monster movie. Polanski managed the Herculean feat of *not* making a monster movie yet still scaring the pants off of audiences. Then Evans and his team did their part by devising one of the great movie-advertising campaigns of the era and cutting a horrific trailer that in some ways betters the movie. The end result was a massive hit that made Roman Polanski not only one of the hottest directors in the business but a pop-cultural icon (he's mentioned in the lyrics of the rock musical *Hair*) and the first genuine rock-star movie director.

And here he is, in the flesh, with his hot-ass wife, Rick's next-door neighbor. *Talk about a guy who has the world by the fucking balls*, Rick thinks.

Then the electronic gate in front of Roman and Sharon

opens up and the Roadster, as quickly as it zoomed into view, zooms out.

"Holy shit," Rick says to himself, "that was Polanski." Then to Cliff, "That was Roman Polanski! He's lived here a month now; this is the first time I've seen him."

Rick opens the car door and steps out, chuckling. Cliff chuckles to himself as well: This is yet another example of Rick's furious mood swings.

As Rick walks across his front lawn toward his front door, his entire demeanor has changed since he saw Polanski. He says excitedly over his shoulder to his buddy, "What did I always say? Most important thing in this town, when you're making money: Buy a house in town. Don't rent. Eddie O'Brien taught me that," referring to the intense character actor Edmond O'Brien, who Rick met when he once guested on a first-season episode of *Bounty Law*. As Rick continues, his strut gets more pronounced. "Hollywood real estate means you live here. You're not visiting. You're not passing through. You fuckin' live here!" As he steps up the first three steps that lead to his front entrance, "I mean, here I am, flat on my ass, and who do I got livin' next door to me?"

He sticks his house key in the lock, twists it, then, turning to his buddy to finish his point and answer his own question, "The director of *Rosemary's* fuckin' *Baby*, that's who. Polanski's the hottest director in town—probably the world—and he's my next-door neighbor." Rick steps fully inside his house as he finishes his thought: "I could be one pool party away from starring in the new Polanski movie!"

Cliff wants to jet, so he stays in the doorway, not wanting to step into the house. "So you're feeling better?" Cliff sarcastically asks.

"Oh, yeah, buddy," Rick says. "Sorry 'bout that, take care of that fuckin' *Comanche Uprising* thing whenever you get the chance."

Cliff indicates *got it*, then asks, "You need me for anything else?"

Rick waves him away. "No no no. I got a lotta lines to learn for tomorrow."

Cliff asks, "You need me to run lines witcha?"

"No, don't worry about that," Rick tells him. "I'll do it with my tape recorder."

"Okay," Cliff says. "If you don't need me, I'm gonna get my carcass on home."

"Naw, I don't need you," Rick says.

Cliff starts walking backward to get out of there quick before Rick changes his mind. "Okay, leave tomorrow morning, seven-fifteen."

Rick repeats, "Got it, seven-fifteen."

Cliff clarifies, "That's seven-fifteen—out the door, in the car."

Rick repeats, "Got it, seven-fifteen, out the door, in the car. See ya, buddy."

Rick closes his front door. Cliff trips over to the car that's parked next to his boss's Cadillac in the driveway. It's his in-need-of-a-wash light-blue Volkswagen convertible Karmann Ghia. The stuntman hops in, sticks his key in the ignition, and twists. The little Volkswagen engine rumbles to life. As the engine sparks, so does the sound of the Los Angeles radio station 93 KHJ. Billy Stewart is doing his scat-like improv vocal at the conclusion of his version of *Summertime* as Cliff reverses out of the driveway, gives the steering wheel a quick yank, which jerks the nose of the Karmann Ghia away from the house and points it down the hill on Cielo Drive. The blond driver revs the gas three times with Billy Jack's boot, then, in time with Billy Stewart's vocal gymnastics, throws the stick into gear and hits the gas, shooting down the residential Hollywood Hill, taking each hairpin turn at break-his-fucking-neck speed, heading to his home, three freeways away in the city of Van Nuys.

Chapter Four

Brandy, You're a Fine Girl

After Cliff became a widower, he never had another serious relationship with a woman for the rest of his life. He fucked girls. He took advantage of all that *free pussy/free love* that was floating around in the late sixties. But no serious girlfriends and definitely no wives. But Cliff did have one female in his life that he loved and who loved him back. His flat-head bent-eared pitbull with a reddish-brown coat, Brandy.

The dog waits anxiously by the door to Cliff's trailer home for the sound of her master's Karmann Ghia pulling up outside. The moment she hears it, her little nub of a tail starts quickly moving from left to right, and she instinctively whines and scratches at the door with her paw. While Cliff is gone all day, he leaves his little rabbit-eared black-and-white television set on so Brandy won't get lonely. On television at the moment is the February 7, 1969, episode of the ABC Friday-night variety show *The Hollywood Palace*. Each episode every week would have a new guest host introducing a new lineup of visiting guests. Last week the host was comedic pianist Victor Borge. This week it's *Camelot*'s Broadway crooner Robert Goulet. Goulet is tearing into a dramatic interpretation of Jimmy Webb's metaphysical classic *MacArthur Park*.

> *MacArthur Park is melting*
> *in the dark*
> *All the sweet green icing*
> *flowing down*

The front door to the dwelling flies open, and there stands Cliff Booth in his full Billy Jack blue-denim regalia. As she does every night when Cliff comes home, Brandy loses her goddamn mind. Cliff, who treats Brandy with a firm hand ("She likes a firm hand," he tells Rick), allows her to get her jumping up on him out of her system. But tonight Cliff has a happy surprise for his little lady. Cliff and Rick had lunch today at Musso and Frank, and the stuntman had steak and carried the steak bone in the pocket of his Levi's jacket, wrapped up in one of the restaurant's white cloth dinner napkins, all day long. After he gives her a few moments to get her welcome-home happy jig out of her system, he barks at her, "Okay, down down down." She sits down on her hind legs, snout pointed up at him. Now that he has her undivided attention, he removes the white cloth napkin with the meaty T-bone inside from the pocket of his cool blue jacket.

"Look what I got for you," he taunts her.

Something for me? Brandy thinks.

As he unwraps it, he says, "It's gonna blow your mind,

man." Then out of the napkin emerges the steak bone. Brandy, excited, hops up on her hind legs, her front paws pressed against Cliff's waist. Cliff chuckles at Brandy's appreciation. You could take a woman out to Musso and Frank, order the same goddamn steak, add a bottle of red wine, and top it off with a piece of cheesecake, and she wouldn't show anywhere near this level of appreciation. This just goes to Cliff's theory about the mercenary mindset of girls. Cliff theorizes what other people call courtship is all just a goddamn transaction. Girls would rather go out with some rich fuck, who the bill doesn't mean shit to, than some lovesick dope, who's saved up and is spending his last dollar on them.

But not *this* girl. He holds out his gift and the dog jumps up in the air, catching the bone in her mighty jaws. Cliff lets go, and Brandy retreats to her corner with her little pillow and privately gnaws on the bovine bone.

How Cliff and Brandy came to be acquainted is kind of an interesting story. It was a little over two years ago. Cliff was sitting in his trailer home behind the Van Nuys Drive-In when his phone rang. On the other end was Cliff's ne'er-do-well stuntman friend, Buster Cooley. Cooley owed Cliff thirty-two hundred dollars. This amount had racked up over the last five or six years. Four hundred here, five hundred and fifty there. He first lent his friend some cash during the time Cliff was doing better than he ever had. It was during the time his partnership with Rick was allowing him to double the leading man in a series of studio action movies. Rick bitches and moans about this time, but for Cliff, these were his salad days. Actually having money for the first time in his life was kind of a mind fuck for the hand-to-mouth Booth. His big purchase was a nice little boat that he bought, lived on, and kept docked in Marina del Rey. It was during these flush days that he lent Cooley the lion share of the cash. Now, Cliff wasn't an idiot, Cooley might have been taking advantage of him, but he wasn't scamming him. Every time Buster borrowed money from him, he really did need it. They were going to repossess his car, his TV, kick him out of his apartment, his car again; he needed to pay off his Union 76 gas card, his first and last month's rent to get a new apartment. Now, Buster Cooley may have been a mooch, but he wasn't a chiseler. If he had the money, he would have paid Cliff, and Cliff knew that. There was no point in Cliff calling Buster up on the phone and humiliating him. One, he wouldn't get his money any faster that way; two, Buster would just avoid him from that time on; and three, the day would come when the two men did run into each other (L.A. is a small town). And if Cliff put the pressure on Cooley and then Cooley tried to duck him, when they did bump into each other, Cliff would be forced to confront him about it. And that's when things between two men of this type could turn ugly real quick. Cliff knew if Buster ever came into cash, he'd get at least some of it. But he also knew Buster was never going to come into cash. So mentally, two years ago, he kissed that money goodbye. And while, sure, he could use it now, he was still glad that when he had it he could help out an old friend. Maybe not to the tune of three thousand dollars, but, hey, at the time, if he couldn't have afforded it, he wouldn't have lent it.

So Cliff was pleasantly surprised when he heard Cooley's voice on the other end of the telephone receiver. And was even more surprised when Buster asked Cliff could he drive out to Van Nuys and see him that very day. It was a little over an hour later when Buster's 1961 red Datsun pickup truck pulled up in front of Cliff's trailer. Cliff offered his friend a beer, and after they both popped the top on two cans of Old Chattanooga, Cooley brought up to his old buddy the debt he owed. "Okay, about that three thousand dollars I owe ya—"

"Three thousand and two hundred dollars," Cliff corrected.

"Three thousand two hundred? Are you sure?" Cooley asked.

"Positive," Cliff said.

"Well, you know best. Three thousand and two hundred dollars," Cooley said. "About that, I don't got it "

Cliff made no reply, just sipped his beer.

Cooley continued, "But don't despair, I got somethin' even better."

"Something better than three thousand and two hundred dollars in green American foldin' money?" Cliff asked skeptically.

"You bet your sweet ass," Cooley said confidently.

Cliff knew the only thing better than money was painkillers, so unless Cooley had brought with him a suitcase filled with ibuprofen, he was unenthused.

"Pray tell, Buster, what do you have that's better than money?"

With his thumb jerking toward the door, Cooley said, "Come outside and take a look."

The two men stepped outside of the trailer, still drinking their cans of Old Chattanooga, and Buster led Cliff to the rear end of his truck. Standing on all fours in the flatbed of Buster's Datsun, in a wire-mesh cage, stood Brandy.

While Cliff was partial to dogs, and especially female dogs, and Brandy *was* a pretty girl, he at first was unimpressed.

Skeptic Cliff asked, "You mean to tell me this bitch is worth thirty-two hundred dollars?"

"Nope." Cooley smiled and said, "She ain't worth thirty-two hundred dollars." Then added with a wider grin, "She's worth anywhere from seventeen thousand up to twenty thousand dollars."

"Really," asked a doubtful Cliff, "and why is that?"

Cooley answered with conviction, "This dog is the best fighting dog on this side of the fuckin' Western Hemisphere."

That raised Cliff's eyebrows.

Buster continued, "This bitch can take on all comers. Pit bulls, Dobermans, German shepherds, two dogs at once, don't matter. This bitch will chew their ass up."

Cliff looked down at the dog in the cage, silently assessing her as Buster continued, "This bitch ain't just a dog. She's money in the bank. She's a grub steak whenever you need it. She's like owning five falling horses!"

A falling horse was a horse you taught to fall on the ground and not get hurt or not get scared. And in a Hollywood that made hundreds of western movies and television shows, if you owned a horse that knew how to fall on the ground and then get back up again, you owned a little mini printing press of money. The only easier money was lucking out and having a kid who became a successful child actor.

"'member Ned Glass?" Buster reminded Cliff. "Had that falling horse Blue Belle?"

"Yeah?" Cliff said.

"'member how much he made off that jughead?"

"Yeah," Cliff remembered. "He made a small fortune."

"This bitch"—pointing to the bitch in the cage—"is like owning four Blue Belles."

"Okay, Buster," Cliff said, "you got my attention. What's your proposal?"

"Look, I can't give you cash," Cooley honestly stated, "at least not three thousand dollars. But what I can give you is a half interest in the Sonny-fucking-Liston of dogs."

Cliff listened as Buster illustrated his plan: "I got twelve hundred dollars. We put her in a dogfight they got running in Lomita. Bet the twelve hundred on her and just sit back and watch her go to work. Once you see her in action, you'll realize her potential. Then me and you take her on the dogfight circuit, pool our winnings, by fight number six we could both have fifteen thousand each."

Cliff knew Cooley wasn't conning him. He believed everything he just said. But Cooley was selling this as a sure thing, and Cliff never believed in sure things. Plus, dogfighting was illegal, not to mention distasteful, and there was just too much that could go wrong.

"Jesus, Buster," Cliff complained, "I don't wanna fight

69

fuckin' dogs, I just want my money. If you got twelve hundred to bet, why don't you just give me that?" Cliff negotiated.

Buster answered honestly, "Because you and I both know I give you twelve hundred dollars, that's all you're ever gonna get." Buster stressed, "I don't want to pay you back thirty-five cents on the dollar. You were a straight-up fucking cat when I needed help, and I want you to make a profit!" Buster bargained, "At least go with me to the first fight in Lomita. Just watch her fight. Trust me, Cliff, it's one of the most thrilling things you've ever experienced. She wins, that's twenty-four hundred dollars. You don't want to continue, the twenty-four hundred dollars is yours."

Cliff took another swig from his can of beer as he looked at the little muscle man in the wire-mesh cage.

Buster finished his spiel: "Now, you know me, so you know I'm not scamming you. If I say it, I believe it. So trust me—at least this first fight, this bitch can win."

Cliff looked to the little bitch in the cage, then to the son of a bitch standing before him with a beer can in his hand. Then he lowered on his haunches and brought his face parallel with the dog on the other side of the wire mesh. Both Cliff and the dog got into a staring contest. When the little lady could no longer handle the man's forceful gaze, she growled and snapped at Cliff. The wire mesh stopped the canine's teeth from puncturing Cliff's handsome face. Cliff Booth turned and looked up at Buster Cooley. "What's her name?"

Cliff, Buster, and Brandy went to the first fight in Lomita. And everything Buster said came true. Brandy was the real deal, and she killed that other dog in less than a minute.

They won twenty-four hundred dollars that night. Cliff couldn't believe how incredibly thrilling the experience was. *Fuck the Kentucky Derby*, he thought, *this is the most exciting forty-five seconds in sports.*

Cliff was hooked.

For the next six months, they went on the dogfight circuit all over Los Angeles County, Kern County, and the Inland Empire. They fought Brandy in fights in Compton, Alhambra, Taft, and Chino. And Brandy won them all and won *most* of them easy. Only a few times did she get hurt, and even then, never *too* bad. And whenever she did get hurt, they took the time to let her recover. But after those first five fights, where Brandy seemed indestructible, the bets became bigger and the competition more fierce. Those fights took them to Montebello, Inglewood, Los Gatos, and Bellflower. Brandy kept winning, but the fights became excruciatingly longer, far bloodier, she got far more hurt, and it took her far longer to recover.

That was the downside. The upside was tougher dogs meant much more money when she won.

After nine fights, Cliff and Buster had made about fourteen thousand each. But Buster, knowing a good thing when he finally fell into it, had a number in mind. Twenty thousand dollars each for him and Cliff. Then Brandy could retire. But it was during her tenth fight, in San Diego, where the young lady fought a pit bull named Caesar, that she got hurt and hurt bad. The fight was called off with no winner declared. And Cliff knew it was lucky for Brandy that it was called off. Because if it had gone on twenty minutes more, Caesar would have killed her. In both wartime and peacetime, Cliff had seen loved ones cut asunder. But the agony he experienced watching Brandy taking the punishment she took from the vicious Caesar was more than he could bear.

So he was shocked when Buster booked Brandy in another competition in Watts, against a male monster named Augie Doggie, before she had fully recovered from the last beating she took.

But Buster was sure of himself. "Hey, man, I promised you twenty thousand dollars, and I promised myself twenty thousand dollars, and we're right there, man! This fight is the last fuckin' fight!"

"No shit it's the last fucking fight!" Cliff shouted. "There's no fucking way she can win against that beast Augie Doggie in her condition."

"That's the beauty of it," Buster animatedly expressed. "She ain't gotta win. It's about her undefeated reputation. We enter her in the fight and bet on the other dog."

That's when Cliff attacked Buster. They grappled in savage combat inside of Cliff's trailer for about four minutes, till Cliff broke Buster Cooley's neck.

Killing him.

They fought around five in the afternoon. Cliff watched TV next to Buster's dead body till about two in the morning. Then, after the drive-in closed, Cliff crammed the dead body in the trunk of Cooley's car, a used white 1965 Impala Sport Coupe he'd bought with his Brandy winnings. With Brandy in the passenger seat, Cliff drove to Compton and abandoned the car there with the keys placed in the sun visor. He walked Brandy away from the car all night till daybreak. And when the sun came up, he and his dog hopped on a bus back home to Van Nuys.

This wasn't the first time Cliff committed murder and got away with it. The first time was in Cleveland in the fifties. The second time was when Cliff killed his wife two years earlier. This was his third time, and Cliff got away with this one too. He never heard a word about what eventually happened to Buster Cooley or his car. In fact, nobody he knew ever brought Buster up again. That was last year. And since that time Cliff's only fought Brandy twice, when he was really hard up for cash. But after the last time, Cliff promised Brandy, even though Brandy didn't understand, he'd never fight her again. And that was a promise Cliff intended to keep.

In Cliff's trailer on Friday night, February 7, 1969, he snaps his fingers and points at a chair. Next to Cliff's recliner sits a wooden chair with a little dog pillow on it. Brandy hops on top of it and takes her position on her hind legs, waiting for Cliff to prepare her dinner. Cliff takes his time preparing Brandy's dinner, even though he knows this is torture for the dog. But that's okay—Cliff knows better than most that torture can build character. Before he prepares her meal, he first opens his refrigerator and removes from a plastic six-pack ring a can of Old Chattanooga beer.

His small black-and-white rabbit-eared television is tuned to the local ABC affiliate, KABC Channel 7. A commercial for Cliff's brand of cigarettes, Red Apple, plays on the little monochromatic screen. A sixties-era regular guy with Bryl-creemed hair in a black suit and tie stares into the camera in a head-and-shoulders frame.

An off-screen announcer asks the guy, "Would you take a bite of a Red Apple?"

The regular man answers enthusiastically, "You bet I would!"

Then, from below frame, he brings a big red apple up to his mouth and bites into it with a healthy crunch.

Cliff takes a sip of his Old Chattanooga and then lays the can on the kitchen counter. He opens his kitchen cabinet and removes two cans of Wolf's Tooth dog food (*Good Food for Mean Dogs*). Cliff opens the cans with a cheapy hand-crank can opener, then dunks the muck, still in the shape of the can, into Brandy's dog dish. Knowing it's feeding time and watching the food slither out of the can and plop into her dish, it's killing Brandy to stay in her chair and not make a noise. But Cliff's trained her and trained her well. She might not know much, but she knows what's expected of her during feeding time. And she knows *damn well* that she *must* stay in that chair and sit *without whining* till her master gives her the signal that she can eat.

On the little black-and-white television screen, a sixties-era female Marlo Thomas type with a small bouffant hairdo stares into the camera in a head-and-shoulders shot as an off-screen announcer asks her, "Would you take a bite of a Red Apple?"

She answers, "You bet I would!" Then she brings a huge red apple up to her mouth and takes a big crunchy bite.

In her chair, Brandy wags her tail furiously from left

to right, while her muscled body vibrates with excitement, anticipation, and canine instinct. Now that Cliff is through plopping both cans of dog food into Brandy's dog dish, he turns his attention to the stove and removes the pot of boiling water from the burner. Cliff pours the pot of steaming-hot noodles into a strainer, then, after giving the strainer a couple of shakes to lose the excess water, he dumps the noodles back into the pot.

On the TV screen, a pretty young black woman with naked shoulders and a big round Afro looks into the camera as the off-screen announcer asks, "Would you take a bite of a Red Apple?" She looks at the off-screen announcer and says, "You bet I would." Then the Afro gal brings a lit cigarette up from below frame, takes a big drag, and lets out a long stream of smoke with a pleasurable moan, then says, "Take a bite and feel all right, take a bite of a Red Apple."

Cliff takes the cheese-powder packet from the ripped-open box of Kraft Macaroni and Cheese, tears it open, and pours it on top of the noodles in the pot. He stirs up the orange powder with a big wooden spoon and a lot of muscle. The directions say to add milk and butter, but Cliff thinks if you can afford to add milk and butter you can afford to eat something else. As Cliff prepares his dinner, he hears a whine escape from a vibrating and twitching Brandy. Cliff looks at her. Placing the pot with the mac and cheese on the counter, he turns and gives Brandy his full attention.

"Did I just hear a whine?" Cliff asks the canine. Brandy knows she's not supposed to whine, she just couldn't help it, she's a dog. Cliff continues to address the excited dog with an authoritative tone. "What did I tell you about whining? You whine, you don't eat," Cliff instructs, "and I throw all this shit in the trash," referring to the two cans of Wolf's Tooth dog food piled in her dog dish. "I don't want to, but I will." Cliff clarifies, "Do you understand?"

Brandy answers with a distinct "Woof!"

"You better," Cliff tells her.

He then picks up a big bag of Gravy Train, a very popular dry dog food of the era, and pours it on top of the wet food in the dog dish. It brings the mountain of dog food to a peak. Cliff could give a shit if the dry kibble spills out of the bowl all over the kitchen floor, because no matter where it goes, Brandy will find it and eat it.

On the television, after the off-screen announcer has described all the different assortments of fine Red Apple tobacco products, the commercial cuts to a head-and-shoulders shot of famous actor Burt Reynolds, smoking a Red Apple plastic-tip cigar.

The off-screen announcer gets his attention: "Hey, Burt Reynolds, would you take a bite of a Red Apple?"

Burt looks at the camera and says, "Oh, you bet I would." He takes a drag from the cigar and blows it out, then says the Red Apple Tobacco slogan: "Take a bite and feel all right, take a bite . . . of a Red Apple."

Cliff grabs the pot by the handle and goes into the living room and sits in his recliner in front of the TV set. Brandy is all eyes and ears. Once Cliff is settled in his chair and eats his first forkful of Kraft Macaroni and Cheese, he makes a small clicking noise with the side of his mouth.

That's Brandy's signal—she leaps out of the chair, bounds into the kitchen area, and wolfishly devours the food in her dog dish. Cliff changes the channel on his little TV set from KABC Channel 7 to KCBS Channel 2 and the Friday-night detective show *Mannix*, starring Mike Connors and Gail Fisher as detective Joe Mannix and his black secretary, Peggy. On the TV screen, Peggy seems worried as she relates the incidents of last night to her boss, Joe Mannix, as he sits behind his desk.

"Okay, Peggy, what's up?" Mannix asks. "We were all groovin' in the club last night," Peggy tells him, "then, wham, a sudden change." Joe tries to explain it away: "You know how these musicians are; they're temperamental cats. Who knows what got into him."

Cliff likes *Mannix*, both the show and the dude Mannix. Joe Mannix is his kind of guy. In fact, there's a part of Cliff that kinda wishes he *was* Mannix. And if he *was* Mannix, the first thing he'd do is *fuck* Peggy. Cliff is also a big fan of the secret agent character Matt Helm. Not those insipid Dean Martin movies that are beyond asinine, but the books written by Donald Hamilton. As a character, Matt Helm is unconsciously racist, consciously misogynistic, and Cliff loves him. Cliff quotes pulp-fiction heroes like Matt Helm, Shell Scott, and Nick Carter the way the British quote Keats and the French quote Camus.

When he went to see the first Matt Helm movie at the cinema, *The Silencers*, he irately asked the box-office girl for his money back after the first fifteen minutes. If it made *him* sick, he could only imagine what it must have done to the author, Donald Hamilton. Dean Martin was a fucking terrible Matt Helm! But if the movies had been done like the books, Mike Connors would have been terrific. Even the drawing of *Matt* on the cover of the books looks like Connors.

As *Mannix* and *Peggy* continue their scene, Cliff puts down the cooking pot filled with noodles and picks up the issue of *TV Guide*. As Brandy wolfs down her mountain of food, Cliff looks up this week's episode of *Mannix* and reads the synopsis out loud:

"'Death in a Minor Key: Mannix searches for Peggy's missing boyfriend, a Negro musician who escaped from a road gang. Heading south, the detective faces a run-in with an enigmatic police chief, a bigoted witness, and a ubiquitous interloper.'"

Cliff tosses the *TV Guide* aside, picks the pot of orange and yellow food back up, and sticks a forkful in his mouth. As he chews, he asks himself and Brandy, "What's a *ubiquitous interloper*?"

Approximately twenty miles away, in Chatsworth, California, on what's left of the dilapidated western-town movie set known as Spahn Movie Ranch, the eighty-year-old George Spahn sits in his house, in his bathrobe and pajamas, on his couch, watching the same *Mannix* episode at the same time. He watches the show with his twenty-one-year-old red-headed and freckle-faced caretaker, "Squeaky." They watch TV like this every night. He sits on his couch in his bathrobe and pajamas, while she lays sprawled out on the couch with her head in his lap. Since George is blind, Squeaky describes the action on the television screen to the sightless old man. "So that nigger that works for Mannix is asking Joe to help find that nigger trumpet player boyfriend of hers from the first scene."

"Peggy's a nigger?" George squawks with surprise.

Squeaky rolls her eyes and says, "I tell you that every week."

Chapter Five

Pussycat's Kreepy Krawl

Pasadena, California
February 7, 1969
2:20 A.M.

It's two o'clock in the morning on Greenbriar Lane in a suburban housing tract in an affluent section of Pasadena, California.

Up and down both sides of the cul-de-sac street runs a collection of suburban houses with manicured front lawns with upper-middle-class white people inside. At this time of night, except for a random cat, or a bold coyote who ventured down out of the hills to eat out of trash cans, there is no movement in the neighborhood whatsoever. All the residents of this street seem fast asleep, safe behind locked doors, in their comfy beds with soft-purring air conditioners.

Standing on the sidewalk in front of one dark house with a homey mailbox in front that reads *The Hirshbergs* are five members of Charlie Manson's "Family." Chipped-front-tooth "Clem"; "Sadie"; "Froggy"; one of the youngest Family members, Debra Jo Hillhouse (aka "Pussycat"); and Charlie himself.

Charlie stands behind Debra Jo; his two hands rest on her shoulders as he quietly and softly speaks into her ear.

"Okay, Pussycat," Charlie purrs, "it's your time. Time to cross the line. Time to face fear. Time to face fear in the face. And now, honeychile . . . it's time you do it by your lonesome."

Debra Jo reminds him that this isn't her first "kreepy krawl." Her spiritual leader acknowledges, yes, she has, but not on her own. He reminds her of "the Family" philosophy of there being strength in numbers.

As he explains it, "That's why we do what we do, how we do it, and why how we live is ultimately important." But then he clarifies as his fingers gently massage her shoulder blades under her dirty black T-shirt, "But also important is *individual achievement*. Testing one's self. Facing one's fears. And one only faces one's fears by themselves. That's why I'm compelling you to do this, Debra Jo."

Charlie is the only person on God's green earth, other than her father, that she still allows to call her by her born name rather than her adopted one.

"I want to do this," Debra Jo says, not too convincingly.

"Why do you want to do this?" Charlie asks.

"Because you want me to," she answers.

"Yes, I do want you to," Charlie agrees. "But I don't want you to do it for me. And I don't want you to do it for them," jerking his head toward the other kids. "I want you to do it for yourself."

Charlie's fingertips on her shoulder blades feel the slight trembling of Debra Jo's body.

"I can feel you trembling, pretty girl."

"I'm not scared," she protests.

"Shhh," he hushes her. "It's okay. No need to lie."

He explains to the dark-haired beauty, "Ninety-seven percent of everybody you've ever met in your life, and ninety-seven percent of everybody you'll ever meet in your life, have spent ninety-seven percent of their lives running away from fear. But not you, pretty girl," he whispers. "You're walking *toward* fear. *Fear* is the point. Without *fear*, there is no point."

While Debra Jo's trembling doesn't subside, her body under Charlie's touch does seem to relax. Standing behind her, Charlie leans forward and into her right ear asks in a soft whisper, "Do you trust me?"

"You know I do," she says. "I love you."

"And I love you, Debra Jo," Charlie tells her, "and it's that love that ever so slightly nudges you toward greatness. I'm in your heart, 'Pussycat,' I'm in your paws, I'm in your tail, I'm in your nose, and I'm in your pussycat skull."

Charlie's fingers come off her shoulders, and he wraps his arms around the young girl, embracing her from behind. She leans her weight back against him. And they both slowly sway from side to side, shifting their weight from their left foot to their right foot, rocking her like a baby in his arms.

"Allow me the privilege of guiding you through this. And the girl who emerges from that house will be gargantuanly more powerful than the girl who enters it."

Then Charlie unwraps his arms from around her waist, takes a small step backward, and slaps the ass of her blue-jean cutoffs, moving her forward toward the Hirshberg house.

In 1968, Terry Melcher, record producer of the Byrds, the brainchild behind Paul Revere and the Raiders, and boy wonder of Columbia Records, spent a good amount of time around Charlie Manson and his "Family" when they were encamped at the Hollywood home of Dennis Wilson and sponging off the Beach Boy. Terry Melcher was never quite as convinced of Charlie's musical talent as Wilson was. When it came to Manson's musical aspirations, Terry didn't think Charlie was without talent. Terry's honest opinion of Charlie's music was that Manson was very very very *not bad*.

But if Charlie Manson *did* have anything to offer, it was that of a folkie singer-songwriter type. And in that plentiful congregation, Charlie couldn't hold a flickering birthday next to Neil Young, Phil Ochs, Dave Van Ronk, Ramblin' Jack Elliott, Mickey Newbury, Lee Dresser, Sammy Walker, or frankly any of the known folk names of the time. Also, the folk scene, as it existed only a few short years earlier, was dead. By that time, all the folkies who had made a name for themselves were plugging into amps and trying to be rock stars.

And since Terry Melcher represented Columbia Records and they already had Bob Dylan, they didn't need Charlie Manson. Besides, Melcher wasn't in the acoustic singer-songwriter business anymore (*as if* he ever was). Paul Revere and the Raiders had made him one of the kings of Top 40 radio pop. He wasn't raiding the Vanguard Records label, trying to poach talent for Columbia. He was looking for the next gimmicky band of cute shaggy-haired boys who could produce catchy novelty records, play on *American Bandstand* and all the other local-TV-station rock shows (*Groovy, Boss City, The Real Don Steele Show, Where the Action Is, It's Happening*), and vie for space inside the pages of *Sixteen* and *Tiger Beat* magazines. That might have been Bobby Beausoleil, but it sure wasn't Charles Manson.

It wasn't that Charlie didn't have *talent*—he had a *little* talent. But what he *didn't* have was the discipline to nurture the talent that he *did* have. If Charlie had a stronger songbook, it wouldn't have persuaded Terry to record a Manson album for Columbia. But it might have resulted in Melcher bringing one of Charlie's songs to Linda Ronstadt to record.

Terry did think Charlie was one interesting far-out cat. But even in those regards, Terry wasn't as fascinated with him as his other friends (Dennis Wilson and Greg Jakobson) were. The real reason Terry Melcher spent so much time with Charlie and "the Family" when they were encamped at Dennis Wilson's pad wasn't due to any potential that the record producer saw in Manson in a business sense. It was due to the fact that Terry loved fucking a fifteen-year-old dark-haired angel named Debra Jo Hillhouse, who had taken up with "the Family." When Terry first met her, she still went by her real name, Debra Jo. But shortly afterward she only answered to her "Family" name, "Pussycat."

Debra Jo had joined Charlie's Family when she was fifteen, at the time the youngest of the bunch, and she was undoubtedly the beauty of the bunch. Only statuesque Leslie Van Houten gave her any competition. And Terry Melcher wasn't the only one—Dennis Wilson loved fucking Debra Jo too. In fact, the only serious connections Manson ever made in the Los Angeles music scene weren't due to Charlie's music but due to the allure of Debra Jo Hillhouse's pubescent pussy. Debra Jo held a special place in the heart of Terry Melcher. (If Debra Jo could sing, she's the one who would have gotten a record deal.)

And bear in mind all this was occurring during the time that Terry Melcher was living with sixties-era zeitgeist beauty Candice Bergen.

But even with beautiful blond Candy Bergen at home, Terry couldn't pass up Pussycat encounters. At one point his affection got so brazen that he tried to hire Debra Jo as a house girl and move her into his Cielo Drive home with Candy and himself. (Candice Bergen might've been oblivious about a lot of things, but she knew enough to squash that idea.)

Debra Jo Hillhouse had an unaffected little kitten quality (that's why Charlie named her Pussycat) that left many older men smitten. Including a few members of the Straight Satans, the motorcycle gang that hung out with Charlie and the Family when they lived at Spahn Ranch.

Something that made Debra Jo unique from all the other girls that Charlie collected was, Debra Jo still had a relationship with her father, and her father had a relationship with Charlie. All the other girls, to one degree or another, joined Charlie's Family in response to their damaged relationship with their family. Disowning your parents, divorcing your real family, becoming a member of your new Family, with Charlie as your *daddy*, that was all part of Manson's spiel. But in Debra Jo Hillhouse's case, it was through her father that she first met Charlie a year earlier.

One afternoon after having sex in Dennis Wilson's billiard room, while they shared a joint and drank ice-cold bottles of Mexican beer, Terry Melcher quizzed Debra Jo about how she came to first be acquainted with Charles Manson.

Debra Jo told him. "My dad picked him up hitchhiking."

"Wait a minute," a surprised Terry said, "you met Charlie through your dad?"

She nodded her bushy brunette head yes. "Charlie was hitching," she repeated. "Dad picked him up, they started talking. They grooved. So Dad brought him home for dinner. That's when we first met."

Terry took a big hit off the joint and passed it to Debra Jo. While holding the reefer smoke in his lungs, he asked her, "How long after that did you go off with Charlie?"

"That night," she told him. "I snuck out of the house and we balled in Dad's car. Then I got the car keys and we took the car and drove off together."

Holy shit, Terry thought. *How the fuck does a little runt like Charlie pull that off? I mean, some of those ugly hippie sluts like Mary Brunner or Patty Krenwinkel, okay. But a little hot piece of ass like Debra Jo?*

Then Debra Jo told him the whole wild tale of Manson and the Hillhouses. Ending with her father asking Charlie if he could join "the Family."

To which Terry exclaimed, "You gotta be fuckin' kidding me!"

Debra Jo smiled and shook her head no. But then added, "But even Charlie thought *that* was too weird."

Jesus-fucking-Christ, Terry thought, he couldn't even get Candy Bergen to agree to a female hippie maid, while Charlie apparently had no problem influencing everybody he met to do whatever he needed them to do. Whatever charm Charlie possessed might be lost on Terry, but it was obvious to even Melcher that he had *something*. In his day he'd seen rock stars manipulate hippie girls to do some pretty outrageous shit. But their fathers? That was a whole other level of influence. Terry doubted even Mick Jagger could pull that shit off.

Debra Jo, knees visibly shaking, slowly approaches the Hirshberg house. She crosses the dew-covered front lawn. She feels the wetness of the grass against the soles of her huge bare feet, and the slight chill is invigorating. When she steps off the lawn onto the concrete pathway that leads toward the backyard gate, she leaves a trail of wet footprints behind her.

She reaches her hand over the wooden gate door and, quietly as she can, lifts the rusty metal hinge on the other side, pushes the door open, and enters the backyard. Her friends watching from the sidewalk slowly disappear from view.

Now Pussycat is by herself on the Hirshbergs' private property. She scans the surroundings. There's a kidney-shaped pool. Green grass. A big tree. A couple of picnic tables. And a couple of heavily-played-with children's Big Wheels. But other than the Big Wheels, the backyard is as nice and neat and manicured as the front of the house.

Then the voice of Charlie whispers in her ear, *How's your heart?*

She quietly answers the voice in her head out loud: "Beating like a jackhammer."

Calm it down, Pussycat, he purrs. *Them jungle drums will wake up the whole damn block. Get a hold of it*, he instructs, *and get a hold of yourself. Take in your surroundings.*

She examines the backyard with a touch more thoughtfulness, her rapid heartbeat ever so slightly decreasing.

Who lives there? he asks her.

"I don't know—the Hirshbergs, I guess."

Not their names, he whispers sharply. *Who are they? Do they have kids? Do you see toys?*

She looks at the Big Wheels and nods her head yes.

A lot of toys? he asks. *A swing set?*

"No," she answers, "just a couple of Big Wheels."

What does that tell you? he asks.

"I don't know, what should it tell me?"

Hey, pretty girl, he gently scolds her, *I'm the one talking in question marks. You're the one answering in periods. Got it?*

She nods her head yes.

So they either have kids or they know kids, Charlie figures. *Like maybe Grandma and Grandpa? We'll answer that question later. Are they rich?*

She nods her head yes.

How do you know? Charlie challenges.

"They live here, don't they?" she says somewhat sarcastically.

Not so fast, Pussycat, Charlie warns. *Don't judge a book by its cover, little darling. They could be renters. They could be four stewardesses or cocktail waitresses living together, pooling the rent.* Then he suddenly asks, *Do they have a pool?*

"Yes," she says.

Touch the water, he orders.

Pussycat creeps across the grass covering most of the backyard, over to the swimming pool. And then dips her fingers in the water.

Once her hand feels the wetness, the voice inside her head asks, *Is it warm?*

She nods her head yes.

Then they're rich, Charlie explains. *Only rich people can afford to heat their pool all the time.*

That makes sense, Pussycat thinks.

Are you ready to enter the house? Charlie whispers.

She nods her head yes.

Charlie gets sharp: *Don't nod your head, bitch! I asked you a question! Are you ready to enter the house?*

"Yes," she says.

Yes what? he asks.

"Yes, sir?" she guesses.

He gets loud and irate. *Not "yes, sir," goddammit, and what the fuck did I tell you about those question marks?*

Then she answers, louder than she should considering the situation, "Yes, I am!"

A jubilant Charlie answers back in her brain, *There ya go! That's my pretty girl! What kinda door they got leading from the backyard to the house?*

She looks at the house and answers, "Sliding-glass door."

Well, then you're in luck, kiddo. Them the kinda doors the safe and secure tend to forget to bolt. Now, creep on over and see how lucky you are.

As her bare feet inch over the wet grass toward the concrete of the backyard patio, Debra Jo thinks, *If I'm really lucky, the door will be bolted shut and I can go home.* She reaches the glass door and lowers on her haunches. She peers inside. Everything is dark. No movement. She listens intently. Except for the jungle drums of her tom-tom-ing heartbeat, which has resumed rhythmically beating again, she hears no sound. With one arm she reaches up and yanks on the heavy sliding-glass door. It doesn't slide open.

Charlie pops back in her head again. *Those doors can be a little heavy. Try again, harder, and with both hands.*

This time she grabs the handle with both hands and gives the door a bigger yank. It slides partially open. Once she saw it actually move, she caught her breath.

Oh shit, she thinks. *I'm going to have to go in there.*

She can hear Charlie's grin in her brain. Then he enters her soul to co-pilot her through the next phase of the kreepy krawl. *Now, before you enter the house, squash your ego. Cease to exist. Keep on all fours like the pussycat you are. You ain't got no more energy than a neighborhood cat explorin' a house that left a back door open. Understand?*

She nods her head yes.

Keep the sliding door open, he tells her, *in case you hafta make a fast getaway.*

Pussycat moves aside the curtain, and while on all fours, she crawls inside the house. She enters on her hands and

90

knees and moves across the hard, cool linoleum floor of the kitchen into the shag-carpeted living room area.

Once in the middle of the living room, she sits her ass on the floor, lets her eyes adjust to the darkness, taking in her surroundings.

Charlie continues with his question marks.

Who are these people? Are they old? Are they middle age? Are they parents or grandparents?

"I don't know," she answers.

Look at the furniture, he tells her, *look at the knickknacks*.

Pussycat scans the room. She looks at the framed pictures on the wall, on the TV, the doodads on the mantel above the fireplace; she sees the hi-fi stereo unit with a stack of LPs leaned up against the wall.

She crawls over to the records and flips through the stack.

Rudy Vallée.

Kate Smith.

Jackie Gleason.

Frankie Laine.

Jack Jones.

John Gary.

Broadway cast albums: *South Pacific*; *Fiddler on the Roof*; *No, No, Nanette*. *Exodus* motion picture soundtrack.

"They're old," Pussycat tells Charlie. "I'm guessin' grandparents."

Well, let's not guess, Debra Jo, let's deduce. He asks, *Do children live there?*

She says, "I don't know."

Well, look around, he says.

She does—the place is definitely tidy.

Pussycat responds, "There's a few toys in the backyard, but I don't think kids live here."

Why not? Charlie asks.

"Because the people who live here are old," she's decided. "Old people are clean. Tidy. Everything in its place. That's a luxury folks with children don't have."

Good for you, Pussycat. She can feel Charlie's smile shoot through her entire body. *How's that heart of yours doin'?*

"Calm."

I believe you. Can you see the stairs?

She nods her head yes.

How's that ego?

"Nonexistent."

Then you might be ready to rise off the floor and stand.

Pussycat rises from the floor to a standing position. The room looks very different standing at her full height. She pulls her black T-shirt off over her head and through her bushy hair, letting it fall to the shag-carpet floor. She then unbuttons and unzips her Levi's cutoffs and slides them quietly down her long bare legs. Then finally she peels off her filthy panties and drops them on her pile of discarded clothes. Once she's shed all her clothes, the naked girl bends down, lifts the cutoffs out of the pile, reaches in the bulbous side pocket, and yanks out one red light bulb. She places the red light bulb in her mouth, her lips wrapping around the silver metal coil.

Then, naked on all fours, she crawls up the carpeted stairway that leads to the house's second floor. Her nude feline body softly and quietly slinks up toward where the bedrooms are.

Once she reaches the top of the stairs, her head slowly turns to the right and then to the left, and it's to the left where she makes out the door that appears to be the entrance of the master bedroom. No more Charlie in her head now, Debra Jo is completely on her own. On her knuckles and knees, she prances down the hall like her nicknamed namesake, toward the half-open bedroom door.

With her ego-less energy, she silently pokes her head through the doorway and peers into the dark bedroom. From her vantage point on the floor, Pussycat discovers she deduced correctly, that yes indeed this is the master bedroom, and the couple who lie asleep in their marital Craftmatic king-sized bed are grandparent age.

Pussycat crawls into the room, twisting her naked body to fit through the open space, careful not to brush up against the bedroom door lest she be betrayed by a squeaky hinge. Once her hands and her knees have maneuvered her feet inside the room, her eyes rise to the surface of the bed. The old man asleep in his bed, dressed in blue pajamas with up-and-down white stripes, is lying on the closest side to her and the door.

The room has the fragrance of Ben-Gay, Pine-Sol evergreen air freshener, Old Spice, and foot odor. The air conditioner sticking out of the far-right bedroom window hums a good solid baseline noise that helps mask her subtle movements. That's the good part. The bad part is it's much colder in the master bedroom than it was in the living room and the upstairs hallway. Chill bumps sprout up across her exposed skin like hives. The goosebumps that pop up on her naked derriere give the young girl that Charlie christened

Pussycat the feeling of what having a tail might be like. Indulging in the whole house-cat masquerade, she gives her bony ass a little wiggle. Yet the chilly temperature doesn't act as an obstacle. Instead, like the cool bracing waters of a mountain stream, after the initial sensation of cold air making contact with warm flesh, she finds the shudder that runs through her body invigorating.

She inches closer to the side of the bed. Then Debra Jo slowly rises from her all-fours feline position to her knees. Her face is very close to the face of the sleeping old man reclining in his bed. The red light bulb sticking out of her mouth gives the young girl an inhuman expressionless demeanor, sort of a cross between a robot and a blow-up fuck doll. Only her pronounced dark eyebrows, which verge on one long unibrow, indicate any sense of expression.

She examines the face of the sleeping old man. His labored breathing that veers ever so close to snoring. His wispy white hair strands that spring up from his bulbous skull, every single strand going its own way. The sunken lips on his toothless mouth. She looks over at the bedside end table and, sure enough, next to a pair of glasses, a lamp, and a small clock sit a set of false teeth soaking in a cloudy glass of water.

Her curious gaze goes from the dentures to the sleeping old fart, to his elderly female companion sleeping next to him. She's a touch on the fat side when compared to her bony, ghoul-like husband. Unlike the old man's every white stringy follicle for itself, the old lady has her bright-orange-dyed hair done up in tight curls that obviously must require weekly beauty-shop visits and quarter jars of Dippity-do to maintain.

Debra Jo takes her hand and places it above the sleeping old man's face and wiggles her fingers. He doesn't stir in the slightest, just continues his loud rhythmic breathing. She's feeling confident now, so she slowly rises to a standing position off her two knees onto her two feet. After all the time she's spent close to the ground in her cat-like posture, standing upright at her full height gives her the sensation of being a *Gulliver*-like giant.

Using the balls of her feet, she silently pads away from the bed and its inhabitants, across the room, over to the bedroom window that faces the front of the house. The curtains to the window are open, and she looks through the glass and sees Charlie and her friends standing together in front of the house on the sidewalk. Froggy is the first one to spot her and jumps up and gives Debra Jo an excited wave. The rest of the group wave up at her like they're restaging the closing credits of *The Beverly Hillbillies*.

Debra Jo, red light bulb sticking out of her mouth, looks down at them through the Hirshbergs' bedroom window and waves back. Quietly, she moves over to a wooden chair parked in front of the woman of the house's vanity table, lifts it off the floor, and brings it up to the window. Also by the window is a bedroom lamp. Sneaking a quick glance at the sleeping couple to make sure she hasn't disturbed them, she begins to slowly unscrew the top of the lamp that holds the shade in place. Once she's done that and has placed the screw top on the table, she silently lifts the lampshade from its home base and quietly places it on the floor. All the while watching the couple in bed for any sign of consciousness creeping up. So far, so good. Keeping both eyes peeled on the old fogies for a reaction, she unscrews the light bulb.

This is by far the noisiest thing she's done, yet the couple's rhythmic breathing, the air conditioner, and her squashed ego keep the equilibrium in the room from changing drastically. Once she is through her final rotation, Debra Jo lifts the light bulb clear of the lamp. Then places it noiselessly on the couple's carpeted bedroom floor. The brunette intruder removes the red light bulb from her mouth and screws it into the lamp's light socket. Once it can turn no farther, she knows she's accomplished her task.

She twists the tiny knob on the lamp till it clicks and the room is bathed in a glowing red light. She watches the couple in bed for a reaction to the change in atmosphere, ready to race out of there if the red light has disturbed their REM. But the low-watt red bulb is still dark enough not to disrupt their slumber.

So she climbs up onto the chair by the window, her naked body framed in the windowsill, backlit by a red-hued Amsterdam-like tableau in the middle of Pasadena. She smiles down at her friends below on the sidewalk, who jump up and down in excitement at Debra Jo's accomplishment. The sixteen-year-old brunette begins gyrating a go-go dance in the window for the amusement of her friends outside. They applaud and cheer her on. She undulates up and down, dancing wilder and wilder, while her friends whoop and whistle, till she jumps off the chair, runs across the floor, and leaps into the bed with the sleeping old couple with a cackling "Geronimo!"

The old couple wakes to find this naked brunette teenager rolling around in bed with them, laughing like a lunatic. The old woman lets out a bloodcurdling scream, as the old man sputters, "What the hell?"

Debra Jo throws her arms around the old man's neck and plants a big kiss on his toothless mouth. When he tries to scream, she shoves her tongue inside of it. Then she lets go, hops out of the bed, runs out of the room, down the stairs, through the living room (snatching her clothes as she goes by), out the open sliding-glass door, through the backyard and the backyard gate, across the front lawn, and down Greenbriar Lane with her "Family," laughing.

Chapter Six

"Hollywood or Bust"

Outside of Dallas, Texas
Four Years Earlier

The rodeo cowboy in the dirty white '59 Cadillac Coupe de Ville, pulling a dirty white horse trailer with a dusty brown horse in it, spotted the young lady with her thumb sticking out on the side of the road on the highway heading out of Dallas about a quarter of a mile before he reached her. She sported a tight pink T-shirt, a banana-colored miniskirt, long bare legs and bare feet, a big white sun hat, and a canvas duffel bag. Once the cowboy got closer, he saw that tight pink T-shirt covered two large bouncing boobs, and her long bare legs were uncommonly white.

When he pulled over to the side of the road and she bent down to look at him through the passenger-side car-door window, he noted she had long golden-blond hair hanging down from the white sun hat; she was about twenty-two and a goddamn good-looking gal.

"Need a lift?" he asked rhetorically.

"I sure do," said the blonde, sans Texas accent.

The cowboy turned down Merle Haggard crooning about *Tulare Dust* on the radio and said, "Where y'all goin'?"

"California," was the big-boobed blonde's reply.

Spitting snuff juice into an empty Texaco paper coffee cup a tenth filled with brown saliva, the cowboy chuckled, "California? Well, that's a ways away."

"I know," she said, nodding. "Can you help me out?"

"I don't know 'bout California," the cowboy qualified, "but I intend to get outta Texas by seven this evening. I could drop ya off in New Mexico."

"That's a start, cowboy." She smiled.

"Well, get in, cowgirl." He smiled back.

Before she committed to climbing into the fella's Caddy, she examined the cowboy more closely. He was somewhere around forty-seven, handsome but weather-beaten (sorta like his Cadillac); he wore a white straw cowboy hat on his head, a cream-colored snap-button country-and-western-type shirt with armpit stains, and had a big pinch of snuff under his lip. She looked in the backseat, which had a duffel bag in it not too different from hers. Except his had an olive-green military look to it, while hers was black and had the 7 Up logo on it. She looked past the fins of the Cadillac at the horse trailer attached to the back hitch and asked, "You got a horse in that trailer?"

"You know I do," he said.

"What's his name?" she asked.

"*Her* name is Honeychilde," he drawled.

"Well," she said, smiling, "I suppose a fella names his mare Honeychilde ain't gonna rape me."

"Well, that's your first mistake." He grinned at her. "A

dude with a big black stallion named Boston Strangler, now, that's a fella you can trust." He winked.

"Well," the blonde said, "here goes nothin'," throwing her duffel bag in the backseat next to his. She opened the door and climbed into the Cadillac.

"That door is kinda fucked up," the cowboy instructed. "You gotta slam it real hard."

She opened the door again and followed his instructions, slamming it real hard.

"That's the spirit," he said, as he pulled back on to the highway.

The cowboy driver got the conversation started. "So where ya goin' in California?" He turned Merle Haggard back up to a decent volume. "L.A., San Francisco, or Pomona?"

The blond girl asked, "Who would hitch from Texas to Pomona?"

"Well, I just might," the cowboy confessed. "But I ain't no blond bathin' beauty."

"Los Angeles," she said.

"You goin' to be a surfer?" the cowboy asked. "Like Annette Funicello?"

"I don't think she's a real surfer," said the blonde. "In fact, neither her or Frankie even got a tan. You got more of a tan than they got."

"Yeah, I got 'bout five more lines in my forehead than they got too." Looking at his pretty passenger, he said, "And bless your sweet heart callin' my sun damage a *tan*."

The young hitcher introduced herself to the older cowboy; they traded names and shook hands.

"So where ya goin'?" the cowboy asked again.

"Los Angeles. My boyfriend is waiting for me."

The blonde had no boyfriend waiting for her in Los Angeles. That's just what she planned to tell lone men who might give her a ride. She then proceeded to talk for the next forty-five minutes about her imaginary boyfriend, which was all part of her method of hitchhiking. She gave him the name Tony.

It was during her Tony spiel that she started trusting the white-hatted cowboy somewhat, because he was neither disappointed nor uninterested in her new life in L.A. with Anthony.

"Well, if ya ask me," he drawled, "this Tony's one lucky fella!"

"Where are you and Honeychilde off to?" the blonde asked.

Now it was the cowboy's turn to be a little cagey. He and Honeychilde were off to Prescott, Arizona. See, the cowboy was a rodeo rider; he'd just finished one rodeo over the weekend in Dallas, called Wild West Weekend, where he won zip-a-dee doo-dah and banged up everything that wasn't already busted to begin with. Now he was off to Prescott, his hometown, for another rodeo the weekend after next. The Prescott Frontier Days was the first rodeo ever held, back in 1888, and the cowboy would be damned if he was gonna lose in front of his hometown audience. All this he kept mum with the leggy blonde sitting Indian style on his passenger seat, 'cause, frankly, he didn't know if he wanted her company that long. So he talked in detail about the rodeo in Dallas he'd just left and vaguely about where he and his horse were off to. But as the two drove and talked, they got to know each other better, and little by little their defenses dropped away.

Being from Texas and the daughter of a military man, she liked this witty shitkicker good ol' boy. And he liked her too, and not just to look at. She was very bright—that was clear from just a casual conversation. As they talked more, she even revealed she spoke fluent Italian, due to a time her family was stationed in Italy because of her father's military career. Which was enough for the cowboy to classify her as a genius, especially since most of the gals he went for could barely speak English (he was partial to Mexican girls).

The barefoot blonde would have to be dim to not realize how pretty she was. But she didn't define her personality by how she looked. She defined it by her sweet disposition, her curiosity about other people, and her genuine excitement about adventure, and while a touch cautious about the dangers that could befall a young woman on the road, she was nevertheless thrilled. And you could color the cowboy charmed. In fact, it was fair to say he even got a crush on her. But since this young gal was probably no more than twenty-two, she fell outside of the range of his morally approved parameters. He had a rule to never engage in slap and tickle with anybody younger than his twenty-five-year-old daughter. Now his *rule* might be downgraded to a *guideline* if his passenger insisted. But he was aware enough to know how unlikely that was. Their relationship was that of pretty half-dressed passenger and friendly driver, and that was alright by him.

They stopped for dinner at a choke and puke once they

crossed the Texas state line into New Mexico. If she had been broke, he would have offered to buy her a bowl of chili, but since she wasn't, he didn't. They drove two more hours, till he pulled into a motel around nine at night.

Okay, the blonde thought, *if the cowboy's gonna make a play, now's the time.*

But she didn't give him the opportunity. Before he could even offer the backseat of his car for her to sleep in, she had her duffel bag out of the back and was hugging him goodbye. He watched her bare feet walk her off into the dark distance.

During their time together (about six hours), once she got comfortable with him, she revealed her real reason for going to Los Angeles. It was to be an actress and work in movies, or at least television. She admitted she didn't want to say it before because it was such a cliché. Also, it sounded like such a pie-in-the-sky daydream coming from a Texas beauty-pageant winner that it even made her look a little stupid. And *if* people thought that, they wouldn't be alone. Because that's exactly what her father thought.

But the cowboy spit out snuff juice into his little paper cup and disagreed. He told her, a gal out in Los Angeles that was as goddamn good-lookin' as her would hafta be stupid *not* to try a career in pictures. Not only that, he told her, he liked her chances. "Now, if my cousin Sherry wanted to go to Hollywood and be the next Sophia Loren, *that* would be pie in the sky. But a pretty little gal like you," he speculated, "I wouldn't be surprised I don't see you actin' opposite Tony Curtis 'fore long."

* * *

As she disappeared into the night, just before she got out of earshot and he checked himself into the motel, he yelled to her one last note of encouragement: "'member what I said—when you're actin' opposite Tony Curtis, you tell 'em hello for me."

The blonde turned around and shouted back to the cowboy, "Sure thing, Ace, see ya in the movies." She waved one last time and walked off.

And when Sharon Tate eventually made her motion-picture debut opposite Tony Curtis in the silly comedy *Don't Make Waves*, she told Tony Curtis, "Ace Woody says hello."

Chapter Seven

"Good Morgan, Boss Angeles!"

Saturday, February 8, 1969
6:30 A.M.

Cliff's Karmann Ghia drives down the practically deserted street known throughout the world as the Sunset Strip. For Cliff, this is the start of *his* working day, driving his car to his boss's house, to drive his boss to Twentieth Century Fox Studios for his eight o'clock call time. As Cliff pushes the little Volkswagen engine down Sunset Boulevard at six thirty in the morning, he thinks, *If New York is the city that never sleeps, Los Angeles in the middle of the night and early wee hours of the morning turns back into the desert it was before it got paved over with concrete.* A lone coyote digging through a public garbage pail demonstrates how correct that thought is. On the car radio Cliff hears the voice of Robert W. Morgan ("the Boss Tripper"), the early-morning disc jockey of AM radio's 93 KHJ, yelling to his audience of early risers, *"Good Morgan, Boss Angeles!"*

In the sixties and early seventies, all of Los Angeles pulsed to the beat of 93 KHJ. It was known as Boss Radio and it was known for playing the Boss Sounds by the Boss Jocks in Boss Angeles. That is, unless you lived in Watts, Compton, or Inglewood. In that case, you pulsed to the soul beat of KJLH.

KHJ played the groovy sixties' sounds of the Beatles, the Rolling Stones, the Monkees, Paul Revere and the Raiders, the Mamas and the Papas, the Box Tops, the Lovin' Spoonful, as well as later-forgotten groups of the era like the Royal Guardsmen, the Buchanan Brothers, Tompall and the Glaser Brothers, the 1910 Fruitgum Company, the Ohio Express, the Mojo Men, the Love Generation, and others of their ilk. Plus the station had an all-star lineup of disc jockeys, including, along with Morgan, Sam Riddle, Bobby Tripp, Humble Harve (who, like Cliff, would later kill his wife. But Harve wouldn't get away with it), Johnny Williams, Charlie Tuna, and the number-one disc jockey in America, the Real Don Steele. Also, Robert W. Morgan, Sam Riddle, and Don Steele all had local Los Angeles music shows on KHJ-TV Channel 9. Morgan hosted *Groovy*, Riddle hosted *Boss City*, and Steele had, naturally, *The Real Don Steele Show*.

The KHJ radio and TV stations dominated the market with their zeitgeist sounds, crazy promotional contests, wild station-sponsored concerts, and a genuine sense of humor emanating from their on-air cast of cutups.

Sam Riddle would greet his nine-A.M.-till-noon listeners with his catchphrase, "Hello, music lovers!" And the Real Don Steele would constantly remind listeners that "Tina Delgado is alive!" (his most popular and never-explained running joke).

As Cliff drives up one of the residential hills of Hollywood, while Robert W. Morgan's live commercial for Tanya Tanning Butter blends into the melodic *do do do* opening of Simon and Garfunkel's ubiquitous Top 40 hit *Mrs. Robinson*, he sees four young hippie girls, age ranged sixteen to early twenties, cross the neighborhood street in front of his car at a stop sign. The girls look dirty, and not just normal unbathed hippie dirt but like they've been having an orgy in a garbage pail.

All the young ladies seem to be lugging some bundles of food. One girl carries a crate of cabbage heads, another three packages of hot dog buns, still another cradles a bunch of carrots. But the fourth—a sexy, tall, thin, bushy-haired brunette flower-child type, in a crochet halter top, short-short cutoff jeans that show off her long dirty white legs, and filthy big bare feet—waddles in caboose position of this hippie-chick train, lugging a big round jar of giant green pickles as if it were a papoose.

The dirty brunette beauty glances in Cliff's direction and sees him through the windshield of the rumbling Karmann Ghia. A smile spreads across her pretty face in the blond dude's direction. Cliff smiles back. The brunette hoists the pickle jar up to one arm by her right breast, leaving the other arm free to flash the Karmann Ghia driver the peace sign with her two fingers.

Cliff holds up two fingers, flashing it back.

They share a moment together, then the moment's over, she's on the other side of the street, and the filthy females baby-elephant-walk their way down the residential sidewalk. Cliff watches hippie pickle girl from behind as she walks away, willing her to take one glance back at him.

One . . . two . . . three, he counts in his head, then she takes one more look back at him over her shoulder. *Victory*. He smiles to her and himself and presses down on the gas pedal with his moccasin-covered foot and zooms uphill.

6:45 A.M.

When Rick's clock radio wakes him up to the voice of 93 KHJ's morning disc jockey, Robert W. Morgan, he immediately feels that his pillow is soaked cold with alcohol sweat. Today will be his first day of work on a new CBS western pilot named *Lancer*. Naturally, he plays the heavy. A kidnapping, cold-blooded, murdering leader of a bunch of cattle rustlers, which the script refers to as "land pirates."

It's a pretty good script and a darn good part, even though Rick thinks he should be playing the series lead, Johnny Lancer. Rick inquired who got the part—it's some fella named James Stacy, who had guested on a good *Gunsmoke*, that CBS decided to give a show of his own. The other regulars are rugged horse-faced Andrew Duggan as the father, Murdock Lancer, and Wayne Maunder, who recently starred in a canceled series on ABC about Custer, as the other brother, Scott Lancer.

The script is not only good but he has good dialogue, including a lot of dialogue on the first day. So he was up late last night running lines with his tape recorder.

He usually does that floating in his swimming pool, in his floaty chair, while he smokes and drinks whiskey sours. He makes the whiskey sours and pours them into one of the German beer steins from his German beer stein collection. *How many did I have?* he thinks as he lies in bed, nursing a hangover that feels closer to polio and a belly full of last night's booze.

The beer stein holds two barsized whiskey sour cocktails.

How many steins?

Four.

Four?

Four!

That's when he vomited all over himself in his bed.

Most actors and actresses in the sixties had a couple of cocktails or glasses of wine to wind down with once they got home. But Rick turned a couple of whiskey sours at the end of the day into eight whiskey sours, till he blacked out. Rick had no memory of leaving the pool or taking his clothes off or climbing into bed. He just woke up in bed with no idea of how he got there. He looks down at the disgusting mess he made of himself, then glances at the clock radio beside the bed. It reads 6:52. Cliff's going to be there in about twenty minutes, so he better get his shit together. The bad part about barfing on yourself when you wake up in the morning is you feel like a disgusting-pig pathetic-loser. The good part is without all that poison sloshing around in your belly you feel much better.

What Rick didn't know, and wouldn't know for years, is he suffered from a condition that was not commonly known at the time. Since high school, Rick had experienced violent mood swings. His blues were bluer than most, and his highs could border on manic. But since completion of the Universal four-picture deal (and specifically *Salty, the Talking Sea Otter*), his downswings seemed to find a deeper basement than before. Especially alone at home at night, when loneliness, boredom, and self-pity combined to create a toxic self-detest fest, with whiskey sour cocktails his only form of relief-inducing medication.

Seven months later, after Rick returned from the Marvin Schwarz–arranged trip to Italy, with a brand-spanking-new Italian wife, he would get a call from his old mentor-director Paul Wendkos. They hadn't talked in three years, and Rick was glad to hear from him.

"Hello," Rick said into the phone receiver.

"Dalton, you ol' sack, it's Wendkos."

"Hey, Paul, how ya doin'?"

"How am I doin', how the hell are you doin'?" Wendkos said. "I heard some fuckin' hippies busted in your place and you went all *Mike Lewis* on them."

Rick gave a humble no-big-deal kinda laugh and said, "All I did was realize the distance between me and Mike Lewis. He kills a hundred and fifty Nazis and doesn't change his expression. I torched one small hippie girl and I practically shit my pants."

"Well, honestly, Rick," Paul said, "when Lewis killed those guys and his expression didn't change, that wasn't because he was so brave. It was because you can't act."

They both laughed it up on each side of the phone.

What Wendkos was referring to: No sooner did Rick and his new bride arrive from Rome to his house in Benedict Canyon than three hippies (two girls and a guy) broke into his home, brandishing butcher knives and a pistol, threatening his family. Rick and Cliff made short order of the housebreakers, killing all three in a brutal fight. Cliff, in the living room, protecting Rick's new wife, Francesca, bashed in the faces of the guy and one of the girls. Rick, who was

110

in his floaty chair in the swimming pool at the time of the attack, was almost shot by the hippie girl with the pistol. He later told authorities, "That goddamn hippie almost blew my fuckin' head off!"

And in a scene straight out of Wendkos's picture *The Fourteen Fists of McCluskey*, Rick set the assailant on fire with the practice flamethrower left over from *McCluskey*, which he had in his toolshed. ("I burnt that goddamn hippie to a crisp," he later told his neighbor.)

What the armed intruders' intentions were was never made clear. But their intentions sounded both deadly and evil. When Cliff asked the male intruder what he wanted, the young man invoked Satan, saying, "I'm the devil, and I've come here to do the devil's business."

The LAPD theorized the hippie intruders were frying on acid and were out to perform a Satanic ritual. What isn't a matter of theory is, those fucking hippies sure picked the wrong house.

The next day, Rick's adventures hit the news, and it became the talk of the town. It went from local news to the network evening news and finally the world. Something about Jake Cahill killing three long-haired hippie bad guys with his flamethrower from *The Fourteen Fists of McCluskey* just seized the imagination. Till pretty soon the whole ghastly night of violence became heavy with symbolic weight—turning Rick, the former TV cowboy, into a folkloric hero of Nixon's "silent majority."

All this newfound attention wasn't lost on the industry either. Shortly afterward, Dalton was offered a guest-star gig on one of the biggest shows on TV, Bruce Geller's *Mis-*

sion: Impossible. After the flamethrower incident, *TV Guide* did an inside profile on him (his third profile in the magazine). And he was asked to appear for the first time on *The Tonight Show Starring Johnny Carson.* Rick proved a big hit in Johnny's guest chair. And throughout the seventies, Carson had him back on whenever Dalton had a film role, TV movie, high-profile guest shot, or new series to promote. Dalton later confessed to his buddy Cliff, "All in all, those goddamn hippies did me a favor."

Paul Wendkos wasn't just calling Rick up to shoot the shit. He was making the phone call that every actor wants to get. He was calling about Rick's availability. The director was just about to start filming a World War Two programmer based out of England and to be shot in Malta. And not only had the hippie flamethrower incident raised Dalton's profile, but it also raised the profile of the Wendkos film *The Fourteen Fists of McCluskey.*

Wendkos was preparing a film for a small British production company called Oakmont Productions, which had an international distribution deal through MGM. Oakmont specialized in modestly budgeted World War Two action-adventure vehicles featuring British casts, except for the lead, who was usually an American actor known from television. Some examples were Boris Sagal's *The Thousand Plane Raid* starring Christopher (*Rat Patrol*) George; *Mosquito Squadron* starring David (*Man from U.N.C.L.E.*) McCallum; Billy Graham's *Submarine X-1,* starring a pre-*Godfather,* post-*El Dorado* James Caan; Walter Grauman's *The Last Escape,* starring Stuart (*Cimarron Strip*) Whitman; and Wendkos's *Attack on the Iron Coast,* starring Lloyd (*Sea Hunt*) Bridges. Wendkos was gearing up to do one more, a Navy-based adventure with the pulpy title *Hell Boats*. The movie was initially set to star the blond television actor James (*Mr. Novak*) Franciscus. But when Franciscus's starring role in Twentieth Century Fox's *Beneath the Planet of the Apes* went over schedule, Wendkos was forced to go looking for another TV-famous American. And just like he did on *McCluskey* when he lost Fabian due to a broken shoulder, Wendkos thought of Rick Dalton. So next thing Rick knew, he and Cliff were on a plane flying to London, then Malta, for a five-week shoot on *Hell Boats*.

All the Oakmont Productions were pretty much the same, with *Mosquito Squadron* and *Attack on the Iron Coast* being the pick of the litter. But for what they were, they weren't bad. They were pretty entertaining if unmemorable potboilers. When *Hell Boats* played theatrically in America in 1970, it was on the lower half of a double feature with Phil (*Hellfire, Texas*) Karlson's exciting Italian-made World War Two action flick *Hornets' Nest*, with Rock Hudson and Sylva Koscina. Which pretty much had the exact same story as *The Fourteen Fists of McCluskey*, except instead of Rod Taylor leading a gang of brutes to blow up a dam and flood a Nazi stronghold, it was Rock Hudson leading a band of war-orphaned children to blow up a dam and flood a Nazi stronghold. All in all, a pretty entertaining night at the movies in 1970.

Along with another lead role in a studio production, *Hell Boats* offered Dalton a chance to reestablish his relationship with director and mentor Paul Wendkos. And Wendkos wasted no time plugging Dalton into his next picture. A few years earlier, when Wendkos was making for the Mirisch Company the third of their *Magnificent Seven* movies, he wanted Dalton for what in essence was the McQueen part. But since Rick was stuck over at Universal working alongside an aquatic rodent, he had to pass. Wendkos did such a good job with that assignment, the Mirisch Company offered Paul the fourth film in the series, at the time titled *Cannons for the Magnificent Seven*. The script was written by Stephen Kandel, who also wrote Wendkos's film *Battle of the Coral Sea*, which was where Dalton first worked with the filmmaker. The script deals with the character of Chris (Yul Brynner in the first two films and George Kennedy in Wendkos's third flick) and his six other compadres fighting a Mexican bandit who poses as a revolutionary named Córdoba. Córdoba's army is one hundred men strong, and he has six cannons he swiped from the United States military.

Chris and his Magnificent Seven, sent by none other than General John J. Pershing, were to go into Mexico, infiltrate Córdoba's impenetrable fortress, destroy the cannons, capture Córdoba, and bring him back to the United States to stand trial. Like General Pershing tells Chris, sounding similar to one of Jim Phelps's self-destructing tapes on *Mission: Impossible*, "If you agree to go, you'll be without authority, without orders, without uniforms. If you're caught, you'll be shot." The whole story has a western *Mission: Impossible* vibe, which shouldn't be surprising since Kandel was the head story editor on that series at that time. When Kandel was writing his script, he just assumed big George Kennedy would be reprising his role as team leader Chris. All through the screenplay, his prose kept referring to Chris's behemoth-like stature. But once the writer turned in the script to the Mirisch brothers, they liked it so much, they figured they could do better than George Kennedy. Instead, they offered the film to George Peppard. Peppard responded to the material, but with a caveat. He'd be damned if he was going to be the third guy in the fourth *Magnificent Seven* film to play Chris. So he instructed them to lose *The Magnificent Seven* connection and name his character anything other than Chris. Kandel rewrote the script, and Peppard's character went from Chris to Rod. And the team went from the Magnificent Seven to the Magnificent Five. And the title was changed to *Cannon for Cordoba*. Wendkos offered Dalton the part of the second-most-important team member, Jackson Harkness. However, this time the second-lieutenant role wasn't a McQueen copy. Rod and Jackson shared a similar dynamic with Gregory Peck and Anthony Quinn in *The Guns of Navarone*. Dalton's Jackson blames Peppard's Rod, his former friend, for the death of his brother. While Rick's character agrees to go on the mission to Mexico to destroy Córdoba and his cannons, Jackson vows to kill Rod —*if* they live through it.

While all through the sixties it bugged Dalton to be in McQueen's shadow, it really stuck a weed up his ass to be in Peppard's. However, by this late date, the two former swinging dicks had been sufficiently humbled. The two men got along in Mexico both on screen and off. They matched up well together, and the antagonistic dynamic between them had real power. In fact, Peppard later got Dalton to guest on his TV series *Banacek*.

But it was another actor in *Cannon for Cordoba* that Rick Dalton really hit it off with. Pete Duel was a handsome thirty-one-year-old actor, who had already acted in two television series. He played Gidget's brother-in-law opposite Sally Field on *Gidget*. And he starred in a sitcom titled *Love on a Rooftop* alongside Burt Reynolds's wife, Judy Carne. He was part of the team's Magnificent Five. Two years later he would become an exciting TV star with his hit western series on ABC, *Alias Smith and Jones* (a TV-series knockoff of *Butch Cassidy and the Sundance Kid*. But a really really good knockoff). Dalton and Duel, on location in Mexico, both enjoyed drinking tequila, chasing Mexican poontang, bitching about Hollywood, and each other's company. But they shared something else, something neither knew intellectually but both sensed internally. Both Dalton and Duel were undiagnosed bipolar. And drinking alcohol was their only form of self-medication. But since neither man knew this, to them their drinking was a sign of internal weakness.

But Pete Duel was far worse than Rick, culminating with—at the height of his *Alias Smith and Jones* success—Pete Duel shooting himself in the middle of the night. The whole town wondered why Duel did it. But Rick, in his heart of hearts, felt he knew the answer. After Duel's death in 1971, Dalton would do the hard work it took to not lean so heavily on booze. By 1973, when Dalton shot the revenge western *The Deadly Trackers* opposite Richard Harris in Durango, Mexico, both men (heavy drinkers) had reached an equilibrium while on location. They stayed off the sauce Monday through Thursday. But starting on Friday night into Sunday afternoon, the two men drank enough tequila, sangria, margaritas, and Bloody Marys to float a boat.

As Rick looks into his bathroom mirror, putting the final touches on his pompadour, he hears Cliff's Karmann

Ghia zoom up into his driveway. He looks at the watch on his wrist: seven-fifteen on the dot. While barfing when he woke up initially made him feel better, it didn't clean out his pipes completely. There's still enough of last night's old booze swirling around in his stomach to keep his belly feeling ill, his face sweaty, and his complexion a little green. He's just going to have to nurse coffee and smoke cigarettes till about one or two in the afternoon. *But, Jesus Christ, Rick thinks, that's seven hours from now? I bet James fuckin' Stacy ain't startin' his first day on his new TV show hungover as fuck.*

He looks at himself in the bathroom mirror and says out loud, "And you fuckin' wonder why CBS is starring him in a new series and not you! Because they think that prick's got potential. The only potential you got is potentially fucking up your life!"

Cliff knocks on his front door. Rick yells from the bathroom, "Yeah, I'm comin'!" He takes one more look at the pathetic fuckup in his bathroom mirror. "Don't worry, Rick," he says intimately to his reflection, "it's the first day. It's gonna take 'em a while to get their shit together. Just take it one cup of coffee at a time." Then, putting on his "show must go on" face, he pumps himself up by saying Jackie Gleason's catchphrase at the time, "And away we go!" Before he exits the bathroom, he spits in the sink, then looks down and sees a little red blood mixed in with the saliva. Rick examines the spit wad closer and asks, "Now what?"

7:10 A.M.

Squeaky's filthy petite bare feet pad their way across the dirty cracked linoleum floor of George's kitchen, over the dusty wood boards of the living room, and down the matted carpet of the hallway leading to George's bedroom at the end of the corridor. She knocks on the door and says cheerfully, "Good morning."

She hears bedsprings squeak as the old man rustles awake. Then, after a moment, she hears his grumpy voice come from the other side of the door.

"Yeah?"

She asks, "Can I come in, George?"

Old man Spahn has his de rigueur morning coughing fit, then says a phlegmy "Come in, sweetheart."

She twists the doorknob and steps inside the eighty-year-old man's stuffy bedroom. George, lying under the covers in his bed, turns in the young girl's direction. Squeaky leans against the doorframe, balances her right foot against her left knee, and tells the old man, "Good morning, honey, I've got eggs cooking on the stove. Do you want Jimmy Dean sausage or Farmer John bacon?"

"Jimmy Dean," says the old man.

She continues with her questions: "Do you want to eat breakfast casual and comfortable, or would you like me to help you get dressed and make y'all handsome?"

George thinks about it for a moment, then decides, "I think I'd like to get dressed."

A smile breaks across her pixieish face. "Ahh, trying to steal my heart, getting all spruced up."

"Stop it," George grunts.

She instructs him, "Lay back down for a second, honey. I'll take the eggs off the stove and come back and get you lookin' all sharp." Squeaky adds, "You'll melt all the girls' hearts, you handsome devil."

"Stop teasing me, honey," George whines.

"Oh, you love it," Squeaky flirts, as she heads back up the hallway, through the living room, and into the kitchen, removing the bubbling eggs in the frying pan from the stove burner. She walks over to the General Electric radio plugged into the wall on the kitchen counter and switches it on. Barbara Fairchild's heartbreaking novelty country hit *The Teddy Bear Song* fills the kitchen.

> *I wish I had button eyes and a red felt nose*
> *Shaggy cotton skin and just one set of clothes*
> *Sittin' on a shelf in a local department store*
> *With no dreams to dream and nothing to be sorry for*

Whenever George is awake, the radio is always playing KZLA, Los Angeles's country music station.

> *I wish I was a teddy bear*
> *Not living nor lovin' or goin' nowhere*
> *I wish I was a teddy bear*
> *And I'm wishin' that I hadn't fallen in love with you*

It's been Squeaky's job to take care of this blind old man for the last few months. The man who leads her commune, Charlie, impressed on her how important her job was. After their Family had moved all around Los Angeles like a nomadic tribe for months, George Spahn's old western movie

119

set and ranch finally offered them a home. A home from which they could lay down roots and test Charlie's societal theories, expand their numbers, and, who knows, hopefully create a new world order.

She was to be the blind old man's cook, his nurse, his friendly companion, and if she wouldn't mind masturbating him every once in a while, that would go a long way to securing "the Family's" position on the ranch. Or, as Charlie said as he broke the news to the twenty-one-year-old, "Sometimes, kiddo, ya gotta take one for the team."

The night Charlie told her she was going to have to jack this old man off periodically, and maybe do even more than that, was the only time during her tenure with Charles Manson she ever considered hightailing it back to San Francisco and maybe patching things up with her parents. But then a funny thing happened that Squeaky never could have foreseen. She fell in love with this blind old bastard. Not Romeo-and-Juliet type of love, but a *deep* love nevertheless. This grouchy old bastard wasn't really a bastard at all. He was just lonely and forgotten.

The industry that used his ranch to make their B-westerns and TV shows for four decades had forgotten him. His family had forgotten him, leaving him to die in a dilapidated rat trap amongst horseshit and hay. Squeaky offered the old man the one thing that his socked-away money couldn't buy. A loving touch, a sweet voice, and a sensitive ear. When Squeaky told George, or anybody else, she loved the old man, that wasn't just hippie singsong. That was Squeaky sincerely expressing her inner emotions about the old man it was her pleasure to look after.

When she returns to the bedroom, she helps the blind old man get into a crisp white western-style shirt, then she does up the little buttons. She holds out some tan slacks that he steps into one leg at a time. The young caretaker ties a western bolo tie around his stiff shirt collar. And combs the wispy white hair on his head with a brush. Then, taking him by the wrist and elbow, she assists him through the house toward the kitchen table. As they make their way at George's slow steady pace, Squeaky tells him, "Now see, you look so handsome. I'm such a lucky girl that you always want to look so attractive for me."

"Stop teasing me," George mock-complains.

"Who's teasing?" Squeaky asks. "You know breakfast tastes better when you put in the effort to take care of yourself."

She eases the old man into a chair at the kitchen table. She lays her hands on his stooped shoulders and asks in his ear, "Sanka or Postum?"

"Postum," says George.

"I swear, you're gonna turn into a cup of Postum," Squeaky kids. "Now, I started making scrambled eggs 'cause that's what I've made lately. But maybe you're getting tired of that and would like something different?"

"You mean like scrambled eggs and carnitas?" George asks.

"No," Squeaky smiles. "I was thinking more like do you want scrambled or sunny-side up."

The old man thinks a moment and says, "Sunny-side up."

She kisses him on the top of his head and goes about fixing his breakfast.

On KZLA, a Sav-on drugstore radio commercial plays out of the speaker:

"Join the Sav-on hit parade, on all these items you can save, Sav-on drugstore, Sav-on drugstore, BOOM BOOM! SAV-ON!"

The redhead takes a jar of Postum (a cheap coffee-flavored substitute that old people like) down from the kitchen cabinet. The powder in the jar has dried as solid as a rock. She has to stab it with the handle of the spoon to break off a chunk.

She drops the rock of Postum into George's coffee cup and pours hot water on it. She puts the cup down in front of George and places his hands on the handle, warning him, "Be careful, it's hot."

"You say that every morning," says George.

"It's hot every morning," says Squeaky.

She drops two new eggs into a piping-hot skillet coated with melted bubbling butter. She cuts off three pieces of Jimmy Dean pure pork sausage from the cookie dough–like plastic container into another frying pan. They sizzle. With a spatula, Squeaky moves the two sunny-side up eggs onto a breakfast plate. After adding the sausages, Squeaky places the plate in front of George.

"Would you like me to cut up your sausage and bust your yolk for you?" George makes an affirmative grunt. Squatting down, with a knife and fork, Squeaky cuts up the round sausage patties into bite-size pieces. Then takes George's fork and busts one yellow yolk, then the other.

"Okay, you're ready to go," she informs him. Then throws her arms around his neck from behind and whispers into his ear, "Enjoy, darling. It was made with love." She kisses him on the side of his head and pads out of the room to let George eat his breakfast in peace.

On KZLA, Sonny James sings the folkloric love story of *Running Bear*.

> *Running Bear loved Little White Dove with a love big as*
> * the sky*
> *Running Bear loved Little White Dove with a love that*
> * couldn't die*

7:30 A.M.

Jay Sebring, the man responsible for creating a revolution in men's hair design, and whose preeminence in Hollywood hairstyling is undisputed, lies in his bed in his black silk pajamas, watching the Hanna-Barbera cartoon adventure show *Jonny Quest*. On the television screen, Jonny's turban-wearing sidekick, Hadji, is casting one of his mystic spells, using his magic word, "Sim sim salabim!"

A slight tap on Jay's closed bedroom door gets his attention.

"Yes, Raymond," Jay calls to the knocker.

A voice with a proper British accent calls from behind the boudoir barrier, "Ready for your morning coffee, sir?"

Scooching up to a sitting position, Jay calls back, "Yes, I am. Come in."

The bedroom door opens and Raymond, Jay's British gentleman's gentleman, dressed in classic butler attire and carrying in both hands a silver-service breakfast-in-bed tray, enters the room with a cheerful "Good morning, Master Sebring."

"Good morning, Raymond," Jay replies.

Crossing the room toward the man in bed, Raymond inquires, "Did you enjoy yourself yesterday evening, sir?"

"Yes, I did," Jay answers. "Thank you for asking."

The butler places the tray in front of his master, and Jay examines the service set before him. It contains a chic silver coffeepot, a china teacup on a saucer, a bowl of sugar cubes, a miniature silver pitcher of heavy cream, a warm croissant on a plate, a dish with a pat of butter, a collection of different-flavored jams in tiny jars, and one long-stem red rose in a skinny silver vase.

"Everything looks delish," says the young man. "What's for breakfast this morning?"

As Raymond walks to the big picture window and throws open the blackout curtains, flooding the dark room with sudden sunlight, he says, "I was thinking of a nice savory salmon scramble with a side of cottage cheese and half a grapefruit."

Jay makes a face and says, "That might be too much for me this morning. We had late-night chili burgers at Tommy's last night."

Now it's Raymond's turn to make a face. The butler has the same regard for Jay ending his night with Tommy's chili burgers as he does when his master starts his day with a big bowl of Cap'n Crunch, and he responds to this new information with droll sarcasm. "Well, in that case, with a *chili burger* still digesting in your belly, I can't imagine you want to have a *savory* anything."

Raymond leaves the picture window and returns to his master's bedside and asks, "Shall I pour the coffee, sir?"

Jay nods his head and says, "That would be nice, Raymond."

Raymond lifts up the silver coffeepot and pours the java into the china teacup, as he says, "Very well, sir. Why don't we change that half a grapefruit into a small glass of grapefruit juice." The butler lifts the small pitcher of half-and-half and pours it into the teacup, and asks, "And shall we continue with coffee, or possibly move on to hot chocolate?"

As Jay ponders this decision, Raymond lifts a tiny spoon off the tray and stirs the cream into the java until it turns the color that Master Sebring prefers.

"I think hot chocolate," Jay pronounces with aplomb.

Then, with equal theatricality, Raymond says, "Then hot chocolate it is. Would you care to remain in bed watching *cartoons*, or should the hot chocolate precipitate a change in venue?"

Jay puts on his thinking face and ponders. "Well, I *was* watching *Jonny Quest*. But we could?" Looking up at his valet, he inquires, "What do you think, Raymond?"

"Well," Raymond says, gesturing toward the bright morning sunshine outside his window, "as you can see for yourself, it's a very sunny, pleasant California morning. If one lived in London and was fortunate enough to wake up on a day like this, one wouldn't stay in bed and watch *cartoons*. A day this nice, you wouldn't even go into work. So may I suggest hot chocolate in your garden so you can thoroughly enjoy it?" Then adding, "You know how you do love your morning beverage with the ghost of Jean Harlow in the garden."

The house that Jay bought three years ago was once owned by Jean Harlow and her director husband, Paul Bern, in the thirties, and they both died there. And Jay insists that the ghosts of Jean and Paul haunt the house. Even his ex-fiancée, Sharon Tate, believes she witnessed something mysterious and spooky one night.

"Raymond," Jay grandly proclaims, "you've convinced me. I'll have hot chocolate, under the sun, in the garden."

To which Raymond replies, "Splendid."

7:45 A.M.

Roman Polanski steps out into his Hollywood Hills home backyard and the vivid view of Downtown L.A. it offers its successful residents. The diminutive Polanski sports bed head on his cranium, a silk robe across his shoulders, and in one hand an empty coffee cup and in the other a French-press coffeepot. As he putters across the wet grass of his backyard, his hard-plastic slippers make *pop-pop* sounds against his bare heels.

He's followed eagerly by Dr. Sapirstein, his wife's little Yorkshire terrier, named after the sinister pediatrician that Ralph Bellamy played in Roman's film *Rosemary's Baby*. Later that year, when Sharon was away in Montreal making a movie, Roman's old friend and houseguest Voytek Frykowski would accidentally kill Dr. Sapirstein by running over the little dog while backing his car out of the driveway. Roman was in his office working on the script for his next movie, *The Day of the Dolphin*, when Voytek appeared in his doorway.

"Roman," Voytek sheepishly said. Polanski turned around in his chair to face his old friend. Voytek admitted, "I think I just accidentally killed Sharon's dog." Roman's face exploded like a bad actor in a silent movie. "You killed Dr. Sapirstein!"

Roman was out of his chair and rushed by his friend, lamenting with panic anxiety, "Oh my god, what have you done?" When the director reached the open front door, he saw the little hairy body lying dead in the car park in front of their house. His hands went to his head and he began pacing in circles, saying to Voytek in Polish, "Oh my god, what have you done? What have you done?"

Voytek felt a little bad, but he didn't expect Roman to react like this. In Polish, he said, "I'm sorry, Roman, it was an accident."

Roman spun around to face him, screaming in Polish, "You know what you've done? You've ruined my fucking life! She loves this dog!"

"Don't worry," Voytek assured him, "I'll tell her it was my fault."

Roman yelled in response, "No, you won't tell her! She'll never forgive you!" Roman tried to explain Americans to his Polish friend: "Don't you understand, she's an American! Americans love their fucking dogs more than they love their children! You might as well have dropped her fucking baby down the stairs!"

Sharon never did learn what really happened to Dr. Sapirstein. In order to save his friend the wrath and scorn of the Texas-born Army brat, Roman told Sharon that Dr. Sapirstein ran away and must have either gotten lost or run afoul of a coyote. Alone in her hotel room on location in Montreal, Sharon cried all night long.

But today Dr. Sapirstein is still alive, and when the little dog comes running up to Roman with a little red ball in his mouth, he wants the little man to play with him. Roman presses down on the French-press plunger and ignores the dog.

Roman's a little grumpy this morning; like his next-door neighbor Rick Dalton (who he's never met), he's a little hungover as well. But, unlike Rick, it is not due to a night of heavy drinking by himself. Last night Roman and Sharon, along with friends Jay Sebring and Michelle Phillips and Cass Elliot, went to a party at Hugh Hefner's Playboy Mansion. Then afterward they went someplace else around three in the morning to eat disgusting chili hamburgers amongst sketchy L.A. types (Mexicans in their uniform street clothes and outrageously painted cars alongside white biker hoodlums on their noisy motorcycles). In Europe, they'd end the night with fine cognac and Cuban cigars or a late-night wine cellar and finish off the evening with a twenty-year-old Bordeaux. But these childish Americans think it's *cool* to end the night with oily chili burgers and Coca-Cola. Not only that, but Roman was also pretty sure nobody liked those fat, greasy burgers. He's positive Sharon didn't, though she'd never admit it. But, naturally, everybody acted like they were having the best time in the world. Sharon tried to even order a hamburger without chili, and Jay wouldn't hear of it. So Sharon gave in to the peer pressure, saying, "Fine, fine, fine," telling the man behind the counter wearing the paper hat, "I'll have a chili burger." Which sat in her stomach like a cannonball, making her feel ill the whole ride back to Cielo Drive. Roman loved his American friends but was always a little surprised at the juvenile things they took delight in, or in this case, *pretended* to take delight in.

Not only that, but he also had to make nice with that asshole Steve McQueen most of the night. Roman and McQueen don't like each other, but since Steve is one of Sharon's oldest friends in Los Angeles, they tolerate each other.

It's obvious Sharon and McQueen fucked before. He's never confirmed this with Sharon, but he knows McQueen's the kind of guy who wouldn't *still* be Sharon's friend if he hadn't fucked her a few times in the past. Normally that wouldn't bother Roman. Jay was engaged to Sharon—they fucked all the time. And Roman has *some* sexual past with more than half the women in his orbit. But McQueen makes a point of it by the way he smirks at Roman. Every glance of those blue eyes and grin of that little mouth seems to say, *I fucked your wife.*

Also, Roman doesn't like the way McQueen manhandles Sharon, like picking the big blonde up off her feet and spinning her around till she goes, "Whee!" like a little girl. Activities that Roman is physically too small to do. And McQueen knows that, and that's why McQueen does it.

The guy's just an asshole, Roman thinks.

After being purposely ignored for the last twenty seconds, the little dog barks to get the little man's attention. *This fucking dog*, Roman thinks, *I can't even enjoy a cup of coffee in peace without this little tyrant spoiling it.* He throws the ball and the little dog runs after it. Roman doesn't hate Dr. Sapirstein like he hates Steve McQueen. He's just grouchy this morning. One, because he's hungover, and two, because Sharon woke him up.

You see, Sharon snores.

Chapter Eight

Lancer

Pulled by six horses, the Butterfield Wells Fargo passenger stagecoach rounded the corner where the adobe-walled mission stood and thundered down the dusty dirt main drag of the Spanish-style town of Royo del Oro, sixty miles on the north side of the Mexican border in California. The hard hooves of the sweaty beasts tore at the dirt main street, creating a cloud of brown powder in their wake.

Monty Armbruster, the white-haired forty-year veteran of the Butterfield line, pulled on the leather reins in his gloved hands, yanking the horses' heads back from the bits embedded in their mouths, making the six powerful equines come to a gentle stop directly in front of the Hotel Lancaster. With his light Texas twang, Monty sang out, "Royo del Oro, last stop!" The backlit sunshine rays filtered through the gauze-like brown dust in the way, a hundred years from now, all cinematographers of western movies would hope to duplicate.

Eight-year-old Mirabella Lancer, the short in stature but wise for her years daughter of Murdock Lancer, the owner and operator of the biggest cattle ranch in the territory, leaped off the wooden barrel she had been perched on. In excited anticipation, she turned to the Mexican vaquero who was only a few inches taller than her but sported a comically large sombrero on top of his head and chirped, "Come on, Ernesto!"

Taking the child's hand, the vaquero Ernesto led the young girl down the main street of the town toward the Butterfield stagecoach. Since her father was the richest man in the territory, Mirabella had known every business owner in Royo del Oro since she was old enough to say anything more meaningful than "goo-goo," resulting in a series of smiles and waves as she made her way down the business district of the town. A horse-drawn wagon piled high with wooden barrels of beer passed in front of her and the little vaquero. They stopped on the wooden walkway till the beer wagon cleared their path. Crossing the dirt street, approaching the stagecoach from behind, Mirabella prepared herself for her first glimpse of either of the two brothers she'd never known. Her father's long lost sons had both sent word they would soon be traveling to Lancer Ranch. However, exactly which brother was going to step off the Butterfield stagecoach was a mystery to both her and Murdock Lancer's ranch hand Ernesto. The ranch had received a wire indicating that the son of Murdock Lancer had climbed aboard a Butterfield stagecoach leaving Tucson, Arizona, two days ago and, minus any hardships, should be arriving in Royo del Oro around twelve this afternoon. Not included in the wire was *which* son exactly was arriving.

Unlike a train, a stagecoach arriving three hours later than scheduled was practically on time. So it was three o'clock in the afternoon when the Butterfield stagecoach stopped in front of the Hotel Lancaster. Mirabella and Ernesto stood in the street, waiting for the stagecoach door to open and see which of her brothers would emerge.

Both brothers were born on the Lancer Ranch, but neither had met the other. And neither had seen their cattle-ranching father since they were small children. Like Mirabella, both of Murdock Lancer's sons were the product of different deceased mothers.

Scott Foster Lancer, who was raised by his mother's (Diane Foster Lancer Axelrod) wealthy family in Boston, was a Harvard graduate and an ex-military man, having ridden with the British Cavalry in India (the Bengal Lancers).

Murdock's other son, Johnny Lancer, was raised in Mexico by his mother, Marta Conchita Louisa Galvadon Lancer. Marta had no family in Mexico, wealthy or otherwise. The only money Marta made was made dancing and fucking and playing castanets in a series of cantinas throughout half the cutthroat hamlets south of the border. Johnny's whole childhood, he thought sex was something men paid women to do, like dance and sing, cook food, or wash their clothes.

Scott's mother, Diane, retreated to her Beacon Hill family back east when it became apparent that life on a cattle ranch surrounded by horseshit, cowshit, cowboys, and Mexicans was not for her or her baby boy. Scott was three years old when he boarded the Royo del Oro stage out of town.

Johnny was younger than Scott, but older when he left the Lancer Ranch. He lived with his father and his mother at the ranch until he was ten. Then one dark rainy night, with her ten-year-old son in tow, Marta climbed aboard a fancy buggy that Murdock had purchased her for her birthday and rode it sixty miles across the border into Mexico. And that was the last time little John ever saw Murdock Lancer, the sprawling Lancer Ranch, the opulent Lancer Ranch house, and the town of Royo del Oro. Johnny went from being the son of the wealthiest man in the valley, being taught his school learning by a private tutor, eating the best Black Angus on china plates prepared by a French chef, and sleeping on a feather bed, to being the son of a Mexican whore, who existed on beans and hardtack served on clay plates, who drank cactus juice the way he used to drink milk, who ate jerky the way he used to eat peppermint sticks, who was taught dirty jokes by motherfuckers, slept on sacks of coffee beans in the back of cantinas, and learned how to defend himself against both rat attacks and molestation-minded prairie scum in the middle of the night. Until, in one of those cutthroat hamlets, a wealthy dissatisfied customer from Mexico City cut Marta's throat. Johnny was twelve years old when he dug the hole in the hard-packed dirt that he buried his mother in. The rich man stood trial for the murder of his mother and was acquitted by a biased jury. Two years later, Johnny killed the man who murdered his mother. And even though it took him a decade, he eventually killed every member of that crooked jury as well.

Johnny never knew why his mother spirited him off in the middle of that wet night, but he could guess. He guessed Murdock Lancer got tired of playing house with a Mexican chili pepper and her half-greaser son. So one night he told her to *vamos!*

Johnny knew if he ever went back to the Lancer Ranch, he'd blow his father's fucking head off for throwing him and his mother out in the rain. But he also knew Murdock Lancer was a very important white American. And if he shot his father, Johnny Lancer would eventually hang by the neck for it. Luckily, Murdock wasn't going anywhere. It's one of the few drawbacks to being a wealthy landowner. Anyone who wants you can find you. Johnny put his mother in the ground, and one day he'd do the same for his father. And if the cost of avenging his mother was to be the forfeiture of his life, so be it. Still, Johnny was in no hurry to forfeit his life. That rich bastard would wait. In the meantime, there was gold to be stolen, pussy to be laid, and tequila to be guzzled. So imagine Johnny's surprise when a telegram showed up at the Hotel Felix, a contact place where he received job offers, usually of the nefarious type.

IN CARE OF JOHN LANCER—STOP—JOB OFFER—
STOP—TRAVEL TO LANCER RANCH OUTSIDE OF
ROYO DEL ORO CALIFORNIA—STOP—PAY ONE
THOUSAND DOLLARS UPON ARRIVAL—STOP—
PAYMENT FOR CONSIDERATION OF JOB OFFER—
STOP—NO OBLIGATION—STOP—MURDOCK LANCER

Along with the telegram was a wire for fifty dollars to pay for the passage to Royo del Oro. *Fuck me swinging*, thought Johnny. But the real lure wasn't the offer of a thousand dollars. It was the opportunity, after all these years, to look in the face of Murdock Lancer—the man who made a money-grubbing whore out of his mother—and blow his brains out of the back of his skull.

Mirabella Lancer caught her breath as the Butterfield stage-coach door finally opened and out stepped a fancy black-and-white spat shoe onto the footwell. Her eyes widened as a very handsome blond-haired man emerged from the passenger coach, dressed in the fanciest bluest clothes she'd ever seen on a man. Having been raised on a cattle ranch, she was used to the attire of men who worked for a living. Even when the businessmen in town got dressed up to go to church or the ranch hands slicked their hair back and put on their Sunday-go-to-meeting duds to attend a dance in town, *their* fancy clothes were charcoal black, dull gray, or drab brown. This blond-haired Eastern dandy's three-piece suit was bright baby blue with gold thread woven into his vest. As he disembarked from the Butterfield stagecoach, he placed a large name-colored top hat on his head. The base of the hat was circled by a cream-colored silk sash. The striking stranger walked with a limp in his left leg, leaning on a silver dog-headed cane. But despite this impediment, or maybe because of it, he moved with impeccable posture and grace. The blue Bostonian removed a brush from his inside jacket pocket and began slowly and meticulously brushing the dust from his baby-blue lapels and cuffs and shoulders.

Color Mirabella impressed. With a quick glance up to Ernesto, her pleased expression said, *That's my brother Scott.*

Just as the little girl swallowed her spit and opened her

mouth to greet her long-lost relative, another passenger emerged from the stagecoach.

This one too was compellingly impressive but in a completely different way. While the blond-haired man was storybook dashing and incredibly dignified, this new man was a devilishly handsome roguish-looking south-of-the-border-styled cowboy with a thick snatch of fudge-colored hair that framed his face in a way that Mirabella could only describe as *dreamy*. This brunette cowboy's clothes weren't as fancy as the blond passenger's, but they were just as colorful and, in their own right, just as snazzy. The dark-haired passenger wore a Latin-styled sangria-red ruffled shirt with a brown leather short coat and black jeans with big silver studs down the pant leg. As he stepped out of the coach, he placed a short brown cowboy hat on his head. Which functioned not to keep the sun out of his eyes but to complement his killer look. After stretching his long silver-studded legs, the rough cowboy in the rouge-colored shirt sauntered over to Monty the stagecoach driver and asked in Spanish for him to toss down his saddle, which sat perched on top of the stage. Monty tossed the handcrafted saddle, heaving it by the horn over the side of the stagecoach roof. It fell heavy into the outstretched arms of the ruffled-shirt stranger.

The top-hatted dandy in baby blue inquired of Ramon, the shotgun-cradling second rider who sat next to Monty on top of the stagecoach, about his paisley embroidered garment bag. Top Hat received the valise from the shotgun-riding Mexican and thanked him with a gringo-accented *gracias*.

Now both the little girl Mirabella and the little Mexican

136

Ernesto showed confusion on their perplexed faces. Neither of them knew, for sure, which one to approach. The little eight-year-old gave a shoulder shrug and, thinking, *Oh well, here goes nothing*, loudly cleared her throat to get the two handsome passengers' attention.

"Mr. Lancer?" she inquired with a big question mark.

The men answered in unison, Top Hat saying, "Yes?" and Red Ruffles saying, "Yeah?" Each man instinctively jerked toward the other with an annoyed expression on his face.

More confusion clouded the little girl's face, till she suddenly understood.

"Oh my goodness," she exclaimed excitedly, "this is great! Both of you came together!"

After the two men shared another uneasy glance at each other, the one with the top hat asked the little girl, in his Harvard-educated diction, "What do you mean, 'both of you'?"

"Well, we knew you were coming," she explained, "but we didn't know you'd be traveling together."

Since Scott hadn't any knowledge of his father's life since his mother hightailed it to Boston, save for the fact he owned a cattle empire, he was a little slow to pick up the little girl's implication. "You were expecting both of us?" pointing to the man at his side in the red ruffled shirt.

"Yeah," she said happily. "You're Johnny," pointing her finger at the dark-haired one in the red ruffles, "and you're Scott," moving her finger in the direction of the blond man in blue.

Well, that was their names. The two men shared another

uneasy look at the other, as the reality of the situation became obvious.

Johnny pointed his finger at the pint-sized provocateur and asked, "And who are you?"

"I'm Mirabella Lancer, and you're my brothers!" And with that declaration, she charged like a runaway wagon at Johnny, wrapping her little arms around his waist and knocking him back on the heels of his cowboy boots.

A look of dread crossed the face of Johnny Lancer. He'd contemplated many variables when he imagined the moment he would be reunited with his father, but an apple-cheeked, ecstatic eight-year-old half sister wasn't one of them. Before Scott could inquire about the meaning of all this, Mirabella had untangled herself from Johnny and had now wrapped her arms around Scott, squeezing his pelvic area, surprisingly strong for such a small fry. Trying to maintain some decorum and hold off, if only for a few seconds more, the inevitable conclusion of her revelation, Scott said, "Look, little girl—"

Mirabella interrupted him by clarifying her name a second time. "Mirabella."

"Mirabella," he continued, "my mother never had any other children."

"No," Johnny said, pointing out the obvious, "but apparently your father did."

Scott turned toward Johnny and said, "You mean *our* father?"

Johnny answered, "Yeah, *our father*, Murdock Lancer. Look, I don't know why you made the trip, Top Hat, but the

138

old man said he'd give me a thousand dollars if I came to see him."

"He made the same offer to me," Scott confirmed.

"I want that thousand dollars," Johnny said, "and after I get it, I'm going to give him a belly full." A belly full of what, Johnny left unspoken.

Apparently, Scott had the same idea. "You and me both, *brother*."

Johnny shook his head. "Don't call me *brother*."

"Are you ready to go?" Mirabella interjected pleasantly.

They both turned to her and said in unison, "Go where?" Which annoyed both of them, and they gave a dirty look to each other.

But their little sister thought it was funny, and she giggled out loud, "Where do you think? Lancer Ranch, you silly goose."

Mirabella turned on her heels, and she and the vaquero Ernesto led the way down the street toward the wagon that Ernesto had driven ten miles into town.

Scott hooked the handle of his silver dog-headed cane through the hardwood handle of his valise and lifted it up to his free hand, while Johnny pitched the saddle over his shoulder. The two brothers followed their sister, who proceeded to paint a picture of what they could expect when they met their father. "Now, Daddy won't *act* like it at first," she warned them, "and he can be a bit of a mule head, but no matter what he says, he's happy both of you came."

Johnny snorted sarcastically, "Yeah, well, we'll see if he still feels that way after our little *family reunion*."

As Scott limped beside him, he concurred, "You know, *brother*, that's the first thing you said I agree with."

That fucking did it, Johnny thought, and stopped in his tracks, pointing his finger in Scott's baby-blue chest. "I done tole' you, don't call me *brother*, *Top Hat*."

Scott's eyes went down to the aggressive finger, then rose up to the aggressive face, and he warned, "Don't point your finger at me, *Ruffles*."

"Boys?"

The two brothers turned away from each other toward their little sister, as she gestured toward the wagon and asked, condescendingly, "Can we go?"

The two men gave each other a look that suggested, *To be continued*, but for the sake of this little sweetheart, they'd drop their fighting stance, and Johnny gestured toward the wagon.

"Lead the way, *sis*."

Chapter Nine

"Think Less Hippie, More Hells Angels"

Cliff drives Rick's Cadillac past the front gate on the Twentieth Century Fox lot. The guard at the gate gives him directions to the Spanish-western-town back lot where the *Lancer* pilot is being shot: "Drive straight to the second left, make a turn at Tyrone Power Boulevard; drive past the man-made lake and the set of *Hello, Dolly!* Turn right on Linda Darnell Avenue, and you can't miss it." In the passenger seat next to him, Rick wears big dark glasses to shield his eyes from the sun and smokes down a Capitol W cigarette to shield his tongue from taste. When Cliff jerks the car to a stop, Rick knows they have arrived.

The actor glances out the passenger-side window, and through his dark glasses he sees a western town; a few horses and wagons; a film crew; some asshole director perched on top of a Chapman crane; a cowboy actor who obviously thinks he's sexy, dressed in a bright-red Las Vegas–style shirt and short brown cowboy hat; some comically dressed fancy-pants dude in a bright-blue three-piece suit, complete with a top hat that looks like he drifted over from the set of *Meet Me in St. Louis*; a period-dressed little girl;

and a Mexican runt in a large sombrero. *Welcome to fucking Lancer*, Rick thinks. He opens the car door and steps out from the vehicle on shaky legs. Upon standing upright, he's struck by a coughing fit that brings up some stomach acid to the back of his esophagus.

He spits out a green loogie mixed with red and turns back to Cliff behind the wheel. The actor leans down and talks to his assistant through the open passenger window. "I think the wind blew down my TV antenna last night. You think you'd mind goin' home and fixin' it?"

"I can and I will," Cliff assures him. Then, asking Rick as nonchalantly as he can, "Could you talk to the stunt gaffer about me today? That way I know if I'm workin' this week or not?"

There was a time when Cliff's involvement on one of Rick's projects was contractually negotiated. *If* Rick was playing the role, then Cliff *was* doubling him. On the Universal films, it was negotiated into Rick's contract and there was a chair on the set with Cliff's name on it. But it ain't been that *time* in a long *time*. Now that Rick is guesting on other people's television shows, Cliff isn't guaranteed jack shit. Most TV-show stunt gaffers had their own crew, and most TV-show stunt gaffers' first priority was looking after their crew. If Cliff was going to get a couple of days on *Tarzan* or *Bingo Martin*, it was because Rick had a word with the stunt gaffer and talked him into it.

Rick sighs. "Yeah, I been meaning to tell you"—*avoid it* was closer to the truth—"the guy who gaffs this show is best friends with Randy. You know, the gaffer from *The Green Hornet*?"

Knowing what that means, Cliff says, "Fuck!"

"So, there really ain't no point," Rick says pragmatically.

Cliff curses bitterly, "That fuckin' little nip." Then he turns his bitterness onto himself. "Why do I care if the Green Hornet's fuckin' chauffeur thinks he can wipe Ali's ass? I mean, Jesus-fuckin'-Christ, the heavyweight champion of the world needs me to fuckin' defend him?"

"Especially at the expense of your career and my fuckin' reputation," Rick adds, getting irritated all over again. "I practically had to suck Randy's cock to get you that gig," Rick remembers. "And what do you do? You practically break that little big mouth's back. End result, you get blackballed from three-quarters of the shows in town and I look like a fuckin' asshole. But you showed him," Rick finishes sarcastically.

"Look, man," the stuntman raises his palms flat out in surrender, "when you're right you're right, and you're right."

Rick tells Cliff an old acting story, oblivious to the fact that he's told Cliff this *exact same* story three times before.

Listening to Rick tell the same stories and anecdotes, pretending to be unaware of the repetition, is practically part of Cliff's job description. And, to be ungenerous, a sign of Rick's low intelligence.

"I'm doin' my first decent part in a feature," Rick begins, *"Battle of the Coral Sea* with Cliff Robertson, directed by Paul Wendkos. I'm doing one of my first real parts, for the guy who's gonna turn out being my favorite director. In a real studio movie, Columbia Pictures—a Columbia B-movie, but still, not Republic, not AIP, fuckin' Columbia Pictures."

Cliff looks up from the driver's seat at his boss, settling himself in to hear the same story for the fourth time.

"So anyway, I'm excited as all fuckin' hell. Except there's this fuckin' 2nd AD on the picture, who's a real horse's ass. And this fucker is fuckin' with me the whole time. Not Tommy Laughlin, definitely not Cliff Robertson—he's practically suckin' Cliff's cock! He's not fucking with anybody else. Just me!"

Rick continues, "It's shitty, it's unfair, and finally I've fuckin' had it. So I'm having lunch with this chubby guy on the movie, a William Witney regular, Gordon Jones. Been around a real long time, been in eighty fuckin' movies, a real good cat. So I tell Jones I'm waiting for this fuckin' prick to say one more word to me, *just one more fuckin' word*, and I'm gonna fuckin' lay 'em out!"

Now Rick gets to the moral of the story: "And Jones tells me, yeah, you could do that. And yeah, you could probably take 'em. And yeah, he deserves it. But, before you lay him out on the job, take your SAG card outta your wallet, light a match, and set it on fire. Because, since basically that's what you'll be doin', you might as well go all the way."

Cliff repeats the sentiment from before. "I get it, I get it. Who fuckin' cares what that little prick says?"

"I mean, Jesus Christ on a fuckin' crutch," Rick says. "If every time a series lead made a big claim about something they *obviously* couldn't do, somebody took a poke at them, no work would ever get done. Bob Conrad and Darren McGavin wouldn't be able to get through a fuckin' week without some wrangler brainin' them." Rick illustrates, "That midget playing Kato, he's a fucking *actor*! Any *actor* claiming to do *anything*, except saying lines other people wrote, is full of fucking shit. And most of them can't even fucking do that!"

Rick counts off on his fingers the actors who know what they're talking about. "You wanna talk to Audie Murphy about killing dudes, he could tell ya. You wanna talk to Jim Brown about running touchdowns, he could tell ya. You wanna talk to Sonja Henie about ice skating, she could tell ya. You wanna talk to Esther Williams about fucking swimming, go ahead. But everybody else is fuckin' faking it. And if anybody should fucking know that, it's a goddamn war-hero stuntman!"

Cliff smiles up at his boss and repeats in his Zen-like manner, "Like I said, when you're right, you're right."

"Darn tootin' I'm right," Rick says.

Changing the subject, Cliff asks, "Well, if you don't need me for anything else, I'll just pick you up at wrap?"

"Naw," Rick confirms. "Just see what you can do about that damn antenna and I'll see you at wrap." Then Rick asks, "When's wrap today?"

"Seven-thirty," Cliff says.

"See ya then," and Rick walks off toward the *Lancer* set.

Then, after a moment, Cliff calls out to him.

Rick turns around and, from behind the wheel of the Cadillac, his buddy points a strong finger at him and says, "Just remember, you're *Rick-fucking-Dalton*! Don't you forget that!"

That makes the actor smile. He gives his buddy a little salute, then the Coupe de Ville drives away and the actor reports for work.

Sitting in a chair in front of a vanity mirror in the *Lancer* makeup trailer, Rick dunks his face in a bowl of ice water.

Supposedly, Paul Newman does this every morning. But for Newman, it's part of his beauty regimen. For Rick, it's to stimulate his senses out of the queasy numbness of last night's alcohol. When his face emerges from the freezing water, he takes a couple of cubes in his hand and rubs them across his face and on the back of his neck.

Sonya, the makeup-and-hair girl on this pilot, who supplied Rick with the bowl of ice water, sits in a makeup chair three stations away, smoking a Chesterfield. Sitting in the chair next to her, waiting for the director to arrive so they can discuss Rick's costume, is the show's fleshy, big-haired cutie-pie costume designer, Rebekkah. If she were wearing pigtails, the outfit she has on could nab her third prize in a Wednesday Addams look-alike contest. Over the Wednesday Addams outfit, she wears a big "Wild Ones"–like black leather motorcycle jacket.

While Sonya doesn't let on, she clearly knows the difference between a beauty ritual (Paul Newman be damned) and a hangover assistance. For one, there's less moaning in a beauty ritual.

Just as the ice-cold stimulation is starting to penetrate Rick's face, the door to the makeup trailer flies open, banging against the back wall, and the director of the *Lancer* pilot steps into the trailer with the huge theatrical flamboyance that is his customary method of entering a room.

Greeting Rick as if he were projecting to the back row of the Old Vic, the director announces, "Rick Dalton? Sam Wanamaker!"

The director shoots his hand out to the seated, slightly

discombobulated, wet-faced actor, who instinctively completes the handshake greeting with a dripping-wet paw.

Clearing his voice, Rick sputters, "Good to meetcha—uh—uh—uh—Sam. Sorry 'bout the wet hand."

Sam dismisses the wet-hand comment. "No worries, I'm used to it with Yul," referencing the exotic Hollywood movie star Yul Brynner, who Wanamaker became friends with when the two acted together in the historical action picture *Taras Bulba*. Recently, Yul Brynner had backed Wanamaker's move behind the camera by starring in Sam's first feature, *The File of the Golden Goose*.

Wanamaker continues with Dalton, "I want you to know, Rick, I'm the one who cast you, and I couldn't be more thrilled about you doing this."

The director is dealing with Rick with a tank of high octane, while the quart-low actor is struggling to catch his equilibrium. Rick's nerves kick in and his slight stammer starts making its first appearance of the day.

"Well-well, thanks, S-S-Sam, I appreciate it." Then, finally getting a hold of the sentence, "It's a good part."

"Have you met the series lead, Jim Stacy?" Wanamaker asks, referring to the actor playing the role of Johnny Lancer.

"N-n-no, not yet," Rick stutters.

Does this fucking guy stutter? Sam thinks.

"You guys are gonna be dynamite together," Sam says.

"Well . . ." Rick looks for the right word, then gives up and just says, "That sounds exciting."

Wanamaker says confidentially, even though Sonya and Rebekkah can hear everything he's saying, "Just between

147

you and me, the network cast the series leads, Jim and Wayne." Wayne is the series co-lead, Wayne Maunder, who plays the Boston-raised Lancer brother, Scott.

"And they did a fine job. But nevertheless, the network chose them. But I chose *you*. Primarily because I can foresee possible gorilla magic between you and Stacy. And I want *you* to exploit that."

Sam leans over Rick, the massive gold Zodiac medallion (Gemini) the director wears around his neck swinging in the air back and forth over Rick in the makeup chair. "That doesn't mean I want you to be anything less than professional. But you're the seasoned pro. I want to work with *you*"—pointing a finger down at Rick—"to help me get what I need out of *him*"—jerking his thumb over his shoulder at Stacy somewhere outside the makeup trailer. "When the two of you are in costume, I want *you*"—again pointing down at Rick in his chair—"to subtextually keep the cock-measuring contest continuing between the two of you."

Waving his hands in front of him in order to frame a picture in the air for Dalton to imagine: "Think of a confrontation between a silverback gorilla and a Kodiak bear."

Rick chuckles, "Well . . . Sam . . . that's some image."

Wanamaker agrees, "I know."

"Which one am I," Rick asks, "the gorilla or the bear?"

"Which one has the biggest cock?" Wanamaker answers.

"Well," Dalton deduces, "that would probably be the gorilla."

"Have you ever seen a fully erect Kodiak bear?" Wanamaker challenges.

"I can't say I have," Dalton confides.

"Then don't be so sure," Wanamaker warns.

"When the two of you are in scenes," Wanamaker directs, "I want you to goad him. You think you can do that, Rick?"

"Whaddaya mean, 'goad him'?" Dalton asks.

"*Goad him,*" Wanamaker repeats. "Poke the bear, get his dander up. You goad him as if you're trying to convince the network executives to fire Stacy and reshoot the pilot with you as Johnny Lancer. You go at him like that," Wanamaker assures Dalton, "you'll be doing both him and the show a favor. Not to mention capturing lightning in a bottle."

Wanamaker finds Sonya behind him in the reflection in the mirror, sitting in her chair, smoking her Chesterfield. He doesn't turn to address her; he just speaks to her reflection.

"Sonya," he dictates, "first off, I want to give Caleb a mustache. A big, long, droopy Zapata-like mustache."

Oh, great, Rick thinks. He hates fake beards and mustaches. It's like trying to act with a caterpillar glued to your upper lip and a beaver attached to your face. Not to mention he hates spirit gum slathered on his mug.

After Wanamaker mentions the "Zapata-like mustache," the director bursts out laughing and tells Rick, "And trust me, when Stacy gets a look at that goddamn mustache, he's gonna flip his fucking wig!" The director explains, "We both wanted Johnny Lancer to have a mustache. I told the network we need facial hair like that to make the genre feel modern. Like what the Italians are doing in Europe."

Rick winces.

Wanamaker continues, too wrapped up in his story to clock Rick's reaction, "Well, CBS said no fucking way. You

149

want to put a mustache on somebody, you put it on the heavy. And that means you, Rick," Sam says with a big grin.

Rick doesn't dig wearing phony mustaches, but if the lead wants it and can't get it but he *can*? That could be a horse of a different color.

"So Stacy wanted to wear a mustache?" Rick confirms.

Wanamaker answers, "Yes."

"Is that gonna bother Stacy?" Rick asks.

"Are you kidding? He's gonna go fucking apeshit! But he knows what the network said. So it'll just add another subtextual layer to the antagonism between you two."

Then he turns around and addresses Rebekkah: "Now, Rebekkah darling, I want a different look for Rick's character, Caleb. I don't want him costumed like they costumed the heavies on *Bonanza* and *The Big Valley* for the last decade. I want a zeitgeist flair to the costume—nothing anachronistic. But where does 1969 and 1889 meet? I want a costume he could wear into the London Fog tonight and be the hippest guy in the place."

The counterculture-savvy costume designer gives the hip director the answer he wants. "We got a Custer jacket, fringes all down the arm. It's tan now, but I dye it dark brown, he could hit the Strip in it tonight."

That's what Wanamaker wants to hear. He runs a finger down her cheek and says, "That's my girl."

Rebekkah smiles back, and at that moment Rick knows Sam and Rebekkah are fucking.

Wanamaker spins back in Rick's direction. "Now, Rick, about your hair."

A touch too defensively, Rick asks, "What about my hair?"

Wanamaker answers back, "The Brylcreem-boy generation is dead." Sam explains, "It's very Eisenhower. I want Caleb to have a different hairdo."

"How different?" Rick asks.

"Something more hippie-ish," Sam tells him.

You want me to look like some goddamn hippie? Rick thinks.

"You want me to look like a goddamn hippie?" Rick questions with a skeptical face.

"Think less hippie," Sam clarifies, "more Hells Angels."

Sam's eyes find Sonya again in the reflection of the mirror. "I wanna get an Indian wig, long hair, put it on his head, then cut it into a hippie hairstyle."

Then, quickly turning to Rick, "But scary hippie," he assures the actor.

Rick interrupts Sam's creative flow with a question. "Sam . . . uh . . . Sam?"

Sam turns toward his actor, giving him his full attention. "Yes, Rick?"

Rick tries, without sounding like a temperamental horse's ass, to slow Sam's roll somewhat with a practical question: "Look . . . uh . . . uh . . . Sam, if you got my face covered up in all this . . . uh . . . uh," he searches for the right word, "*junk*, nobody's gonna know it's me."

Sam Wanamaker takes a beat, then answers the actor, "Well, there are those, *dear boy*, that call that *acting*."

Chapter Ten

Misadventure

The minute Cliff shot his wife with the shark gun, he knew it was a bad idea.

The impact hit her a little below the belly button, tearing her in half, both pieces hitting the deck of the boat with a splash. Cliff Booth had despised this woman for what seemed like years, but the moment he saw her ripped in two, two separate halves lying on the deck of his boat, years of ill will and resentment evaporated in an instant. He rushed to her side, cradling her, holding the two separate pieces of her torso together, expelling frantic heartfelt statements of remorse and regret.

He held her that way, keeping her alive, for seven hours. He didn't risk leaving her side for one minute to call the Coast Guard, for fear without his applied pressure she'd come apart. So for seven hours he held her close and tight, cradling her, calming her down, keeping her alive. If he hadn't shot her in the first place, the effort would have been heroic.

On the bloody deck of the boat he had named after her (*Billie's Boat*), amongst the guts, blood, and intestines seeping out of Billie Booth, the husband and wife, on the brink of death, had the seven-hour conversation they could never have in life. So she wouldn't dwell on the extremity of her dilemma, he kept her talking.

What did they talk about? Their love story.

In those seven hours, they recounted their whole life together.

As the Coast Guard ship finally approached, somewhere around hour six, the husband and wife were communicating in baby talk like two helplessly-in-love fourteen-year-olds away at summer camp. Each trying to outdo the other in a game of remembering the smallest detail of their first meeting and first date. As the Coast Guard boarded the vessel and drove her into port, Cliff continued holding Billie's two separate halves together. All the while assuring her that she was going to be okay. "Hey, I ain't gonna lie," he said, "you're gonna have the King Kong of scars. But you're gonna be just fine."

Cliff tried so hard to convince Billie of this that, after six hours of committed line readings, he talked himself into it too. So the pragmatic Cliff Booth was, surprisingly, surprised when in the Coast Guard's efforts to transfer Billie from the boat to the dock and an awaiting ambulance . . . she fell apart.

Oh well.

Inside the stunt community of Hollywood in the sixties, Cliff Booth was greatly admired for his distinguished military career and his status as one of World War Two's great war heroes. But there existed widespread speculation that Cliff Booth murdered his wife and got away with it. No one really knew for sure if he shot her on purpose. It could have been just a tragic mishandling of diving equipment, which is what Cliff always claimed. But anybody who had ever seen a drunken Billie Booth berate Cliff in public in front of his colleagues didn't buy that. And since a lot of people in the Hollywood stunt community *had* seen that, they thought he just fucking killed her.

Cliff even admitted to the authorities his wife had been drinking at the time of the accident. Since the authorities didn't know Billie, they didn't know what that meant. But stuntmen and their wives did.

That *probably* meant Billie was being belligerent. And that *probably* meant she said one fucking thing too many. And that *probably* meant Cliff got fed up and, in a moment of weakness, he did something drastic. Something once he did, he couldn't undo.

How did Cliff get away with it? Easy. His story was plausible and it couldn't be disproven. Cliff felt real bad about what he did to Billie. But as much regret and remorse as he felt, it never occurred to him *not* to try to get away with murder.

After all, Cliff had always been a practical what's-done-is-done type. While taking the whole matter seriously, he also observed it from a pragmatic point of view. He didn't need to spend twenty years in jail—Cliff could do an adequate job punishing himself for his reckless moment. After all, it wasn't like he was a criminal. It wasn't like he plotted her murder. It was *practically* the accident he claimed it was. When his finger pulled the trigger, was it a conscious decision?

Not exactly.

One, it was a hair trigger. Two, it was more *instinct* than a *decision*. Three, was it a *pull*, or was it closer to a *twitch*? Four, it wasn't like anybody was gonna miss Billie Booth. She was a fucking cunt. Did she deserve to be ripped in two? Maybe not. But to say without Billie Booth on this earth the sweet life goes on unabated would be an understatement. Really, only her sister Natalie was upset, and she was even a bigger fucking cunt than Billie. And she was really only upset for a while. So Cliff carried the guilt, Cliff carried the remorse, and Cliff vowed to do better. What more does society want? The countless numbers of American soldiers he saved by killing Japs were definitely worth one Billie Booth.

Now, the law-enforcement agencies that investigated the case were not as aware of Cliff Booth's violent tendencies as the Hollywood stunt community was. And Cliff's story of a tragic mishandling of diving equipment was very plausible.

Also, as it turned out, proving *exactly* what happened when two people were alone, in a boat, out in the middle of the ocean, wasn't so easy. The authorities had to prove it *didn't* happen the way Cliff said it did. So, armed with a story that couldn't be disproven, Billie Booth's death was labeled *misadventure*.

And from that day forward, Cliff became the most infamous man on any Hollywood set he set foot on. Because no matter what set he set foot on, he was always the only man on that set that everybody in the know knew *got away with murder*.

Chapter Eleven

The Twinkie Truck

As Charles Manson negotiates the twisty roads leading up toward Terry Melcher's house on Cielo Drive, in the beat-up Hostess Twinkies Continental Bakery truck, he knows he's taking a chance.

When Charlie drove out from San Francisco to Los Angeles, it was with the purpose of getting his music published, his songs recorded with him singing them, landing a recording contract, and then finally becoming a rock-and-roll star. This whole being a spiritual leader to a bunch of zonked-out kids and a guru to a harem of runaway girls was just supposed to be something he did in the meantime. And at first, it worked. In fact, at first, it worked *really* well. His girls led him to create a relationship with the Beach Boys' drummer, Dennis Wilson, a real honest-to-goodness rock star. Which led Manson into a relationship with Wilson's friends Gregg Jakobson and Doris Day's son, Terry Melcher.

And that led to happenings, shindigs, toke parties, and jam sessions with other successful musicians on the L.A. rock-music scene. Before Charlie knew it, he was sharing a joint with the lead singer of the Raiders, Mark Lindsay, hobnobbing with Mike Nesmith of the Monkees and Buffy Sainte-Marie, and jamming on guitar with Neil Young. Neil fucking Young!

Charlie not only jammed with him; his musical improvisation skills seriously impressed Young. (That night jamming with Neil Young was the closest to legitimacy Manson ever got.) Charlie hoped his jam session with Young would lead to a meeting with Bob Dylan, but Bobby proved elusive. The closest Charlie ever got to meeting Dylan was trading a few words with Bob's sidekick at the time, Bobby Neuwirth, at the London Fog. No doubt about it, during the time when Charlie Manson and his "Family" were hanging out at Dennis Wilson's pad, his musical aspirations had forward momentum. There was even a recording session where Charlie put some of his tunes down on three-quarter-inch tape. It's doubtful that Melcher ever really entertained the idea of signing Charlie to Columbia Records. But it's not out of the realm of possibility that he entertained the idea of recording some of Charlie's songs for other artists. For all of Charlie's jailhouse wisdom and philosophical savvy, Manson was almost charmingly naïve when it came to the music business. Charlie knew Terry Melcher was wishy-washy about his record-selling potential. But he never allowed himself to get discouraged by it. To an admirable degree, when it came to the subject of himself, Charlie was always the eternal optimist. A foot in the door was all he ever said he wanted. And a foot in the door is what he got when Terry Melcher assured him that, at some point, he would sit down and let Charlie play him some of his music on his guitar.

Did Manson turn his relationship with Melcher into more than it was? Absolutely.

Was Melcher *somewhat* intrigued by Charlie? Maybe.

But Charlie's hottest prospect for gaining a record deal was his close relationship to Dennis Wilson. Dennis was the only *real* rock star of the Beach Boys. Brian was fat and getting fatter, Al Jardine looked like a skeleton, and Mike Love had been going bald since he was eighteen. Dennis was a sexy dreamboat, who even in the early sixties gave off a Zen late-sixties vibe. For a while, Dennis Wilson truly believed in Charlie's musical potential. He shared late-night trip sessions with Charlie, where Manson's philosophy and view of the world honestly impressed Dennis (Wilson also shared Manson's distrust and fear of black males). During jam sessions at his house, Dennis bore witness to Charlie's undeniable gift for in-the-moment improvisation behind a guitar. Still, it's dubious to think the untrained, undisciplined, loosey-goosey Manson would have ever gotten the hang of capturing his music in the pressure-filled, anxiety-inducing, sterile environment of a professional recording studio. (In that regard, Charlie would have some serious musical-genius company. Recordings of Woody Guthrie and Leadbelly serve more as historical records than as evocative representations of their musical talent.) But it's not out of the question to imagine, in an earlier time, Charles Manson making his way and learning the ropes in the pass-the-hat Greenwich Village coffeehouse scene of the late fifties and early sixties and on the hootenanny circuit, where his gift for musical improvisation, skill with a guitar, and prison background would've all been assets. For a while, Dennis

Wilson sincerely encouraged Charlie's musical dreams, even going so far as recording one of Charlie's songs (*Cease to Exist*, his signature Family tune), rewritten under the title *Never Learn Not to Love*, and putting it on the Beach Boys' *20/20* album.

And while the idea of Terry Melcher signing Charlie to make an album for Columbia Records was always far-fetched, the Beach Boys started their own record label, Brother Records, and a Charles Manson album for that label *could've* happened. The reason it didn't all stemmed from the aggravation and eventual fear Dennis Wilson felt for the sketchy characters he let take root in his home. It was the girls that first lured Dennis into the "Family" fold. Then later it was his genuine fellowship with Charlie that kept Dennis in the "Family" orbit. But it was Wilson's exasperation at Charlie's pinhead family of hippies that eventually led to burning the Beach Boys bridge just as Charlie was preparing to cross it.

The share-and-share-alike anti-establishment ethos of the Topanga Canyon Hollywood hippie entertainment clann of the late sixties was what Dennis Wilson offered these ragamuffins. However, pretty quickly, these garbage-eating, acid-tripping, clap-ridden, singsong-sounding runaways proved themselves to be a bunch of freeloading ingrates. They wrecked Wilson's pad and cost him thousands of dollars in venereal-disease medicine and lost, stolen, and damaged property. Until, finally, Wilson just moved out of the house and left it to his business manager to evict the squalid squatters.

* * *

If the "Family" hadn't turned Dennis's house into a zoo, causing his bandmates to worry and lose respect for him, Charles Manson would have been a perfect prospect for the Beach Boys' new record label. One doubts much would have happened with the disc or even if Manson, with his peculiarities, would have been capable of completing a full album. But it's entirely possible that, if the other band members hadn't associated Charlie with that group of freaks freeloading off of sweet Dennis, Manson could have parlayed his association into *something*.

But the way it was, the "Family" cost Dennis so much money that, even when the Beach Boys did record one of Charlie's songs, they kept his name off the publishing, figuring the costly antics of his acolytes were payment enough. (Rumors exist that in lieu of putting Charlie's name on the copyright, Wilson gave him a motorcycle.)

So by February 8, 1969, all of Charlie's once-promising musical connections have dried up. Only one remains—that vague commitment that Terry Melcher once made about someday sitting down and letting Charlie play his music for him. Only he's lost contact with Terry. There was a time when Charlie saw Terry, if not often, often enough to plan a meeting. But that was before he became persona non grata at Dennis Wilson's pad. And even Charlie knows that's reason enough to squash any possible deal. But, then again, maybe not? Charlie *did* get one of his songs on the new Beach Boys album. Now, true, he didn't get credit for it. But one of the few people who knows it originated from his song *Cease to Exist* is Melcher. So now Terry can legitimately think of

Manson as a music composer worthy of producing commercial music, instead of as the shaggy pimp who supplied the record producer with syphilis-ridden jailbait.

Now, Terry Melcher had already agreed to come out to Spahn Ranch and give Charlie's songs a listen. A date was set, a time was agreed to, an appointment was confirmed, and a whole shindig was put into place at the ranch . . . then Terry was a no-show.

For Charles Manson to be stood up like that was devastating on a few different fronts. One, Charlie had planned all week for this opportunity to finally perform his music for Terry. The Family had decked out and decorated the ranch for this big whoop-de-do, including practicing with background instruments and half-naked girls harmonizing and dancing in the background . . . then Terry didn't show.

Also, that day was *the* day.

Charlie was on fire *that* day.

Manson never forgave himself for letting his nerves get the better of him during his one professional recording session.

But *this* day would be different.

On *this* day Charlie was perfectly on point, his mind was calm, his heart was full, and his music was at his fingertips.

This day was the day he'd been dreaming about since he first started listening to the Beatles in prison.

On *this* day all Charlie's dreams would become a reality and his life would be changed forever.

On *this* day the music was going to come flooding out of him. He owned his creativity. He couldn't play a wrong note.

He was at one with his talent, at one with his muse, and at one with God . . . then Terry didn't show.

Terry's no-show not only thwarted Manson's creativity and frankly hurt his feelings, but it also compromised him with his kids.

The kids at the ranch weren't hip to exactly how much Charlie wanted to be a rock star. How much he wanted fame, money, and recognition. Because to them, Charlie preached against those base desires.

They thought Charlie was on a spiritual path to enlightenment.

They thought Charlie's true desire was to pass on that enlightenment.

They thought Charlie's goal was to create a new world order guided by that enlightenment and love for all mankind.

They believed Charlie had a higher purpose, because he told them he did, and they believed him. It never would have occurred to them that he'd ditch all that horseshit in a minute to put on a Revolutionary War outfit and trade places with Mark Lindsay.

It never would have occurred to them that he'd say goodbye to all of them, all that he created, and all he taught them, to trade places with Micky Dolenz and join the Monkees.

They thought the only reason Charlie wanted a recording contract in the first place was to expand his influence. To bring his enlightenment to a larger audience, a worldwide audience on a planet starving for it.

Like the Beatles. Like Jesus Christ. Like Charlie.

He didn't want fame for himself; he wanted fame for what his music would mean to others. But the music would simply be an entry point for the planet earth to get to know Charlie. With God working through him, Charlie would write some of the greatest music ever written, the way Jesus Christ wrote some of the greatest poetry ever written. Not to have framed platinum albums on his walls, like Dennis Wilson. Not to own sports cars, like Dennis Wilson. Not to be on the cover of *Crawdaddy* magazine. Not to have a song on the *Easy Rider* soundtrack. Not to join the Real Don Steele in crazy promotional contests on KHJ. But to save all mankind.

Their first glimpse that Charlie's motives and desires may have been less pure than their own was when he couldn't help but reveal his anxiety over the Terry Melcher audition.

Everybody wanted everything to go well, but nobody else at the ranch thought *everything* was riding on it.

It goes . . . it doesn't go. Don't sweat it, baby. What's supposed to happen will happen. Men plan, God laughs. That's what Charlie taught them.

So then why was Charlie stressing out so much about what Terry Melcher thought of him?

Why was Charlie freaking fucking out about whether or not Terry Melcher liked his music or had a good time?

Why was Charlie flipping fucking out trying to make a good impression on Terry "Fucking" Melcher?

But as Terry Melcher's three-thirty appointment turned to three-forty, then three-fifty, then four o'clock, then four-ten, then four-twenty, then four-thirty, and it became apparent to all that Terry Melcher wasn't going to show, it became apparent to all how badly Charlie felt. Terry's no-show made Manson look weak in front of his kids. Nothing that took place in front of "the Family" ever made Charlie look weak. Not irate parents, sometimes carrying shotguns; not former members, who sometimes came back to the ranch accompanied by friends demanding money, cars, or babies. Not the Black Panthers. Not even the pigs. Charlie faced them all down with a wink and a smile. Secure in the knowledge that God was on his side. But not this time. This time it was Charlie who looked foolish. Something else that day also became apparent, something the kids at Spahn Ranch had never considered before. Maybe Charlie was just another long-haired hippie with a guitar, trying to get on the radio. They couldn't believe it and they wouldn't believe it. But for the first time, it occurred to some of them.

Somehow, Melcher got word to Charlie that he didn't stand him up out of disrespect. He's a busy man and something important came up. But that was a little while ago. Since then, there's been no effort made to reschedule. And now Charlie and Terry don't run in the same circles. The idea of just bumping into him and setting up another time for another audition doesn't seem likely.

In a way, Charlie was getting a good education in what the entertainment business is like. People fall in and out of social circles. Somebody you seriously hung with yesterday rates no more than a wave today. Promising opportunities just don't pan out. Or as Pauline Kael once wrote: "In Hollywood, you could die of encouragement."

Well, since Mohammed wasn't going to just bump into the mountain at the Whisky a Go Go, drinking Cutty Sark, Mohammed would have to go to the mountain, or in this case the Hollywood Hills.

This is Charlie's last card.

Since he's been to Terry Melcher's house before, he remembers where he lives. He's even partied there. So him just popping up at his gate to say hi, while bad form, isn't completely out of the question.

This is a desperate move, and it feels like a desperate move. And Charlie is pretty fucking sure Terry will read it as a desperate move. But the way things are, it's the only move he has left. Terry *had* said he'd listen to Charlie's music one day. And Terry did *owe* him after standing him up before. And Charlie *isn't* going to just bump into him at Wilson's pad anymore. The only chance Charlie has of rescuing this lost opportunity is lucking out and catching Terry at home and putting the bite on him. A soft bite. Just enough to make him feel too guilty to say no to Charlie's face. But without the bite, Charlie's never gonna see Terry again. And when this doesn't work, which it probably won't, at least Charlie can say he tried.

When Charlie pulls up to the front of Terry's house on Cielo Drive, he sees the gate is open. These people leave their gates open most days they have a lot of deliveries, so they don't have to keep running to the intercom to buzz people in. Charlie had thought he'd get the brush-off at the call-box speaker located on the metal pole next to the driveway, outside the front gate.

Hi, is Terry there?

Who's asking?

It's his friend Charlie.

Charlie who?

Charlie Manson.

He ain't here.

That's how Charlie imagined the conversation would go, even if it was Terry at the intercom, pretending to be some-body who worked for him. So the gate being open counts as a stroke of luck. Some say luck is when preparation meets opportunity. The preparation part is picking Saturday late morning/early afternoon to pay his visit. If he's going to catch Terry bopping around his house, it's going to be Sat-urday late morning/early afternoon. Who knows, he might get a face-to-face with the man yet.

He considers driving the Twinkie truck up the long curvy driveway, but that's way too bold. Better to be hum-ble. Approach the house on foot, with open palms and a big smile.

Leave a soft footprint.

Charlie climbs out of the bakery truck. Terry lives on top of a hill at the end of a cul-de-sac. The only other human being in sight is a blond guy with his shirt off, working on an antenna on the roof of the house next door. Charlie pays him no mind as he walks up the driveway toward Terry's front door.

Sharon places the phonograph needle on the first track of the Paul Revere and the Raiders' album *The Spirit of '67*. The creator of the band and the producer of the album used to rent the house on Cielo Drive that Sharon and Roman are now renting from the owner, Rudi Altobelli, who lives in the guesthouse out back by the swimming pool. When the former tenant, Terry Melcher, moved out, he was living with the actress Candice Bergen. But before Candy moved

166

in, Terry shared the pad with Raiders lead singer Mark Lindsay. So it makes sense Sharon found a whole stack of cellophane-covered copies of *The Spirit of '67* tucked away in the guest room closet. She mentioned finding the records to her husband, Roman, who made a face and said, "I hate that bubble-gum garbage."

Sharon didn't argue, but she didn't agree either. She liked the bubble-gum hits she heard on KHJ. She liked that song *Yummy Yummy Yummy* and the follow-up song by the same group, *Chewy Chewy*. She liked Bobby Sherman and that *Julie* song. She loved that *Snoopy vs. the Red Baron* song.

She wouldn't tell this to Roman or any of their hip friends like John and Michelle Phillips or Cass Elliot or Warren Beatty, but to be completely honest, she liked the Monkees more than the Beatles.

She knows they're not even a real group. They're just a TV show made to capitalize on the popularity of the Beatles. Nevertheless, in her heart of hearts, she prefers them. She thinks Davy Jones is cuter than Paul McCartney (as evidenced by her attraction to Roman and Jay, Sharon does have a thing for cute short guys who look like twelve-year-old boys). She thinks Micky Dolenz is funnier than Ringo Starr. She's more attracted to Mike Nesmith's "quiet one" than to George Harrison. And Peter Tork seems just as much of a hippie as John Lennon but less pretentious and probably a nicer fellow. Yeah, sure, the Beatles write all their own music, but what the fuck does Sharon care about that?

If she likes *Last Train to Clarksville* better than *A Day in the Life*, she likes it better; she doesn't care who wrote it. Anyway, Paul Revere and the Raiders are sorta like the

Monkees. They sing catchy groovy songs, they're funny, and they're on TV all the time. She really likes their songs *Kicks, Hungry*, and especially *Good Thing*. Rudi Altobelli told her Mark Lindsay and Terry Melcher wrote *Good Thing* on the white piano in their living room. Cool. She thinks about that as she places the needle on the vinyl and listens to the cool opening guitar riff come out of her speakers. She starts immediately moving her shoulders and hips to the bubble-gum beat. Then she goes back to what she was doing before. Which is packing Roman's suitcase. Roman's leaving for London tomorrow, and she always packs his suitcase for him. It's just a sweet thing she started doing for him, and now it's just a sweet thing she does.

Her ex-fiancé, Jay Sebring, is in the kitchen, making himself a sandwich before he drives Sharon over to his salon on Fairfax and does her hair for a TV appearance Roman and Sharon have to do tonight (Jay exclusively does men's hair. Sharon is the only woman he does). They all attended a party at Hugh Hefner's Playboy Mansion last night. And during the night Hefner hit up Roman to appear on his quasi-talk show, *Playboy After Dark*, filmed on top of the 9000 building, toward the end of the Sunset Strip. Sharon was irritated that Roman committed them to two things in a row without consulting her. Not only that, but she's also reading a really good book, Gore Vidal's *Myra Breckinridge*, and Roman knows she'd rather spend the evening in bed alongside him reading it. Instead, she's going to have to get all dolled up for the second night in a row and do her "sexy little me" act ("sexy little me" is Sharon's self-deprecating nickname for her sixties-starlet persona).

As she folds the white turtleneck sweater she bought for Roman when they were in Switzerland and places it inside the suitcase laid open on the guest room bed, she doesn't see the shaggy-haired dark little hippie fellow in the long untucked blue-denim shirt with the brown rawhide vest over it, the Jesus sandals, and the dirty dungarees emerge from her foliage and wander into the cement parking area in front of her house. But Jay spots him through the kitchen window as he takes a bite of his Wonder Bread turkey-and-tomato sandwich. As Jay follows with his eyes the dark little hippie's path from the driveway to the front of the house, he thinks, *Who's this shaggy asshole walking around the property as if he owns it?*

Sharon, packing at the far end of the house, hears Jay's voice by the front door say to somebody authoritatively, "Hello? Can I help you?"

Then, from outside the house, she hears a muffled answer from a voice she isn't familiar with. "Yeah, hey, man, I'm lookin' for Terry. I'm a friend of Terry and Dennis Wilson's."

Who the hell is that? she thinks, keeping her ears peeled.

Then she hears Jay's response to the stranger: "Well, Terry and Candy don't live here anymore. This is the Polanski residence now."

Sharon puts down the paisley shirt she's holding and leaves the guest bedroom to investigate who Jay's talking to. As she walks through the carpeted hallway leading to the living room, in bare feet and Levi's cutoffs, she hears the stranger say with surprise and disappointment, "Really? He moved? Dang it! You know where?"

Sharon turns the corner leading to the entry hall with

The Fearless Vampire Killers one-sheet framed on the wall. (Roman thought it was embarrassing and juvenile to hang up in their house the posters for movies they'd done. But then Sharon reminded him he knew she was embarrassing and juvenile when he married her.)

The front door is wide open, and Jay has moved outside to talk with this creepy-looking dude with a mop of shaggy hair and a two-day growth of dark stubble on his face.

She reaches the door and calls out to her former fiancé, "Who is it, Jay?"

The shaggy stranger's eyes rise to the beautiful blonde in the doorway. Her radiant eyes look past Jay's for a moment to lock with the dark little man's.

Jay turns toward her and says, "It's okay, honey. It's a friend of Terry's." Then he turns back to the shaggy stranger and directs him to where the owner of the house lives. "I'm not sure where Terry moved to, but the owner of the property, Rudi, might know. He's in the guesthouse." With his hand, Jay points the way. "Take the back path."

The shaggy stranger smiles and says, "Thank you kindly."

As he turns to leave, he lifts his eyes again to the golden blonde in the doorway with the long legs, wearing a striped T-shirt that looks like she bought it in the little boys' section of a department store. His hand rises in a wave gesture and he says, "Ma'am."

Even though she finds this dark little intruder creepy, she nods at him and returns a slight smile. As the little man makes his way around the back of the property, Sharon's eyes follow him until he disappears from view.

* * *

Rudi Altobelli has just stepped out of his shower when he hears his dog, Bandit, pitching a bitch at somebody by his open front door. He knows it's a *somebody* rather than a *something* because, when it comes to intruders intruding on the property, the dog has three distinct barks. Cats get one bark, lizards, raccoons, and other varmints get another, and humans the dog doesn't know get a third. Rudi throws a towel on top of his head, puts his naked, still-wet body in a terry-cloth bathrobe, and steps out of his bathroom, heading toward the front door to investigate.

Altobelli is a small-time Hollywood manager, who—once upon a time—represented (in some capacity) Katharine Hepburn and Henry Fonda. But these days his client list boasts Christopher Jones, Olivia Hussey, Sally Kellerman, and two out of the three members of the pop trio Dino, Desi & Billy (he repped the Juniors, Desi Arnaz and Dean Martin). The property was a pretty good investment; he lives in the guesthouse out back and rents out the big house to Hollywood highfliers. As he approaches the wide-open front door, which is really the side door, the television set plays a black-and-white rerun of the TV series *Combat!* The opening credits of the show flash across the screen, and the series' military theme blares out of the speakers. The deep-voiced announcer announces:

"*Combat!* Starring Rick Jason. And Vic Morrow."

His dog is excitedly barking at the small-in-stature shaggy figure on the other side of the screen door. As Rudi reaches the visitor, he shouts at Bandit to calm down, grabs him by his collar, and pulls him out of the way. The damp man in the bathrobe looks through the screen door and realizes he recognizes the man on his doorstep.

"Rudi?" Charlie asks.

"Yeah?" answering a one-word question with a one-word answer.

Charlie goes right into it: "Hey, Rudi, I don't know if you remember me, I'm a friend of Terry Melcher's and Dennis Wilson's—"

"I know who you are, Charlie," Rudi tells him without any warmth. "What do you want?"

This dude ain't too friendly, Charlie thinks, *but at least he knows I know Terry.*

"Well, I came down to talk to Terry, and the dude at the house said Terry moved?"

"Yeah, they moved about a month ago," Rudi confirms.

Charlie does a little frustrated dance, kicking at the grass in the ground, cursing, "Gosh dang it, dagnabit! Looks like I came all the way down here for nothing." He then turns back to the man behind the screen door and asks with a big open face, "You know where he moved to or his number? I really got to get in touch with him. It's kinda an emergency." Which, from Charlie's perspective, isn't a lie.

But Rudi lies to Charlie when he tells him, "Yeah, sorry, Charlie, I can't help you with that. I don't know."

"Well, that's a drag," Charlie says.

Changing his tone, Charlie asks the man behind the screen a question he already knows the answer to. "What do you do for a livin', Rudi?"

"I'm a manager, Charlie," adding, "you know that."

As Vic Morrow, Rick Jason, and Jack Hogan blast Nazis in the background, Charlie goes right into his rap, before Rudi Altobelli can give him the brush-off.

172

"Well, the reason I gotta get in touch with Terry is, Terry was arranging an audition for me with Columbia Records and Tapes. But the truth of the matter is, I don't have representation, so if all goes well with this audition and they want to sign me to a contract, I'm all by my lonesome. And you know that ain't the best situation for an artist. Especially against some commercial giant like Columbia Records and Tapes.

"So maybe I could come back, play you some tapes of my songs. Maybe play for you a little on my guitar.

"You like what you hear, you sign me up and I start my relationship with Columbia Records and Tapes on the right foot."

Charlie sees Rudi isn't interested, so it's time to bring out the catnip.

"I hang out with a bunch of girls. Maybe bring them around, they sing background. Everybody always has a good time with my girls. You ask Terry. You ask Terry—he's had himself a goddamn good time with my girls."

Rudi starts to open his mouth, but before anything can come out, Charlie shoots him a question. "Have you heard the new Beach Boys album, *20/20*?"

"No."

"Well, I got a song on it," Charlie informs him. "I wrote the song," he qualifies, "and Dennis Wilson tinkered with it, fucked it up, and the Beach Boys fucked it up even more."

"Look—" Rudi tries to cut in, but Charlie doesn't let him.

"In fact, they fucked it up so much I'd rather you not listen to it. I'd rather play my version of it. Maybe come back, play my tapes for you. Play a little on my guitar. You

know, just make up some songs. I'm real good at that,"
Charlie says sincerely.

Finally, Rudi gets out, "Well, I'd like to talk to you longer,
Charlie, but I'm leaving for Europe tomorrow and I gotta
pack."

A big smile spreads across Charlie's face, and he says
with a giggle in his voice, "Well, I guess this is just my shit-
luck day, ain't it?"

Now it's Rudi's turn to change the subject. "How did you
know to come back here?"

Charlie jerks his thumb over his shoulder. "Dude at the
main house sent me back here."

"Look," Rudi Altobelli sternly instructs, "I don't like my
tenants to be disturbed. So from here on in, you don't bother
them again, you got it, Charlie?"

Charlie grins wide and waves his hand in compliance. "I
get it, I got it, and I'm good," Charlie assures him. "I don't
want to be no bother." Trying to wrap up this whole ex-
change with a little dignity, Charlie says, "So I'm gonna go
track down Terry—or he'll track me down. And maybe at
another time I can play you some of my songs?"

Finally! Rudi thinks.

"Yeah," Rudi says, "sure thing, Charlie."

Charlie gives the man behind the screen a big wave and
an even bigger smile and says, "Happy trails!"

Up on top of Rick's roof, Cliff has got Rick's TV antenna back
up again. He's twisting some wire around the base with a
pair of pliers to keep it in place when he spots the little hippie dude he saw drive up in the Twinkie truck leaving the

Polanski residence, walking back down the driveway in the direction of the automobile. As Cliff continues to twist the pliers, he follows this sketchy dude with his eyes.

Charlie's just about to climb aboard the Twinkie truck when he feels eyeballs on his shoulders. He pauses. Then turns around. He sees staring down at him from the roof of the house on the opposite side of the street a blond guy with his shirt off, working behind a TV antenna.

The men are too far away to get a good glimpse of each other.

Charlie smiles one of his big face-covering smiles and gives the shirtless blond bloke a big wave.

Cliff doesn't smile or wave back. He just stares holes through the dark little hippie while he twists the wire around the antenna with a pair of pliers.

The smile disappears from Charlie's face.

Then suddenly Charlie breaks into one of his "ooga-booga" dances, complete with yelled Manson gibberish. When Mr. Manson finishes his spastic dance performance for Cliff, he flips off the asshole on the roof. "Fuck you, Jack!"

Mr. Manson climbs back in the Twinkie truck, starts it up, shoves the broom-like stick shift into gear, and pops and coughs down the hill of Cielo Drive.

Cliff watches him leave.

Then says to himself, out loud, "What the fuck was that?"

175

Chapter Twelve

"You Can Call Me Mirabella"

The door of the makeup trailer on the set of *Lancer* flies open, and out steps Rick Dalton. Except he doesn't look much like Rick Dalton anymore. Sonya put a brown Indian wig on his head, which she cut into shoulder-length locks, and spirit-gummed a "big droopy Zapata-like mustache" around his mouth. And Rebekkah put him in a groovy brown rawhide jacket with a Custer-like fringe dangling off the arms that wouldn't be out of place if Rick was performing onstage at Woodstock with Country Joe and the Fish. In other words, Caleb DeCoteau, à la Sam Wanamaker.

Sam, Sonya, and Rebekkah couldn't be happier. Rick ain't so convinced.

But Sam is so enthusiastic about both Rick as an actor and his conception of a counterculture Caleb that the actor thought it best not to rock the boat. So he decided the best plan of action was to be as good an actor as Sam thinks he is by *acting* as if he's as enthusiastic as the other three about the development of Caleb's look. In reality, Rick thinks, *I look like a cross between a goddamn hippie faggot and the Cowardly Lion from The Wizard of Oz*. And he's not quite sure which of the two he dislikes most.

Sonya pops her head out of the makeup trailer door and warns him, "Rick I know it's lunch, but you need to wait at least an hour before you eat. Give that glue holding your mustache on your lip a chance to dry."

Nice-guy Rick gives her a *no sweat, baby,* look, pulls a western paperback out of his back pocket, and waves it at her in demonstration. "No worries, honey, I got my book."

Great, Rick thinks, *I'm fucking starving and now I gotta miss lunch.*

One of the things Rick likes about working on a set is they have to feed you. Rick thinks any meal not paid for or prepared by him is a good meal. A lot of actors he crosses paths with on a set are ingrate sons-a-bitches. What's not to love? They pay you a lot of money for pretending, they feed you, they fly you places, they put you up, give you spending cash, and do their best to make you look good? And still some actors complain. *Aww, what, chicken again today?* Rick has never understood it.

So during his lunch half hour, when he can't eat, he might as well get himself familiar with the saloon set, where the gang of rustlers his character leads hangs out. Rick, in his full Caleb DeCoteau regalia, walks the Twentieth Century Fox western back lot, which on this show is called Royo del Oro. When lunch is over, this place will be teeming with crew members, cowboys, filming equipment, and horses. But during lunch it turns into a ghost town. It's not completely deserted—random crew members cut through the western set as a shortcut on their way to somewhere else. But by and large it's deserted.

As the actor walks in his costume and his boots down the dirt main street, surrounded by Wild West–type businesses (livery stables, general stores, a coffin maker, a fancy hotel, a shitty hotel), he starts getting a feel for Caleb DeCoteau.

In the pilot, Caleb was the leader of a gang of bloodthirsty cattle rustlers—which the show referred to by the fancy moniker of "land pirates"—who'd moved into the Royo del Oro territory, poaching the cows of the biggest cattle rancher in the valley, Murdock Lancer, at will. And with no law in the town to speak of, the nearest federal marshal over a hundred and fifty miles away, and nothing but old man Lancer and a few Mexican ranch hands to shoo them off, that situation didn't look like it was going to change anytime in the near future. However, as if the unabated poaching of Murdock Lancer's cows wasn't bad enough, events had recently taken a turn for the lethal worst, with Caleb sending snipers at night to rain rifle fire upon the Lancer Ranch house (where Murdock's precious eight-year-old daughter, Mirabella, slept) and the bunkhouse (where the ranch hands slept), resulting in the murder of George Gomez, the Lancer Ranch ramrod and Murdock's oldest friend, and scaring off a quarter of Murdock's men.

Murdock Lancer was desperate. And desperate times called for desperate measures. It would appear Murdock's only alternative would be to hire a bunch of cutthroats of his own and engage in a bloody ranch war, which would leave many men dead (not to mention put his daughter in harm's way). Not only did Murdock feel his money was not meant to finance murder (even scum like the men of DeCoteau), ultimately old man Lancer felt the murder of men wasn't worth the price of bovine.

So instead of doing the obvious, Murdock Lancer took a turn toward the unique.

The old man had two sons by two different mothers (shades of *Bonanza*), who he hadn't seen since they were children. And if their reputations could be trusted, both men seemed more than capable when it came to handling firearms.

The oldest of the two, Scott Lancer, was the most impressive in the old man's eyes, educated inside the hallowed halls of Harvard and raised in wealth, culture, and honor by the Fosters, his mother's distinguished Boston family.

Currently, in Murdock's opinion, he was pissing away that pedigree by living the life of a riverboat gambler. There were also rumors of him killing the son of a United States senator in a pistol duel over the compromising of the honor of a beautiful Southern belle.

However, the young man had a distinguished military career, riding with the British Cavalry in India. When he left Calcutta and set sail for home, he returned with two medals for bravery in the face of the enemy and a limp in his right leg.

John Lancer, Murdock's youngest boy, was another case entirely. The last time Murdock saw him was when the boy was ten years old. After his mother, Marta Conchita Louisa Galvadon Lancer, had sex with one of her husband's ranch hands, she took their young son and fled into the night. Marta was a tramp the way other people are drunks. It was what she was but not necessarily what she wanted to be. But like a true honest-to-goodness drunk on the wagon, she might lay off her prowess at seduction and her susceptibility to same for a week or two, or a month or two, or a year or two, but her eventual fall was inevitable. In Marta's case, as Murdock Lancer's wife and John Lancer's mother, she laid off for ten years (after the birth of her son). But, eventually, the time came where she gave in to her true nature.

The first time Marta saw handsome Lazaro Lopez astride a saddle, roping steers, she knew her fall from grace, wealth, and position was simply a matter of time. Marta might not have loved her husband, but as Tina Turner was later to sing, "what's love got to do with it?" Fifteen-year-old girls fall in love with stable boys, who don't have a pot to piss in or a window to throw it out of, when wealthy landowners would gladly trade twelve good horses for their hand in marriage. Love is for young girls with their brains in their ass. What Marta felt for Murdock was far more meaningful: *respect*.

When she humiliated him in his home, in the eyes of his men, she pulverized the thing that made his spine stand straight, his pride. She had played house for ten years, but now he saw her for what she was. A filthy whore who could not be trusted. When he confronted her with her treachery, she saw in his eyes that the life they had created together on the Lancer Ranch was destroyed. Even if he did forgive her, he'd never forget. But even more catastrophic was the re-spect in herself she'd lost and would never regain. Murdock Lancer had his problems, but he was a good man. And he didn't deserve a tramp who'd toss away the life he gave her for no better reason than a roll in the hay with some cocksure bronco buster. So once her husband went to sleep, she took their ten-year-old son and the buggy Murdock had given her for her twenty-eighth birthday and ran off to Mexico.

In the border towns of Mexico, she could stop pretending to be something other than what she was born to be. Unbeknownst to their little boy, Murdock spent five years searching for his runaway wife and young son. All to a fruitless outcome. After a dissatisfied customer slit her throat two years later in the back room of an Ensenada cantina, Marta finally received the peace she'd craved since her transgression. Her self-degradation could come to an end, her husband's pride could finally find restitution, and her son could finally be rid of the weight tied to his ankle that dragged him down to the lower depths of humanity. Since Jesus Christ was the only one who knew how badly she felt about what she had done, maybe he'd forgive her like he always promised he would. Then she could finally leave behind the shacks, cantina back rooms, and whorehouses. A paradise, where her sins would be washed away, was what lay before her (if this whole Jesus business was to be believed).

In some ways, Marta Lancer was the more fortunate one, because Murdock never found peace with his sons lost to him. The old man felt terrible bitterness toward his first wife, Diane Foster Lancer, for her weakness and lack of fortitude. Making vows in the eyes of God at their wedding ceremony she hadn't the strength of character to keep. To keep a promise was a test of one's self. A test that these women he brought into his life failed and failed horribly. But at least in Scott's case the old man knew he was safe, secure, and well fed. He might grow up a dude as opposed to a cattleman and the heir to a self-made empire, but at least he would be well looked after by his China-plate Beacon Hill relatives.

But poor John—God only knew what he'd lived through. After five years of searching, one of Lancer's Pinkerton detectives finally located Marta Galvadon Lancer's final resting place in a boot-hill graveyard in Ensenada, Mexico. It was obvious that the wooden cross and her name carved on the board was carved by her surviving twelve-year-old son. The old man journeyed to Ensenada. The last record of his son was his appearance at the murder trial of her killer, a Mexico City citizen of wealth and prestige. The affluent Mexican was acquitted under prejudicial circumstances by the biased jury, who seemed to have it in for Marta. The throat-slitting parasite could have set Marta on fire and that jury wouldn't have found him guilty. And though Murdock continued to search for the boy, all his efforts were in vain. When Murdock Lancer signed his last check to the Pinkerton detective agency, it was with the bitter resolve that his son was dead. And that, apparently, was that.

It was sometime around fifteen years later that the reputation of a deadly half white/half Mexican gunfighter named Johnny Madrid reached the ears of Californians. The reputation was that of a scoundrel, but a scoundrel with lightning-fast prowess with a *pistola*. From the accounts of eyewitnesses and dime-store pulp writers, he had the quickness in killing of Tom Horn, the accuracy of aim of Annie Oakley, the nasty disposition of John Wesley Hardin, and the lack of human empathy of William H. Bonney. He was one of the most feared killers who rode the Mexican side of the border, known by the peons in the pueblos he passed through as El Asesino de Rojo (translation: "The Murderer in Red"), due to the fancy red ruffled shirt he always wore.

But it wasn't till three years ago that one of Lancer's former Pinkerton detectives sent him a telegram that informed the cattle baron that his long-lost son was indeed alive and living under the name *Johnny Madrid*.

The old man cried for three days, with nobody on the ranch understanding why.

However, now that Murdock Lancer's battle with Caleb DeCoteau and his land pirates had graduated from the simple loss of cows to the tragic loss of life, it was only a matter of time before the cattle baron hired killers of his own. But before that inevitable day arrived, Murdock had one crazy idea. He would track down and get word to his two long-lost sons, John and Scott. He'd wire them enough money to travel to Lancer Ranch, with an offer of a thousand dollars apiece for just listening to his proposition.

His offer was simple. Help him defend the ranch against Caleb and his killers, and once they'd driven off these pirates, Murdock would equally share his entire empire with his two sons. It was a generous offer, but it was no gift. They'd have to earn it. And they'd have to keep from getting killed by Caleb and his boys.

But if they were willing to help Murdock prevail against these rascals and were willing to put in the blood, sweat, and tears it took to run a successful ranch this size, all three Lancer men would be equal partners. And if all these things miraculously worked out, Murdock Lancer and his long-lost sons would finally, at long last, be a family.

All in all, not a bad premise for a TV series, Rick thought. Good story and good characters.

A little reminiscent of *Bonanza* and *The High Chaparral*, but darker and more violent, more cynical.

For one, Murdock Lancer is no Ben Cartwright–like, stern but fair and compassionate patriarch. He's a real uncompromising son of a bitch. You could imagine both former wives getting fed up with his shit real quick and hightailing it away from this bitter bastard first chance they got. And the horse-faced actor Andrew Duggan (who Rick did a play with once) they got to play Murdock doesn't have a folksy bone in his body. He's hard as a bar of iron and about as lovable. The character of Scott Lancer is more the likable good guy found on sixties' western shows. But his fancy Eastern-dandy wardrobe definitely gives him a different look. He makes earlier dandies like Bat Masterson and Yancy Derringer look like saddle tramps. And his past as a former Bengal Lancer is an intriguing backstory. But it's Johnny Lancer/ Johnny Madrid that is the no-shit unique western-TV-series lead. Dalton's Jake Cahill was about as antihero as western-TV-series leads ever got. But Johnny Lancer/Johnny Madrid, at least in the pilot script, goes far further than Jake was ever allowed to go.

The handsome, roguish, mysterious Johnny Lancer who steps off the Royo del Oro stage is the type of character that usually guest-stars on western TV shows, not stars in them. That type of character usually shows up on *Bonanza*'s Ponderosa Ranch, or *The Big Valley*'s Barkley Ranch, or

The Virginian's Shiloh Ranch, and they're young, cocky, sexy, and a little dubious. They make friends with Little Joe, or Heath, or Trampas, but at some point, usually in the first act, we learn they have some sort of dark secret. They're either on the run from somebody or from something, or they're running from who they were or something they did or didn't do. Or they're in the area for some clandestine reason (usually revenge, planning a robbery, or to meet somebody from their past). We (the audience) know they're shady. But we also know we'll have to wait till the third act before we find out: Is the character a bad guy or a misunderstood good guy? And in the third act, Michael Landon or Lee Majors or Doug McClure either helps them redeem themselves or shoots them dead. These characters are always the best roles on the show, and the guys who specialized in playing them usually went on to become stars (Charles Bronson, James Coburn, Darren McGavin, Vic Morrow, Robert Culp, Brian Keith, and David Carradine).

But the role of Johnny Lancer, while written like a guest star, is the no-shit lead of the fucking series. And he's not anything like any of the other cowboys riding the range on the big three networks.

Whoever this fucking guy Jim Stacy is, Rick thinks, *he sure fell into a big piss pot full of luck when he landed this role.*

But Caleb DeCoteau isn't just a standard-issue heavy either. It's a damn good part and he has some of the script's best dialogue. As he walks the dusty deserted streets of Royo del Oro, Rick goes over some of his lines, making his way to the saloon on the western back-lot set. As he walks by one of the western businesses on the main drag, he catches a glimpse of his reflection in the glass of one of the windows. The sight makes him stop for a moment and examine it.

Looking at the end result in the makeup-trailer mirror, surrounded by the wig girl and the wardrobe girl and the director, he wasn't that keen on the results. *Unless somebody reads it in TV Guide, who the fuck's gonna even know it's me*, is what Rick really thought. But now he's gotten a little more used to it, walking around (*the boots feel good*), seeing himself reflected in the western-styled picture window surrounded by a Wild West environment, *this look ain't bad*. He liked the hat from the get-go, but it's the brown hippie jacket that's really growing on him. The fringe hanging off the sleeves is pretty swell. He starts pointing and gesturing with his arms and watching the effect in the window reflection. The way the dangling fringe emphasizes his movements is pretty neat. He can do a lot with that. *Not too shabby, Rebekkah*, Rick thinks. He also thinks:

It doesn't look like me. But maybe Sam's right, that ain't such a bad thing. It does look like Caleb. Maybe not the Caleb I pictured in my mind when I first read the script. That Caleb just looked like me. I mean, if they want me, they want it to look like me, right?

But maybe Sam has a point. At least when Johnny Lancer kills me, he won't be killing Jake Cahill.

But staring at Caleb in the window staring back at Rick, he sees something else. He sees a little of what Marvin Schwarz was talking to him about in his office yesterday. At one point he called Rick "an Eisenhower actor in a Dennis Hopper Hollywood."

Looking at his reflection in his whole Caleb DeCoteau regalia, he understands a little more clearly, and a little less defensively, what Marvin Schwarz was getting at. Shaggy-haired guys are the style of the day. And that guy in the window in the fringe jacket could be Michael Sarrazin. Sans pompadour, Rick looks not only like a different character but a different actor. He's worn his hair the same way for so long, somewhere along the line the pompadour *became* him. But now? Examining his reflection in the window without it? He doesn't look so much like an aging cowboy actor from the fifties anymore. He kinda looks like a with-it modern actor. *This guy* isn't an Eisenhower relic. *This guy* could be in a Sam Peckinpah movie.

After Rick tears himself away from his own reflection in the window and the reflections about his career in his head, he spots Caleb's commandeered saloon, the Gilded Lily, out of which his character runs his murderous gang of rustlers. As he approaches the front porch of the saloon set, he sees a director's chair with his character's name on it. On TV shows, series regulars get a director's chair with the actor's name written on it. But guest stars usually get chairs with their character's name on it, because oftentimes they're not cast till a few days before.

Sitting next to his empty director's chair on the wooden walkway directly in front of the swinging saloon doors is the little girl dressed in the period clothes he saw talking to Sam when he first arrived. He doesn't know her real name and can't remember her character's name, but she plays Murdock Lancer's eight-year-old daughter (by yet another mother, but this one didn't skedaddle the first chance she got. Instead, she tragically broke her neck when she was thrown from the beautiful strawberry roan Murdock gifted her for their third-year anniversary. The same strawberry roan Murdock Lancer shot in the head once he got home from her funeral).

Later in the script, Caleb will kidnap the little girl and hold her for ten-thousand-dollars ransom.

The kidnapping of the child will end up being the emotional turning point in the story. While Johnny Lancer was brought to town by his father to defend the ranch against Caleb and his men, the screenwriters of the pilot had a twist in store for that standard scenario. One, Johnny hates the father he hasn't seen since he was ten years old. And two, as luck would have it, unbeknownst to anybody on the ranch, Johnny Madrid and Caleb DeCoteau both know and like each other. At any rate he likes Caleb a damn sight better than the father he blames for the death of his mother. Getting revenge for his mother by killing his father has been a dream of the son since he buried her eighteen years earlier in the Ensenada dirt.

A revenge that Caleb DeCoteau is quite successfully executing. Which ends up putting Johnny in the difficult, but dramatically rewarding, position of having to decide not only which side is he on but who is he? Lancer or Madrid? With Caleb's kidnapping of the child being the emotional catalyst that ultimately pushes Johnny over to the side of the angels and sets him up for a weekly western television show alongside his newfound family.

Rick has a scene with the young actress later today where he negotiates his ransom demands with Scott Lancer, as the little girl sits on his lap with a pistol barrel pressed against the side of her temple. But it's tomorrow when he and the little girl will have their biggest scene together. As he examines the little dishwater blonde from a distance, sitting in her director's chair reading a big black hardcover book, she looks to be about twelve years old. She's spending her lunchtime sitting on the set by herself, with no adult guardian or no sign of a lunch. She doesn't raise her eyes from the book she's reading when he walks up to the saloon's front-porch steps. Not even after he clears his throat and says, "Hello?"

Oh boy, he thinks, *this little bitch is gonna be a pip.* Hitting his greeting much harder, he repeats, "Hello?"

Raising her eyes from the book opened up in her lap, apparently annoyed, she says, "Hello," to the hairy cowboy standing at the bottom of the porch steps.

Holding up the western paperback in his hand, he asks her, "Would it bother you if I sat next to you and read my book too?"

She looks at him, poker-faced, with the bitchy timing of a pint-sized Bette Davis. "I don't know. Would you bother me?"

That was pretty clever, Rick thinks. *What, does this little squirt walk around with a team of gag writers supplying her bitchy comebacks to rhetorical questions?*

"I'll try not to," Rick softly replies.

She lays the big black book on her lap and examines him for a moment, then turns to the empty director's chair, examines it, and looks back at Rick again. "That's your chair, ain't it?"

"Yep," Rick says.

"Who am I to tell *you* not to sit in *your* chair?"

Removing his cowboy hat and giving her a gracious bow,

"Nevertheless," he says, pouring on the charm, "I thank you kindly."

She neither giggles nor smiles, just lowers her eyes back to her reading material.

Fuck this fucking little cunt, Rick thinks. So, noisier than need be, his cowboy boots clomp up the wooden steps of the porch. He heads to his director's chair, climbs himself backward into the seat, making the slight moaning sound he always makes when he climbs himself backward into his director's chair.

She ignores him.

He then removes his fucked-up pack of cigarettes from his black Levi's pants pocket, takes one from the sweaty crumpled pack, and sticks it in his mouth underneath the horsetail glued to his upper lip. He lights his cancer stick with his silver Zippo in the flashy (noisy) way of a fifties-era cool daddy-o. After he's accomplished setting the end on fire, he slams the lid of the Zippo closed with what looks like a diagonal karate chop; metal slams down on metal with a loud *snap*.

She ignores him.

He takes a big drag of his cigarette, filling his lungs with smoke, the way when he was a younger actor he used to watch Michael Parks do, only in hungover Rick's case the exhale triggers a coughing fit, which causes him to cough up another one of his green-mixed-with-crimson loogies, which splatters in a colorful glob on the wooden walkway.

That she doesn't ignore.

A look of horror crosses the little lady's little face, as if

Rick just pissed in her Wheaties; she stares in disbelief at both Rick and the gooey loogie refuse on the ground.

Okay, that was a little too much, Rick thinks, so he sincerely apologizes to his little co-star. She tries to blink the image out of her eyes as her head lowers back down to find the place in the big black book where she left off.

The fact is, after assuring her he'd try not to bother her while she was reading, he's frankly done nothing but. And he's still not through. Pretending to read his paperback, as he tries to mask that he's digging a stubborn booger lodged up his nose, he asks her casually, "You don't eat lunch?"

She answers back flatly, "I've got a scene after lunch."

Rick asks her, "Yeah?" As if he's saying, *So?*

Now he finally gets her attention, so she closes the book, lays it in her lap, and turns to explain to him her methodology.

"Eating lunch before I do a scene makes me sluggish I believe it's the job of an actor—and I say *actor*, not *actress*, because the word *'actress'* is nonsensical—it's the actor's job to avoid impediments to their performance. It's the actor's job to strive for one hundred percent effectiveness. Naturally we never succeed, but it's the pursuit that's meaningful."

Rick just stares at her for a beat or two without saying anything, till he finally says, "Who are you?"

"You can call me Mirabella," she says.

"Mirabella what?" he asks.

"Mirabella Lancer," she says obviously.

Rick waves that away with his hand and asks, "No no no, I mean, what's your real name?"

Again she answers in a tutorial-like fashion. "When we're on set, I'd prefer to only be referred to by my character's name. It helps me invest in the reality of the story. I've tried it both ways, and I'm just a tiny bit better when I don't break character. And if I can be a tiny bit better, I want to be."

Rick doesn't really have anything to say back to that. So he just smokes.

The young girl who calls herself Mirabella Lancer looks the cowboy bedecked in the fringe rawhide jacket up and down with her eyeballs and says, "You're the bad guy, Caleb DeCoteau," she says—not asks—and she pronounces the name like *Jean Cocteau*.

Rick blows out some more cigarette smoke and says, "I thought it was pronounced Caleb *Da-kota*."

As she turns back to her big black book, Mirabella says like a know-it-all smarty-pants, "I'm pretty sure it's pronounced day-coc-too."

Watching her read her book, he asks her sarcastically, "What's so interesting?"

She looks up from the book, not getting the sarcasm, "Huh?"

"What are you reading?" he asks again, minus the sarcasm.

The serious little girl does a serious spike in girlish enthusiasm, as she excitedly bubbles, "It's a biography on Walt Disney! It's fascinating," she reviews. Then she opines to her fellow actor, "He's a genius, you know. I mean a once in every fifty or hundred years kinda genius."

Finally Rick asks the question he's dying to know: "What are you, twelve?"

She shakes her head no. She's used to adults making that mistake, and she likes it when they do. "I'm eight." She hands the big black book about Walt Disney over to Rick for him to examine. He looks down at the book and thumbs through the pages, asking her, "You understand all these words?"

"Not all of them," she admits. "But half the time the context of the sentence gives you a pretty good idea of the meaning. And the words I really, really can't figure out, I make a list of and ask my mom."

Impressed, as he hands the book back to the little girl he says, "Not too shabby, eight years old—your own series."

As she retrieves the book to her lap, she qualifies his compliment: "*Lancer*'s *hardly* my series. It's Jim, Wayne, and Andy's series. I'm just the *'little tyke'* series regular." Then, pointing her tiny index finger at the actor, she tells him, "But just you wait, one of these days I'm gonna get a series of my own. And when I do," she warns, "watch out."

This little girl is un-fucking-believable, Rick thinks. In his career he's met and worked with a lot of unbelievable child actors. But before Lillie Langtry here, the most unbelievable one he ever saw was an eleven-year-old boy, whose name he sure as shit don't remember but who he'll never forget. The year before he landed *Bounty Law*, he was cast in a series pilot that never was picked up; it was called *Big Sky Country*. And it starred boring fifties' leading man Frank Lovejoy. It was the story of a widowed town sheriff (Frank Lovejoy) and his family. Rick played the oldest son, and there was an eleven-year-old brother and a nine-year-old sister. The show was passed on by the network, but it was produced by the television production company Four Star Productions and was screened once for the makers at their screening room. At the screening, which Rick attended, he bumped into the eleven-year-old little boy who played his younger sibling, in the men's room at Four Star. Rick headed for the urinal as the little boy finished washing his hands in the sink. If the series had been picked up, and if it had been success- ful, these two would have worked together for the next five years or longer. Rick would've watched this little boy turn into a teenager and maybe a man before his eyes. The young lad would become like either a real brother to him or just an annoying younger colleague, or maybe both. Because of this association, they *coulda* been linked together for the rest of their lives. Or, like what happened, the show doesn't get picked up, and this is the last time in their lives they'll ever see each other. As Rick removed his pecker from his pants and pointed it at the urinal wall, he asked over his shoulder how his young co-star was doing. The little actor told him, as he harshly wiped the wetness from his hands with a pa- per towel, "Well, I'll tell you one thing. I'm getting rid of my fuckin' agent, that's for goddamn sure!"

As Rick remembers *that* kid, *this* kid asks him, "What are you reading?" referring to the paperback western in his hand.

He shrugs his shoulders and tells her, "It's just a western."

"What does that mean?" she asks, not understanding the initial dismissal. "Is it any good?" she inquires.

He answers, far less enthusiastic about his book than she is with hers, "Yeah, it's pretty good."

She wants more. "What's the story?"

"I ain't finished it yet," he answers.

Jeez, she thinks, *this guy is so literal*.

"I didn't ask for the *whole* story," she emphasizes. Trying another avenue of investigation: "What's the premise of the story?"

The book is called *Ride a Wild Bronc*, and it's written by Marvin H. Albert, who wrote a pretty good book about the Apache Wars that Rick liked, called *Apache Rising*, which was turned into a pretty mediocre movie with James Garner and Sidney Poitier, titled *Duel at Diablo*. So Rick thinks about the story of this new book for a moment, gets the facts in the right order, and then proceeds to relate them to the young girl.

"Well, it's about this guy who was a bronco buster. And it's the story of his life. Guy's name is Tom Breezy. But everybody just calls him 'Easy Breezy.'

"So when Easy Breezy was in his twenties and young and good lookin', he could break any horse you could throw at 'em. Back then, well . . . uh, he just had a way. You know what I mean?"

"Yeah," she answers. "He had a gift for breaking horses."

"Yeah, that's right," he tells her. "He had a gift. So, anyway, he gets into his late thirties, and he takes a bad fall. . . . Now he ain't crippled or anything like that, but his lower section ain't ever the same. Now he's got spine problems he never had before. Now he spends more of his days in pain than he ever did before—"

"Jeepers," she interjects, "this sounds like a good novel."

He sorta concurs. "It ain't bad."

"Where are you in it?" she asks.

"About midway," he answers.

She asks, "What's happening to Easy Breezy now?"

Rick has been reading pulp western paperbacks since he was twelve years old. And ever since he became an actor, it's what he does in between takes and in his trailer waiting for the 2nd AD to summon him to set. He'll mix it up a little with a detective story or a mystery or World War Two adventure, but the pulps he keeps returning to are the westerns. Even though he likes them, he doesn't really remember them. He remembers the names of the authors he likes—the aforementioned Albert, Elmore Leonard, T. V. Olsen, Ralph Hayes—but not the book titles. Considering how generic those titles were—*The Texan*, *Gringo*, *The Outlaw*, *Ambush*, *Two Guns for Texas*—that's perfectly understandable. But all the years sitting around on sets reading westerns, while somebody may have asked him what he was reading, nobody ever asked him to recite the story. Though Rick never really thought about it before, he kinda now realizes that reading western paperbacks is one of the most solitary activities that he partakes in. So being asked to explain to somebody what's happening now in the book he's reading is not something he's used to articulating.

But for her sake, he tries his best.

"Well, he's not the best anymore." Clarifying, "In fact, far from it. And he's coming to terms with . . ." Rick thinks what's the right word to describe Easy Breezy's conundrum. "What it's like to become . . . uh . . . slightly more . . . uh—" He opens his mouth to say the word "useless," but the only thing that comes out of his mouth is a loud sob.

The sob catches Rick by surprise and gets Mirabella's

attention. He opens his mouth and tries again to say "use-less," but the word sticks in his throat. On his third attempt, he croaks out, "Useless—each day," followed by a stream of tears that leak out of his eyes and run down his hairy face, folding him up like a jackknife.

Oh, great, he thinks, *now I'm crying in front of children about my fucked-up life? Holy shit, I've turned into my Uncle Dave.*

As fast as she can, Mirabella is out of her director's chair and on her knees at Rick's feet, patting his right kneecap in an effort to comfort him. As his fist violently wipes away the wetness around his eyes, with both embarrassment and self-loathing, he chuckles to indicate to the small child he's okay. "Heh heh, boy, I must be getting old. I can't talk 'bout nothin' touchin' wit'out gettin' all choked up, heh heh."

The little girl *thinks* she understands and continues to console the weepy cowboy, who is now, in her eyes, starting to resemble the Cowardly Lion.

"It's okay, Caleb. It's okay," she assures him. "It sounds like a really sad book." Shaking her head in sympathy: "Poor Easy Breezy." She shrugs her shoulders and says, "I'm practically crying and I haven't even read it."

He says under his breath, "Wait till you're fifteen, you'll be livin' it."

She doesn't understand and asks, "What?"

He plasters a smile under his glued-on mustache and says, "Nothin', Pumpkin Puss, I'm just teasing." Then, holding up his western paperback, he proclaims, "And you know, you might be right. Maybe this book hits harder than I gave it credit for."

The little girl's eyes narrow, and she gets back on her

feet, rising to her full height, and informs him, "I don't like names like 'Pumpkin Puss.' But since you're upset, we'll talk about that some other time."

He laughs slightly to himself at her reaction, as she climbs back into her director's chair next to him. Once she's back sitting comfortably in her chair, she looks Rick up and down in all his hairy-faced, brown rawhide-fringed-jacket glory.

"So this is your Caleb DeCoteau look, huh?"

"Yeah. What do you think? Do you not like it?"

"No, you look groovy."

Yeah, she's right. It's not so bad, he thinks.

"It's just . . . I didn't know Caleb was supposed to look groovy."

Oh shit, I fucking knew it, Rick thinks.

"Do I look too much like a hippie?"

"Well," the little actor contemplates, "I wouldn't say, *too much*."

"But I look like a hippie?" the big actor clarifies.

"Well," she asks, confused, "that's the idea, ain't it?"

"Apparently," Rick dismissively snorts.

The little actor gives a more elaborate evaluation of her first impression. "Look, that's not what I thought when I first read the script, but it's not a *bad idea*." Taking him in more with both her eyes and her eye toward characterization, "In fact, the more I look at it, the more I like it."

"Really?" Rick asks. Then he challenges her, "Why?"

"Well . . ." The eight-year-old thinks. "Just for me, I find hippies . . . kinda sexy . . . kinda creepy . . . and kinda scary.

And sexy, creepy, and scary is a pretty strong choice for Caleb."

Rick snorts again and thinks, *What does this little twerp know about sexy?* But her words do calm him down about his anxiety over his Caleb DeCoteau look.

Now that Rick's questions have been answered, Mirabella's got a few questions of her own. "Caleb, may I ask you something personal?"

His one-word answer is, "Shoot."

She asks a question of her fellow actor that she seriously would like to know the answer to: "What's it like playing the bad guy?"

"Well, it's actually pretty new for me," he tells her. "I used to have my own cowboy show once. And on that show I played the good guy."

"Which do you like playing better?" she asks.

"The good guy," he says without any ambiguity.

"But," the little girl counters, "Charles Laughton said that villains are the best parts."

Of course that's what that fat queer would say, Rick thinks. But instead of talking to a little girl about fat fags, he tries to explain to her why he prefers playing the good guy.

"Look, when I was a kid and played cowboys and Indians, I didn't pretend I was some damn Injun. I was the cowboy. Besides, the hero gets to kiss the lead actress or, in the case of a TV series, that week's female guest star. Heroes get the love scenes. Closest thing to a love scene a villain gets is when they let you rape somebody. And the bad guy always loses the fight to the good guy."

"So what?" she says. "It's not a real fight."

"Yeah, but people watch it," he explains, "and now they think that guy can beat me up."

She rolls her little eyes and says, "Well, then, good—that means they believe the story."

"It's embarrassing," he emphasizes.

Oh my god, she thinks, *this guy is incredible.*

"How old are *you*?" she asks him in exasperation. "I'm sure too old to be thinking like that."

"Hey hey hey, calm down," he tells her. "When people ask me what I like better, I assume there ain't no right or wrong answer."

That actually makes sense to the young actor's sense of fair play.

"You know what, Caleb, you're a hundred percent right."

He gives her a head nod that serves as a thank-you.

Then she reminds him of something: "You know our big scene is tomorrow?"

"Yeah," remembering, "our big scene together *is* tomorrow, isn't it?"

"Yes, it is. And in that scene, you yell at me and grab me and scare me."

He assures her, "Don't be scared. I won't hurt you."

She qualifies her instruction with the caveat, "Well, I don't want you to really hurt me," then she zeroes in on Rick and points her little finger at him. "But I *want* you to scare me." She continues intensely, "Yell at me as loud as you want. Grab me, grab me hard. Shake me—shake the shit out of me. Scare me. Don't make me *act* scared, make me *react* scared. Anything less," she explains, "and you're treating me like a baby, and I don't like it when adults treat me like a baby." After her intense finger-pointing, she slips back to her normal snotty demeanor. "The scene we do tomorrow, I want to put on my reel. And the only reason I can't put scenes on my reel that I want to is because the adults in the scenes aren't good enough. Don't use my age as an excuse to be anything less than great—okay?"

"Okay," he says.

"Promise?" she insists.

"I promise," he assures her.

"Let's shake on it," she suggests.

Having reached an understanding, the two actors shake hands.

Chapter Thirteen

"The Sweet Body of Deborah"

While everybody in the stunt community knows Cliff Booth is Rick Dalton's stunt double, it's not the thing he's *most* known for. It's just the most *legitimate* thing in the stunt community he's known for. On the list of things that Cliff Booth is known for, it ranks about number four. The number-one thing he *used* to be known for was his incredible military record. Having more confirmed kills of Japanese enemy soldiers than any other American serviceman fighting in the Pacific theater is one hell of a feat. And that's just confirmed kills. Ask any of his Filipino-brother resistance fighters how many unconfirmed kills of Japanese enemy soldiers Cliff Booth was responsible for, their answer would be, *Who fucking knows?*

But once there was widespread speculation that in 1966 Cliff Booth killed his wife, his status as a war hero became the second thing he was most known for inside the stunt community.

Number three on the list of things that Cliff Booth was known for inside the stunt community were his talents as a "ringer."

As a ringer, Cliff Booth was the best in the sixties' film industry.

What's a ringer? Don't try looking it up; it's an unofficial term.

Well, say you're a stunt gaffer and you're working with a real asshole director who yells at your dudes all the time. Or with some fucking dickhead actor who keeps tagging your dudes and blames *them* for his mistake. Now, the stunt gaffer or anyone on his team can't knock the director's block off or punch the actor back when they get tagged.

But what the stunt gaffer can do is hire a stunt player for the day (not one of the gaffer's team). And that dude is a ringer.

And he can do what the stunt team can't. Which is basically fuck the shit outta the asshole, preferably in front of the whole crew.

Say you're working in the broiling-hot sun of Mississippi for a year with that bald Nazi bastard Otto Preminger on *Hurry Sundown*. And that sadistic prick has belittled and berated crew members in front of the whole company for an entire year. So you hire Cliff Booth as a stunt day player and have him purposely fuck up a shot in front of Otto. Then you and the crew just sit back and enjoy the show.

Booth socked Preminger, mid-tirade, in the jaw, knocking him flat in the Mississippi mud. Cliff's excuse was, as a World War Two hero, he experienced a wartime flashback when Preminger yelled at him in his German Gestapo accent, and he forgot where he was. And when the production manager gave him his bus ticket home the next day, Cliff left Mississippi with an extra (off the books) seven hundred dollars in his back pocket. And that night, celebrating with the crew at the hotel bar, he never had to pay for a drink.

Or say you're part of the stunt team on the western TV series *The Wild Wild West*. Now, series lead Robert Conrad prides himself on doing (a lot) of his own stunts. Well, that may be, more or less, true.

But while performing his own stunts, he didn't really mind how many stuntmen got hurt in the process. Especially when it comes to tagging stuntmen during fistfights ("tagging" definition: accidentally punching somebody for real in a staged fight). Which he never took responsibility for. It was always *their* fault. *They* weren't where they were supposed to be. *They* were the ones that were unprofessional. It was *their* fault he hurt *his* hand. He did this to such a degree that, in the stunt community, he earned the name Robert Never-Met-a-Stuntman-He-Couldn't-Blame Conrad.

So it was considered a grand and glorious day when Cliff Booth—with an "accidentally" mistimed haymaker—knocked Bob on the ass of his skintight pants.

A couple of stuntmen wept.

Again, Cliff Booth left the set with seven hundred extra dollars in his back pocket and a case of beer in the trunk of his car.

Then, while shooting *100 Rifles* on location in Almeria, Spain, in a bar, he became the only known white man to ever win a fistfight with Jim Brown. Now, as cool as the Jim Brown story is, it's the one that might be mythic horseshit. For one, it's doubtful during the time Jim Brown and Burt Reynolds were in Spain making *100 Rifles* that Cliff was there as well. He was probably with Rick shooting his *Bingo*

Martin episode (later in 1969 both Rick and Cliff would go to Almeria to shoot *Red Blood, Red Skin* with Telly Savalas). Also, the legend of a white man winning a fistfight with Jim Brown might just be that: a legend. Supposedly, it's either: (a) Cliff in a bar in Spain on *100 Rifles*; (b) Rod Taylor in Kenya on the set of *Dark of the Sun*; (c) Rod Taylor again, not on the set of *Dark of the Sun* but at the Playboy Mansion in front of the fountain; or (d) it never happened.

But the set fight Cliff was most infamous for was the "friendly contest" between himself and the most renowned martial artist of all time, Bruce Lee.

At the time of what came to be known in Cliff's career as "the Bruce Lee Incident," Bruce wasn't as yet either a movie superstar or a legend. He was just the actor who played the Green Hornet's sidekick, Kato, on the TV series *The Green Hornet*, a cheap-jack show made to cash in on the popularity of the *Batman* TV series. But in the Hollywood community, even more than for his role on the TV show, Bruce Lee was mostly known as "karate coach" to the rich and famous ("karate coach" is how Hollywood would have referred to him, not how Bruce would have referred to himself). The way celebrities would later work out with personal trainers in their backyards for one-hour sessions is how Steve McQueen, James Coburn, Roman Polanski, Jay Sebring, and Stirling Silliphant all took classes with Bruce at home. It's a little funny to think that one of the most talented martial artists of all time would choose to spend his time teaching Roman Polanski, Jay Sebring, and Stirling Silliphant how to throw a straight-leg kick. It's a little like if Muhammad Ali spent a large portion of his time giving James Garner,

Tom Smothers, and Bill Cosby boxing lessons. But Bruce Lee had a game plan in mind. Like Charles Manson, this spiritual *sifu* stuff was just a side gig. The way Charles Manson wanted to be a rock star, Bruce Lee wanted to be a movie star. James Coburn and Stirling Silliphant were *his* Dennis Wilson. Steve McQueen and Roman Polanski were *his* Terry Melcher. Every fourth training session with Roman Polanski, Bruce brought up *The Silent Flute*, the script he was trying to get made with Oscar-winning screenwriter Stirling Silliphant (who, like Dennis Wilson with Charlie, truly believed in Bruce's potential), which would star James Coburn and Bruce (playing four different roles). Bruce even accompanied Roman and Sharon on a ski trip to Switzerland to try and get Roman to commit to the project.

As if Roman Polanski would follow up *Rosemary's Baby* with a pretentious James Coburn action picture. Roman seriously liked and respected Bruce. He even admired him. But whenever Bruce brought up *The Silent Flute*, he diminished himself in Roman's eyes. In fact, it made Roman think about how Hollywood brought out the worst in people.

One difference between Lee and Manson was, Bruce had what it took to be a phenomenon. Not at the time he was acting on *The Green Hornet*. But a few years later, first in his Hong Kong movies with Lo Wei, then in his big Warner Bros. martial-arts extravaganza, *Enter the Dragon*.

But back in 1966, when he was still playing the Green Hornet's sidekick, Kato, Bruce Lee had a reputation amongst the American stuntmen who worked on his show.

A bad one.

Bruce Lee didn't have much regard or respect for American stuntmen. And the actor went out of his way to make that disrespect obvious. One of those ways was tagging them with his flying fist and feet during fight scenes. He was warned about this time and time again, and like Robert Conrad, he always had an excuse that made it *their* fault. To such a degree, a whole host of stunt players refused to work with him.

Now, truth be told, Cliff didn't like Lee from the first moment he laid eyes on him. Which was before Rick started shooting his guest-villain gig on the show. The first time Cliff witnessed Lee's screen-fighting technique was when the stuntman drove Rick to the Twentieth Century Fox lot for his wardrobe fitting for the following week's episode. The two men stood back away from everybody and watched Bruce and his co-star, Van Williams, shoot an outdoor fight scene, where Lee performed a lot of dazzling quicksilver kicks and Nureyev-like leaps. When Lee was finished, the crew broke into applause. Rick was definitely impressed and turned to Cliff and said, "That guy's really somethin', huh?"

Uncharacteristically, Cliff snorted dismissively, "That guy ain't fuckin' shit! It might as well be Russ Tamblyn out there. The guy's just a fuckin' dancer. Send Twinkle Toes back to *West Side Story*."

Rick countered, "That guy's fast as fuck. Those kicks are great."

"They look great—in a movie," Cliff schooled. "There ain't no power in that shit. Yeah, he's fast, I'll give you that. But fast patty-cake is still patty-cake. None of these karate faggots are worth a shit in a *real fight*. Judo's a little different. With judo, you deal with a guy who don't know what he's doing, you can toss him around a little bit. But none of these karate faggots have any power in their kicks, and not a single one of them can take a punch to save their life." Then Cliff points at Kato for emphasis. "Least of all that midget there."

Cliff rarely went on a tear, so when he did, Rick let him rant himself out.

"Hand-to-hand combat, man. That's where it's at. A fucking Green Beret would scramble his eggs. Everything he does is for show.

"Everything Ali or Jerry Quarry does is to inflict punishment. Everything a Green Beret does is to kill. I'd like to see that faggot in the jungle, fightin' a Jap who outweighs him by thirty pounds with a knife in his hand and murder on his mind." Cliff snorted, "That happens, the Green Hornet's lookin' for a new chauffeur."

"Okay, look," Rick offered, "maybe in a kill-or-be-killed situation you might be right—"

"I am right," Cliff interrupted.

"Nevertheless," Rick continued, "those fast kicks are impressive."

"Stretching," Cliff said dismissively. "It's all stretching. I come over to your house and stretch you out for three hours a day, Monday through Friday. In three months you can do every fuckin' thing he can do."

Rick gave him a skeptical look, and Cliff backtracked a bit.

"Okay, maybe not *everything*. But close enough."

* * *

The fight between Cliff and Bruce occurred when Cliff was on the set of *The Green Hornet*, doubling for Rick. Bruce, as usual, was holding court with the crew about his prowess. And then somebody asked him the single question that people asked Bruce all the time: Who would win in a fight between him and Ali? Bruce was constantly asked this question. And depending on the time and his mood, his answer was different. Later, on the set of *Enter the Dragon*, when John Saxon asked him the question, Bruce supposedly said, "His fists are bigger than my head." But Bruce admired Ali's ability and made it a point to study 16mm films of Ali's fights. And in examining those films, he had made a discovery: *Ali dropped his left.*

In a boxing ring, he knew, Ali would murder him.

But frankly, Bruce felt there was nobody he *couldn't* defeat in a fight. The trick would be to fight Ali without boxing gloves and to allow Bruce kicking privileges.

So when asked on the set of *The Green Hornet* that day, he said, "If put in a room and told anything goes? I'd beat him senseless."

And Cliff—this day-player stuntman—laughed.

Bruce asked him, "What was so funny?"

For one small moment Cliff tried to deflect the confrontation. "Hey, man, I'm just here to do a job."

But that wasn't good enough for Bruce. "But you're laughing at what I'm saying, but I didn't say anything funny."

"Yeah, ya kinda did." Cliff smirked.

A pissed-off Bruce asked the stuntman, "What do you think is so funny?"

Okay, here it goes, Cliff thought.

"I *think* you ought to be embarrassed to suggest you'd be anything but a stain on the seat of Muhammad Ali's trunks."

All eyes on the set shifted to Bruce.

But Cliff, who knew from this point on his job was kaput, felt he might as well get his money's worth, so he continued, "A little squirt like you is gonna beat the heavyweight champion of the world senseless? A fucking *actor* is going to beat Ali senseless? Fuck Ali—Jerry Quarry would pound you like a nail! Let me ask you something, Kato: Have you *ever* taken a serious punch?"

An angry Bruce answered back, "No, I haven't, *stuntman*. Because people can't hit me!"

"That's what I thought you'd say," Cliff said.

Cliff looked to the wide-eyed crew members watching all this. "I can't believe you buy the horseshit this squirt's dishing out."

Turning back to Bruce, "Get real, man. You're a *fucking actor*! You get a black eye, the fight's over. You get a loose tooth, the fight's over. Jerry Quarry will fight five rounds with fucking Muhammad Ali with a broken jaw! You know why? Because he's got somethin' you don't know shit about—*heart*!"

Bruce, in his chauffeur's outfit, took a cool-guy pose, looked at the ground, shook his head, then looked at the stuntman and smiled, saying, "You got a big mouth, *stuntman*. And I'd really love closing it, especially in front of all my friends. But, you see, my hands are registered as lethal weapons. That means, we get into a fight and I accidentally kill you, I go to jail."

Cliff came back with, "Anybody accidentally kills anybody in a fight they go to jail. It's called manslaughter. And I think all that 'lethal weapon' horseshit is just an excuse so you *dancers* never hafta get into a real fight."

Okay, now that was an actual challenge, made in front of a handful of Bruce's colleagues. So Bruce offered Cliff a "friendly contest." Two out of three falls. Nobody tries to hurt anybody. Who just ends up on their butt.

"You've got it, Kato," was Cliff's reply.

Under the excited eyes of the crew, the two men prepared to face off against each other. What Bruce didn't know was, Cliff loved two-out-of-three challenges. Though they usually took place in the parking lots of bars at one in the morning. Whenever Cliff engaged in this style of contest, especially with somebody who had some fight training, he deployed a sneaky technique that was so obvious he's surprised it always works.

The technique is simple.

He gives them the first fall.

He offers very little resistance and prepares himself to withstand whatever they give. He offers so little resistance that the opponent, especially if they're a skilled fighter, assumes Cliff is just some barroom tough guy in way over his head.

Cliff also knows in this type of contest his opponent will use whatever moves, or combination of moves, he's the most confident with. So after the first fall, Cliff's opponent has usually shown him his *big move*.

And if Cliff appears untrained and the guy's confident about putting Cliff away, nineteen times outta twenty the other guy will use the exact same move again. And now that

Cliff knows what it is, he waits for it, counters it, and drops the fucker on his ass.

From Bruce's perspective, he had no intention of hurting this loudmouth honky. He just wanted to shut his big mouth and make him look a little foolish in front of the crew. For one, it would mean big trouble for Bruce if he hurt this guy. The stuntmen were already complaining about Bruce hitting them and were informing Randy Lloyd, the stunt gaffer, that they didn't want to work with him. Plus, from showing off on the set, Bruce had accidentally dislocated a set designer's jaw with a mistimed kick. If Bruce broke anybody else's jaw on the set, his ass would be grass.

So the Little Dragon decided the best plan of action was something that would look good but ultimately wouldn't hurt the guy. Just knock him off-balance. But at the same time show this asshole a demonstration of who he was dealing with.

A spinning roundhouse kick to the ear would take this fucker's head off, and maybe make it hard for him to do arithmetic from that point on. A straight-leg power kick would knock him clean over that car behind him, and God knows what would get broken? But, along with Rudolf Nureyev, Bruce Lee had the ability to hang in the air unlike few who had ever lived. Nureyev and Lee seemed to sail through the air, accomplish their task, and, when *they* wanted to, land softly on the ground.

So Bruce decided a sail-through-the-air leap that contained a lot of height but little forward thrust was the safest move. He could catch air, look damn cool, then stop his flight by tapping his foot on this asshole's chest area, knocking him backward, dropping him on his butt, and teaching this motherfucker a lesson.

And that's exactly what he did. Knocking Cliff right on his butt, to the applause of the crew. The blond stuntman looked up from the ground with a goofy smile on his face and said, "Nice leap, Twinkle Toes." Then as he got off the ground he said, "Do it again."

Okay, now I'm gonna put my foot through this fucker's chest, Bruce thought. *I just gotta make sure this asshole doesn't break his tailbone when he hits the ground.*

So, with less height and more forward thrust, he took his second leap at the stuntman, who pivoted his body at the last minute. And the master martial artist practically fell into his waiting arms. Then Cliff, holding on to his leg and belt, swung the martial artist like a cat, hard, into a parked car on the set.

Bruce heard a crunch sound emit from his lower spine when he smashed into the automobile and his shoulder blade caught the passenger-door handle. He was really hurt. Looking up from the cement pavement, Bruce saw the honky stuntman smiling down at him.

Bruce really didn't want to hurt Cliff. He just wanted to show him up. But Cliff *wanted* to hurt Bruce. If by slamming him into that car he had fucked up Bruce's back and neck for the rest of his life, Cliff would have been fine with that.

As Bruce picked himself off the ground, he watched Cliff take his fighting stance for the third round. And he recognized it as a military hand-to-hand-combat stance.

Bruce was mad as hell at this fucker for hurting him. But also, for the first time, he saw his opponent for what he was. He wasn't just some cowboy stuntman redneck. Bruce knew Cliff knew what he was doing. Bruce realized Cliff had suckered him into taking him lightly and into doing the same move twice. Bruce could have gone at Cliff in fourteen different ways that the stuntman never could have blocked. But by pretending to be an untrained lunkhead, Cliff caused Bruce to go the lazy way and play right into the stuntman's hands. If Cliff's response hadn't've been so vicious, Bruce could have almost admired it.

Bruce also quickly recognized that, while Cliff wasn't anywhere near as skilled as the opponents he fought in any of his martial-arts tournaments, he *was* something they *weren't*.

He was a *killer*.

Bruce could see Cliff *had* killed men before with his bare hands.

He could see Cliff wasn't *fighting* Bruce Lee.

Cliff was *fighting* his instinct to *kill* Bruce Lee.

The martial artist often wondered, if the day came that he found himself in a kill-or-be-killed situation with a skilled fighter, how would he respond? Well, it looked like *that* day was *today*.

Fortunately, the third round was broken up by the stunt gaffer's wife, just as it got started. And, as he knew he would be, Cliff was quickly fired. The problem with all this was when Cliff was brought on the set of *The Green Hornet,* it wasn't as a day-player ringer meant to give Kato a public spanking. He was just meant to double Rick during the actor's guest-star gig. The stunt gaffer, Randy Lloyd, didn't want to hire Cliff in the first place—because Randy believed Cliff was guilty of killing his wife. And Randy worked with *his* wife, Janet, who very much believed Cliff was guilty of killing his wife. And, frankly, they'd rather hire somebody for a job who they didn't think was guilty of killing his wife. There were a lot of transgressions people could forgive, especially in the sixties. But a stuntman who killed his wife *and* tried to break the back of the TV-show lead in front of the crew wasn't one of them. After the Bruce Lee Incident, for all intents and purposes, Cliff stopped being Rick's stunt double and started being his gofer.

Rick was so mad about that whole Bruce Lee Incident that Cliff thought he was going to fire him too. But then who would drive Rick to work? Sure, he could find *somebody* to do it. But at the end of the day, it was just easier to forgive Cliff. Rick paid Cliff a nominal salary to drive him places, do odd jobs, and be available when he needed him. A salary that was *supposed* to be augmented by getting stunt gigs. But after the Bruce Lee Incident, the already meager stunt work he got, due to the speculation in town that he was a murderer, dried up even more. The Hollywood stunt community didn't need *another* reason not to hire Cliff, but now they had one, and it was Cliff who gave it to them. Rick's little story that morning about the prick AD on *Battle of the Coral Sea* was actually quite apropos.

However, Cliff knew that one of the most interesting things about Hollywood was, ultimately, it was a small fucking town. One of these days, on the street, in a parking lot, in a restaurant, or at a red light, he was going to see that little prick Bruce Lee again. And on that day, ain't nobody except the police gonna be breaking it up!

* * *

Having finished putting back Rick's TV antenna, and with nothing better to do until around seven-thirty, when he'll pick his boss up from the set, Cliff is driving Rick's Cadillac down Sunset Boulevard, on his way to the movies.

As Cliff sits parked at a red light, visualizing knocking Bruce Lee's block off, he glances to his right at the Aquarius Theater with its huge colorful painted mural of the hit stage show *Hair*. And he spots two of the same hippie girls he saw this morning, including the saucy tall brunette number with the pickles who locked eyes with him and flashed the peace sign. Both girls stand in front of the Aquarius with their thumbs stuck out, trying to hitch a ride. The brunette is still dressed the same way she was this morning—cutoff Levi's, crochet halter top, bare feet, and a coat of filthy grime.

The brunette hippie pickle girl spots Cliff, in a different car from this morning, across the street, going in the opposite direction.

She smiles, waves, points at him, and squawks, "Hey, you!"

He smiles at her and waves back.

She yells across traffic at him, "What happened to your Volkswagen?"

He yells across traffic back at her, "This is my boss's car!"

She holds out her thumb. "How about a lift?" Tugging her thumb.

Cliff points his finger in the opposite direction. "Not goin' my way."

She shakes her head sadly and yells, "Big mistake!"

He yells back, "Probably!"

"You're gonna think about me all day!" she warns.

He yells back, "Probably!"

The light on Sunset Boulevard turns green, and traffic starts moving again.

He gives her a little salute, and she gives him a sad-little-girl bye-bye wave as the cream-yellow Cadillac drives off.

When he gets to Sunset and La Brea, he makes a left and drives down La Brea Boulevard. Sam Riddle, the lunchtime disc jockey on KHJ radio, reads the copy for a commercial for Tanya Tanning Butter. Not tanning lotion, which protects you from the sun's harmful rays, but tanning butter, which accelerates burning. Cliff drives past Pink's Hot Dogs, on the corner of La Brea and Melrose. There are so many people outside crowded around the hot-dog stand, you'd think they were giving away free pussy, not selling overpriced chili dogs. Cliff moves the Cadillac into the right-hand lane and makes a right when he gets to Beverly Boulevard. He drives a short distance down Beverly and pulls up in front of a little movie theater and parks the car.

In the thirties, the cinema was a vaudeville house called Slapsy Maxie's.

In the fifties, it was where Martin and Lewis first performed in Los Angeles.

Later, in 1978, it will become a revival house called the New Beverly Cinema, showing repertory films. But in 1969 it's called the Eros Cinema, and it is one of the erotic cinemas of Hollywood (the Vista, located where Hollywood Boulevard and Sunset Boulevard meet, is another).

Not pornographic films, which would later be labeled "Triple XXX."

But just sexy movies, usually from Europe or Scandinavia. The Eros marquee reads:

CARROLL BAKER DOUBLE FEATURE
THE SWEET BODY OF DEBORAH RATED R
PLUS
PARANOIA RATED X

Cliff climbs out of the Cadillac and buys a ticket for the show at the box office. He makes his way down the darkened aisle and finds a seat in the middle of the fourth row. On the Eros's silver screen, Carroll Baker is doing a sexy dance to tom-tom drums, dressed in a skintight emerald catsuit. Cliff throws his moccasin-covered feet over the back of the chair in front of him. As he settles down in his seat, he looks up at Carroll Baker sashaying her big green hips from side to side.

My god, he thinks, *she's as big as a horse!* Then he smiles. *Just the way I like 'em.*

Chapter Fourteen

"The Wrecking Crew"

The 8-track tape player in Sharon Tate's black Porsche is playing Françoise Hardy's first album in English, *Loving*. The track that's coming out of the sports car's stereo speakers is Hardy's version of the Phil Ochs song *There but for Fortune*. Sharon loves this song, and as she sits behind the wheel of the Porsche, driving down Wilshire Boulevard on her way to Westwood Village, she sings along with it.

> *Show me the prison, show me the jail.*
> *Show me the prisoner whose face is growing pale.*
> *And I'll show you a young man with so many reasons why,*
> *And there but for fortune, may go you or I.*

Tears run down her cheeks as she sings. The actress is out running a few errands. She picked up some dry-cleaning. Three short mod-ish dresses, whose hems reach down to Sharon's upper thigh, and Roman's blue double-breasted blazer hang on clothes hangers wrapped in clear plastic on a hook behind the passenger seat. She also picked up a pair of chunky-heeled platform shoes from a tiny shoe repair shop

219

located on Little Santa Monica Boulevard. And now she's off to run her final errand of the day. She ordered a first edition of Thomas Hardy's *Tess of the d'Urbervilles* as a present for Roman. And the sweet old man who runs the store called the house yesterday to tell her it had arrived. So, singing along with Mademoiselle Hardy, enjoying an anxiety-free cry, Sharon races toward Westwood Village.

She spots the young hippie girl standing on the side of the road with her thumb stuck out about a mile after she turns onto Wilshire from Santa Monica Boulevard. The waify hippie looks pleasant, and Sharon is in a pleasant mood, so she thinks, *Why not?*

A year later, the answer to that question would be: because that hitchhiker could murder you. But in February 1969, even people who have something to steal, like Sharon in her cool black Porsche, don't feel that way.

She pulls up to the curb in front of the sweet-looking freckle-faced hippie, hits the button to lower the passenger-side window, and informs the hitchhiker, "I'm only going as far as Westwood Village."

The young girl bends over with her butt stuck out to look through the window frame at the driver. This young girl may be a free spirit, but she's not just going to climb into anybody's car. But upon seeing the beautiful blonde behind the wheel, the hippie's smile grows wider and she says, "Hey, beggars can't be choosers."

Sharon smiles back at her and tells her to climb in.

The two young women chat easily together during the thirteen minutes it takes for Sharon to get to Westwood Village and park her car. The hippie girl calls herself Cheyenne, and she's hitching up to Big Sur to meet up with a bunch of friends. They're going to attend an outdoor music festival where Crosby, Stills and Nash (but no Young) will perform, along with the James Gang, Buffy Sainte-Marie, *and* the 1910 Fruitgum Company. Sharon thinks it sounds like a lot of fun. If it was two days later, after Roman left for London, she'd consider driving Cheyenne to Big Sur and joining her and her friends for the concert. She might not actually do it, but she would consider it. Sharon has always had an impulsive streak. Roman does not, and it's one of the few things that make her cooler than her hip movie-director husband. As they drive the thirteen minutes together, they speak of Big Sur and Crosby, Stills and Nash, listen to Françoise Hardy, and eat sunflower seeds out of Cheyenne's small leather pouch.

"Well, bye-bye, have fun at Big Sur," are Sharon's last words to Cheyenne as she hugs her farewell in the pay parking lot behind the Westwood Village Theatre, where a large six-sheet poster for Roman's friend Michael Sarne's film *Joanna* is fly-posted on the wall. Then, while Sharon strides into Westwood Village to complete her errands, heading west, the little hippie girl continues on her California adventure, heading north.

As Sharon's white patent-leather go-go boots walk past head shops, coffeehouses, pizza parlors, and newspaper vending machines giving away the *Los Angeles Free Press*, she removes the big black bug sunglasses from her purse and puts them on to shield her eyes from the glare of the California sun. As she moves toward her destination, she notices her new movie, the Matt Helm secret-agent adventure film comedy, *The Wrecking Crew*, is playing at the Bruin Cinema, directly in front of her. The big marquee reads:

DEAN MARTIN AS MATT HELM
IN
THE WRECKING CREW
E. SOMMER   S. TATE   N. KWAN   T. LOUISE

Smiling as she crosses the street, she stops in front of the drawing of herself on the film's poster. She looks down the poster to the credit block and finds her name. She reaches out with her finger and traces it. After enjoying seeing her name, looking at an artist's rendering of her swinging on a wrecking ball by a cartoon Dean Martin, and appreciating that the movie is playing at one of the premier Westwood houses, she trots past the cinema to the bookstore, four shops away. In Arthur's Rare Books for Sale, the sound of the Classics IV's *Stormy* emanates from the radio behind the counter. The moment Sharon walks through the door and hears Dennis Yost's lead vocal, her body relaxes in response. Along with Art Garfunkel, Dennis Yost of the Classics IV has the prettiest voice in current rock 'n' roll, Sharon thinks. And she thinks David Clayton-Thomas of Blood, Sweat and Tears has the sexiest.

"What can I do for you, young lady?" asks Arthur.

As she removes the sunglasses from her face, she greets the old man behind the counter. "Yes, hello, I'm here to pick up a first edition you called me about?"

"What book?" he asks.

"Thomas Hardy's *Tess of the d'Urbervilles*. I ordered it

a couple of weeks ago." Then she clarifies, "It's under 'Po-lanski.'"

"Whoa boy," Arthur says, "now you're talkin' books, kiddo."

She lights up. "I know, isn't it wonderful? I'm getting it as a gift for my husband."

"Well, your husband's a lucky fella," says Arthur. "One, I wish I could read *Tess of the d'Urbervilles* for the first time again. And two, I wish I was young enough to be married to a pretty little gal like you."

Sharon smiles once more and reaches out across the counter to touch the old man's spotted hand. He smiles too.

As the Classics IV continue to play in her head, Sharon exits Arthur's store and walks back to her car. Her long coltish legs move her white miniskirt down the Westwood Boulevard sidewalk, approaching the cinema where her movie is playing. Sharon starts to move past the cinema and cross the street, but she doesn't make the green light on the corner, forcing her to cool the black heels of her white go-go boots. With her back to the cinema, the rare first edition in her hand, staring at the red traffic light, something snags Sharon from behind. Something that keeps her from crossing the street when the light finally turns green. Almost like a trout caught on an invisible fishing line, she turns around and walks into the courtyard of the Bruin and examines the lobby-card display out in front of the cinema. One lobby card has Dean with Elke Sommer. The lobby card next to it is her and Dean peering over a wall, spying something intriguing. In the photo, Sharon's dressed in the cute baby-blue outfit with the adorable blue cap with the fluffy ball on top, which she wore through the whole last forty-five minutes of the picture. The next lobby card is another one of her and Dean. It's a photo of her first entrance in the movie. On the lobby card, she's lying on her back in the middle of a hotel lobby in Denmark, having just performed a comedic pratfall, with Dean bending down to assist her. Boy, she remembers that day. She was so nervous. None of her other acting jobs had ever required her to be funny, let alone perform slapstick! This was a first. And being a klutzy bumbler was the entire conception of her character. It's why she took the part. But that didn't make her any less nervous the first time she was meant to fall on her ass for comic effect. Not only that, but she also had to do it in front of Dean Martin, who spent twenty years watching Jerry Lewis fall on his ass. So if she fucked it up, Dean was going to know it. Now, both Dean and director Phil said she did a good job with the pratfall. And they should know, right? Still, both of them were such gentlemen, even if she had done a bad job, it's not like they were going to tell her. Sharon isn't insecure about the *whole* comedic performance. She does think she eventually got the hang of the slapstick. She's just not so sure of that first tumble. Is she really funny or is she "sexy little me" trying to be funny? How's a bombshell to know?

The audience, dingbat, she thinks. *The audience either laughs at the gag or they don't.*

The sign on the box-office-booth window reads that the showtime is 3:30. She checks the thin gold watch on her slender wrist, and it reads 3:55. Well, that's okay, that's around when she enters the picture. *Holy shit, really?* Sharon thinks. *Do I really have time to watch The Wrecking Crew in the middle of the late afternoon and still get ready for this Playboy After Dark horseshit I have to do tonight? Well, now, wait a minute, Sharon, just forty minutes ago you were pumping yourself up about how spontaneous you are when compared to Roman. If not for Roman you'd be driving to Big Sur right now with Cheyenne and dancing barefoot in the mud to Crosby, Stills and Nash. But you're going to stand out on the sidewalk and have a debate with yourself for twelve minutes about whether or not you're going to go see your own movie? Sharon,* she thinks, *you're a goddamn hypocrite.*

"One please," she asks the cute curly-haired rubber-faced girl enclosed behind the glass cube in the box-office booth.

"Seventy-five cents," she answers back through the metal vent in the middle of the glass box.

Sharon starts to dig in her purse to produce three quarters, then stops herself when a thought enters her mind. "Ummm . . . what . . . uh . . . if I'm in the movie?"

The curly-haired box-office girl's forehead shows thinking lines. "What do you mean?" she asks.

"I mean," she explains, "I'm in the movie. I'm Sharon Tate. My name's on your marquee—I'm 'S. Tate.'"

The curly-haired box-office girl's eyes raise. "You're in this?" she asks slightly incredulously.

Sharon smiles and nods her head. "Yes," then adds, "I play Miss Carlson, the klutz."

She moves over to where the lobby cards are on display and points at the one with her and Dean peering over the wall. "That's me."

225

The box-office girl squints through the glass in the box-office booth at the lobby-card picture, then back up to the smiling blonde. "That's you?"

Sharon nods her head. "Uh-huh."

"But that's the girl from *Valley of the Dolls*," the curly-haired girl points out.

Sharon smiles again and shrugs her shoulders and says, "Well, that's me, the girl from *Valley of the Dolls*."

The curly-haired box-office girl is starting to see it, but she has one last issue. She points at the lobby card and says, "But you have red hair in that."

"They dyed my hair," Sharon tells her.

"Why?" the curly-haired box-office girl asks.

"The director wanted the character to have red hair," she answers.

"Wow!" the curly-haired box-office girl exclaims. "You look prettier in real life."

Now, for the record, if you're ever walking down the street and you see an actress you recognize in real life, and you think she looks prettier than she does in movies or on television, fight the temptation to tell her so. Because it's not something actresses like to hear. It makes them feel insecure. But Sharon knows how pretty she is, so while it bugs her a bit, at the end of the day she doesn't really mind.

"Well," giving the box-office girl an excuse, "I just got my hair done."

The box-office girl yells out the open back door of the box-office booth at the day manager, Rubin, who's standing in the Bruin lobby, "Hey, Rubin, come out here!"

Rubin steps outside into the Bruin courtyard, as the curly-haired box-office girl points her finger at Sharon and says, "This is the girl from *Valley of the Dolls*."

Rubin stops and looks at Sharon and asks the box-office girl, "Patty Duke?"

She shakes her curly head and says, "No, the other one."

"The girl from *Peyton Place*?" he asks.

She shakes her curly head again. "No, the other one."

Sharon chimes in on the guessing game, "The one that ends up doing dirty movies."

Rubin recognizes her. "Oh!"

"She's in our movie," the curly-haired girl tells him.

"Oh!" says Rubin again.

"She's 'S. Tate,'" says the curly-haired box-office girl.

"Sharon Tate," the actress corrects, then corrects herself, "Sharon Polanski, actually."

Now fully up to speed, Rubin turns into the gracious manager greeting a celebrity patron. "Welcome to the Bruin, Miss Tate. Thank you for coming to our theater. Would you like to come in and see the show?"

"Could I?" she graciously asks.

"By all means," he says as he makes a sweeping gesture with his hand to the cinema's open front door.

Sharon walks through the lobby and opens the door leading to the darkened auditorium. As she was dicking around with the curly-haired box-office girl in the glass booth, she prayed she hadn't missed her entrance and her comedic pratfall. As she enters the auditorium, she can hear the rotation of the reels on the film projector in the booth above her and even the slight *tick . . . tick . . . tick . . .* of the 35mm film print running through the projector film gate. She loves that sound.

Back in Texas, when she went to movies at the theater on her dad's Army base, or when she went to the local cinema in town, the Azteca, either with her girlfriends to see something like *Splendor in the Grass*, or when she was enlisted to take her little sister Debra to see the new Disney movie, or at the Starlight Drive-In with a boy to see the new Elvis or *Beach Party* movie (and invariably engage in a slight wrestling match as she tried to watch the movie and he tried to make out), Sharon never thought about movies as "film." Or, frankly, movies as "art." Movies weren't art, not like the Thomas Hardy book in her hand. They were just a fun thing to do. They were entertainment. But being with Roman has convinced her film *can be* art. Roman's *Rosemary's Baby* isn't art like Thomas Hardy's *Tess of the d'Urbervilles* is art, but it's still art, just a different kind. She's read the book of *Rosemary's Baby* and she's seen Roman's movie, and Roman's movie is more *artful*. Nor had she ever realized that certain directors make their films with the same power that great authors do. Not all directors. Not most directors. None of the directors she's ever worked with, except her husband. But some.

She remembers an incident that happened on the set of *Rosemary's Baby*, which drove this point home. The cinematographer, Billy Fraker, had set up a shot; it was of Ruth Gordon's character, Mrs. Castevet. She's in Rosemary's apartment and she asks to use the telephone in the other room. Rosemary tells her to go into the bedroom and make

228

the phone call, so Mrs. Castevet sits on the bed and talks for a moment on the telephone. And the shot was Rosemary's perspective of a quick glance of the old woman in her bedroom making the call. So Billy Fraker set up the camera in the hallway and lined up the camera to shoot Ruth Gordon through the doorway. And the way Fraker lined up the shot, you could clearly see Ruth Gordon framed between the two sides of the door. When Roman looked through the viewfinder, he didn't like it, so he adjusted it. When they did what Roman wanted, Mrs. Castevet wasn't clearly framed. She was obscured by the left side of the doorway. When Sharon looked through the camera viewfinder (she always looked at Roman's shots through the viewfinder), she couldn't understand why Roman changed it. If the shot was meant to be of Mrs. Castevet, it clearly wasn't as good as the earlier one. She was cut in half.

The cinematographer couldn't understand it either. But Roman was the director, so Fraker did what he was told. While Roman sat on an apple box, sipping coffee from a white styrofoam cup, as the camera crew readjusted the camera, Sharon asked him why he changed the shot.

Roman just gave her a knowing elfin grin and said, "You'll see." Then he got up and scooted away.

Whatever the hell that means? Sharon thought. Then she forgot about it till six months later. The two of them were together at the very first audience test screening, which was being held at the Alex Theatre in Glendale, California. Roman and Sharon sat toward the back of the auditorium, holding hands. Roman, who usually liked to sit closer to the screen when he watched other people's movies, liked to sit toward the back when he watched his own—because he was watching the audience even more than he was watching the movie.

The cinema was packed. The scene with Mrs. Castevet in Rosemary's apartment came on. Ruth Gordon asks Mia Farrow if she can use the phone in the other room. Mia says yes and points her toward the bedroom.

Roman leaned closer to his wife and whispered to her, "You remember when you asked me why I changed the shot?"

She had forgotten it, but she remembered now. "Yes."

"Watch this," he said, and pointed, but he didn't point at the screen. He pointed instead at the whole sea of heads that sat before them, about six hundred of them.

On-screen, Mia Farrow as Rosemary takes a glance at the old woman in her bedroom, and the movie cuts to what she sees. Which is the shot of Ruth Gordon as Mrs. Castevet sitting on the bed, talking on the telephone, partly obscured by the left-hand doorframe.

Then suddenly Sharon witnessed all six hundred heads in front of her lean slightly to the right in order to see around the doorframe. Sharon let out a small gasp at the sight. Of course they couldn't see any better by moving their heads— the shot was the shot. Nor did they intellectually know they leaned to the right; they did it instinctively. So Roman had manipulated six hundred people, and soon that number would grow to millions all over the world, to do something they would never do if they were thinking. But they weren't thinking. Roman was doing their thinking for them.

Why did he do it?

Because he could.

She looked at him and he gave her that same knowing elfin grin he had given her on the set *that* day, but *this* day she understood it. The only thought in her head was: *WOW!*

There are times when Sharon knows she didn't just fall in love with and marry a good movie director. She fell in love with and married a cinematic Mozart. That was one of those times.

Yet the 35mm print that is being projected on the Bruin's screen that *she's* in is about as far away from that level of cinematic artistry as the earth was to the moon. *The Wrecking Crew* isn't a film, it's a movie. And it isn't even a *good* movie. That is, unless you get a laugh out of seeing Dean Martin play Matt Helm. And since this is Dean Martin's fourth Matt Helm movie, apparently a lot of people get a laugh out of seeing Dean Martin play Matt Helm. (Dean Martin's deal on the Matt Helm movies was so good that he made more money on the first three than Sean Connery made on the first *five* Bond movies. Which infuriated the Scottish tightwad Connery.)

As Sharon makes her way down the darkened auditorium aisle looking for a seat, she can see that the scene being projected on the screen is the one of Matt Helm landing in Denmark.

Oh, great, she thinks, the hotel scene where she makes her big entrance is next. As she scooches sideways down an empty row, she glances around the dim auditorium. There are about thirty-five to forty people scattered around the huge picture palace.

As she takes a seat toward the middle of the row, on-screen Dean as Matt makes a quip to a sexy stewardess, and the audience laughs.

Good, she thinks, *they're laughers and they're enjoying the movie.* Sharon removes from her purse the huge glasses she wears whenever she watches a movie, puts them on, and settles into her seat just as secret agent Matt Helm, dressed in his turtleneck-and-sport-coat ensemble, enters the lobby of the Danish hotel.

Two different villainous female spies, Elke Sommer and Tina Louise, keep him under surveillance. As Helm speaks to the Danish desk clerk, "*T. Louise*," speaking in what sounds like it's supposed to be a Hungarian accent, approaches the secret agent, making both contact and a date for later that night.

When she slinks away, Matt Helm turns to the desk clerk, quipping in his familiar Dean Martin delivery, "This is some hotel you have here."

Enter Sharon Tate as her clumsy character, undercover secret agent "Freya Carlson" . . .

As Sharon stood off camera, on location in Denmark, waiting for her director, Phil Karlson, to call action, she thought back to when she first read the script, five months earlier.

When she heard she was being offered a part in the new Dean Martin/Matt Helm secret-agent spoof, she naturally assumed she'd be playing a seductive chic-styled spy-film sexpot. And if she'd been offered one of the roles the film's other three leading ladies—Elke Sommer, Nancy Kwan, and Tina Louise—were playing, she would have been correct. But her character, Freya Carlson, was Matt Helm's beautiful but inept and bumbling sidekick. Sharon had already acted in two comedies prior to *The Wrecking Crew*: the Tony Curtis sex farce *Don't Make Waves* and Roman's film *The Fearless Vampire Killers*. But neither comedy allowed her to be funny. While the other actors (Tony Curtis, Roman Polanski, Jack MacGowran) in both films ran around maniacally, did pratfalls, and made faces, Sharon was just asked to act vacant and look alluring (or "sexy little me"). How ridiculously good she looked in a bikini in *Don't Make Waves* was played for some comic effect. But, unlike with Leigh Taylor-Young in *I Love You, Alice B. Toklas!*, the film never took advantage of her character's comic possibilities.

But the role of Freya Carlson was different. In this comedy, she was supposed to be the comic relief. Comic relief opposite Dean Martin, one of the best light comedians in the business. Also since her character was a klutz, a performance built around physical comedy (pratfalls, falling in mud puddles, knocking over things), in essence she was being asked to play the Jerry Lewis part opposite Dean Martin! Sharon jumped at the opportunity.

But that was then, this is now.

Now, on location in Denmark, standing in the lobby of a Danish hotel, waiting for the director to call action, then make her character's entrance by running into the shot and performing her first comedic pratfall, Sharon was terrified. Not of hurting herself, though she was a little concerned at first of smacking the back of her head against the hard floor of the hotel lobby. The stunt gaffer, Jeff, had told her to tuck her chin into her chest when she fell and she'd be all right. They slipped a pad under her outfit to protect her keister and the small of her back. And Jeff gave her a few different things to hold in her head: tuck her chin into her chest as she fell, keep the champagne bottle in her hand held high during the fall so it didn't shatter against the floor and shower her with glass. Also, the camera would be pointed right up her dress, so if once she hit the floor her legs go wild, she should close them. But the most terrifying part of all was performing a giant comedic pratfall in front of Jerry Lewis's old partner.

As Sharon stood in the wings waiting for her cue to enter, arms loaded down with junk, her head full of things to remember to do, she'd never felt more at one with a character. Like Freya, she felt out of her depth (Freya as a secret agent, Sharon as a comedian) and intimidated by her more experienced partner (Matt Helm, after James Bond the world's greatest secret agent, and Dean Martin, one half of one of the screen's greatest comedy teams). Also, like Freya, she was eager to do a good job but also a little afraid of screwing it up. Somebody told her at one point they considered Carol Burnett for the role of Freya. It was obvious why they decided to go a different way. But whether or not they'd regret the way they went would all depend on how Sharon performed this gag.

The sweet gentleman Phil Karlson, who was the director of this picture, told her this was the moment that defined her character for the audience. At one point there was talk that maybe her character should be introduced as another slinky sexpot, like the other female leads in the film. Then, after the audience judged her by her sixties-starlet cover, that's when it would be revealed that she's a comic klutz. But, much to Sharon's delight, Phil rejected that approach. "You're the best character in this whole silly movie," he told her. In fact,

Karlson revised the whole idea. Not until mid-movie would her character wear anything even remotely sexy. Her long blond hair was dyed red and tied up on the back of her head. As opposed to Sommer, Kwan, and Louise, who were all introduced in outlandish stylish fashions, Sharon made her entrance in the uniform of a Danish tourist-board representative. They stuck big comic glasses on her face and she spent the first half of the movie wearing a collection of silly hats on her head. "As far as I'm concerned," her director told her, "the real movie doesn't start till you enter. So when you enter, you have to enter with a bang."

Naturally, at the time, she was thrilled at her director's confidence in her, but *bang time* was now, and she hoped she'd make a big bang and not a pitiful pop.

On the Bruin screen, Sharon as Freya Carlson comes running into the scene, carrying a bottle of champagne and screeching her co-star's character name: *"Mr. Helm, Mr. Helm, Mr. Helm!"* When Dean turns to look at her, she falls backward over his camera case, landing flat on her ass.

The whole matinee audience at the Bruin does a belly laugh at Sharon's pratfall. *Wow! That felt nice,* she thinks. She even turns around in her seat to look at the smiles on their faces. If she could have, she would have shaken all their hands and thanked them all individually. As she turns back to the screen, she wears an ear-to-ear grin on her lovely face. *This was a good idea,* she thinks. She unzips her white go-go boots, slips her bare feet out of them, throws her long legs over the back of the chair in front of her, and settles back to enjoy the show.

Chapter Fifteen

"You're a Natural-Born Edmund"

Actor Rick Dalton, dressed in his Caleb DeCoteau costume, and his director, Sam Wanamaker, sit in their director's chairs on the *Lancer* set, discussing Dalton's character.

"I want you to think about a rattlesnake," Sam says. "I think a rattlesnake is your spirit animal."

Normally, directors on TV shows are so busy trying to make their day, they don't have time to talk about spirit animals. But Sam is one of those serious British-theater-type directors. And since he seems to be so enthusiastic about Rick, Rick thinks he should probably talk that way too.

"Well, it's funny you say that," Rick lies. "I was looking for a spirit animal for Caleb."

"Well, go with the snake," Sam says, then points at *Lancer* series lead Jim Stacy sitting across the set with the little actress playing Mirabella Lancer, Trudi Frazer, in his lap. "Think of him as the mongoose. It's a duel. We're going to shoot that scene later today with the two of you. And I want it all in the eyes."

I want it all in the eyes? What the fuck does that mean? Rick thinks.

So Rick thoughtfully repeats aloud, "All in the eyes."

Sam reminds him, "You remember when I said 'Hells Angels' before?"

Rick nods his head.

"Think about you're on a great big chopper"—Sam points again at Stacy across the set in his red ruffled shirt— "and that guy over there wants to join your gang. And you would put him through the exact same test that a Hells Angels boss would put one of their people through."

"I see that," Rick asks. "So the horses are almost like motorbikes?"

"They are," Sam agrees. "They're the motorbikes of their day."

Nodding his head, Rick says, "Right."

"And your gang is a bike gang," Sam directs.

Nodding his head, "Right."

"And they've taken over this town just like a motorcycle gang takes over a town and scares the living shit out of everybody," Sam says.

Even though Jim Stacy's sitting across the set and can't overhear them, Rick leans closer to Sam and asks in a confidential manner, "So Stacy really wanted the mustache?"

Laughing, Sam says, "Believe you me, I can't tell you the fights I had about that damn mustache. He wanted Johnny Madrid to have a mustache so badly. To him, that *was* the character. You see, Stacy, like Madrid, has got an edge. But not some broody Actors Studio edge. Like one day maybe he'll go to jail kinda edge," Sam says provocatively. "And, yes, of course he wants to do this series. But he doesn't want to be like Doug McClure or Michael Landon. So the mustache made him different. And then CBS shit-canned the whole mustache idea."

Rick hates wearing this furry fucking caterpillar stuck to his face. But, admittedly, the fact that Stacy wants it so bad is making Rick warm up to it more and more.

Sam continues, "Speaking of fake mustaches, the last time I had a fake mustache was when I was doing *Lear* onstage—with Olivier. And he used to come off every night after the storm scene dripping wet from the rain and drenched in perspiration. Then he'd take one look at me—I was playing the Duke of Cornwall—" As if suddenly seized by inspiration: "Rick, dear boy, have you ever done Shakespeare?"

Rick laughs, then realizes, *Oh shit, he ain't kidding.* "Me?" Rick asks.

"Yes," says Sam.

Do I fucking look like I've done Shakespeare?

"No," Rick says, "I ain't done much theater."

"Well, I think you're a born Edmund," Sam says.

Rick asks, "Ed-Edmund?"

"He's the bastard son," Sam reminds him. "He's the bastard son who's been resentful his whole life."

Any resentful character could be called a character that Rick was born to play. "Well, I can get behind that," Rick says sincerely.

"He's resentful because the king excluded him," Sam explains.

"Right," Rick says.

Sam declares, "You would be a killer Edmund."

Really? Rick thinks.

"Well, thank you," Rick says, "I'm flattered you think so."

Rick can't even read Shakespeare, no less speak it, no less know what he's saying when he says it.

"And I would be honored to direct you in it," Sam declares.

Practically blushing, Rick repeats, "Well, again, I'm flattered."

Sam starts web-spinning: "I mean, it could be something we do together. I think the time has come that I have enough gray in my hair to be right for *Lear*."

Rick admits honestly, "Well, I'd hafta do some reading up. I gotta be honest, I ain't read much Shakespeare."

Or any, Rick thinks.

"That's not an issue," Sam insists. "I can work with you on that."

"Would I hafta do it in a British accent?" Rick asks.

"Oh dear lord, no! I wouldn't allow that." Sam explains, "I know it seems as if the Brits have a monopoly on the Bard."

Who's the Bard? Rick thinks.

"But in my opinion," Sam proclaims, "it's actually American English that is closer to the English spoken in Will's day."

Rick asks, "Will who? Oh shit, Shakespeare!"

Sam continues, "Yes, not that pompy hammy purple prose of the Maurice Evans school."

Pompy hammy purple what? Maurice who?

"The best Shakespearean actors are American actors. Actually, truth be told, Spanish or Mexican actors—when they do it in English—are the best Shakespearean actors. Ricardo Montalban's *Macbeth*—amazing! But Americans

239

come closest to capturing the poetry of the streets that is what Shakespeare truly is when it's done correctly—which it rarely is. That is, unless the American actor's trying to do it in a British accent. That's the worst."

"Yeah, I hate that," a lying Rick agrees. "Well, like I said, I ain't done much Shakespeare. I mostly been cast in westerns."

"Well, you'd be surprised how many westerns the plot is Shakespearean," Sam tells him. Then he points again at James Stacy, across the set with little Trudi Frazer still sitting in his lap, and says, "You see, whenever there's a struggle for power or who's going to be the leader, that's pure Shakespearean."

Rick nods his head and says, "Yes, I see."

"And that's the relationship you two have—Caleb and Johnny—a struggle for power. And when we do your final scene today, the ransom scene with the little girl, we can have a discussion about *Hamlet*."

Rick asks, "You mean Caleb is like Hamlet?"

"And an Edmund."

"Well, I'm afraid I don't know the difference."

"Well, they're both angry, conflicted young men. And that's why I cast you in this. But underneath Hamlet, underneath Edmund, there's a rattlesnake."

"A rattlesnake?"

"On a motorcycle."

Chapter Sixteen

James Stacy

Jim Stacy had waited for a little over ten years to get his own series. And now, on the first day of production, on the pilot for his new series *Lancer*, that day has finally arrived.

In the mid-sixties he starred in two pilots: A half-hour sitcom where he played a young pediatrician, titled *And Baby Makes Three*, which featured Joan Blondell and a pre–Mary Tyler Moore Gavin MacLeod in the supporting cast. And a half-hour action show called *The Sheriff*, about a beach-town sheriff played by Mexican movie star Gilbert Roland and a gang of rowdy surfers led by Stacy. Neither show was picked up for a full series. But *Lancer*, which was produced by Twentieth Century Fox for CBS, was an expensive pilot and a sure pickup for the fall schedule.

The man now known as James Stacy was born Maurice Elias in Los Angeles. The roguishly handsome football-playing tough guy came to acting via an origin story similar to that of a lot of young men of his era. Maurice had already become a star at his high school due to his combination of good looks and gridiron success. His idolization of James Dean (also like a lot of other young men of his era) led him to adopt his idea of a Dean-like brooding persona and take a few acting classes. And, like a lot of other young men and women who were the best-looking people at their high school, Maurice decided to move to Hollywood and give acting a try. Being from Glendale, the handsome hunk didn't have far to go.

Maurice Elias changed his name to James Stacy. First name in tribute to James Dean, second name in tribute to his favorite uncle, Stacy. He put some grease in his hair, wore tight jeans, and hung around Schwab's drugstore, waiting to be discovered.

His first real part was a recurring character as one of Ricky Nelson's buddies on *The Adventures of Ozzie and Harriet*. For seven years he hung around the local malt shop as part of Ricky's crew, eating hamburgers and drinking milkshakes. And appeared in the background of military-themed movies with other future TV stars: *Lafayette Escadrille* with Tom (*Billy Jack*) Laughlin, Clint (*Rawhide*) Eastwood, David (*Richard Diamond*) Janssen, and Will (*Sugarfoot*) Hutchins. And in *South Pacific*, also with Tom Laughlin, Doug (*Overland Trail*) McClure, and Ron (*Tarzan*) Ely.

Stacy received his first real roles guesting on episodic TV shows: *Have Gun–Will Travel*, *Perry Mason*, *Cheyenne*, and *Hazel*. His first featured role in a major motion picture was alongside Hayley Mills in Disney's *Summer Magic*.

Later he and the *Lafayette Escadrille* director's son, William Wellman Jr., would star in two beach-party-type flicks that wouldn't take place on a beach. In 1964's *Winter A-Go-Go*, which takes place at a Lake Tahoe ski resort, Stacy canoodles with sixties' pussycat Beverly Adams (who would later marry Vidal Sassoon). Jim even sings a snazzy number called *Hip Square Dance*, written by those Monkees hit-makers Boyce and Hart. Then a year later he'd again join "Wild Bill" Wellman Jr. in *A Swingin' Summer*, which takes place at Lake Arrowhead. This one includes a good guest bit by the Righteous Brothers, doing the only real rocker in their songbook, *Justine*. But the real reason anybody remembers the flick is an early appearance by Raquel Welch, who steals the show as a bespectacled bookworm who tosses off her Buddy Holly glasses and turns into a sex bomb as she sings her big number, *I'm Ready to Groove,* backed by Gary Lewis and the Playboys!

During this time, Stacy married one of the sixties' most charming actresses, Connie Stevens; the marriage lasted four years. Then, after numerous guest shots in the late sixties, Stacy would do the project that set him up for TV stardom.

At the time, one of the most popular shows on the CBS schedule was *Gunsmoke*. But by the late sixties, *Gunsmoke* star James Arness tried to appear on the show as little as possible. Even though Arness only made guest appearances on his own show, the series was such a staple of the network that it never affected viewership. So CBS let him get away with it (Arness didn't want to leave and do movies, he just didn't want to work). But that allowed CBS the opportunity to build episodes around exciting guest stars. And if those guest stars scored on their *Gunsmoke* episode, they were pretty much guaranteed a show of their own on the next season's CBS fall schedule.

Well, James Stacy scored one of the best episodes in the entire run of the series. Which, considering that *Gunsmoke* was one of the highest-quality shows of its day, is saying something.

The episode that James Stacy did in the thirteenth season of the series was entitled *Vengeance*. It was written by Calvin Clements, one of the great TV-western episodic writers of his time, and directed by Richard C. Sarafian, a talented episodic-TV director just before he made his leap to feature films with cult classics like *Vanishing Point* and *Man in the Wilderness* (Barry Newman is okay in his button-down white shirt and his Jew-fro as the Dodge Challenger driver Kowalski in *Vanishing Point*, but James Stacy would have been both way sexier and way cooler). *Vengeance* was a two-part episode that guest-starred Stacy, John Ireland, Paul Fix, Morgan Woodward, Buck Taylor (just before he joined the show as Marshal Dillon's deputy Newly O'Brien), and Kim Darby one year before *True Grit*.

Stacy plays Bob Johnson, who along with his older brother, Zack (Morgan Woodward), and his foster-father figure, Hiller (James Anderson), are saddle bums riding the range. Being seasoned saddle tramps, they're aware that the unwritten law of the range is that wounded calves must be slaughtered in order not to draw wolves to the herd. So, when riding through a herd of cattle they come across a wounded little animal, the three men do their duty and prepare to partake in a free steak dinner. That's when the low-rent cattle baron Parker (John Ireland), flanked by his sons, his ranch hands, and his puppet sheriff (Paul Fix), ride up. The calf they found was Parker's and was found on Parker's land. The Johnson brothers try to explain the situation. But Parker deems them cattle rustlers.

They kill Hiller, paralyze Zack, and leave a wounded Bob for dead, with Parker's bought-and-paid-for sheriff legally officiating over all of it (shades of *The Ox-Bow Incident*).

Bob survives and gets himself and his brother to the nearby town of Dodge City, where series star U.S. Marshal Matt Dillon (James Arness) presides. Marshal Dillon informs the Johnson brothers that Parker owns his own town, called Parkertown, which was supposed to rival Dodge as a municipality. But where Dodge grew and became a stagecoach stop, Parkertown remained a one-dog town run by a wealthy family of Wild West Borgias. While Marshal Dillon believes the Johnson brothers' story and knows full well that Parker is completely capable of doing what they claim, the fact remains they *were* on Parker's land and it *was* Parker's calf. And the sheriff who presided over the execution, although a weak-willed puppet of Parker, *is* the legal law of Parkertown. So, as unjust as it is, the execution was legal.

Marshal Dillon instructs Bob to sit tight and heal up from his wound and let Doc (Milburn Stone) care for his bedridden brother.

But what nobody in either Dodge or Parkertown knows is, Bob Johnson possesses a lightning-fast gun hand. Now, Bob is aware enough to know he can't just go out and kill Parker and his sons without hanging for it. But he also knows he can bait Parker's asshole son Leonard (Buck Taylor) into a gunfight, where he can kill him legally. So Bob starts running down the Parkers to everyone in Dodge, in order to lure Leonard into town. And Bob's plan works. By playing a psychological game with Parker's idiot son, he gets Leonard to draw on him in the middle of town, at a town dance, surrounded by practically every resident of Dodge City.

Legally shooting him dead.

Naturally, Parker and his men ride into town loaded for bear and demanding retribution. But Marshal Dillon informs the bloodthirsty cattle baron what's good for the goose is good for the gander. While legally he couldn't interfere with the initial murder over the calf, neither can he interfere with this killing, because Bob has the whole town as his witness that he was defending himself.

Nevertheless, Matt Dillon knows full well Bob orchestrated the whole damn incident. And he doesn't appreciate saddle tramps coming into Dodge City and turning his main street into a killing ground for their own private vendetta. So he tells Bob that once his brother is fit enough to travel, he wants them the fuck outta Dodge. Unfortunately, Bob's brother Zack will never leave Dodge. Parker sends an assassin in the night to murder Bob's bedridden brother.

Everybody knows Parker is responsible, but proving it is another matter.

So as *Vengeance, Part 1* comes to a close, we witness James Stacy (all alone) riding into the shithole known as Parkertown to face down John Ireland's Parker and all his men.

Wow! What a cliffhanger!

Vengeance, Part 2, also written by Clements and directed by Sarafian, picks up right where *Part 1* left off. And what follows is one of the most exciting shootouts ever filmed for a sixties' western television show. The beginning of *Vengeance, Part 2* doesn't feel like an episode of *Gunsmoke* but like the exciting climax of a terrific seventies' revenge western movie.

What happens? What do you think? Bob kills every son of a bitch in that town.

Hooray! Fuck those motherfuckers!

And you don't have to wait for it, it just happens—*bam*—right off the bat. Now, after the opening of *Part 2*, as anybody familiar with the structure of a *Gunsmoke* episode could have told you, the show falls off a cliff. Because from that point on we know Matt Dillon's going to have to kill Bob Johnson, and we just kill time waiting for it to happen. And then, just before the end, that's exactly what happens. *Stay tuned for scenes from next week's exciting episode of Gunsmoke!*

Every young budding leading man in town wanted to play Bob Johnson. Rick Dalton would have given his back molars to play the part. Instead, the week Jim Stacy shot *Vengeance*, Rick was fucking around on a botanical garden, wearing a pith helmet, playing scenes with a practically naked Ron Ely as Tarzan. But once you see the episode, it's hard imagining anybody else but Jim Stacy.

Another storyline on the episode included Bob's burgeoning romance with an innocent young Dodge City girl played by Kim Darby. On the show, Darby played a sweet girl who fell for the troubled rascal Johnson. And while filming the show, sweet girl Kim Darby fell for troubled rascal Jim Stacy. The two were married after filming and divorced a year later.

* * *

The suits at CBS knew they had a hot property in Stacy when they cast him in the coveted *Gunsmoke* guest-star slot. Now that they've seen the results, they are positive.

CUT TO Jim Stacy, dressed in Johnny Lancer's sangria-red ruffled shirt with a brown leather short coat, sitting in a wooden chair out in front of the Hotel Lancaster on the Twentieth Century Fox western back lot, filming the first day of the pilot for his new series. His silver-studded legs stretched out before him, he takes sips from a tiny green bottle of 7 Up.

At that moment, he feels an ever-so-slight irritation. The reason is the sight of Rick Dalton's mustache. When he first heard that Rick Dalton—Jake Cahill himself—was going to be playing the heavy Caleb DeCoteau on the pilot of his show, he was thrilled.

For a few different reasons. One, he's always dug Dalton. Both on *Bounty Law* and in *The Fourteen Fists of McCluskey* (he also liked him in that western he did with Ralph Meeker, but he couldn't remember its name).

Two, the fact that both Fox and CBS were spending the money to get a legitimate TV star to play the heavy in the pilot meant they were serious about the show's potential. And from an ego standpoint, number three, the day had finally come where somebody like Rick Dalton was the heavy to Jim Stacy's hero. It also was a dynamic way to launch his Johnny Lancer character. At the end, when Johnny defeats Caleb, he's not just coming out on top with that week's bad guy. The audience is going to see Johnny Lancer going up against Jake Cahill (an icon of western television) and

Lancer emerging triumphant. He remembers discussing it with the pilot episode's director, Sam Wanamaker. For the role of Caleb DeCoteau, it was between two choices. One was Dalton, the high-profile guest-star route. The other was an exciting young actor named Joe Don Baker, who had been one of the convicts in *Cool Hand Luke* and one of the seven in that last *Magnificent Seven* sequel with George Kennedy (Jim had read for the McQueen role but lost it to Monte Markham). And Wanamaker liked Baker. He looked like a movie actor, and Sam liked his size (Baker was bigger than Stacy). But the idea of taking a known TV cowboy and subverting his image was just too delicious for Wanamaker to pass up. Wanamaker didn't want this series to look like *Bonanza* or *The Big Valley* or any of the dozen other sixties' western shows on TV. The spaghetti westerns out of Italy had introduced a gritty new look that was finally catching up to their American counterparts. Yeah, there was still the Andrew McLaglen and Burt Kennedy–directed junk starring Wayne, Stewart, Fonda, Mitchum, and all the other old fucks who were still cranking out nostalgia-based vehicles for their ever-dwindling audience. But the American westerns of 1969 started having a different flavor. Partly in response to Eastwood's startling sex appeal in the Leone westerns, the stars started being younger. They dressed with far more panache than was the standard wardrobe over at Western Costumes on Santa Monica Boulevard. And, more often than not, they fell into the "antihero" category. To such a degree, some of the older stars left over from the Eisenhower era sought to subvert their personas.

William Holden in *The Wild Bunch* led a band of bastard murderers. His first line in the film, in regard to the innocent customers of the bank they're robbing: "If they move, kill 'em!"

Henry Fonda started his performance in Leone's *Once Upon a Time in the West* by shooting a five-year-old boy in the face.

Actors who had spent their careers playing villains in both western movies and practically every western show on television, like Lee Marvin, Charles Bronson, Lee Van Cleef, and James Coburn, were now suddenly the heroes . . . and the movie stars!

And the villains of these new westerns weren't just bad men; they were bloodthirsty, sadistic maniacs. And any parallel with hot-button political issues of the time was encouraged. In *Little Big Man* and *Soldier Blue*, they fought the Vietnam War. In *Tell Them Willie Boy Is Here*, Robert Blake's Indian on the run from "the man" was a de facto Black Panther. And when characters got killed in these movies, they didn't just clutch their bellies, grimace and groan, then slowly fall to the ground. They got the shit blown out of them and the blood sprayed across the screen. If Sam Peckinpah was behind the camera, they got the shit blown out of them at a hundred and twenty frames per second, and the spurting red blood squibs achieved a visual poetry beyond mere Don Siegel–style brutality.

Naturally, Sam Wanamaker couldn't achieve much of that for a CBS television series airing at 7:30 on Sunday nights. But he could strive for the ambiance of this new style of western. And he intended to do it in two ways. One was the look, especially in regard to the costumes. And two was in the personification of one of his three series leads, Jim Stacy's character Johnny Lancer aka Johnny Madrid. Of all the western series on television during that time (and actually *Lancer* marked the beginning of the end of that time), Johnny Lancer was hands down the closest thing to an antihero in the entire genre.

It was this shady aspect to the character that excited both Stacy and Wanamaker. And an idea that both men had to exploit this aspect of the character was to give Johnny Lancer a mustache. Now, Jim Stacy wanted Johnny Lancer to have a mustache for more than just integrity-of-characterization concerns. One of the clichés of the sixties' western TV series was when casting the two leads, almost always, one had dark hair and one had light. Stacy's co-star Wayne Maunder, who played his half brother, Scott Lancer, was the light-haired lead. And Jim was the brunette. But Jim also knew if he wore a mustache he'd draw the audience's attention away from his co-star even more and break further new ground.

The network told both Stacy and Wanamaker, "Nice try. But no fucking way. You want to put a mustache on somebody, you put it on the heavy."

And now here we are, first day on the set and Rick Dalton looking fly as fuck in his brown rawhide fringe-style jacket, sporting a fabulous soup catcher that they'd never let Stacy wear in a million years. *Those fucking assholes,* Stacy thinks. *One of these days they're going to let some numbnuts wear a mustache on his show; then everybody's going to be wearing mustaches. And that numbnuts could be me!*

But there's more in Stacy's racing mind than just Rick's mustache. He was going over his lines last night for their big scene together, and it hit Jim that Dalton had all the best lines. Sam acted contrite to Stacy when the network nixed the mustache idea. But the director couldn't hide his excitement at the news that they were casting Rick Dalton as Caleb.

So much so that now Jim thinks, rather than introducing Johnny Lancer, it's subverting Rick Dalton's persona that his director is the most excited about. And it's this thought that can't help but run through the actor's mind as he sits on *his* set, on the first day of *his* series, and he watches Rick Dalton and *his* director sitting in director's chairs, laughing it up and chatting away like this is their fifth film together. *What the fuck's up between these guys?* Stacy wonders as he sips his soda.

Right then, Trudi Frazer, the little actor who plays his half sister, Mirabella Lancer, comes skipping up to Jim and plops herself in his lap.

"What's up, doc?" she asks. She notices he's staring in the direction of the actor playing Caleb and the director Sam, sitting in their director's chairs, gregariously shooting the breeze.

"Sizing up your competition?" she cheekily inquires.

Tearing his eyes away, he looks down at the little girl in his lap and says, "What's up, squirt?"

"Well," she observes, "I could see you getting all puffy-chested over Caleb from across the set. So I thought I'd come over here and give your feathers a few loving pets."

He doesn't protest to the child that he's not bugged looking at his dramatic antagonist. Instead, he tells her, "I can't believe they put that goddamn mustache on him." Stacy spits out, "I wanted Johnny Madrid to have a mustache. Fuckin' know-nothings at the network wouldn't go for it."

She asks Jim, "Have you met the actor playing Caleb?"

"Not yet," he says.

"Well"—extending her arm toward the furry-faced actor—"He's right over there. What are you waiting for?" she challenges. "This is your show. He's your guest. Go over and introduce yourself and welcome him aboard."

"I will, honey," he promises. "He's talking to Sam right now."

She shakes her head from side to side in a tsk-tsk manner, then murmurs under her breath, "Excuses, excuses, excuses."

"Hey, squirt, I'm gonna do it," he says, getting irritated. "Get off my back."

Trudi puts up her hands. "Okay, okay, okay," she says. "It's your show, you know what you're doing. Take your time."

Jim Stacy huffs and takes a swig from the small green 7 Up bottle.

Trudi wiggles in his lap and asks, "Do you know Caleb as an actor?"

"As an actor?" he repeats. "Of course I do—"

She quickly interrupts him. "Don't tell me his real name," she warns. "I want him to just be Caleb to me!"

"Well, in that case," he explains, "*Caleb* had a cowboy show of his own about six years ago."

She asks Jim Stacy sincerely, "Was he good on it?"

Jim glances over at Rick Dalton looking really hip and

really different in his Caleb costume, wearing the mustache he wanted to wear, getting on like a house on fire with his director, and says, more to himself than to her, "He wasn't bad."

Rick Dalton sits in his director's chair, in the shade, in his Caleb costume, reading his paperback, *Ride a Wild Bronc*. As he reads, killing time before his first big scene (the 1st AD told him they'd probably get to it in about an hour and a half), he contemplates the book more seriously than he'd done before his emotional encounter with the little girl. The little girl was right, this is a pretty frickin' good novel. And Tom "Easy" Breezy is a pretty frickin' good character. Like maybe it might be worth trying to get the rights and make a movie out of it, with Rick playing Easy Breezy. Maybe he could talk Paul Wendkos into directing it.

His first scene of the day is also his first appearance in the story. And it's a pretty nifty introduction scene. Before we meet his character, he's been talked about by a lot of the other characters. And that always sets up excitement for when the character is finally revealed to the audience. If this were a movie, he would have demanded that this scene not be shot on the first fucking day! But this is TV, and on TV they don't shoot a script, they shoot a schedule. And if your big scene makes sense to do the first day—even first thing in the morning—that's how they're doing it. In the scene, he deals with two actors, James Stacy playing series lead Johnny Lancer, and Bruce Dern playing his henchman Bob "the Businessman" Gilbert. Rick has known Bruce going on a few years now (everybody knows fucking Bruce Dern).

And Rick knows the co-lead Wayne Maunder from when Wayne starred in his earlier show, where he played Custer. Rick never appeared on it, but his buddy Ralph Meeker did. And one night when Dalton and Meeker were sippin' sauce at the Riverbottom Bar and Grill (across the street from Burbank Studios), Maunder came in and joined Rick and Ralph for a couple of drinks. Rick and Wayne hadn't seen each other since that night, so they traded hellos and Wayne welcomed him on the show. As did Andrew Duggan, who plays patriarch Murdock Lancer (Duggan had appeared twice on *Bounty Law*). Once Dalton got out of the makeup trailer, he and Duggan smoked cigarettes and caught up. Dalton congratulated Duggan on what looks to be a successful new series. But Rick Dalton has yet to officially meet his co-star, James Stacy.

He saw him across the set earlier. But set protocol dictates that when an established actor—especially one who used to have his own hit television series—is guest-starring on your show, it's the lead of the series' obligation to approach the visiting actor and thank him for appearing on the show.

Just like Rick did when Darren McGavin guested on *Bounty Law*, and Edward G. Robinson, and Howard Duff, and Rory Calhoun, and Louis Hayward, and even Douglas Fairbanks Jr. It had been Rick's place to welcome them aboard and thank them for their contribution. But as of two o'clock in the afternoon, Jim Stacy has yet to introduce himself and welcome Rick. Van Williams did on *The Green Hornet*. Ron Ely did on *Tarzan*. Gary Conway did on *Land of the Giants*. Efrem Zimbalist Jr. did on *The FBI*. But that little cocksucker Scott Brown on *Bingo Martin* didn't. If you're somebody and the series lead hasn't introduced himself to you before you're standing in front of the camera, you've just been told, in front of the whole crew, *Fuck you!*

Both men have been on the set long enough that Jim *should* have introduced himself by now. But Dalton is prepared to cut Stacy a little slack. This is the first day of his first series. He could be legitimately nervous. But if he doesn't get his shit together soon, he's going to have an enemy for life.

Well, Rick wouldn't have long to wait. As he reads his paperback, he spots over the top of the pages CBS's new swingin' dick, in his red ruffled shirt and black jeans with the silver studs down the pant leg, making his way across the dusty Twentieth Century Fox western back lot, heading in his direction.

Well, it's about fucking time, Rick thinks. The actor acts like he doesn't see Jim approaching and continues reading his book.

When the devilishly handsome series lead reaches Rick's chair, he says his name with a question mark at the end.

"Rick Dalton?"

Rick's eyes rise from the paperback western, and he lowers the book into his lap. "You bet," is his answer.

Jim Stacy sticks out his hand and says, "Jim Stacy. This is my show; welcome aboard."

Rick smiles and shakes the swingin' dick's hand.

Stacy says, "We're real glad to have a pro like you playin' the heavy on the pilot. I just want you to know I was a big fan of *Bounty Law*. That was a damn good show, and you should be really proud of it."

"Well, thank ya, Jim," was Rick's reply to Stacy. "Yes it was and yes I am."

"And gotta tell you," Jim Stacy continues, "I came damn close to joining you in *The Fourteen Fists of McCluskey*."

"No kidding?" Rick says.

"Yeah," Stacy tells him. "I was up for the Kaz Garas part. I mean, I didn't stand a chance against him. He'd already starred in a Henry Hathaway movie by that time, but I wanted it real bad."

Good-natured Dalton counters with, "Well, let me tell ya, I just got my part by sheer luck. Up until two weeks before shootin', *Fabian* was in my role. Then he breaks his shoulder doin' a *Virginian*—that's how I got it. The director, Paul Wendkos, worked with me in the early days and he did a few *Bounty Laws*, so he suggested me to Columbia."

Jim Stacy sits down in the empty director's chair next to Rick that Sam formerly occupied, leans toward the *Bounty Law* star, and asks in a confidential manner, "Rick, I gotta ask you somethin' I heard about. Was it true you almost got the McQueen role in *The Great Escape*?"

Oh boy, Rick thinks, *here we go again. The same stupid swingin' dick, askin' the same stupid passive-aggressive question.*

Rick remembers sitting on the set of *The Green Hornet*, when series lead Van Williams, dressed in his full Green Hornet regalia, asked him about that same rumor. Or Ron Ely, practically naked, in his skimpy Tarzan loincloth. And in neither case were they good enough actors to hide the pity they held in the corner of their eyes.

Rick gives Jim Stacy the short-version answer to the question Marvin Schwarz asked him yesterday.

"Never had an audition, never had a meeting, never met John Sturges. Don't think you can say I almost got the part—"

Rick stops short, but an implied "but" hangs in the air and Stacy says it. ". . . *But*?"

Rick reluctantly continues, "*But* . . . the story goes . . . for a brief moment, McQueen almost passed on the movie. And during that brief moment, I—apparently—was on a list of four."

Stacy's eyebrows rise and he leans in even closer. "You and who?"

"Me and the three Georges: Peppard, Maharis, and Chakiris."

Stacy winces in pain and instinctively hits Rick on his shoulder and says, "Oh man, that's gotta hurt. Against those three faggots, you would've definitely got it. I mean Paul Newman—maybe not—but the fuckin' Georges?"

A fed-up Rick answers quickly back, "Well, I didn't get it. McQueen did it. And frankly . . . I never stood a chance."

Stacy laughs and nods his head, but then says, "Still . . ." and pantomimes sticking a knife in his heart and twisting the blade.

Rick looks at the grinning prick sitting next to him for a beat or two, then asks him:

"Hey, Jim, I was wonderin' . . . whaddaya think of my mustache?"

Chapter Seventeen

The Medal of Valor

When Cliff was discharged from the military after World War Two, he had money and two Medals of Valor in his pocket. He also had to decide what he wanted to do with the rest of his life. Which, frankly, for the last few years wasn't a decision he ever really thought he'd have to make. While Cliff was in Sicily during the war, he thought it was very likely he would die over there. However, once he was transferred to the Philippines to fight alongside the Filipino guerrillas against the occupying Japanese military, he was fucking positive he was never going to see home again. And then, once he was captured by the Japanese and put in their makeshift POW camp in the Filipino jungle, Cliff Booth considered himself a walking dead man. If, in his mind, Cliff hadn't already kissed his life goodbye, he never would have attempted the daring escape from the camp that allowed him to lead the Filipino prisoners to overthrow their captors and execute all the camp personnel, escape into the jungle, and rejoin their brother resistance fighters.

Their escape was so daring and exciting that Columbia Pictures made a nifty little wartime action flick about it directed by Paul Wendkos, titled *Battle of the Coral Sea*. The Wendkos film was a highly entertaining but hugely fictionalized account of the escape. In the movie, it wasn't Cliff and a bunch of Filipinos that pulled off the successful escape from the prison camp. It was an American submarine crew, led by their captain, played by Cliff Robertson, who performed the heroic adventure. And in a strange coincidence, way before Cliff Booth knew him, Rick Dalton played one of Robertson's men.

The movie dispensed with a lot of the real-life details. It left out Cliff Booth, it left out the Filipinos, and the Japanese in the movie didn't make a practice of cutting off most of the cast's heads, the way they did in real life. Nor did it show the surviving prisoners decapitating the heads of the Japanese camp personnel once the tables were turned. Neither was the brutish Japanese commander of the camp as sophisticated, debonair, intellectual, and honorable as the one portrayed in the movie.

Shit, Cliff thought when he saw the movie, *if that sadistic rock-headed bastard was that cool, I woulda stayed put till the war was over.* In fact, Cliff Booth thought Cliff Robertson was the prick in the movie. He later admitted to Rick (who *loved* the movie), "The goddamn movie practically had me rootin' fer the fuckin' Japs."

Nevertheless, the details of the escape itself were more or less accurate. However, since Cliff was damn near positive he was never gonna leave the jungle alive, now that he had, his survival proved to be a mite inconvenient. When it came to what he was going to do with the rest of his life, Cliff knew fuck all.

First things first, he wasn't in any hurry to return to the United States. So once he was discharged, he thought he'd visit Paris. And it was from hanging around Paris a few months, eating cheese and baguettes and drinking red wine like it was Coca-Cola, that he was first introduced to a profession that before the war he was completely ignorant of: "gentleman of leisure."

A profession more commonly referred to as "pimp." Like a lot of American men of Cliff's era, the whole concept of pimping was completely foreign to them. They understood the concept of a madam who ran a brothel. But in Paris, Cliff met these French fellas called *le maquereau*, or *Maqs* for short (pronounced in English as "macs"). These French fellas dressed sharp, hung around in bars all day, and put women on the street to sell their pussy for money, who then gave the money to the *maq*. To an American male at the time, the idea of a woman selling her pussy, then giving the money to a man, was a mind-blower. But these French fellas had it all worked out to a science. Due to Cliff's good looks, he'd been manipulating women to do things against their best interests his whole life. Getting them to offer up the pink, that was easy. But to get them to *sell* the pink, and then give *him* the cash? Man, that was manipulation on a whole other level. If he could figure out how these French fellas were doing it, this was something he could do when he got back home. So Cliff got to know a couple of these cats.

"What does the girl get out of the arrangement?" Cliff asked. The French fella explained it to Cliff like this:

"The women pay you to take care of them. And you *do* take care of them. You protect them. From customers, cops, hoodlums, and other women. You take them out and you show them off. Yeah, they give you money, but you spend a lot of the money on them. You could just give them a cut of what they make, but that's not romantic. And eventually they'll wise up, and when they wise up, they resent it. But if you take the money *they* make and spend a lot of it on *them*, buying them stuff they like, dresses, perfume, jewelry, wigs, pantyhose, magazines, chocolate, and take them to places they like to go, restaurants, bars, cinemas, dancing, they forget it's *their* money. As long as they do what Daddy *says*, Daddy takes care of them."

"There's gotta be more to it than that?" Cliff asked.

"Do not underestimate the desire for a woman to have a daddy take care of them," the French *maq* said.

"Nevertheless, you're right," the *maq* admitted. "There is more to it than that. There's one thing more important than anything else. For instance, finding the right type of girl is important. But even as important as that is, there's one thing more important.

"There are a lotta guys out there who can turn a woman out, but to keep them turned out? That's the mark of a true *maq*. And then turn out multiple women, and keep them turned out? That's a real motherfucking *maq*. And to do that, it requires you to do one thing above everything else."

"What's the secret?" Cliff asked.

"Simple," said the *maq*. "Fuck 'em good. Fuck 'em real good. And fuck 'em real good real often."

Cliff smiled, but the French fella assured him, "Hey, that's harder than it sounds. You can't fuck 'em like you fuck your girlfriend. You can't fuck 'em like you fuck your best friend's girlfriend. You can't fuck 'em like you fuck your father's mistress. That's fucking for fun. This is *work*. For work, they fuck customers for money. For work, you fuck *them* for money. And trust me, *they're* harder to please. If you want to keep 'em in line, you better fuck 'em good, and you better fuck 'em a lot. Which means you're gonna hafta fuck 'em when you don't wanna fuck 'em. But even when you don't wanna fuck 'em, you hafta fuck 'em, and you hafta fuck 'em good. And the more bitches you have, the more fuckin' you're gonna do. More *bitches* means more *fuckin'*. No sleepin' on the job. You get lazy even four goddamn days, that bitch is gonna wake the fuck up. The spell will be broken. And when the spell's broken, it's not like, *Okay, I guess that was that; see ya later.* When the spell's broken, that bitch fuckin' hates you. And that bitch doesn't just hate you, that bitch wants to see you dead. And *maybe* she tries to kill you. And *maybe* she tries to steal your shit. And *maybe* she calls her father, *maybe* she calls her brother, or *maybe* calls the boyfriend she had when she was a little girl and asks him to save her. And now it's him coming after you with a knife, or her brother coming at you with a pistol, or her father coming at you with a fuckin' shotgun.

"Or she takes the pussy *you* taught her how to use, to recruit some joker to kill your ass.

"In other words, a *maq* ain't got no days off. There ain't no fuck-free holiday for a true *maq*.

"You fuck her, and you keep fuckin' her, you can never stop fuckin' her, and you can never stop fuckin' her good.

"You can't be bored, you can't resent it, nobody gives a shit if you're in the mood. You're her *man* and you take her there *every fuckin' time*.

"And the key: different positions. You don't hafta fuck her *better* than any other man, you hafta fuck her *different* than any other man.

"You wanna know what she gets out of it? *That's* what she gets out of it. And you know what, it's a good fuckin' deal. She takes care of you, and you *better* fuckin' take care of her. Yeah, she gives you money, but, *mon ami*, you're gonna fuckin' earn it."

Cliff understood. He understood really well. He also understood he didn't want to work that hard. He'd rather drive a car into a brick wall at sixty miles an hour (like he was later paid to do) than fuck a bitch he didn't want to fuck. It's like that old expression, the only people who don't like riding horses are cowboys.

So once Cliff realized he wasn't cut out for being a pimp, he returned to the States and bummed around America for a few years, eventually finding his way to Cleveland, Ohio. While there, he looked up an old chum from high school, Abigail Pendergast. Abigail was a peroxide beauty who was one of the mistresses of the Mafia-connected hoodlum Rudolfo "Patsyface" Genovese.

Cliff Booth and Miss Pendergast were sitting in a Gay Nineties pizza joint, with sawdust on the floor, checkered tablecloths on the tables, music coming from a piano roll inside a player piano, and a 16mm Charlie Chaplin movie projected on the wall.

As Miss Pendergast bit into a pizza slice and gooey mozzarella dribbled down her chin, she twisted around in her chair to ask the waiter for a napkin. That's when she spotted them: Pat Cardella and Mike Zitto, sitting at the bar, sipping beers, and making faces at her table.

Oh shit, the platinum-blond bombshell thought.

She turned to her date, who, since he didn't eat the crust, had polished off his pizza slice in two and a half bites.

She leaned to Cliff across the table, "We're not alone."

With a mouthful of gooey pizza pie, Cliff asked, "What?"

Her eyeballs shifted to the bar. "Those two guys at the bar."

He started to twist in his seat to look at the bar, when her hand reached out and grabbed his wrist and she whispered, "Don't look."

His eyebrows rose in a question mark.

She whispered, "That's Pat and Mike. They work for Rudy."

Then, despite her protest, he twisted around to get a good look at the two rough-looking customers sitting on barstools, sipping beer. They gave the former soldier a clear fuck-you look.

He turned back around and disconnected another slice of pizza, as she told him, "At some point they're going to come over here and chase you away."

He raised his eyes from the pizza slice in his hand to the pale-skinned bottle blonde across the table. "Oh, they are, are they?"

Abigail made a guilty face and apologized. "I'm sorry, Cliff, I didn't think Rudy would react this way. I mean, it's not like I'm his fuckin' wife or he doesn't have eight other girlfriends."

"Yeah," Cliff said, "but you're probably his favorite. I can see that."

That made Abby blush.

Then he told her to excuse herself and go to the little girls' room. She started to protest, and he repeated his order to her: "Excuse yourself and go to the little girls' room. Lock the door and don't open it till I tell you it's okay."

She didn't understand.

"Do it," he commanded.

She followed orders, standing up, excusing herself, going into the ladies' room, and locking the door.

Once Miss Pendergast had exited the dining room, the two Italian hoodlums made their way over to Cliff's table.

Mike Zitto sat in Abigail's vacant chair, and Pat Cardella took a chair from an unoccupied table and slid it over.

Cliff looked away from Charlie Chaplin on the wall and up at the two linebacker-like fellows joining him at his table, as he took another bite of his pizza.

Pat placed his glass of beer on the table and said to Cliff, "Okay, fruitcake, here's what's gonna happen. You're gonna get up from the table, you're gonna take your ass out that door"—jerking his thumb behind him, pointing at the door—"and if either me or him"—moving his thumb between Mike and himself—"sees you hangin' 'round Miss Abigail again, you're gonna visit the hospital for a long time."

Cliff continued chewing his slice of pizza.

"You understand, pizza-face?" Mike asked.

Cliff swallowed his food and took the pizza in his hand and placed it back on his plate. He grabbed a napkin, and as he wiped the grease from his fingers, he asked the two fellows, "You two gentlemen wouldn't by chance be of *Italian descent*, would you?"

The two dark-haired men instinctively gave each other a look, then looked back to the blond guy. "Yeah," Pat said.

Cliff pointed his outstretched finger back and forth between them. "Both of you?"

Mike puffed up his chest and said, "Yeah, we're both Italian, what of it?"

A grin spread across Cliff's face as he leaned forward and said, "Do you know how many *Italians* I've killed?"

Pat leaned forward and asked in a whisper, "Excuse me?"

Cliff said, "Oh, you didn't hear me? Let me repeat it." Then he asked for a second time, "*Do you have any idea how many Italians I've killed?*"

Cliff reached into his front jacket pocket as he said, "Let me give you an idea."

Pat and Mike watched him pull the Medal of Valor out of his pocket and drop it on the table between them. It landed hard on the wooden table, with a loud *bang*.

"For the day I got that"—pointing at the Medal of Valor—"I killed at least seven. Maybe as many as nine. But at least seven." Cliff continued, "And that was just one fuckin' day. When I was in Sicily, I killed Italians every day."

Sitting back in his chair, he said, "And I was in Sicily a long, long time."

The two Italian gangsters' faces turned red.

"In fact," Cliff continued, "I killed so many Italians, they made me a war hero. Consequently, because I'm a war hero, I got a license to carry this."

Cliff removed a snub-nose .38 from his other jacket pocket and placed it, loud, on the table next to the Medal of Valor. Pat and Mike jumped in their seats when they saw him take out the pistol and lay it on the table.

Cliff leaned forward and whispered across the table to the two torpedoes, "You know what? I betcha I could take that pistol there and shoot both of you dead—right now—in this shitty little pizza parlor. Right in front of the owner, the waiters, the customers, and Charlie Chaplin. And you know what?

"I betcha, I just betcha, I'd get away with it. Because I'm a war hero. And you two are just degenerate guinea garbage."

Mike Zitto had had enough, and now it was time for him to do the talking. He pointed an angry finger at the blond smart aleck. "You listen to me, you Army faggot—"

Cliff interrupted him by snatching his snub-nose .38 off the table and firing one bullet each into the skulls of Pat and Mike. Red blood shot out of the holes he'd just made in their craniums, spraying across the tabletop, across the front of Cliff's shirt and face, and practically across the room.

The female customers screamed as the male customers hit the ground. Both gangsters tipped over out of their chairs, collapsing on the sawdust-covered floor. Once they were on the ground, Cliff shot them twice more for good measure.

Later, when the Cleveland Police Department questioned Cliff about the incident, he told them, "Well, they tried to kidnap myself and Miss Pendergast. The fatter one said he intended to shoot me and throw acid in Miss Pendergast's face to teach her a lesson." Adding, "I didn't know what to do. I was so scared."

Cliff's theory proved to be right. The Cleveland cops knew exactly who Pat Cardella and Mike Zitto were. And if a World War Two hero wanted to shoot 'em dead in a pizza parlor, the police would pay for the pizza. Cliff's story didn't even need to be convincing. It just needed to be plausible.

And that was how Cliff Booth got away with murder . . . the first time.

Chapter Eighteen

The Name Ain't Jughead

Caleb DeCoteau.

When Murdock Lancer mentioned that the name of the ringleader of the land pirates who'd been stealing his cattle was Caleb DeCoteau, it took all of Johnny's poker-playing skills not to show a reaction on his face. This proud, bitter old bastard Murdock Lancer, his father, was desperate. And it was Caleb DeCoteau who was the cause of his desperation. When Johnny and his half brother, Scott, traveled from different locations to their former childhood home, it was to receive the thousand dollars their father offered them if they would listen to a proposal. Neither of the men figured they'd be interested in anything the father they hadn't seen since they were children had to propose.

Both men were wrong.

For about two hundred miles, their father, Murdock Lancer, was the wealthiest man on the American side of the California-Mexico border. He had the biggest ranch, he owned the biggest home, and he had more cattle than any other man in the Monterey Valley. But now this rich, proud man was desperate, and desperation was not an emotion he was accustomed to. It didn't make him look weak. Murdock Lancer had the strength, the dignity, and the face of a stagecoach relay horse. But it did make him look worried. Things were definitely bad, but the worry he wore on his face was the acknowledgment that they could get far worse.

Ever since Caleb DeCoteau and his gang of rascals had moved into the area of Royo del Oro, they'd zeroed in on Murdock's cows to such a degree it would appear Caleb had a personal vendetta against the man for some past transgression. But, actually, nothing could be further from the truth. It was simply that, in a field of poppies, Murdock Lancer was the tall poppy, and it's the tall poppy that gets cut down to size.

It started with the pilfering of a few head every night. In the beginning, Murdock posted a couple of ranch hands to act as guards spending the night in bedrolls to discourage overzealous steak lovers. That seemed to work at first. But then the ranch hand Pedro was descended upon by eight of Caleb's brutal boys. They beat poor Pedro to a bloody pulp, then tied him to a tree and horsewhipped him damn near to death. The bastards herded off twenty steers that night and shot six more just for spite.

The problem with being the biggest landowner in the territory was, unless you maintained a personal army of gun-toting mean motherfuckers, it was damn near impossible to police an assault this aggressive in nature. The nearest law was a federal marshal over one hundred and fifty miles away. (And the truth of the matter was, protecting the property of rich men drew very little sympathy from law-enforcement agents paid fifty dollars a month.) Not only was Caleb herding off significant numbers of steers during the night, but he was also openly selling them at cattle pens sixty miles away (Lancer Ranch brand on their hide and all).

Then Caleb and his men moved into the town nearest the Lancer Ranch, Royo del Oro. First they took over the town's saloon, turning its owner, Pepe, into a terrorized servant in his own establishment.

The mayor, a man who took his commitment to the civics of his community as a duty, tried to talk to Caleb. He was bullwhipped in the middle of Main Street for his efforts. The land pirates informed the merchants of Royo del Oro that unless they wanted their little red schoolhouse burned down to the ground and their women molested on a daily basis, when it came to Pepe and his place and Murdock and his cows, to mind their own fucking beeswax.

Then Caleb moved into the presidential suite of the Hotel Lancaster. And it wasn't too long after that the land pirates started a weekly tax collection from all the business owners in the town.

Caleb's plan was simple. A slow, steady, but relentlessly constant experiment of seeing how much guff Murdock and the citizens of Royo del Oro were willing to swallow. And experiment after experiment proved the community had a seemingly bottomless appetite.

Now, Caleb wasn't so drunk with power that he thought this type of terrorism could last indefinitely. At some point, the Army would be called in. But they were a three-day march away. So by the time the blue bellies arrived, Caleb and his men would be long gone. Caleb only had one obstacle: Murdock Lancer's money. When a man of principle battles a scoundrel, the scoundrel always at first has the upper hand. Because there are some things the man of principle won't do. While the scoundrel will do whatever it takes. That is, until the man of principle is pushed past his breaking point and beyond his nature. Most of Greek tragedy, half of all English theater, and three-quarters of American cinema operated from this premise.

Other than leave town, the citizens of Royo del Oro had no recourse. But Murdock's money offered him options. He could spend it buying scoundrels of his own. And with Caleb's last transgression—the sniper killing of Murdock's trusted ramrod, George Gomez—he finally pushed the old man over his self-imposed line.

The proposal Murdock Lancer proposed his sons was simple. Split his entire empire three ways with them. That meant cattle, that meant land holdings, that meant the ranch house, that meant bank accounts. In order to get it, they had to agree to two things: Help Murdock repel Caleb and his killing thieves from the area. And work the ranch and tend to the business of running a cattle empire for ten years. After ten years, if they wanted to leave and cash in their shares, they were free to do so. Both young men had been living hand to mouth for the last couple of years—Scott, a riverboat gambler, living from one poker hand to another, and Johnny from selling his gun arm to the highest bidder, keeping one horse length away from a posse. In both cases the brothers were risking more than they would ever hope to gain. There was no love lost between the brothers and their father, but both men had to consider his offer, because there was no other scenario on God's green earth where either man could make the money Murdock was offering them. Not legally or illegally. Murdock Lancer wasn't just rich. Murdock Lancer possessed *wealth*. Murdock Lancer didn't just have a lot of land and a successful business—he had an empire. An empire he said he was willing to split three ways.

As far as Johnny was concerned, there was only one problem. He *hated* the fucker. This was the same fucker who threw him and his mother out in the rain. The same fucker who turned his mother into a money-grubbing whore. The same fucker who was ultimately responsible for putting her in that hotel room with that other wealthy fucker who slit her throat. Johnny was twelve years old when *that* fucker stood trial for the killing of his mother and was found not guilty. He was fourteen when he killed that fucker. And he spent the next ten years killing every member of that fucking jury who acquitted that motherfucker. Johnny slit all their throats, so they'd know how his momma died. Gurgling blood, unable to speak, dying slowly, terrified as they looked up at their killer. Then Johnny would smile at their agony and tell them, "Marta Conchita Louisa Galvadon Lancer says *hola*."

It took ten years to kill those thirteen people, but finally Marta Galvadon Lancer was avenged. But the last person left who had yet to pay the final price for his momma's murder was the man who sent her on her path of degradation. His father. Murdock Lancer.

Still, that was a lotta cows, a lotta land, a lotta ranch, and a lotta money. More than Johnny could make on his own in ten lifetimes. And all he had to do to get it was keep from killing his old man and from getting killed by a murderous gang of rustlers. But Johnny had a secret. Something neither Murdock nor Scott nor anybody else at the Lancer Ranch knew.

Johnny Madrid and Caleb DeCoteau were friends.

Johnny Madrid rode his horse down Royo del Oro's main drag. When he rode in on the Butterfield Wells Fargo stage two days ago, it seemed a town like a hundred others he'd seen before. But that was before knowing the narrative that Murdock told him and his half brother. Now Johnny saw what separated Royo del Oro from other towns: This town was terrified. When he first arrived, he noticed the town's big saloon, and he noticed the collection of owl hoots collected in front of it. Now, a lotta towns had saloons with a lotta owl hoots collecting in front of them. But Johnny knew these weren't just *any* owl hoots. These were some of the men Johnny had been lured into town to shoo off or kill. These men were the men responsible for Murdock's misery. These were the land pirates that worked for Caleb DeCoteau.

As he rode past the Gilded Lily, he felt their eyes follow him. Out of the corner of his squinty eye he counted four owl hoots. One was a black fella dressed like a bandito. Two were banditos dressed like banditos. But it was the fourth man that caught Johnny's eye. A big white man, older than the rest. While the other three adopted the dress of Mexican scum, he wore a tailored western black suit and fancy cowboy boots of black leather. He sported a crisp big black cowboy hat on his head and a big soup catcher on his upper lip, slathered with a generous application of mustache wax. The big man sat in a rocking chair on the porch of the Gilded Lily, carving a wooden horse figurine with a pocketknife. Tiny flecks of wood collected in a small pile by his shiny boot. Aside from both his age and his dress, he was different from the other three owl hoots on the porch. They were henchmen; he was a cowboy of quality. Johnny couldn't place him. But even if he didn't know *who* he was, he knew *what* he was. The big man in the black suit with the black boots and the big mustache was a big name with a big reputation. These other prairie dogs divvied up slices of pie for the havoc they caused and the ruckus they raised. The big man was paid a sack of gold by Caleb personally before any work was done.

In a gangster story, he'd have been known as an "Out-of-Town Torpedo." In an earlier chapter of the big man's story, he could have been the hero, and he had been. But on this page—today—he sold his gun arm to the highest bidder. And in *this* story, *that* bidder was Caleb DeCoteau.

Johnny climbed down from his horse and tied it to the hitching post located in front of the Hotel Lancaster. The big man in black folded up his pocketknife and put it away in his pocket. Johnny started crossing the main street of Royo del Oro in the direction of the saloon. The big man in black placed the little horse figurine he was carving on a tiny barrel in front of him and rose out of the rocking chair, moving toward the front of the patio. Johnny was nine steps away from the bottom stair of the three-stair porch steps that led to the saloon's front porch when he heard the big man in black call out, "That's far enough, Jughead."

Johnny stopped walking. "Name's not Jughead," Johnny corrected.

"Whatcha doin' round here, boy?" the big man asked.

"I'm thirsty," Johnny answered, pointing his finger at the establishment. "That's a saloon, ain't it?"

The big man in black turned around and glanced up at the big sign that read SALOON, hung up over the entrance, then turned back to Johnny and said, "Yeah, that's a saloon. Only you can't come in."

"Why?" Johnny asked. "Y'all closed?"

The big man smiled and patted the grip of his pistol, which rested in the waistband of his trousers, right up against his belly. "Oh no, we're open for business."

Johnny, getting the picture, smiled right back and asked, "So it's just *me* can't come in?"

The big man smiled even wider, this time showing teeth, and said, "That's right."

Johnny asked, "Why?"

The big man in black explained, "Well, you see, we only serve *ladies* on *Ladies' Night*."

The other three owl hoots on the porch laughed at his little joke.

Johnny laughed a little too and said, "That's a good one. I'm gonna hafta remember that one."

The big man warned, "You take another step near this saloon, you ain't gonna be remembering nothin' ever again." Placing his hands on his hips, the gunfighter in black explained to the young man in the sangria-red ruffled shirt the immediate future.

"Now, looky here, Jughead, you're gonna climb back up on that nag you rode in on, and you're gonna hightail your ass outta here—you hear me, boy?"

Johnny squinted his eyes and said, "Oh, I hear just fine, but apparently you don't. 'Cause I done tole' you, the—name—ain't—Jughead."

That's when Johnny's hand lowered to the pistol that sat in the holster on his hip, and he unhooked the tiny leather loop wrapped around the hammer of his widow-maker.

In response, the big man's hand lowered down his front, where the grip of his smoke wagon rested inside the waistband of his trousers.

Then, as the porch, the street, the town, and the state got quiet while the two men twitched into their killing stances—SUDDENLY—the squeaky batwing doors of the saloon were flung open and out stepped the villain of this piece, Caleb DeCoteau.

The outlaw gang leader was dressed in a brown rawhide jacket with leather fringe running down the sleeves, and he was eating a fried-chicken drumstick. Johnny felt Caleb step out on the porch, but he was committed to his staring contest with the troublemaker, so he didn't raise his eyes to greet his old friend.

"Mr. Gilbert," Caleb said, addressing the big man from behind his back, "don't let me stop you from earnin' the money I pay you—I know how bored and restless you get when you run outta *tamales.*" Caleb took a big bite out of the chicken leg, and as he chewed the greasy meat he said with

278

his mouth full, "But if I were you, I'd find out that Jughead's name."

Gilbert asked his boss, "Who is he, Caleb?"

Caleb leaned in the doorway of the saloon, swallowed the meat in his mouth, and said, "Allow me to introduce the two of ya."

Pointing at the man in black's back with his chicken bone, Caleb said, "This here is Bob Gilbert."

So that's the Businessman, Johnny thought.

"The Businessman?" Johnny asked.

"That's right," Bob said. "Business Bob Gilbert. And who might you be?"

Before Johnny could answer, Caleb tore with his teeth another big piece of meat and skin off the chicken bone and said, "That's a fella named Madrid. *Johnny Madrid.*"

"Who's *Johnny Madrid*?" Bob asked sarcastically, repeating the name in a mocking ridiculous fashion. The other three porch owl hoots laughed, until Caleb shot them a shut-the-fuck-up-when-grown-folks-are-talking look. They piped down.

Business Bob was confused, irritated, and beginning to get a little concerned. He was hired by Caleb to shoo off or kill fellas like this jughead in red. And he was paid handsomely in gold coin to do it. So why, all of the sudden, is the man who paid him actin' all cute?

"I mean it, Caleb, who the hell is this joker?"

Caleb tossed what was left of the chicken bone into the street between the two men and said to his hired gun, "You're about to find out, *Businessman*."

And with that, Caleb disappeared back behind the

batwing doors. Johnny Madrid turned and faced Bob sideways, his showdown stance, demonstrating to the Businessman that Johnny meant business. Bob Gilbert's throat went dry as Johnny, standing still as a statue, said, "Ready when you are, *Gil-bert*."

Bob's hand inched toward his holster.

Johnny blinked.

Bob's body jerked left as his hand grabbed the grip of the pistol, then his body violently jerked right as Johnny's bullet burrowed smack-dab into his pumping heart.

The pistol he had just cleared tumbled out of his useless fingers, bouncing off the wood porch into the powdery brown dirt. The big man dressed in black teeter-tottered on his black shiny bootheels and fell face forward down the steps into the street, tipping over a pickle barrel, spilling pickles and pickle water into the dirt.

And so ends the impressive career of Business Bob Gilbert, Johnny thought. The man in the sangria-red ruffled shirt standing in the street with pickles by his feet pointed the still-smoking barrel of his gun in the direction of the three porch owl hoots, asking them in Spanish, "Anybody else?"

When Johnny entered the saloon, seven of Caleb's other land pirates, who were playing poker at tables, smoking cigars, or drinking booze at the bar, raised their eyes to see the fella in the red ruffled shirt who put Bob outta business. No one looked too angry at the turn of events. I guess Bob didn't make it his *business* to make friends. Then, from way above his head, Johnny Lancer heard shouted out, "Johnny Madrid!"

His eyes rose and he found his ole' buddy Caleb DeCoteau

standing on the second-floor landing, leaning against the impressive wood banister, looking down at him with a smile on his hairy face as big and wide as Texas.

"How long's it been?" the bad man in brown asked the bad man in red.

Johnny didn't have to think; he knew. "Oh, since that time in Juarez. 'Bout three years ago."

Caleb blew out smoke from the cheroot in his mouth and said, "Well, come on in and have a drink."

As Johnny crossed the saloon floor heading toward the foot of the staircase, he asked, "So I don't gotta wait till *Ladies' Night*?"

The two tough guys made their tough-guy jokes. "Well, rules were made to be broken."

Ha ha, Johnny thought. "Well, in that case," Johnny offered, "buy ya a drink, Caleb?"

"Sure, Johnny," Caleb said as he slowly descended the staircase. "How 'bout some *mez-cow*? Like that time in Juarez."

Johnny let out a soft chuckle as he shook his head at the memory and said, "A lot of people died that day."

"Yes, they did," Caleb said as he finished descending the stairs. "But we had a good time, didn't we?"

"Yes, we did," Johnny replied with a conspiratorial smile at the grim but lively memory. Then, gesturing toward the long brown bar across the room, Madrid said, "After you, DeCoteau."

As the two men walked in step toward the bar, Caleb called out to the pathetic wreck that owned the establishment, "Pepe, get your *be-hind* behind that bar—I got a guest!"

As Johnny crossed the length of the floor, his eyes took in the Gilded Lily. It was actually an impressive saloon, befitting a town built by cattle money. He also contemplated his next plan of action. Or at least he would have if he had a plan. Once he learned he'd receive one-third of a fortune for killing an old friend, it just naturally seemed appropriate to reintroduce himself. But to what end, exactly? Well, *exactly*, he hadn't quite figured out yet. Since he knew Caleb, *if* he was backing Murdock's play, it seemed like a smart move to offer DeCoteau his services. Then he could work from the inside. Well, if that was *still* the plan, then it was a good one, provided Caleb wasn't privy to the knowledge that Johnny was Murdock's son. If he was, it would be Johnny's funeral. So *if* the plan was to stop Caleb and get his father's beef, so far so good. But ever since he was twelve and he broke ground on his mother's grave, Johnny had another plan: Make Murdock Lancer pay for what he did to him and his momma. And, frankly, in that department Caleb was doing a better job than Johnny ever could. The old man was at the end of his rope. He was desperate. So the real question was, what did Johnny want more? Money or blood? His father's ranch or his mother's revenge? Security or satisfaction?

Pepe moved behind the bar and took the two men's orders. "Dos mescal," Johnny said. Then the cowboy asked in Spanish, "Any food?" Pepe answered, "Just beans and tortillas."

Johnny turned to Caleb. "How's the beans?"

"I've had worse," was his reply.

Johnny turned to Pepe and said in Spanish, "Give me a plate of beans."

"One dollar," was Pepe's hostile reply in English.

Johnny turned back toward Caleb and remarked, "A dollar for beans is kinda steep, or am I crazy?"

Smashing some peanut shells on the bar with his fist, Caleb justified, "Hey, Pepe's got a right to make a livin' too." He then picked out the peanuts from the pile of smashed shells and popped them in his mouth.

Johnny snorted, "What, your boys aren't big spenders?" Mr. Madrid slapped a big coin on the bar. Pepe noisily slid the coin off and into his hand, made a face at Johnny, and fetched the mescal bottle. He poured it into two clay cups.

"A toast!" Caleb declared, as he raised his cup in the air. Johnny did the same. "To my wife and all my sweethearts—may they never meet." Johnny and Caleb clinked clay cups, then tossed the fiery-tasting booze down their gullets. Caleb gestured to a lone brown table located toward the back of the saloon. "Señor Madrid, would you care to join me at my table where I entertain my guests?" Johnny did a slight bow and assured him, "I would be delighted, Monsieur DeCoteau." Caleb headed toward the table, barking over his shoulder, "Take the bottle witcha." Johnny turned on his heels and snatched the mescal bottle off the bar.

The lead land pirate scraped a wooden chair noisily out from under the table and dropped his ass into it. "So, Johnny, what brings you to Royo del Oro?"

"Oh, you know me, Caleb," he said as he poured both himself and his host another snort of mescal. "Money."

Caleb knocked back his firewater and asked, "Who's payin' you 'round 'ere?"

Johnny took a sip of his drink and said, "I hope you."

283

Giving his guest his full attention, Caleb asked the million-peso question: "And what have you heard about me?"

"I heard about the Lancer Ranch," Johnny told him truthfully. "I heard about all the cattle you've appropriated. Lotta land, lotta cows, lotta money, no law to speak of. And nothin' but an old man and some Mexican ranch hands to shoo ya off."

Pepe arrived with a big plate of runny beans and a big wooden spoon and placed it in front of Johnny.

Caleb poured himself more hooch and asked, "And what pray tell business is that of yours?"

"Same business as Business Bob's. I want me a job," Johnny said, straight no chaser. Then added, "And seein' as you've just had a opening, I'd like to fill it."

"Doin' what?" the outlaw asked.

Johnny took another sip of booze, then, after a small dramatic pause, said "Killin' Murdock Lancer."

That raised his ole' buddy's bushy eyebrows.

Johnny picked up the lime wedge that came with the mescal and squeezed it over his plate of beans. "You pushin' that old man pretty hard. But that old man's got money. And Lancer's wealth is trouble with a capital T when it comes to you, Caleb old boy. 'Cause sure as God made little green apples, sooner or later, one of these days he's gonna hire some guns and *push back*. And that ain't gonna be his fellas versus your fellas, and best fellas win. The name of that game is gonna be *Kill Caleb DeCoteau*."

That statement caused Caleb to make a face.

Johnny picked up a little jug filled with hot sauce and began to sprinkle it over the beans, as he continued, "With you dead? All these prairie dogs you got workin' fer ya will find some new hole to live in. With you dead? Life goes back the way it was. And when you're Murdock goddamn Lancer, life's pretty fuckin' sweet. Yeah," Johnny said, as he scooped up some of the beans he'd just prepared in the big wooden spoon, "Murdock Lancer will pay a pretty penny for that." Johnny put the spoon in his mouth and began to chew.

The outlaw narrowed his eyes at him and said, "Maybe he already has."

"Maybe," Johnny said with his mouth full, then he swallowed and said, "But maybe I don't like Lancer, and maybe I don't like his boots."

"What's not to like about Murdock Lancer's boots?" Caleb asked.

"How he uses them," Johnny replied.

"How's he use 'em?" Caleb asked.

"To step on people," Johnny answered.

Then, pointing his finger across the table at his host, Johnny added, "But you, Caleb, you I like. I'd much rather work for you stickin' a weed up that old man's ass than fight *against* you defending Murdock Lancer's cows." Taking a dramatic pause, Johnny finished, "Provided you can pay my price." After Johnny said that out loud, he realized, *That ain't too far from the truth.*

Caleb smiled and inquired, "What's your price these days, Johnny?"

Johnny stuck the wooden spoon filled with frijoles into his mouth, chewed a bit as he thought, then said with his mouth full, "Well, I think *today* I'm worth more than you paid Business Bob," swallowing and grinning at Caleb.

Caleb smiled back and ordered, "Git your horse. Put him in our stable." He pointed at one of the doors at the top of the stairs. "You'll sleep there tonight. We hit the Lancer Ranch tomorrow morning. I pay quality men in fourteen-karat-gold coin."

"How much?" Johnny asked.

Caleb pantomimed a medium sack of gold with his hands. "Oh, 'bout this much."

All the time Johnny had contemplated killing Murdock Lancer, he'd never contemplated turning a profit on it. But he sure as hell was contemplating it now, as he smiled and said, "I kill Murdock Lancer"—Johnny pantomimed a larger sack with his hands—"I want this much."

Caleb lifted up his clay cup and clinked it against Johnny's cup. Both men brought the fiery liquid up to their lips and drank.

But what *exactly* was he toasting? The execution of a successful undercover operation that placed him on the inside of his father's enemies? Or a newfound collaboration with an old friend against a bitter enemy? What was more important to him, his future or his past? Was he Johnny Lancer or Johnny Madrid? Looked like Johnny had till morning to figure that out.

Chapter Nineteen

"My Friends Call Me Pussycat"

When Cliff noticed the film with Carroll Baker playing at the Eros on Beverly Boulevard was rated X, he thought there was a good chance of seeing Carroll Baker really fucking somebody. No such luck. Unlike *I Am Curious (Yellow)*, where Lena Nyman actually looks like she's fucking on film, the Italian Carroll Baker movie was just movie fucking.

European movie fucking, which was more lurid and violent, but nobody was actually getting fucked on set.

Too bad.

But it was a pretty good mystery anyway, and it had a great twist at the end. All in all, not the worst way to spend an afternoon. However, if he knew Carroll Baker wasn't really fucking on film, he would've probably seen *Ice Station Zebra* at the Cinerama Dome.

On 93 KHJ, the Real Don Steele introduces the new song by Los Bravos (the "Black Is Black" guys), *Bring a Little Lovin'*, as Cliff speeds down Forrest Lawn Drive, makes a right on Hollywood Way, and pulls into the left-hand turn lane. He sits idling, waiting for the light to change to green, at which point he'll negotiate his left-hand turn onto River-side Drive.

Digging the forward momentum of the high-energy Los Bravos tune, Cliff slaps out the song's rhythm against the steering wheel with his fingers.

Then he spots her on the corner of Riverside Drive and Hollywood Way, standing in front of a bus stop advertising local Channel 9 newscaster George Putnam. Just like she was when he saw her standing in front of the Aquarius The-ater, she's hitching a ride.

Except now she's alone.

Jesus, Cliff thinks, *what are the chances of seeing the same hitchhiker three times on the same day in three different parts of Los Angeles?* He thinks, *Who knows, with all the kids hitching rides these days, maybe that's not such a big deal.* It sure seems like a big deal. But this time this slinky little sexpot is going in Cliff's direction. In fact, once he receives his green direc-tional arrow, he's going to turn right into her. A quick ride could easily turn into a behind-the-wheel moving blow job (Cliff's favorite kind). Or at least a twenty-minute French-kissing session. He rises a little bit in the driver's seat at the anticipation of what this ride could lead to.

As Cliff contemplates this thought, the brunette hippie pickle girl spots him idling in the cream-yellow Cadillac.

As soon as she sees him, she leaps in the air and waves frantically. Cliff acknowledges her. She sticks out the little fist that's attached to her long arm and gives her protruding thumb a jerk, which indicates, *Gimme a lift?*

He gives her a pointy salute back, which indicates, *I'll give you a lift.*

In response to his pointy salute, she screeches and does a spastic dance on the street corner. The dance she does could be best described as a combination of a pirouette and jumping jacks.

Look at this little grasshopper on the corner, Cliff thinks. "Grasshopper" is Cliff's name for slinky, sexy, tall girls who are all elbows and kneecaps. He calls them that because when they wrap their long legs and gangly arms around you, it's like fucking a grasshopper.

But Cliff thinks the idea of fucking a grasshopper is sorta sexy. So for him, it's a term of endearment.

Then, as Cliff sits in Rick's Coupe de Ville, waiting for the light to change, he notices a blue Buick Skylark, going in the opposite direction on Hollywood Way, make a right-hand turn at the corner of Riverside Drive, pulling to a stop right next to the brunette hippie pickle girl.

Leaning forward in his seat, Cliff says out loud, "What the fuck?" Across traffic, he watches the hippie girl lean down and talk to the driver through the open car-door window on the passenger side.

After a bit of back and forth between the driver and the hitchhiker, she nods her head yes.

She straightens up for a moment, looks across traffic at the blond guy in the cream-yellow Cadillac, gives him a big shoulder shrug, and dips inside the Skylark.

As pickle girl's car drives away, Cliff's directional arrow turns green. Cliff negotiates his left-hand turn onto Riverside Drive and falls behind the Buick Skylark. The Real Don Steele comes back on the air and reminds listeners, "Tina Delgado is alive!"

Through the Skylark's back window, Cliff can see the outline of both the male driver and the female passenger very clearly. The driver seems to be another hippie type, with long, frizzy, curly red hair. Maybe he's that funny-looking guy who plays Bernie on *Room 222*. He watches the bushy-haired silhouettes talk animatedly with each other. Red-haired shaggy Skylark guy says something and pickle girl laughs, slapping her bare knee in response.

Cliff says to himself, "Okay, now she's just fucking with me."

He yanks the steering wheel to the left, and the Cadillac jerks off of Riverside Drive onto Forman and pulls into an open parking space on the curb across from the big beige carpet store. Cliff twists the ignition key, cutting off the engine and the Real Don Steele, then gets out of the Cadillac and crosses busy Riverside Drive on foot. Passing the Money Tree bar and grill, he walks down the sidewalk, heading for the Toluca Lake record store Hot Waxx.

The Monkees' catchy hit *The Last Train to Clarksville* hits him right in the ears as soon as he pushes open the record-store door. The place smells like most places these days that cater to young people. Sort of a combination of incense and BO. Four other customers, all under twenty-five, poke through the store's inventory.

A black guy in a dashiki examines Richie Havens's self-titled album.

A girl who looks like that chubby flower-child singer Melanie, who Cliff's got a crush on, holds Simon and Garfunkel's *Bookends* in her arms.

A young guy who looks like he could be the son of somebody Cliff was in the Army with riffles through the movie-soundtrack section.

The fourth patron, like the guy in the Buick Skylark, is another frizzy-haired guy who looks like a cross between Jesus Christ and Arlo Guthrie. He's in a discussion with the skinny shovel-faced twenty-two-year-old male who works at the store about the future of Ringo Starr's career post-Beatles.

That Tom Jones song, *Delilah*, has been haunting Cliff ever since he first heard it on the radio three weeks ago. He wants to pay attention to the story part of the song, but the only part that he can remember is the chorus. And just catching it when it comes on the radio isn't working out. Naturally, Cliff is partial to songs about guys who kill their women.

He walks up to the counter and asks Shovel Face where they keep the 8-track tapes.

"Susan's got the key," Shovel Face says. "You need to talk to Susan and get her to open the case for you." Apparently, stores thought 8-track tapes were so valuable that they felt the need to keep them under lock and key. You couldn't just thumb through them, choose the one you wanted, and take it up to the counter. You had to get an employee to open a locked glass case with a key, then they would stand there and watch over you as you scanned the shelf and made your selection. Then keep an eye on you as you walked to the counter and actually bought the fucking thing. Now, true, it was easier to slip an 8-track tape of *Rubber Soul* in your inside jacket pocket than it was an LP. Nevertheless, you would have thought they were trading in diamonds. Also, it's a little odd to assume all your patrons are thieves.

Before Cliff can ask, "Where's Susan?" Shovel Face points at a golden-blond beach-bunny type wearing a buttoned-up Levi's vest and a pair of white skintight jeans with a KEEP ON TRUCKIN' patch on the ass pocket. She's sprucing up the community billboard when Cliff walks up to her and asks, "You Susan?"

Susan turns to face him and instantly gives Cliff the smile Shovel Face has waited six months to get. They both have hair so blond that when their heads are close together Cliff and Susan resemble two different suns from different galaxies orbiting each other. She confirms to her fellow blond that indeed she is Susan.

"Can you open the 8-track case for me?"

She involuntarily makes a face that tells Cliff she thinks these 8-track tapes are a pain in the ass, though Cliff doubts whoever owns this record store pays her to spruce up the community billboard.

In her toneless voice, which seems to go hand in hand with this type of athletic sexy blond Californian beach girl, Susan tells him, "Ahh . . . yeah, sure thing. Let me go get the key." She points over to where the 8-track glass case is. "Meet me by the 8-track tapes."

Cliff watches her tight white jean–covered ass disappear behind a bead curtain to fetch the key, which, since there's only one and she's in charge of it, should be in her pocket, not in a desk drawer in some back room behind a bead curtain.

He can feel Shovel Face's resentment of him as he moves over to the glass case in question. If asked, Cliff would tell Shovel Face that he probably had a chance with Susan four to five months ago. But if he hasn't made his move by now, she probably chalks him up as a dickless wonder and it doesn't matter how much pizza and beer they have after work. And, in Cliff's opinion, his best bet would be to concentrate on good-looking customers.

Cliff scans the 8-track selection through the locked glass, searching for Tom Jones's *Delilah* amongst all the other names. Steppenwolf. The Fifth Dimension. Ian Whitcomb. Crosby, Stills and Nash. *Hair* Broadway soundtrack. *Zorba the Greek* original soundtrack. Arlo Guthrie's *Alice's Restaurant*. Mama Cass's solo record. Two Bill Cosby records. Some comedy team named Hudson and Landry that Cliff has never heard of.

The beach bunny bounces back and unlocks the glass door, sliding it open with a noisy tug. Cliff bends over to better examine the titles. He can feel Susan watching him with her hand on her cocked-out hip. Cliff finds what he's looking for and plucks out *Tom Jones Greatest Hits*. Susan does a slight but audible guffaw and covers her smile with her hand.

His eyebrows rise. "What? Is my choosing Tom Jones funny?"

She nods her golden-blond head as if to say, *Yeah, a little.*

Cliff exits the record store (still a little pissed at Susan), and steps onto the sidewalk, holding a little burgundy bag with the Hot Waxx logo on it. He heads for the corner of Riverside Drive and Forman to cross the street and get back in his vehicle. Then, across traffic, he spots her again. The bushy-haired brunette pickle girl in the cutoff jeans, bare feet, and crochet halter top, apparently waiting for his return, by his cream-yellow Cadillac. When she sees him standing on the corner, ready to cross the street and return to his car, she jumps up and waves frantically at him. As Cliff gets the green light and crosses the busy street heading toward both his car and the bushy-haired barefoot brunette hippie pickle girl, he notices something. This girl is younger than she looked through his dirty windshield. How young, he's not sure. But as they converse, he's going to try and examine that.

Leaning against his Cadillac, the bushy-haired barefoot brunette hippie pickle girl says, "Looks like third time's the charm."

"I count you on Riverside Drive and Hollywood Way being our *third* time," states the blond dude in the yellow Hawaiian shirt. "And it was definitely *not* charmed."

"Picky, picky, picky," the bushy-haired barefoot brunette hippie pickle girl teases. "Okay, Mr. Persnickety, have it your way." Then she gives a very over-enunciated line reading on, "Fourth time's the charm."

How fucking old is she? Cliff thinks.

"How were those pickles?" Cliff asks.

"Real good," the bushy-haired barefoot brunette hippie pickle girl says. "They were the fancy kind."

Cliff raises his eyebrows as if to say, *Good for you.*

"Give me a ride?" she pleads in her cute-girl voice, then bites her bottom lip for effect.

"What happened to Bernie?" he asks her.

"Who?"

"The guy in the Buick Skylark," he says.

She sighs. "Looks like he wasn't goin' my way."

"Which way is *your way*?" Cliff inquires.

She's definitely underage, Cliff has deduced, but *how* underage? She's not fourteen or fifteen. So the question is, is she sixteen or seventeen? Or maybe, who knows, eighteen? And then she would officially *not* be underage, at least as far as the Los Angeles County Sheriff's Department is concerned.

"I'm going to Chatsworth," she tells him.

That makes him involuntarily giggle, "Chatsworth?"

In her puppet body language, she nods her head yes.

With a smirk on his face, Cliff asks her, "So you just hitch up and down Riverside Drive till somebody with a lotta free time and a lotta gas agrees to drive you all the way to fucking Chatsworth?"

She waves away his incredulous reaction. "Shows what you know. Tourists love to drive me. I'm the favorite part of their L.A. vacation. . . ."

As she talks with her hands, he notices how big they are. *My god, her fingers are so long,* he thinks. *They'd feel pretty good wrapped around my cock and squeezing, with that big giant thumb of hers mashing up the head.*

". . . they'll be telling stories about the Hollywood hippie girl . . ."

As she continues to rattle on, he glances down at her feet. *Oh shit, they're huge too.*

". . . gave a ride to the movie ranch to for the rest of their lives."

Beat one.

Beat two.

Beat three.

Beat four.

"Spahn Movie Ranch?" Cliff finally asks.

Debra Jo's face lights up. "Yeah!"

Cliff shifts his weight from his right foot to his left foot and unconsciously shifts the little burgundy Hot Waxx bag with the 8-track tape in it from his left hand to his right hand as he clarifies, "So that's where you're goin', Spahn Movie Ranch?"

Again her bushy head nods in a puppet-like yes, accompanied by an "Uh-huh."

Cliff asks, genuinely curious, "Why you goin' there?"

"That's where I live," she answers.

"Alone?" he asks.

"No," she assures him. "Me and my friends."

What? he thinks. At first, when she said Spahn Movie Ranch, Cliff just assumed she was George Spahn's hippie granddaughter or his hippie caretaker. But when hippies say "friends," they mean "other hippies."

"So," he clarifies, "let me get this straight—*you* and a bunch of friends *like you* all live at Spahn Movie Ranch?"

"Yep."

The stuntman rolls the information around in his brain, then opens the passenger-side car door for her. "Hop in, I'll give you a lift."

"Great!" she hollers, as she folds herself up on the passenger-side front seat.

Cliff slams the door behind her. He contemplates, as he walks around to the driver's side of the Cadillac, the information that the bushy-haired brunette barefoot hippie pickle girl just gave him. If what she says is true, it does sound like something strange is going on at Spahn Ranch. He's sure, ultimately, it's probably nothing. Nevertheless, George Spahn is an old man, and it wouldn't hurt to check up on 'em. All it'll cost him is the drive to Chatsworth. He ain't got anything else better to do this late afternoon. Might as well look in on an old friend. In the meantime, he intends to keep flirting with Elbows and Kneecaps and maybe find out more about these "friends" and where they came from.

Soon they're speeding down Riverside Drive. On the radio, the Real Don Steele is joking his way through a commercial for Tanya Tanning Butter. Debra Jo, who gets a lot of rides, immediately starts going into the directions of how to get to Spahn Ranch. "So you wanna get on the Hollywood Freeway—"

Cliff cuts her off. "I know where it is."

She leans her fuzzy head back in the seat and gives the blond dude in the Hawaiian shirt a curious look.

"Are you some old cowboy dude who used to make movies at the ranch?"

"Whoa," Cliff says, with such enthusiasm it surprises Debra Jo.

"What?" she asks.

He answers as he maneuvers the Cadillac around traffic, "I'm just surprised what an accurate description of me that was. Some old cowboy dude who useta make movies at Spahn Ranch."

Debra Jo laughs, "So you useta make westerns at the ranch?"

He nods his head yes.

"Back in the old-timey days?" she adds.

"Well, if by *old-timey days*, you mean television eight years ago, yeah," he says.

Debra Jo puts her huge dirty feet up on the Cadillac dashboard, pushes her filthy soles into the smooth cold glass of the windshield, and asks, "Were you an actor?"

"No," he tells her. "I'm a stuntman."

"Stuntman?" she repeats excitedly. "That's way better!"

"Really?" he asks. "Why is that 'way better'?"

"Actors are phony," she says with the air of authority. "They just say lines that other people write. They pretend to murder people on their stupid TV shows, while real people are being murdered every day in Vietnam."

Well, that's one way to think about it, Cliff thinks.

She continues, "But stuntmen? You guys are different. You jump off fuckin' buildings. You set yourselves on fire. You embrace fear." Then, going into the philosophy she learned from Charlie, "It's only by embracing fear that one conquers one's self. To conquer fear is to render one unconquerable," she says with a satisfied smile on her pretty face.

Whatever the fuck that means, is what Cliff thinks but doesn't say as he takes the ramp to the northbound Hollywood Freeway.

On KHJ's Big 93, the Box Tops' new song, *Sweet Cream Ladies, Forward March*, comes out of the speakers.

After he successfully merges into traffic, Cliff decides to ask, "What's your name?"

"My friends call me Pussycat."

"What's your real name?"

"You don't want to be my friend?"

"Of course I want to be your friend."

"Then I told you, my friends call me Pussycat."

"Fair enough. Pleased to meetcha, Pussycat."

"Aloha. Did you know 'aloha' means hello *and* goodbye?"

"Actually, I did know that."

Touching the shoulder of his yellow shirt: "Are you Hawaiian?"

"No."

"So what's your name, Mr. Blond?"

"Cliff."

"Cliff?"

"Yeah."

"Clifford or just Cliff?"

"Just Cliff."

"Clifton?"

"Just Cliff."

"You don't like Clifton?"

"It's not my name."

She lowers her legs from the dash and snatches up the little burgundy Hot Waxx bag off the front seat. "What'd ya get?"

Cliff protests, "Hey, wait a minute, Miss Rude. Ask."

She sticks her big hand in the little bag and pulls out the *Tom Jones Greatest Hits* 8-track tape and bursts out laughing.

As opposed to his reaction to the smirking Susan, Cliff smiles at Pussycat's ridicule. "Look, fuck you, you stuck-up hippie bitch. I like the song *Delilah*. You got a problem with that?"

Holding up the 8-track tape with Tom Jones's picture on it, she sarcastically asks, "Whatsamatter, they all outta Engelbert Humperdinck?"

Leaning in close to her: "I like him too, smartass."

She waves her big hands at the end of her long arms to indicate, *No problem.* "Hey, Mark Twain said, 'If people didn't have different opinions, there'd be no such thing as horse races.'"

He asks, "Is that what Mark Twain said?"

She shrugs. "Somethin' like that."

Her long fingers tear at the cellophane that covers the 8-track till she rips it off. She removes the cardboard border that the chunky plastic tape sits in, then reaches over and switches the Cadillac's music system from radio to tape player.

The Box Tops shut off.

While Cliff keeps one eye on her and the other on the Hollywood Freeway, Pussycat shoves the 8-track into the car's tape player. It makes a loud *ca-chunk* sound, then for a moment or two they just hear tape hiss emitting from the car-stereo speakers, then Tom Jones's bombastic *What's New Pussycat?* blares out in full stereo.

"Okay," Pussycat admits. "I do like *this* song."

She reaches out and twists the volume knob louder, as she begins moving her shoulders to the music and performing a sexy little dance for Cliff's pleasure on the passenger-side seat of Rick's Cadillac. She brings her bare legs out from under the floorboards and tucks them under her fanny. Then, as she rises to her knees, she unbuttons the metal button on her Levi's cutoffs.

Cliff, who has still not uttered a word, raises his eyebrows.

Okay, maybe this is worth the gas to Chatsworth, he thinks.

In response to his reaction, the brunette raises her two brown caterpillar eyebrows as she unzips the fly of her cutoffs. Then slides them off her ass and down her legs, till she's holding them in her hand, revealing soiled pink panties with little cherries printed on them. She twirls the short-short Levi's on her finger in time to the calliope-like piano of *What's New Pussycat?* till she tosses them down on the floorboard.

As she shimmies her ass left to right in time with Tom's vocals, Pussycat hooks a thumb under the underwear and slowly slides the dirty pink cherry panties down her legs and off her person. Then she lies back against the passenger-side car door and spreads her legs open, revealing to the driver the mountainous mound of dark pubic hair between her legs. The hair between her legs is as wild and bushy as the hair on her head.

"Like what you see, Cliff?" she asks.

"You bet," Cliff truthfully tells her.

She lies down onto her back on the passenger-side seat of Rick's Coupe de Ville, putting her bushy brown head against the door. She raises her left leg and presses the heel of her foot against the driver's seat headrest and raises her right leg and wedges her other foot between the dashboard and the windshield on Cliff's side, presenting herself spread-eagle to the amused driver.

Then, in time to Tom Jones's song about a pussycat, she licks two of her fingers and begins running them up and down against her clit.

Cliff continues driving down the Hollywood Freeway, keeping one eye on the road and the other eye on Pussycat's dark bushy pussy.

Pussycat closes her eyelids and says in a voice affected by her arousal, "Stick your fingers in me."

"How old are you?" Cliff asks.

Pussycat's eyelids pop open.

It's been so long since anybody cared about that, she wasn't even sure she heard him right. "What?"

"How old are you?" Cliff repeats.

She laughs incredulously as she says, "Wow, man, that's the first time anybody's asked that in a long time."

"What's the answer?" he asks again.

She props herself up on her elbows but keeps her legs spread wide as she tells him sarcastically, "Okay, we're gonna play kiddie games? Eighteen. Feel better?"

Cliff asks her, "Do you got some kinda ID? You know, like a driver's license or something?"

"Are you joking?" her surprised face blurts out.

"No, I'm not," he assures her. "I need to see something official that verifies you're eighteen. Which you don't have, 'cause you're not."

With that, Pussycat closes her legs and rises up into a sitting position, shaking her bushy head in disbelief. "Talk about a bring-down bummer, dude, that's you."

With her pants still off, she stretches out her long legs again and plops her huge feet back on the dashboard, placing her hands behind her head in the full recline position.

"Obviously I'm not too young to fuck you, but obviously *you* are too *old* to fuck me."

Cliff sees this from a different perspective and imparts that perspective to Pussycat.

"What I'm too old to do is go to jail for poontang. Prison has tried to get me my whole life. But it ain't ever got me yet. But the day it does get me, it ain't gonna be because of you. No offense."

So with finger fucking off the table, the young gal that calls herself Pussycat puts her pants back on, and the two chat together on the drive to Chatsworth, Cliff never revealing to his passenger he knows George Spahn personally or his real intention in giving her a ride.

He fishes for more information about these "friends" of hers that live at George's ranch.

And she is only too happy to talk his ear off about them. Especially this dude named Charlie, who she is sure will dig Cliff.

"I can see Charlie really digging you," are her exact words.

At first, Cliff is more interested in this gaggle of chicks in their twenties who believe in and practice free love. But the more she speaks of this Charlie character and the more she recounts his teachings, the less he sounds like a peace-and-love guru and the more he sounds like a pimp.

Yes, it looks like this Charlie fella took the pimpin' playbook and ingeniously rewrote it for a generation of girls pissed off at their folks. As he watches Pussycat sincerely spew this fella's horseshit, Cliff tries to imagine where she came from. If in the fifties he'd followed through with his intentions to give the pimping game a whirl, he never would have gotten

303

close to a pretty, obviously educated gal like this one. But this whole *hippie shit* put the whole world outta whack. Now she's offering up her snatch for a lift to Chatsworth.

Girls who, before, maybe gave you a hand job at the drive-in will now fuck you *and* your friend.

Where those French dudes supplied their girls with champagne, lipstick, pantyhose, and Max Factor, this Charlie dude supplies his with acid and free love and a philosophy that ties it all together.

It's kinda brilliant, Cliff thinks. *I'm kinda lookin' forward to meeting this Charlie fella.*

"So how'd you meet this guy?" Cliff asks.

"Charlie?"

"Yeah, Charlie."

"I first met Charlie when I was fourteen," Pussycat tells him. "I was living in Los Gatos, California, when my father picked him up hitchhiking."

"Wait a minute," a surprised Cliff asks. "You met Charlie through your father?"

"Yeah," Pussycat says. "He picked him up on the side of the road, gave him a lift, then took him home for dinner."

She continues, "So we had dinner. And we were definitely attracted to each other, so we snuck outta the house that night once everybody went to bed. And we fucked in the backseat of my dad's car and then drove off."

Wow, Cliff thinks, *that's a bold motherfucker. Steal a guy's car and his hot little piece of ass fourteen-year-old daughter? Doesn't just fuck her in the night. That would be plenty rude enough. But steals the guy's car and runs off with her?*

Guys get fucking shotgunned from fathers for pullin' far less shit than that. That's a free-of-charge fuckin' murder right there, boy. No cop would arrest you, and no jury would convict you.

"So, what happened?" Cliff asks Pussycat.

"Well, we had two fun days on the road. But then Charlie told me I had to go back. Charlie said my parents probably got the cops looking for me. And if we go any further we'll cross the state line and he can't do that in a stolen car."

This fuckin' dude knows his shit, Cliff thinks.

The Los Gatos girl continues explaining to the Hollywood stuntman: "But Charlie said if I want to be with him, what I gotta do is go back home. Go back to school. Back to my room. Back to watching TV with my family. And then— marry the first jerk I meet. Because once I marry some jerk, I immediately emancipate myself from my parents.

"So I marry some bozo, then I send word to Charlie I'm emancipated. He sends word to me where I can meet him. I split from Dumb Shit and meet up with Charlie."

Cliff never had much sympathy for guys who let girls jerk them around, but even he feels sorry for the poor sap that married this piece of work.

"And then what?" Cliff asks.

"*Then,*" Pussycat explains, "a life that consisted of merely existing transformed itself into a life of purpose."

And it is at that point Debra Jo takes on the glassy-eyed look that all of Charlie's girls take on if they're allowed to babble on long enough.

"So all this happened because your dad picked up a hitch-hiker?" Cliff confirms.

She laughs her big, loud spastic laugh. "I guess so! I never looked at it that way, but yeah, I guess."

"So what does your father have to say about this turn of events?" a curious Cliff queries.

"Well, that's kind of a funny story. My mom left my dad because of it."

That's funny? Cliff thinks.

"And my dad tried to blow Charlie's head off with a shotgun."

Well, it's about fucking time, Cliff thinks.

"I take it he wasn't successful?" Cliff says.

This giggle puss shakes her head from side to side.

Cliff asks, "What happened?"

"What happened," Pussycat explains, "is Charlie *is* love. And you can't kill *love* with a shotgun."

"What does that mean in plain old American?" Cliff wants to know.

"It means Charlie turned my dad's hate to love." Pussycat goes on to describe, "Charlie told my dad he was ready to die, and if it was to be today, so be it. My dad calmed down. Charlie ended up turning my dad on that night. Then he had one of the girls with him—Sadie or Katie, I'm not sure which, I wasn't there—suck his cock. And when they parted the next morning, they parted as friends."

"Turning him on?" Cliff asks. "What does that mean?"

"They dropped acid."

"Your dad dropped acid with the guy that ruined his life?"

"My dad dropped acid with the dude who showed him how groovy life could be," she says. "Later my dad asked Charlie could he join the Family."

"Holy shit, you gotta be fuckin' kidding me!" Cliff exclaims.

Pussycat shakes her head no, she isn't kidding. Then clarifies, "But Charlie thought that was too weird. He said, 'Jesus Christ, we can't do that, he's Pussycat's fucking father.' So my dad isn't a member of the Family, but he's a friend of the Family."

After hearing Pussycat's wild story, Cliff can't help but have a level of respect for this Charlie fella. I mean, manipulating a bunch of hippie-girl runaways, that's one thing. Cliff could probably do that. But Cliff never held much sway with irate shotgun-toting fathers.

So Cliff asks, to sum up, "Okay, let me get this straight: A dude picks up a hippie hitchhiking? He takes the hippie home for dinner with his wife and his fourteen-year-old daughter? The hippie fucks the fourteen-year-old girl and takes off with her in the dude's car? The same car that gave him a lift? Because of the hippie, the daughter gets married at fifteen and then runs off with the hippie? The dude's wife leaves him due to all the chaos he caused by giving that fucking hippie a ride? The dude tracks the hippie down with a shotgun, but instead of blowing his head off, he later drops acid and parties with the hippie? And then later asks to be one of the hippie's disciples?"

Pussycat nods her head. "I'm telling you, Cliff, Charlie's a far-out cat. You're gonna dig 'em, and I know he's gonna dig the fuck outta you."

As Cliff turns all of his attention back on the road, he admits, "Well, I gotta say, I am rather curious to meet this Charlie fella."

Chapter Twenty

Sexy Evil Hamlet

While Rick Dalton, with the use of his reel-to-reel tape recorder, is going over the lines for the next scene, he hears a knock on his trailer door. He pushes the pause button on the machine and the tape reels stop in mid-rotation.

"Yes?" he says to the door.

"Hello, Mr. Dalton," the second-second assistant director says. "If you're ready, Sam would like to have a word with you on set."

"I'll be right out," Rick tells him.

Rick looks around his trailer. *Oh shit, I'm gonna hafta clean this place up before I leave*, he thinks. *And I'm gonna hafta come up with a good excuse why the window's broken.* The actual reason the window is broken is that when he entered the trailer after performing the last scene he shot, he was so angry with himself, he flung his cowboy hat across the room so hard he broke the window. The reason he was so angry with himself was due to an embarrassing moment on set when he kept fucking up his lines. Now, actors go up on their lines all the time. But the reason it caused Rick anguish was how it made him look. For three hours last night, Rick worked hard learning his lines. Rick knew he had a lot of lines to learn for today's shoot. Professionals know their lines, and Rick is a professional.

But professionals don't usually drink eight whiskey sours till they pass out drunk, not remembering how they got to bed. Now, *some* acting professionals do do that. But over the years they've learned how to handle it. But those actors (Richard Burton and Richard Harris) are professional drunks. Rick's still an amateur.

In the generation before drugs and weed became de rigueur among SAG members, alcohol was the monkey on most of their backs. Now, a lot of them started drinking for the same reasons their children would take drugs. They would just drift into it as an escape, till it got out of hand. But some came by their alcoholism honestly.

You must remember a lot of leading men of the fifties served in World War Two. And a lot of men who became actors in the late fifties and early sixties served in Korea. And a lot of those men saw things during the war they could never unsee. And since their generation understood this, their alcoholism was tolerated, to a large degree.

Both World War Two hero Neville Brand and classic World War Two dogface Lee Marvin were allowed to be drunk on set without the insurance company closing down the production. As Marvin got older, he seemed more and more haunted by the ghosts of the soldiers he killed on the battlefield. During the climax of his 1974 western, *The Spikes Gang*, when Marvin's character is supposed to shoot his young co-star Gary Grimes (the young lad from *The Summer of '42*), apparently Grimes's look or age or both brought to mind a young soldier Marvin killed during the war. The Oscar-winning tough guy sat in his trailer and drank himself into a stupor in order to have the courage to face what he had done and what he must now pretend to do. And the proof is in the pudding. The rest of *The Spikes Gang* is an okay seventies' western. Enjoyable enough to watch, but not memorable enough to stay in the mind. Except for that climactic violent shoot-out and the vicious expression on Marvin's totem-pole face.

In George C. Scott's leading-man actor's contract was a stipulation that three days of the production would be lost due to the actor's alcoholism.

Before he practically became a skid-row case in the seventies, even Aldo Ray's excessive drinking was somewhat tolerated by film production companies.

Rick Dalton has no such excuses. His drinking is caused by a three-way combination of self-loathing, self-pity, and boredom.

Rick grabs Caleb's hat, slides into Caleb's brown rawhide fringe jacket, and exits the trailer, making sure the second-second AD doesn't get a good look at the mess he made out of his acting trailer. As the crew hustles and bustles and horses clop their hooves in the dirt, Rick is led down the main street of the Royo del Oro western-town movie set and delivered back to Caleb DeCoteau headquarters, the Gilded Lily saloon. As Rick walks through the batwing doors, he sees the crew setting up the camera on one side of the set. Opposite the 35mm camera lens stands Sam

Wanamaker by himself, next to a handsome high-back mahogany chair. His director summons him over with a hand gesture. "Hey, Rick, come over here a minute, I want to show you something."

"Sure thing, Sam," Rick says, as he double-times it over to Mr. Wanamaker.

Sam stands behind the sturdy wooden chair, lays his hands on the back of it, and says, "Rick, this is the chair from which you'll make your ransom demands for Mirabella."

"Well, great, Sam," Rick drawls. "That's a damn good-lookin' chair."

"But I don't want you to think of it as a chair," Sam corrects.

"You don't want me to think of it as a chair?" a perplexed Rick repeats.

"No, I do not," Sam says.

"What do you want me to think of it as?" Rick questions.

"I want you to think of it as a throne. The throne of Denmark!" he concludes.

Having not read *Hamlet*, Rick has no idea Hamlet was Danish, so he doesn't comprehend the "throne of Denmark" reference.

He repeats to his director, somewhat incredulously, "The throne of Denmark?"

"And you are a sexy evil Hamlet," Sam says with flourish.

Oh Christ, this fucking Hamlet horseshit again, Rick thinks.

But instead of saying that, he just repeats what Sam said. "Sexy evil Hamlet."

Sam points at him with a strong index finger and says,

"Ex-act-ly," as if he's saying, *Eureka!* Then Sam continues with his own Shakespearean performance. "And little Mirabella is your pint-sized Ophelia."

Rick's not sure who Ophelia is, but he assumes she's a character in *Hamlet*, so he just nods along as Sam continues his subtextual *Hamlet* web-spinning. "Caleb, Hamlet. Both in control. Both in power."

"Both in power," Rick repeats.

"Both mad," Sam says.

"Both mad?" Rick asks.

Sam nods his head yes. "In Hamlet's case, due to the murder of his father at the hands of his uncle." Then, as an aside adds, "Who's also fucking his mother."

"Actually, I didn't know that," Rick mumbles under his breath.

"And in Caleb's case—syphilis," Sam says.

"*Syphilis*?" Rick says, surprised. "I got syphilis? I'm crazy?"

Sam nods his head in the affirmative to each question.

"Look, Sam," Rick reminds him, "I told you I ain't read much Shakespeare."

With a dismissive wave of his hand, Sam assures Rick, "That's not important. All you have to do is *seize* the throne."

"Seize the throne?" Ricks repeats.

"You've got to *rule* Denmark," Sam declares.

I guess Hamlet is Danish, Rick thinks.

And Sam finishes his Prince of Denmark analogy: "And you're going to rule it *violent*, rule it *cruel*, you're going to rule it like a cowboy De Sade, but you're going to *rule*!"

De Sade? Who's that, wonders Rick, *another character from Hamlet?*

312

Sam continues with his directorial pep-talk performance. "Mirabella is the most precious thing in the world to these Lancer men."

"She's a beautiful girl," Rick interjects.

"She's purity personified," Sam counters. "And these hard men, who've lived these hard lives, worship this little girl. And now the worst thing that can possibly happen has happened. You, an unscrupulous scoundrel, have taken the most precious shining jewel of their lives! And now you must impress upon them beyond a shadow of a doubt that you will kill her like *that*"—Sam snaps his fingers, and Rick snaps his fingers in response—"unless they dance to your tune. Got it?" the director asks his actor.

"Got it!" the actor answers.

Then, with one final theatrical gesture, Sam points at the wooden chair. "Caleb, assume the throne of Denmark."

Rick steps past his director and lowers himself into the seat of the chair, then, once seated, grips the arms of the chair with his hands, straightens his spine, and does his best to mimic the posture of a king on a throne.

Sam's face lights up, as he declares to the set and the crew, "Behold, Prince Hamlet!"

Rick doesn't understand three-quarters of what Sam just said, but he appreciates Sam's enthusiasm. And apparently Sam has forgotten Rick's fumbling with his lines earlier. The director turns away to deal with his crew, while Rick sits on his throne, goes over the lines in his head, and tries to think of himself as the Prince of Denmark.

The eight-year-old actress playing Mirabella enters the saloon, eating an onion bagel slathered in white fluffy cream cheese, which smears all over her face every time she takes a bite.

"I thought you said you didn't eat on set?" Rick asks her.

"I *said* I don't eat lunch when I have a scene *after* lunch, because it makes me sluggish," she corrects, "but by three or four I hafta eat something or my power will crash."

"Well, you ain't sittin' in my lap till you finish eating that monstrosity and wipe your fingers," he tells her. "I don't want you getting that white shit in my wig."

"You're just jealous you can't have a bite," she teases.

"No shit," he says. "I ain't been able to eat all fuckin' day with this Cowardly Lion shit all over my face. Every bite of chicken I ate during that earlier scene was coated in hair."

That makes the little girl giggle.

"But I gotta admit—that not-eating-lunch idea, especially when you have a scene later when you hafta eat, that ended up being a strong choice."

"See, I told ya."

The 1st AD, Norman, walks over to the two thespians and instructs Mirabella to sit in Rick's lap. She ditches the bagel and climbs aboard. Then hair and wardrobe come by and start fussing and adjusting both actors, preparing them for the take. After vanity sciences finish their priming and shove off, the two actors wait for Sam to finish talking to the crew and give them the cue to start the scene. However, there's a problem with the harsh daylight coming in through the big saloon picture window. So the director holds up the scene while one of the grips tapes a tan gel to the window to cut down the harshness of the afternoon sun.

While the little girl sits in Rick's lap, waiting to perform their first scene together, she asks her scene partner, "Caleb . . . can I ask you a question?"

"Shoot," he says.

"If Murdock Lancer doesn't pay the ransom, or if something happens to the money," she asks, "would you really kill me?"

"But he does pay the money," Rick says matter-of-factly.

"Jeez Louise," she rolls her eyes and says in exasperation, "I'm not talking to Rick, who's read the script, *I'm talking* to *Caleb*, who doesn't know what's going to happen till it happens. So again, *Caleb*, if Murdock Lancer doesn't pay the ransom, would you kill me?"

"Absolutely," he answers immediately.

She's a little surprised by the lack of hesitation in his answer. "Really? Absolutely? No question, no hesitation?"

"None whatsoever," he answers. "That's my thing when I play villains. I make them no-bullshit, real, real bad guys. Like, I did that horseshit *Tarzan* show with Ron Ely. Now, that show's horseshit, but the guy I played was a real bastard. I played a poacher—you know what a poacher is?" he asks the child.

She shakes her head no.

"It's a guy who kills wild animals he shouldn't," he explains. "So I enter the show carrying a flamethrower, setting the jungle on fire so I can stampede the animals to the area where I can kill 'em. Like I said, that show ain't shit, but I dug playing that fuckin' bastard. And same thing here. I commit to Caleb's cruelty. I think it's a strong choice."

Listening to his explanation, she nods her head; then, when he's finished, she offers up her interpretation.

"Well, naturally I understand what you're talking about. I mean, you are the villain of the piece, so your character has storytelling concerns that my character doesn't have. But putting aside the label 'villain,'" she makes air quotes around the word "villain" and continues, "you're still a character, and characters can be affected by a wide array of things that can cause them to act *out* of character."

This is an interesting train of thought, Rick thinks, and he twists his upper body a little closer to her, to indicate he's giving her his full attention.

She gives an example of where she's coming from. "I mean, the way you talk in our big scene we're doing to-morrow, it sounds like you kinda like me. Not this scene," she quickly clarifies. "This scene you don't know me yet. I'm still just Murdock Lancer's little girl. But in our big last scene, we seem to know each other more."

"Well, yeah," he explains, "we've spent a couple of days and nights together on horseback ridin' into Mexico."

"Exactly my point," the little girl insists. "And . . . apparently . . . you like me?"

"Apparently," he concedes.

She fixes her eyes on him, and the moment Trudi does that, there's an audible *click* sound in the air. It might have just been one of the land-pirate extras playing with the ham-mer of his pistol, but the timing was exact.

"What do you like about me?" she asks him.

He gets exasperated at having to be this clever, and says, "Oh, I don't know, Tru—"

She cuts him off before he can say her real name. "Mira-bella!" she interrupts.

Correcting himself, he repeats with contrition, "Oh, I don't know, Mirabella."

"No, that's a cop-out, man. You know. If Caleb likes me, he knows why." Then she instructs, "And you *should* know why."

Rick says, "He likes—"

"*You* like," she interjects.

He rolls his eyes but goes along with the rules of the game as she has decided it must be played. "Excuse me," he corrects himself, "*I like* the fact I don't hafta treat you like a child."

"Ooh, great choice." She claps her hands together in mini applause. "I like that answer."

He smirks. "I bet you do."

Pointing her finger to emphasize her words, she says, "So to get back to my original question: You *will* kill me . . . but you don't *want* to?"

"No," he concedes.

"No *what*?" she fishes.

He gives in and tells her what she wants to hear, and slowly says, "No, I don't want to kill you—"

Then she fires back quickly, "But you will?"

"Yes, I will," he says with conviction.

She holds for a beat, then asks with eyebrows raised, "Are you sure?"

Her question makes him blink.

"Yes . . . I'm *pretty* sure."

Her face lights up. "Oh, so you're just *pretty* sure now, so maybe not?"

"Maybe," he confesses.

Then, in a quiet secret voice, she says, "Do you want to know what I think happens?"

With just a touch of comic bite, he says, "Well, I know you want to tell me, so why don't you tell me."

She continues to talk in her quiet secret voice, but she does get caught up in the momentum of the web she's spinning. "Well, I think you *think* you could kill me. And you tell the other land pirates you could kill me. And you tell yourself you could kill me. But if push came to shove, and you had to do the thing you said you'd do, kill me—you couldn't do it."

"Okay, smarty-pants," he says, "why not?"

"Because," she tells him, "you realized you've fallen in love with me. And you pick me up in your arms and carry me to your horse. And we ride full out—Pony Express style—to the nearest preacher. And at the barrel of a gun, you make him marry us."

That makes Rick smile, but in a mocking way. "Oh, I do, do I?" he says skeptically.

"Yes you do," she says assuredly.

"I'm not gonna marry you," he says dismissively.

"*You're* not going to marry me, or *Caleb's* not going to marry me?" she clarifies.

"Neither of us is marrying you," he tells her.

"Why?" she asks.

"You know why, you're too young," he says.

"Well, today—yeah, I'm too young. But this is western times. People had child brides all the time back then," she correctly explains to him. "I mean—back then—it was nothing to marry a girl thirteen years old."

"You're not thirteen, you're eight," he clarifies.

"And that means something to Caleb DeCoteau?" she asks incredulously. She reminds him, "Five minutes ago, you just talked about how you'd kill me, like *that*." She snaps her fingers to emphasize the word "that." "You told Scott you'd throw me down a fucking well. So killing an eight-year-old's okay, but marrying me, that's where Caleb DeCoteau draws the line?"

Rick's a little lost for a comeback. She sees this and smirks, telling him, "I don't think you've really thought this through."

"Of course I haven't thought this through," he says defensively. "This is your harebrained idea."

"It's not harebrained. It might be *provocative*," she admits, "but it's not harebrained."

Rick gets exasperated and starts to tell her how uncomfortable this whole conversation is making him. "Trudi, I'm not comfortable with—"

But she interrupts him before he can finish. "Jeez Louise, Rick, we're not doing it! It's just a simple character thought experiment. They do it all the time at the Actors Studio. The script is the script. And we're doing the script. In the script, Lancer *does* pay the money. So you never have to make this choice. In the script, Johnny kills you, so none of this will ever happen. But at the Actors Studio they ask the question: What if the script didn't say that? Then what would your character do? Then what choice would your character make? It's simply about understanding who your character is when they're not dictated by the text."

"Well, maybe, just maybe, I don't wanna get married," he counters.

"Well, you see now," she gestures with her hand, "that's a choice." Investigating further: "So then, it's not about my age. And it's not you don't love me—"

He interrupts, "I never said I loved you."

She completely dismisses his last statement. "Don't be ridiculous, of course you love me. So, it's not my age, and it's not you don't love me, it's just Caleb's not a marrying-type guy, right?"

He shrugs. "Yeah, I guess."

"So we're just shackin' up?"

"That's not what I said."

"Well, it just stands to reason," she states logically. "We're together, we're in love, we're not married, so we're shackin' up. I can do that." Then clarifies, "For a little while. But at some point I'd *make* you marry me."

Skeptical, he repeats, "You'd *make me*?"

"Yeah," she explains, "that would be a huge part of our dynamic."

"What would be a huge part?" he asks.

She explains, "That you're the boss, you run the gang. They do whatever you say without question. However, when nobody's around? *I'm the boss!* And you do *whatever* I tell you."

I can't fucking believe this little midget, Rick thinks.

"Oh, I do, do I?"

"Yes, you do."

"And *why* do I do whatever you say?"

"Because of a power I have over you. If I didn't have this power, you'd've thrown me down the well, like you said you would. But it's okay, you *like* the power I have over you. I

320

mean, I'm *the boss*, but I'm a good *boss*, and I would never use my power in a negative way against you. Because I love you. Not as much as you love me. But I still love you."

"Okay," he asks, "what if I don't?"

"What if you don't what?"

Challenging her theory: "What if I don't do what you tell me to?"

"Now, remember," she reminds him, "I would never reveal the power I have over you in front of the gang, or anybody else for that matter. To the world, you're in charge."

"Okay, I get that," he tells her. "But you said, I do whatever you tell me to, right?"

"Yes," she says. "Like a dog. It's a command. And you must obey."

"Really?" he says, smirking. "What if I don't?"

She emphasizes, "But you do."

"Now who's a slave to the text," he counters. "You wanna play *What if?* What if I don't?"

"Well . . ." She thinks about it for a moment. "It stands to reason that there would be a few times—at first—you didn't. And that's when I had to punish you."

"You punish me?" he asks.

She nods her head yes, then concludes, "And after I'm through punishing you, you always do what I want."

And it is at that moment, as Rick is trying to think of something to say to that, that Sam Wanamaker yells to his actors, "Action!"

And Caleb and Mirabella act out the scene.

Chapter Twenty-One

Lady of the House

Squeaky, of all the girls at Spahn Ranch, enjoys an enviable position. The women at the ranch hold a second-class citizenship inside "The Family"; they're definitely considered inferior to the men. But Charlie makes it a point that they are also inferior to the dogs that live on the ranch. Whenever a Family woman wants to eat a bowl of food, she has to offer it to a dog first. Almost none of the females hold any position of authority (least of all Mary Brunner, the first member and the mother of Charlie's child, Pooh Bear).

I say "almost" because two females do hold a special place inside of the Family's hierarchy. One is "Gypsy," who, at thirty-four, is by far the oldest of the Family women. Gypsy's position amounts to an officer in charge of recruitment. Whenever a young lady or man is lured to the ranch, the first stop is to introduce them to Gypsy.

But it is the pixieish Squeaky who holds the closest thing to an authority position inside of the Family's social structure. The reason the Family can stay at Spahn Ranch is due to a deal Charlie made with the property owner, George Spahn. And it is Squeaky's responsibility to take care of George.

George Spahn is an eighty-year-old man, who for decades used to rent his movie ranch, with its back-lot western-town main drag, to Hollywood for movie and TV productions. Back in the day, the Lone Ranger, Zorro, and Jake Cahill rode their horses down the Spahn Ranch main drag. But in recent days, Hollywood has gone elsewhere, and the former movie set has fallen into disrepair. It is still used from time to time for photo shoots for magazines and album covers (the James Gang shot an album cover there). The ranch still has horses, and they still offer follow-the-leader type horseback rides to families through the Santa Susana Canyons.

But now the only movies shooting at the ranch are dirty movies with a western theme or grade-Z Al Adamson exploitation flicks. Also, George Spahn has gone nearly blind. The old man who was forgotten by the industry has found companionship in Charlie Manson's "Family." For the most part, he stays in his little house, which is perched on a hill, overlooking the western-town back lot. The house is cluttered to the gills with old western memorabilia, which George can no longer see, representing the ranch back in its heyday: Framed movie posters of old westerns that used George's ranch as a location, and photos faded from direct sunlight of older actors who shot at the ranch. A western-saddle collection and even a couple of actual George Montgomery–sculpted cowboy and Indian statues.

And presiding over George and the whole household is Squeaky. And when it comes to taking care of George, Squeaky has proved both adept and invaluable.

This has allowed her an autonomy inside the Family dynamic that other ranch women can only dream about. For one, she stays in the house. And she has positioned herself as "the lady of the house." A position even George doesn't challenge. It might be George's ranch, but at some point it became Squeaky's household. The other girls have to do ranch work and dumpster-dive. Squeaky has to cook for George, dress George, take care of his house, and keep him company. The other girls eat rancid garbage, stale bread, ugly vegetables, bruised and rotten fruit, and sometimes have to blow or fuck supermarket employees for the privilege to pick through their trash. Squeaky cooks and eats real food that George buys. Sure, she has to throw a fuck George's way every so often and jerk him off every once in a while. But she doesn't really mind that much. Besides, she'd much rather monkey around with George than fuck those sleazy biker assholes that hang around the ranch. But also, since George plays the country-music radio station all day, Squeaky is really the only Family member with a connection to the outside world. But along with eating real food that comes out of a refrigerator as opposed to a garbage dumpster, the most enviable thing about Squeaky's position, ensconced inside the house with George, is her television privileges.

Charlie doesn't let his kids watch television. When they were children and their parents forbade or restricted their television viewing, they claimed it would rot their brain. Charlie says it will steal their soul.

The truth of the matter is, the only real way Charlie can keep control of these kids is if he controls their environment, and their reality. Charlie isn't worried about them watching TV shows. The allure of *The Beverly Hillbillies*, *Gomer Pyle*,

Get Smart, and *Gilligan's Island* isn't going to challenge his authority. It's the commercials (the real opium of the masses) that Charlie worries about. The seductive reinforcement of forbidden fruit, which they once enjoyed but have now forsaken. He doesn't need short films, made by the geniuses of Madison Avenue, produced with the sole aim to entice, to remind his kids of the life they've left behind. In head-to-head competition with the parents that they distrusted and resented, Charlie would win. In direct competition with the establishment they despised, Charlie would win. In direct competition with a philosophy contrary to Charlie's, Charlie would win. But in direct competition with the remembered pleasures of *Tootsie Rolls*, *Froot Loops*, *Clark Bars*, *Hires root beer*, *Kentucky Fried Chicken*, *Revlon lipstick*, *CoverGirl makeup*, and *Flintstones chewable vitamins*, at some point Charlie would lose.

But Squeaky can watch all the television she wants.

While it may have been the offer of sex with Squeaky that initially sealed the deal with George Spahn, in practice, it's Squeaky's caregiving that makes their position at the ranch secure. Squeaky keeping the old man company. Dressing him, taking him out on walks, cooking for him, watching TV with him, describing to the blind old man what the Cartwrights are doing when they watch *Bonanza*.

But today Charlie and a large group of the kids are away in Santa Barbara. So as they say, when the cat's away, the mice play.

Squeaky invited a group of kids up to the house to watch TV. Seeing as it's Saturday afternoon, they're watching the

Dick Clark rock block on ABC. First *American Bandstand*, hosted by Dick himself, and then the Dick Clark–produced show *It's Happening*, hosted by Paul Revere and the Raiders. Today's guests are Canned Heat.

As befits her position in the house, the freckle-faced Squeaky is sitting in George's comfy reclining chair, in full recline mode, bare ghost-white legs sticking out of Levi's cutoffs stretched out in front of her, watching the television screen through dirty bare feet. The other five Family members, passing a joint amongst each other, lounge on the couch and the floor.

On the television, the theme song to *It's Happening*, performed by Paul Revere and the Raiders, plays out of the little TV speaker, as the show's opening bumper flashes by. It consists of black-and-white footage of Paul Revere and lead singer Mark Lindsay in dune buggies, hopping and bounding over sand dunes rather recklessly (so recklessly Mark Lindsay almost killed himself filming this opening).

While everybody taps their foot and nods their head to the groovy song, Squeaky hears, in the distance, a car pull up to the entrance of the ranch. Immediately, the little woman pushes herself out of recline mode, and her bare feet hit the floor.

"That's a car," she says out loud. She grabs the big chunky remote control, clicks the volume button two times, and listens with intent. She hears distant engine noise and the sound of tires on dirt. "That's a strange car," she deduces.

The young woman snaps out a military-like command: "Snake, go see who's outside."

"Snake," who is the youngest of the Family girls, plops

off the couch and walks from the living room through the kitchen to look out the screen door. The young girl peers through the dirty screen as her eyes search out the automobile. George's house is located on top of a hill at one end of the ranch. From her high perch, Snake can see the whole property. She looks down what's left of the old western movie set and at the beginning of the main drag to where people park their cars. That's where she sees the big vintage yellow-cream-colored Cadillac.

"Do you see anything?" Squeaky squawks from the living room.

"Yeah," Snake calls back, "a really bitchin' yellow Coupe de Ville. It's some old-looking dude in a Hawaiian shirt who just gave Pussycat a ride home," Snake reports to Squeaky.

From the other room: "Did he just give her a lift?"

"Nope," Snake informs her. "She's bringing him down to the ranch to meet everybody. Gypsy just came out to greet them."

Squeaky reclines back in her chair and hits the volume button on the boxy plastic remote, turning the sound on the TV up again. "Stay by the door and tell me if he starts coming this way."

Snake watches Pussycat and the Hawaiian guy talk to Gypsy, as, little by little, other female members of the group join the circle. From Snake's perspective, they all seem sociable, and she can hear laughter and giggles from time to time. Even "Tex" Watson rides up on horseback along with Lulu, speaks a bit to the Hawaiian guy, then rides off.

"What's goin' on?" Squeaky demands.

"The Hawaiian guy seems to be okay," Snake reports.

"Everybody's talkin' all friendly. Tex even came over and checked him out, then rode away with Lulu."

"Keep looking," is Squeaky's order. "If he comes this way, let me know."

Then, about ten minutes after Tex and Lulu ride away, Snake spies a change in dynamic between the Family girls and the strange older male in the Hawaiian shirt. Now the laughing and giggling seem to have stopped. As does the loosey-goosey hippie-dippy body language of the Family girls. They start becoming still, stiff, and defensive. Then Snake sees the Hawaiian guy look up toward the house and even gesture toward it with his finger.

"Something's up," Snake relays. "The girls are acting weird, and the Hawaiian guy is pointing toward the house."

"Motherfucker, I knew it," Squeaky says.

Clem, the chipped-tooth Family boy, asks Squeaky, "Want me to take care of him?"

Squeaky gives Clem a motherly smile and says, "Not yet, honey. I can handle it."

"Oh shit," Snake says.

Although she already knows the answer, Squeaky asks, "What?"

"The old Hawaiian guy's coming this way," Snake says with alarm.

Squeaky straightens out the reclining chair, rises from her throne, and walks into the kitchen to see what Snake sees through the screen door. And she sees the guy in the Hawaiian shirt walking alone toward the stairs that lead up to the door they're looking through.

Squeaky bites her lip and wonders, *Who the fuck is this dude?*

Then, to the other kids, "Okay, you guys, get the hell outta here. I'll handle this fucker."

As Squeaky stands by the screen door, the other kids file out of the house and walk single file down the staircase, passing the approaching stranger in the Hawaiian shirt.

They all give him dirty looks. Once the last Family kid has left the house, Squeaky replaces the hook on the screen door into its metal hole.

The Hawaiian guy climbs the stairs till he's standing on the other side of the filthy screen door, directly in front of Squeaky.

"So you're the mama bear?" he says in a good-natured fashion.

Squeaky considers giving him a sarcastic "aloha" but decides that would be too encouraging. So instead she says, as crisp and brittle as a snapping twig, "Can I help you?"

The Hawaiian guy sticks his hands in his back pockets and says, in a trying-to-be-personable way, "I hope so. I'm an old friend of George's. I thought I'd stop by and say hello."

With the two headlamps she has for eyeballs, she turns the full effect of her big, bulging, unblinking stare on this Hawaiian interloper.

"Well, that's very nice of you. Unfortunately, you picked the wrong time. George is taking a nap right now."

The Hawaiian guy removes his sunglasses and says, "Well, that is *unfortunate*."

"What's your name?"

"Cliff Booth."

"How do you know George?"

"I'm a stuntman. I used to shoot *Bounty Law* here."

"What's that?"

That makes the Hawaiian guy chuckle a bit.

"It's a western TV show we used to shoot out here," he says.

"You don't say?" Squeaky says.

"I do say." Jerking his thumb behind his back at the western town, he tells her, "I think I've been shot off of horses on every inch of that main drag. I think I've fallen into bales of hay from the roof of every building. And gone headfirst through the window of the Rock City Café probably one time too many."

"Really? That's fascinating." Her unblinking eyes challenge this interloper in a manner that would make the stare Ralph Meeker used to employ during acting scenes envious.

"Not bragging, mind you," the Hawaiian guy assures, "just letting you know I know the place."

With the unemotional authoritative demeanor of a highway patrolman, Squeaky asks the Hawaiian guy, "When was the last time you saw George?"

That stumps the intruder, and he has to think a moment. "Oh, let's see, ahh . . . I'd say . . . oh, 'bout eight years ago."

Finally, a smile creeps into the corners of her mouth. "Oh, I'm sorry. I didn't realize you two were so close."

As a fan of face-to-face sarcasm, the Hawaiian guy chuckles.

"Well, when he wakes up," she informs him, "I'll tell him you came by."

The Hawaiian guy looks down to the floor, puts his sunglasses back on for effect, then raises his head and looks through the screen door at her freckled face. "Well, I'd really like to say a quick hello—now—while I'm here. I came a long ways, and I don't really know when I'm gonna get back this way again."

Feigning sympathy, Squeaky says, "Oh, I understand. But I'm afraid that's impossible."

"*Impossible*," Cliff repeats incredulously. "Why is it *impossible*?"

Squeaky bursts out in one breath, "Because me and George like to watch TV on Saturday night—*The Jackie Gleason Show*, *The Lawrence Welk Show*, and *Johnny Cash*. But George finds it hard to keep awake that late. So I make him take a nap around now, so I don't get gypped outta my George TV time."

The Hawaiian guy smiles and takes off his glasses again and says through the screen door, "Look, Freckles, I'm coming in there. And with my own two eyes, I'm gonna take a good look at George. And this"—he taps the screen door right in front of Squeaky's face—"ain't stopping me."

Through the dirty kitchen screen door, Squeaky and the Hawaiian guy share a stare-off, until Squeaky suddenly gives one decisive blink of her eyelids. "Suit yourself."

Then she noisily flips the little hook lock off the screen door, turns her back on the Hawaiian guy, walks into the living room, and plops down in the chair again, leans back into the reclining mode, and picks up the remote and clicks the TV volume louder.

She turns her attention to George's little black-and-white television set that sits on top of his broken cabinet-style

Zenith. On the little screen at the moment, Paul Revere and the Raiders are hopping up and down, performing their song *Mr. Sun/Mr. Moon*.

When it comes to persuading George to do things, Squeaky is usually pretty good. But when it comes to persuading a skinflint blind old man to shell out money for a color television, it would appear Squeaky's powers of persuasion have their limits.

She hears the rusty hinge on the screen door squeak, as the Hawaiian guy pulls it open and steps inside. She doesn't turn her head his way, but she hears him enter the living room.

"Where's his bedroom?" he asks.

Using her bare foot, she points to the hallway. "Door at the end of the hallway," she barks. "You might hafta shake him awake. I fucked his brains out this morning." Then she turns toward the Hawaiian intruder and says with a smirk, "He may be tired."

The Hawaiian guy doesn't give the shocked look she was hoping for, or, for that matter, any reaction at all. He just moves past her, enters the hallway. Just before he disappears from her sight, she tells him, "Oh, Mr. Eight Years Ago? George is blind. You'll probably hafta tell him who you are."

That stops the Hawaiian guy for a beat, then he continues down the hallway, disappearing from sight.

On the little TV set, the Raiders finish their song and Mark Lindsay tells the people out there in TV land to stay tuned for "these Happening messages," followed by a promo for the ABC television show *The FBI*. Squeaky hears the Hawaiian stuntman lightly knock on George's bedroom door and ask, "George, are you awake?"

Squeaky yells loudly from the recliner, "Of course he's not awake, I fuckin' tole' you that! And he won't hear those little-girl knocks either. If your heart is set on waking him up, then open the door, step inside, and shake his fuckin' ass awake!"

She hears the old man's bedroom door open. She grabs the chunky clicker and clicks it twice, lowering the volume on Efrem Zimbalist Jr. narrating *The FBI* promo.

She hears the Hawaiian guy shake George and call his name, then she hears the confused old man wake up with a start. "Wait a minute! What's going on? Who are you? What do you want?"

She hears the Hawaiian guy explain, "It's okay, George. It's okay. Sorry to disturb you. It's Cliff Booth. I just stopped by to say hello and see how you're doin'."

A confused George asks, "Who's that?"

The Hawaiian guy further explains, "Well, I used to shoot *Bounty Law* here. I was Rick Dalton's stunt double."

"Who?" George squawks.

"Rick Dalton," the Hawaiian guy repeats.

George mumbles something Squeaky can't hear from the other room. Then she hears the Hawaiian guy repeat and emphasize the name "Rick—Dalton."

"Who's that?" George asks.

"He was the star of *Bounty Law*," the Hawaiian guy tells him.

Getting confused again, George asks, "Who are you?"

The Hawaiian guy answers, "I was Rick's stunt double."

Squeaky laughs when she hears George say, "Rick who?"

"It doesn't matter, George," she hears the Hawaiian guy in the other room tell George. "I'm an old colleague from the past, and I just wanted to make sure you're okay."

"Well, I'm not okay," George informs him.

"Whatsamatter?" the Hawaiian guy asks.

"I can't fuckin' see shit!" is George's reply, and that makes Squeaky laugh again.

The Hawaiian guy says something she can't hear, then George says something else she can't hear, then the Hawaiian guy says something she can't quite make out, but she can make out the words "little redhead."

Squeaky has no trouble making out George's reply: "I told you I can't see shit! How the fuck am I supposed to know what color the hair is of the girl who hangs around me all the time?"

Then she hears the Hawaiian guy mumble something and George tell him, "Look, I don't remember who you are, but thanks for coming and visiting me . . ." then whatever else the blind old man tells the Hawaiian guy is unintelligible to Squeaky. The next couple of exchanges are just mumbles in different tones, till she hears the Hawaiian guy's voice rise up because he's trying to get through to George. "So you've given all these hippies permission to be here?"

At that question, an angry George answers back, "Just who the fuck are you?"

She hears the Hawaiian guy try one more time to explain why he's here. "I'm Cliff Booth. I'm a stuntman. We used to work together, George. And I just want to make sure you're okay and all these hippies aren't taking advantage of you."

"Squeaky?" George asks. Then answers, "She loves me, sir."

That makes the little redhead smile. She grabs the chunky clicker, hits it three times, and watches Canned Heat perform *Going Up the Country* on *It's Happening*.

About six minutes later the Hawaiian guy comes out of the bedroom and is standing in the living room, looking down at her in the recliner. Without looking at him she asks, "Satisfied?"

He sticks his hands in his pockets and answers, "That wouldn't be the word I'd use."

Her head turns toward him, and she says with a twinkle in her eye and a smile on her face, "I think that's the word George woulda used this morning."

Cliff smirks at her saucy comeback and sits on the love-seat opposite her recliner.

"So you have sex with that old man regular, huh?"

"Yep," she says. "George is great. And I bet he can get hard and stay hard longer than you, Bronco Buster."

"Look," the Hawaiian guy says, "George is an old friend—"

She interrupts him, "He doesn't even know who the fuck you are!"

"Be that as it may," he follows up, "I just want to make sure he's happy and *aware*."

"He's *aware* I have sex with him five times a week and he's *happy* about it." Squeaky points to his room and says, "If you want to embarrass him, you can ask him directly."

The Hawaiian guy removes his sunglasses, leans forward,

and asks, "And the reason you have sex with George five times a week is because you love him?"

Squeaky gives this Hawaiian fucker one of her unblinking stares and tells him, "You bet I do. With all my heart, and everything that I have, and everything that I am, I love George. And whether or not you believe in my capacity for loving George means to me," she lowers her voice to a whisper, "less than nothing."

The Hawaiian fucker meets her unblinking glare with a sarcastic question: "So you're not talking to him about *changing wills* or anything legal like that, are you?"

That question makes Squeaky blink, once. But the blink doesn't break her composure or compromise her righteous indignation.

"No, I'm not talking to him about *changing wills*. I'm talking to him about marriage."

How do you like them apples, smartass?

Squeaky sums up, "So let me get this straight—the last time you saw George was the fucking *fifties*, and now all of a sudden you show up and you're gonna save 'em . . . from marriage? You're gonna save him from sex five times a week? Are you sure when you knew George you were his friend? Do you drive around saving *everybody* from marriage, or is there something special about *George*?"

The Hawaiian guy sits on the love seat listening to this, then says, "You know something . . . you have a point." So he stands up from the love seat and walks through the house and out the screen door and down the staircase. A satisfied Squeaky crosses her legs at the ankles and turns her attention back to the Dick Clark–produced music show.

Chapter Twenty-Two

Aldo Ray

Almeria, Spain
June 1969

As fifties' movie star Aldo Ray sat at the foot of the soiled mattress in the stuffy Spanish hotel room, sweat dripping down his hairy shoulders and back, he wasn't contemplating some of the wrong turns he'd made along the way that were responsible for him occupying this oppressive room. Nor did he torture himself about the days, *once upon a time . . . in Hollywood*, when he worked for directors like George Cukor, Michael Curtiz, Raoul Walsh, Jacques Tourneur, and Anthony Mann. He didn't stress about his long-gone swank apartment at the El Royale, or his little baby Porsche, which, fast as it was, was way too small for the barrel-built beefcake. Nope, sitting in the sweltering un-air-conditioned hotel room in Spain on his first night on location on a new picture, Aldo thought about the thing that Aldo always thought about every night about this time. A bottle of booze.

* * *

Whenever Aldo Ray did a movie on location, the crew, the cast, the hotel employees, and frankly anyone else who could be enlisted was put on *Aldo watch*. When Aldo was put up in a hotel or motel on a film location, he was basically under house arrest. He wasn't allowed to leave the hotel, for fear of him getting a bottle. He was banned from the hotel bar. He wasn't allowed to carry any money. And either he or the building entrances and exits were closely monitored. Every member of the production was given strict orders, in no uncertain terms, no matter how much he begged, pleaded, and cajoled, not to supply Aldo with booze. In David Carradine's autobiography, *Endless Highway*, he recounted the time he made the low-budget Fernando Lamas–helmed film *The Violent Ones* with Aldo. Mr. Carradine wrote about how if any young actor who knew and respected Mr. Ray from his early days did a film with him, they were basically given the job, *Take care of Aldo*.

By the summer of '69, Aldo had fallen pretty far from his former heights during the fifties starring opposite Bogart, Tracy and Hepburn, Rita Hayworth, Anne Bancroft, and Judy Holliday. What wasn't known at the time was how much farther he had to fall. By 1975 he wouldn't be able to handle any role that lasted longer than two days (the longest he could be counted on to stay sober).

As the seventies progressed and turned into the eighties, the man who was discovered by George Cukor—in a screen test that consisted of Aldo tossing playing cards into a hat—could only find employment for schlockmeisters like Al Adamson and Fred Olen Ray (no relation).

He was the first former Hollywood star to ever appear

in a seventies' porno film, making him (so far) the only former Hollywood star to win the best actor award at the Erotic Film Awards, for 1979's *Sweet Savage* with Carol (*Deep Throat*) Connors (in the eighties, Cameron Mitchell would appear in a porno film as well).

Aldo Ray was also the first former Hollywood star to be sued by the Screen Actors Guild for appearing in cheap non-union movies.

Since its inception, Hollywood had seen its fair share of former highfliers who fell on hard times, as evidenced by the films they were doing as opposed to the films they once did (Ramon Novarro, Faith Domergue, Tab Hunter, even poor Ralph Meeker). Still, none could really match Aldo Ray when it came to publicly played-out poignant pity. So as desperate as he was on that night in Spain during the summer of '69, twenty years later that night would seem like the "good ole' days."

But for Mr. Ray it sure as hell didn't seem like the good ole' days. It seemed like the same goddamn fucking night he faced every goddamn fucking night the big man didn't have a bottle.

On the same night, in the same hotel, in the same country, in a different un-air-conditioned room, Cliff Booth poured two fingers of room-temperature gin into a plastic hotel cup. The deep cut above his right eyebrow, which he'd received from the rifle butt of a Winchester earlier that day, was beginning to bleed again and run down his face and drip onto his sweaty wifebeater. Not only that, but his ballooning eyebrow was showing no sign of settling down. If it didn't begin to unpuff at least a little bit, he'd be useless tomorrow on set. Cliff stared at himself in the bathroom mirror. He touched his bulbous eyebrow to see if it still hurt. It did. What he needed to do was ice it, and he needed to do it pretty fast.

And while he was at it, a couple of cubes for the warm gin wouldn't be the worst thing in the world. It's not like he preferred the taste of chilled gin to room-temperature gin. To Cliff, gin tasted like lighter fluid, and gin over ice tasted like chilled lighter fluid. But the addition of a couple of cubes of ice did give one the appearance of drinking a cocktail, as opposed to the depressing sight that drinking warm gin out of a plastic cup provided by a cheap hotel thousands of miles away from home gave. As he walked over to the little table where the little plastic ice bucket the hotel provided sat, he glanced at the little television chained to a heating pipe. On the screen was a black-and-white Mexican melodrama from the early fifties starring Arturo de Córdova and María Félix emoting melodramatically in Spanish. Cliff had no idea who they were.

Cliff had traveled to Europe with his boss, Rick Dalton, and for the first time in a long while, Cliff was stunt-doubling for Rick again. This was the fourth European film they had done in rapid succession. The first two (*Nebraska Jim* and *Kill Me Quick, Ringo, Said the Gringo*) were westerns shot in Italy. The third, a James Bond–wannabe secret-agent flick called *Operation Dyn-O-Mite*, was shot in Athens, Greece. And this one, *Red Blood, Red Skin*, co-starring Telly Savalas and Carroll Baker, was being shot in Spain. When this film finished, Cliff and Rick would be heading back home to Los Angeles.

* * *

The two men enjoyed their whole five-month-long European sojourn tremendously. Rick loved all the attention the paparazzi gave him, and Cliff loved being a stuntman again. They shared a swank apartment in Rome with a really nice view of the Colosseum out the window. Rick was always going out to Italian eateries, swilling cocktails at nightclubs, and generally living the life of an American movie star in Rome, with Cliff as his trusty co-pilot. During their stay, Cliff scored a shitload of Italian pussy. Far more than Rick, but Rick was always pickier. To Cliff, pussy was pussy, but he did have a real fondness for Italian pussy. And while he preferred a naked Italian girl in his bed sucking his cock to sleeping alone with no girl in his bed, he much preferred those naked Italians be different girls. Cliff was never *that* hung up on what a girl looked like. As long as they let him bury his teeth in their ass and enjoyed sucking cock, as far as Cliff was concerned, they were beautiful.

However, the flight going home would be a little different than the flight going to Europe.

While working on the secret-agent movie in Greece, Rick had met a big dark-haired Italian starlet named Francesca Capucci. Then, as Cliff told his friends back home, "Out of the fucking blue, he fucking married the bitch." The minute Cliff realized where this was going, he knew that whatever the deal was that he and Rick shared was kaput. Rick wouldn't need him around, Francesca wouldn't want him around, nor would Rick be able any longer to afford to keep him around.

Now, Cliff wasn't selfish. If he felt Rick and Francesca were good for each other, he'd back out gracefully, no worries. And it wasn't like he thought Francesca was some evil femme fatale preying on his unsuspecting friend. He *thought* they were both a couple of idiots who committed to a massive life change without thinking it through. Cliff gave them two years. That was fine enough for her, but in a few years this was going to really cost Rick in alimony. So much so that he'd probably have to sell his house in the Hollywood Hills. And Cliff knew what that house meant to Rick. Rick was broody enough in *that* house. Rick Dalton living in a condo in Toluca Lake was going to be far worse.

Cliff snatched the small plastic ice bucket provided by the hotel off the little desk it rested on, as well as a hand towel off the bathroom towel rack. Then, opening his hotel room door, he proceeded to squeak and creak his way down the hall toward the ice machine. The filthy carpet under his feet had the consistency of Silly Putty. At the Hotel Splendido— the closest motel to the Wild West–looking rock formations that manage to make Almeria, Spain, pass for Arizona— every room had its door open. Since the establishment had no air-conditioning, every guest in every room had a loud box fan that the Spaniards provided.

As Cliff passed by Room 104, he quickly glanced inside and saw what looked like a very depressed barrel-built old man, a tent-like white linen shirt stuck to his sweat-covered back, sitting on the end of his bed next to the box fan, as he stared down into the filthy carpet beneath his feet.

That was Aldo Ray, Cliff thought as he passed by the doorway. *And that's the ice machine*, Cliff thought he saw at the end of the hall. He scooped a bunch of ice cubes into the plastic bucket that looked more like a wastepaper basket. Then, with his hand, he reached into the ice, yanked out four cubes, and put them in the white handtowel he'd brought with him. Placing the cold compress against his ballooning eyebrow, he trotted back toward his room.

As he passed Aldo Ray's room the second time, he shot a quick glance inside to make sure the big sweaty man was really indeed *Aldo Ray*. But this time, instead of looking down at the carpet, the *Men in War* star was looking right at him. Once Cliff was past the doorway, he heard the star's unmistakable raspy soft sandpaper-like voice call out to him, "Hey?"

The stuntman moved back into the actor's doorframe.

"You American?" that famous rasp croaked out.

"Yes," Cliff said as he held the towel with the ice against the right side of his face.

Aldo asked, "Are you workin' on this western?"

"Yes, I am, Mr. Ray," Cliff said.

That made Mr. Ray smile, and he stuck out five sausage fingers and said, "Call me Aldo. I'm in this picture too."

Cliff stepped inside the actor's room, crossed the difference between the doorway and the bed, and shook hands with the fifties' Warner Bros. leading man.

"Cliff Booth," said Cliff Booth. "I'm Rick Dalton's stunt double."

"Is Dalton in this picture? I knew Telly was and Carroll Baker was, but I didn't know about Dalton. Who's he play?" Aldo asked.

"He plays Telly's brother," said the stuntman.

Aldo guffawed, "Yeah, there's a real family resemblance.

343

Me an' Mantan Moreland might as well play fuckin' brothers."

That made both men laugh.

Both men had served in the Second World War (Aldo as a frogman for the Navy). Ray was about the same age as Booth. But looking at them together that night, you'd never know it. Cliff still had the body of a middleweight boxer, while Aldo Ray's barrel chest had turned into a barrel belly. That strong athletic frame he sported opposite Rita Hayworth in *Miss Sadie Thompson* had gone soft and his broad shoulders had rounded, giving him an ape-like posture. Cliff looked a good ten years younger than he really was, while Aldo looked a good twenty years older. The simian-like Aldo stared up at Cliff's face, finally noticing the huge eyebrow.

"Jesus, kid," Aldo blasphemed. "What the fuck happened to your face?"

"I got hit in the eye with a rifle butt earlier today," said Booth.

"What happened?"

"Well," Booth explained, "we were shooting out on those rocky cliffs, and the shot is, one of those banditos hits me in the face with a Winchester."

Booth continued, "But the Italian guy playin' the Mexican ain't never done no action like that before, so he kept hesitating and missing me by a mile. Five different takes, all no damn good. But each time I'm falling flat on my back on goddamn rock. So finally I go to the 1st AD—who's the only one of the Spanish crew to have halfway-decent English—'Tell this guy to just fuckin' hit me in the face, 'cause I can't take too many more of these rocky fuckin' falls,'" Cliff finished.

"Rang your bell, huh," Aldo stated more than asked.

Cliff shrugged. "It's the job. I'm Rick's *crash and smash*."

"You worked with him a long time?" Ray inquired.

"Rick?"

"Yeah, Dalton."

"Goin' on ten years now."

"Oh, you two must be pals?"

"Yeah, we're pals." Cliff smiled.

Aldo smiled back. "That's nice. It's good to have a buddy on set." Aldo asked Rick's double, "Didja know 'em when he did that George Cukor picture?"

"Yeah," Cliff said, "but I didn't work on it. That's the one film he did that didn't have any stunts."

"Yeah, it was some picture based on a big book at the time. Warner's dumped all their contract players in it. Some not so bad, Jane Fonda was in it—ever meet Hank Fonda?" Aldo asked.

Cliff said, "No."

"Anywho," Aldo continued, "Dalton was one of the ensemble cast members. Now, it was George Cukor who gave me my big break in pictures, with *The Marrying Kind* with Judy Holliday. Then he cast me in *Pat and Mike* with Hepburn and Tracy."

Suddenly switching gears: "You know who was in bit parts in both pictures?"

Cliff shook his head no.

"Charlie fuckin' Bronson," said Ray. "And he was even uglier then than he is now, if such a thing is possible."

Aldo went into his own head for a moment, like he was remembering what it was like working alongside Bronson,

345

back when *Aldo* was the star and Bronson was just a bit player.

After a moment's pause, Ray rasped, "I hear Charlie's doin' pretty good these days. Good for Charlie."

Then Ray jerked up his head toward Booth. "What was I sayin'?"

"Rick and George Cukor," Cliff reminded him.

"Yeah, yeah, yeah, of course—ever meet George Cukor?" Ray asked the stuntman. "Great fella," Ray declared. "Everything I have I owe to him."

"I hear he was the biggest queer in Hollywood," said Cliff.

"Well, George was homosexual," said Ray. "But I don't think he did much about it. He was kinda fat."

Then, as Aldo looked up at Cliff, he turned deep and philosophical. According to David Carradine's autobiography, that was a tendency for the big man.

"You know, people useta ask me all the time, since Cukor started me off, did he ever try anything? And the sad answer to that question is no. But I wish he did."

Aldo mused, "There was an emotional sadness to George that if I coulda cured, I woulda.

"But," Aldo sighed, "I'm afraid by the time I met 'em he was incurable. As far as I know, he was celibate his entire time in Hollywood. I think I got more cock in the Navy than he did his whole forty years in Hollywood."

Aldo paused, then said, "Fuckin' waste if ya ask me."

The big man paused again and asked again, "What was I sayin'?"

"Rick and George Cukor," Cliff reminded again.

346

"Oh yeah. So, Rick Dalton's workin' for Cukor on this dog of a picture. So Dalton's doin' a scene, right? Then all of a sudden Dalton cuts the scene, *cut cut cut cut cut cut*. Trust me, the whole damn set gulps. Nobody on a Cukor set calls cut but George. Kate fuckin' Hepburn wouldn't call fuckin' cut. But Rick Dalton calls fuckin' cut.

"So Cukor looks up from his director's chair and says, 'Is there a problem, Mr. Dalton?' And Dalton says, 'You know, George, I was thinking that right here would be a good place to take a dramatic pause. Whaddaya think?' And Cukor, who's as bitchy as a turtle is crunchy, says"—Aldo, with his raspy voice, tries to imitate Cukor's fey, erudite delivery—"'Mr. Dalton . . . it is my fervent belief that, up to now, your entire career has been one long dramatic pause.'"

The two sweaty he-men laughed it up in the stuffy Spanish hotel room. Rick was Cliff's best friend, but Cliff knew better than most that Rick was proficient in making an ass out of himself—especially back then.

Before Cliff's laughter died down, Aldo looked up at him, suddenly serious and sincere: "Hey, pal, I'm in a bad way. Can you get me a bottle?"

"Oh wow," Cliff said. "I'm sorry, Aldo, you know you're not supposed to drink. They sent out a memo to everybody on the production not to ever give you a bottle. No matter what you say, we're not supposed to give you alcohol."

Aldo sighed and shook his head in despair and said, "They don't let me carry any money. They told the hotel not to serve me. They got a guy watching the door. I'm under house arrest here."

Aldo looked up at Cliff, and his eyeballs grabbed Cliff's

347

eyeballs and pleaded. "Please . . . please, kid, I'm in a bad way. C'mon, be a pal. Please . . . please . . . don't make me beg . . . but I will."

Cliff walked back to his room, grabbed his bottle of gin, made his way back down the hall on the Silly Putty filthy carpet, and handed it to the man in Room 104. Aldo Ray took the bottle of gin from his benefactor and, holding it in his big catcher's mitt of a hand, stared at it intensely.

He's got a bottle.

He's going to be okay tonight.

He's going to drink the whole thing.

And all that is going to start in a moment.

Aldo looked up from the bottle to Cliff. Then he looked back down at the bottle of gin. Then back up to Cliff. His eyes narrowed and he asked, "Are you wearin' a wig?"

Just then Cliff remembered he still had his Rick wig on from earlier today. "Oh yeah, I forgot I still had this on." He took the wig off his head, revealing to Aldo his own blond hair for the first time. Cliff Booth gave the big man a wave and said before splitting, "Have a good night, Aldo."

Aldo Ray looked back at the bottle in his hand and said to the Beefeater fella on the label: "I will."

After killing Cliff's bottle of gin, Aldo was unfit for work the next day, and was put on the first plane home. The Spanish producers tried like hell to find out who supplied Ray with the booze, but thankfully for Cliff they never did. Cliff was so nervous he never even told Rick about it. At least, not until two years later.

"You did what?

"Cliff," Rick hipped him, "when they give you your SAG card at the fuckin' union office, they give you three rules: One, they gotta give you turnaround. Two, don't do any nonunion shoots. And three, if you ever do a film with Aldo Ray, under no circumstances give him a bottle."

If Cliff had to do it again . . . he'd do the same damn thing.

Chapter Twenty-Three

Drinker's Hall of Fame

Staring at himself in his makeup mirror, in his trailer on the *Lancer* set, Rick rubs a small cotton ball doused in spirit-gum remover across his phony mustache and upper lip. He's already removed his long-haired wig, and his natural chocolate-brown hair sits on top of his noggin in a sweaty mess. After thoroughly drenching his upper lip and filling his nostrils with the smell of alcohol fumes, he takes his two fingers and slowly, somewhat painfully, peels the fake horsetail from off his face and lays it down carefully on his makeup table.

On the small TV in his trailer, football star Rosey Grier, on his syndicated variety show *The Rosey Grier Show*, sings Paul McCartney's song *Yesterday*. Half-listening to the song, Rick grabs a jar of Noxzema Medicated Cold Cream, scoops out a big hunk with his fingers, and begins slathering it all over his face. Hearing a tiny *knock-knock* rap, he leans over in his chair, twists the handle on the trailer door, and pushes it open, revealing pint-sized Trudi Frazer standing on the pavement, looking up him. This is the first time Rick's seen what she looks like in her street clothes. Which, in this case, consists of a white button-down shirt with a crisp white collar under beige corduroy overalls. Rather than the twelve-year-old she pretends to be, the outfit makes her more resemble the eight-year-old little girl she actually is.

"Well, I'm leaving right now," she informs him, "and I just wanted you to know I thought you were excellent in our scene today."

"Aw gee, thanks, honey," he says modestly.

"No, I'm not just being polite," she assures him. "It was some of the finest acting I've ever seen in my whole life."

Wow, Rick thinks, that hits him harder than he would have imagined. This time the modesty isn't a put-on. "Well . . . thank you, Mirabella."

"It's after work," she reminds him. "You can call me Trudi."

"Well, thanks a bunch, Trudi," says the cold cream–faced Rick. "And you are one of the most excellent actresses—"

"Actor," she insists.

"Excuse me, *actor*, of any age, I've ever worked with," he sincerely tells her.

"Why, thank you, Rick," she says without cuteness.

"In fact," Rick builds on the compliment, "I have no doubt that the day will come that I brag to people that I got a chance to work with you."

"After I win my first Oscar, you *will* be bragging that you worked with me when I was only eight," Trudi says confidently. "And you'll tell everyone I was just as professional *then* as I am *now*." Then adding under her breath, just to make it clear, "'Now' meaning in the future, when I win an Oscar."

Rick can't help but smile at the moxie of this midget. "I'm sure I will, and I'm sure you will. Just hurry up and do it while I'm still alive to see it."

She smiles back. "I'll do my best."

"Like always," he says.

She nods her head yes. Then her mother's voice yells at her from the waiting car: "Trudi, come on now, stop bothering Mr. Dalton. You'll see him again tomorrow!"

Trudi, annoyed, spins in the direction of her mother and shouts back, "I'm not bothering him, *Mom*!" Gesturing theatrically at him with her arm, "I'm congratulating him on his *performance*!"

"Well, hurry it up!" her mother orders.

Trudi rolls her eyes and turns her attention back to Rick. "Sorry about that. Where was I? Oh, I remember . . . Bravo to you, sir. You did exactly what I asked. You scared me in that scene."

"Oh man, I'm sorry, I didn't mean to," Rick blurts out.

"No, don't apologize, that was what was so exciting about your acting," she stresses, "and consequently that's what made *my* acting so good. You didn't make me *act* scared. You made me *react* scared. Which is exactly what I asked you to do," she reminds him. "You didn't treat me like some little eight-year-old actress. You treated me like an actor colleague. And you didn't baby me. You tried to *win* the scene," she says with admiration.

"Well, thank you, Trudi," now falsely modest again, "but I don't think I *won* the scene."

"Well, of course you did," dismissing his protest. "You

had all the dialogue. But," she warns him, "in our big scene tomorrow, that's another story. So watch out!"

"You watch out," he warns her right back.

She sports a huge grin and says, "That's the spirit! Bye-bye, Rick, see you tomorrow." She waves at him.

He gives her a little salute and says, "Bye-bye, honey."

As Rick turns back around to face the makeup mirror, she starts to close the door for him, but before she completely closes it, she says in an undertone, "Know your lines tomorrow."

That turns Rick back around in his chair, not quite believing what he heard. "What was that?"

Trudi's little face looks at him through the small crack in the almost-closed trailer door. "I said, know your lines tomorrow. You know, I'm very surprised how many adults don't know their lines, when that's what they are paid to do," and adds, a little snot on the end of her observation, "I *always* know my lines."

Rick says back, "Oh, you do, do you?"

Emphasizing each word: *"Yes-I-do."* Then she quickly adds, "If you don't know your lines, I'm going to make you look bad in front of the crew."

Why, this little bitch, he thinks.

He asks her, "Are you threatening me, you little punk?"

"No, I'm fucking with you. Dustin Hoffman does it all the time. Nevertheless, it's not a threat, it's a promise. Bye-bye." She shuts the door before he can say anything back.

Trudi Frazer never did *win* an Academy Award.

But she was nominated three times. The first time was

in 1980, when she was nineteen and she received a best-supporting-actress nomination for playing Timothy Hutton's sort-of girlfriend in Robert Redford's *Ordinary People*. She lost to Mary Steenburgen for *Melvin and Howard*.

Her second best-supporting-actress nomination was in 1985, when she was twenty-four, for the role of Sister Agnes in Norman Jewison's *Agnes of God*. She lost the Academy Award to Anjelica Huston for *Prizzi's Honor*, but she won the Golden Globe for best supporting actress. Frazer's only nomination for the best-lead-actress Oscar was in Quentin Tarantino's 1999 remake of the John Sayles script for the gangster epic *The Lady in Red*. Frazer played thirties' brothel-prostitute-turned-bank-robbery-gang-leader Polly Franklyn, opposite Michael Madsen as public enemy number one, John Dillinger. Losing her last nomination to Hilary Swank in *Boys Don't Cry*.

Rick rooted for her every time.

Forty minutes later, Rick has wiped the cold cream off his face, combed his hair back into a half-ass version of his normal pompadour, climbed into his street clothes, and cleaned up the trailer from his earlier temper tantrum. He lights up a Red Apple cigarette and is getting ready to find Norman, the 1st AD, and tell him a horseshit story about how he accidentally broke the window, when another knock happens against his trailer door. He figures it's the 2nd AD, with tomorrow's call sheet telling him what time he has to be here. So he's a little surprised when he twists the doorknob and finds Jim Stacy standing outside his trailer.

"Oh, hey, man," says Rick.

"Hey, Rick, great job with that last scene, man," Jim Stacy says.

"Oh shit, well, you too, Jim," Rick replies, "and congratulations on the first day of your new show."

"First day of the pilot," Jim corrects.

Rick waves away Stacy's qualification. "Aw, horseshit, you know CBS is gonna pick it up. They wouldn't be spendin' so damn much money if they weren't."

"Famous last words," reminds Stacy.

"*And* . . . it's a good show," Rick adds.

"Well, it's definitely a better one after your two scenes," Stacy says. "Hey, Rick, I was wonderin', you wanna go out and get a drink tonight?"

"Well, shitfire!" Rick exclaims. "You know I do."

Stacy smiles.

"Where ya thinkin' 'bout?" Rick questions.

"I got a little place by my house in San Gabriel," Stacy explains. "They're kinda expecting me to stop by and celebrate my first day. I hope that ain't too far away for ya?"

"Shit, what'd I care," Rick tells him. "My car's in the shop, so my stunt double's giving me a ride."

"Will he mind?" Jim asks.

"No way, man," Rick assures him. "He's cool as hell, you should meet 'em."

"Well, let me get changed, wipe this pancake off my face so people don't think I'm some Kansas City faggot, and why don't you follow me on my bike to the bar?"

With Rick in the passenger seat and Cliff behind the wheel, they follow behind Jim Stacy driving on his motorcycle till he pulls into the parking lot of a bar painted barn red, with the colorful name "the Drinker's Hall of Fame." Painted on the red walls are comic caricatures of famous Hollywood drunks. W. C. Fields, Humphrey Bogart, Buster Keaton, and a drawing of Lee Marvin from *Cat Ballou*.

Jim Stacy pulls his motorbike up the gravel-covered driveway, then cuts off the engine. Cliff pulls Rick's Cadillac next to him. This is obviously one of James Stacy's watering holes.

The three macho guys enter the establishment. At eight in the evening, the dark bar isn't packed, but it's packed with regulars. The Drinker's Hall of Fame is a nostalgia-based cozy watering hole for San Gabriel locals, actors, and musicians. Memorabilia of famous Hollywood citizens who ruined their lives with booze litter the walls. The four biggest framed posters on the wall, the highest place of honor, are reserved for the bar's four patron saints.

W. C. Fields in his gray top hat, looking at a poker hand. Humphrey Bogart, looking sexy in his trench coat and snap-brim fedora. John Barrymore during his handsome silent-film days, showing off his famous profile. And the great stone-face Buster Keaton in his flat pork pie hat and black vest from his silent-movie-star heyday.

Other famous drinkers line the upper area of the bar, over the shelves of bottles, in framed black-and-white eight-by-tens that have turned yellow or brown. Some are publicity shots, some are from specific movies, and some are signed personally to the bar. Lee Marvin in his Liberty Valance white shirt and black vest, giving the camera a grinning leer (signed by Lee to the Hall of Fame). Sam Peckinpah, fiery bandanna on his head, standing next to a movie camera, pointing at something (signed by Sam to the bar). Beefcake Aldo Ray in a sweaty wifebeater in a still from *God's Little Acre* (signed by Aldo to the bartender, Maynard). A fairly recent photo of a big and jowly Lon Chaney Jr. (signed by Lon to the bar). Richard Harris from the movie *Major Dundee* (unsigned). "Big Mouth" Martha Raye staring at the camera with pop eyes and mouth wide open in a comic publicity still from the thirties (unsigned). And Richard Burton in a still from *Night of the Iguana* (unsigned).

Off in the left-hand corner of the bar, clustered around an old-fashioned typewriter, are four standing framed photographs of famous alcoholic authors: F. Scott Fitzgerald, Ernest Hemingway, William Faulkner, and Dorothy Parker (all unsigned).

Other themed bric-a-brac nestled on the shelves behind the bar include a W. C. Fields lamp, which consists of a comic caricature of Fields leaning drunk against a lamppost.

An Aurora model kit of the Wolfman (Lon Chaney Jr.) sits by a tip jar on the bar.

Attached to the men's room door is the Elaine Havelock psychedelic John Barrymore poster. On the ladies' room door is the Elaine Havelock psychedelic poster of Jean Harlow.

In the piano section of the bar, on the wall behind the piano, is a large three sheet of the new film *The Wild Bunch*, directed by regular and Hall of Fame member Sam Peckinpah (signed to the Hall of Fame by Sam, William Holden, and Ernest Borgnine).

On the wall in the area where the pool table is located is the Elaine Havelock psychedelic poster of W. C. Fields and

Mae West, a one-sheet for a new Lee Marvin movie called *Sergeant Ryker*, and that reprinted head-shop poster of the old Bogart flick *All Through the Night*.

Except for the four large posters of Fields, Bogart, Barrymore, and Keaton, none of the other posters are framed. They're just stuck on the walls with thumb tacks.

As the three fellows walk through the door, they hear the piano player playing O. C. Smith's *Little Green Apples*.

> *God didn't make Little Green Apples*
> *And it don't rain in Indianapolis in the summertime*
> *There's no such thing as Dr. Seuss, no Disneyland,*
> *no Mother Goose, no nursery rhymes*

Jim Stacy gives the man behind the piano a wave, and the man behind the piano gives Jim a head nod of recognition. Stacy walks Rick and Cliff up to the bar area, where he greets the bartender with a warm handshake across the bar.

"How ya doin', Maynard?"

The friendly barkeeper says, "How was your first day?"

Still clasping hands, Jim says, "Well, they want me back tomorrow, so I guess it coulda gone worse." Turning toward his two new friends, Jim introduces them to the man to know at the Hall of Fame.

"Boys, this here is Maynard. Maynard"—gesturing toward Rick and Cliff—"these are the boys, Rick Dalton and his stunt double, Cliff."

Maynard shakes hands with both, starting with Cliff. "Cliff."

Cliff repeats the bartender's name. "Maynard."

Then Maynard lights up as he shakes Rick's hand. "Oh hell, *Jake Cahill* himself. Good to meetcha, bounty hunter."

Finishing the handshake, Rick says, "You too, Maynard. Is the doctor in session?"

Maynard guffaws, "The doctor is definitely in session. What can I get ya?"

Rick: "Whiskey sour."

"How 'bout you, stuntman?" the bartender asks.

"What beer ya got?" Cliff inquires.

"Can: Pabst, Schlitz, Hamm's, Coors. Bottle: Bud, Carlsberg, Miller High Life. Tap: Busch, Falstaff, Old Chattanooga, and Country Club."

"Old Chattanooga," says Cliff.

Maynard points a finger at Jim, the regular, and recites his order: "Brandy Alexander for *Lancer* over here." Then the doctor moves off to service his patients.

Jim yells after him, "Make that *Johnny Madrid* to you, asshole!"

All three fellows chuckle.

Another San Gabriel actor saunters up to the three—a craggy-faced, so-ugly-he's-sexy type, with shaggy, feathered-style sandy hair and a black leather jacket. The actor named Warren Vanders joins the three men, cradling a Pabst Blue Ribbon.

Jim and Warren greet each other warmly, then Jim looks to Rick and jerks a thumb back at Warren. "Rick, you know this guy?"

Rick gives a knowing grin. "Shit, you know I do."

Rick and Warren shake hands knowingly, as Rick explains, "Vanders here musta done 'bout three *Bounty Laws*."

"Four, you ungrateful bastard. Once a season I'd go down to Spahn Ranch and get my ass wiped by Rick Dalton," Warren declares. "That's four years *Bounty Law* kept me in cornflakes."

The piano player goes into the instrumental *Alley Cat*.

As Maynard places the customers' drinks down on the bar, the four men mount barstools. The bartender hangs out with them till he's summoned by a thirsty patron.

Cliff and Warren are still working on their beers, but Rick has sucked his whiskey sour through his straw fairly quickly, and Jim has polished off his brandy Alexander.

The bartender returns and asks Jim and Rick, "Another one?"

"Yep," says Jim.

"Whiskey sour," repeats Rick.

The piano player, Curt Zastoupil, finishes up *Alley Cat* as Jim and his three friends, with drinks in their hands, saunter up to his piano station.

"Hey, Curt, how ya doin'?"

Taking a sip of his Harvey Wallbanger, Curt replies, "Just fine, Jim, how's it goin' with you?"

"Goin' real good." Jim tells him, "I did the first day on my pilot today."

"Fuck, man, that's great." Curt begins playing *Happy Days Are Here Again* on the piano.

"Calm it down, Liberace," Jim warns him. "Let's finish the pilot first. Let's see if it's good. Let's see if it makes the CBS fall lineup. Then 'Happy Days Are Here Again.' For a few weeks anyway."

Jim introduces the piano-bar musician to his two new friends. Warren already knows Curt. In fact, Warren gave Curt's son his first dog, named Baron. The actor and the stuntman shake hands with the piano man. Jim brags on his musician buddy: "Curt can play every song of the day on both piano *and* guitar. And he does a good job, especially on *Me and Bobby McGee*. He plays it like a country song—"

"It is a country song," Curt explains.

"I know, but that's not how everybody plays it," Jim says.

"That's 'cause they just do the Janis Joplin arrangement. But if you listen to the song, it's best done on acoustic guitar, as a country song." Then Curt clarifies, "Not Ernest Tubb country. But modern country."

Jim continues to brag to Rick and Cliff about his musician friend, "I'm telling ya, if Curt did *Me and Bobby McGee*, he coulda had a hit with that. Good Creedence Clearwater too. Especially that 'Doo Doo Doo' song."

Curt's confused. "What's the 'Doo Doo Doo' song?"

Jim reminds him, "You know that one." The actor sings, "'Doo doo doo, lookin' out my back door.'"

Curt starts playing the opening of the song on the piano and sings:

Just got home from Illinois
Lock the front door, oh boy
Look at all the happy creatures
Dancing on the lawn
Dinosaur Victrola, listenin' to Buck Owens
Singin' doo doo doo, lookin' out my back door

The four men applaud him. "Great," Rick says.

"Well, not *great*, but not bad," says Curt modestly, then adds, "My son likes that song. So I always do it for him when I'm at home practicing."

"How old's your son?" Cliff asks.

"He's turning six next month," Curt says.

Jim encourages the musician, "Get out from behind that piano and show 'em what you can do with a guitar."

"Okay," Curt agrees, picking up his guitar and putting it in his lap. As he tunes the neck, he tells Rick, "I gotta say, Rick, I'm a big fan. Loved *Bounty Law*. *Bounty Law* and *The Rifleman* are my two favorite shows of that time. I still watch 'em on TV. Also one of your western movies I loved."

"Which one?" Rick asks. "*Tanner*? That's the one most people dig."

Still fiddling with the tuning, Curt asks, "Who else is in that?"

"*Tanner*'s me and Ralph Meeker," says Rick.

"No, it wasn't Meeker—I like Meeker, but it wasn't him." Curt thinks a moment, then it comes to him: "Glenn Ford!"

"Oh, Glenn Ford," Rick says. "That's *Hellfire, Texas*. Yeah, that one ain't so bad. Me and Glenn didn't get along so well. He was less committed to the picture than I was. I mean, you know, a fella can do *too many* movies, and that was Glenn's problem. But, all in all, not a bad picture."

Jim says to Curt, who's finishing up getting his guitar ready to go, "Play somethin' that shows you off a bit."

Curt says, "Oh, so I'm selling myself. I didn't realize that. Thanks for pointing that out."

"Well, it's only fair," teases Rick. "You said you liked my

shit. It's only fair I get to judge you to see if I like your shit."

Curt goes into the recognizable opening chord riff of Johnny Rivers's *The Secret Agent Man Theme*. The other men smile in recognition. Then Curt starts singing the first verse:

There's a man who leads a life of danger
To everyone he meets he stays a stranger
Be careful what you say, you'll give yourself away
Odds are you won't live to see tomorrow
Secret Agent Man
Secret Agent Man
They've given you a number and taken away your name

Curt stops and waits for the cheers he gets. "That's another favorite of my son's." Then, looking at Rick, he asks, "So do we exist on a plane of mutual respect?"

"Abso-bloody-lutely." Rick raises his whiskey sour. "Cheers to the troubadour." They all raise their glasses and bottles and toast Curt.

"Also speakin' of my son and of you, we're both big fans of *The Fourteen Fists of McCluskey*," Curt tells Rick.

"Well, that's one of the good ones," says Rick.

"You know when you watch a movie like that," Curt explains, "about a team of guys doin' some shit, you kinda pick your favorite dude and root for him through the whole movie, hoping he gets through it alive."

The men all involuntarily nod their heads in agreement.

"Well, for my son, you were his favorite dude."

"Aw, that's nice to hear," Rick says.

"In fact, I showed him a *Bounty Law* the other day on

TV," Curt explains. "It was on and I pointed at you and said, 'Hey, Quint'—his name is Quentin—'hey, Quint, you know who that guy is?' He said no, and I said, 'You remember that guy from *The Fourteen Fists of McCluskey* with the eye patch and the flamethrower who burnt the shit outta all them Nazis?' He said yeah and I said, 'That's the same guy.'" Asking rhetorically, "You know what he said? He said, 'So that was back when he had two eyes?'"

They all laugh.

"Can I get you to sign him an autograph?" Curt asks.

"Sure," Rick says. "Ya got a pen?" Curt doesn't, but Warren Vanders does.

So Rick signs a Drinker's Hall of Fame cocktail napkin to Curt's son, Quentin, addressing it to "Private Quentin," making sure to check the spelling, then writes, "Maj McCluskey and Sgt Lewis salute you." Then signs his name, "Rick Dalton," with "Sergeant Mike Lewis" written under it. And then he adds a little drawing of Sgt. Mike Lewis with an eye patch, wearing a shirt that says *Quentin Is Cool*, and then a p.s. with "Burn Nazi Burn!" underneath it.

Jim Stacy groans, "Ugh . . . *Fourteen*-fuckin'-*Fists of McCluskey*. Heartbreak. Kaz-fuckin'-Garas. *Fuck that guy*—sorry, probably a friend of yours," he says to Rick. "But still—*fuck him anyway*."

He explains to Curt, Cliff, and Warren Vanders how he almost got the Kaz Garas part in *McCluskey*. "It got down to three. Garas, Clint Ritchie, and me. But Garas had already starred in a movie for Henry Hathaway at the time. So Hathaway calls up the brass at Columbia to pitch for his boy, and that was all she wrote for me and Ritchie," Stacy says with a sigh.

Warren Vanders asks, "What was the Hathaway picture Garas did?"

"Some African piece of shit with Stewart Granger," Stacy says.

Rick says, "I did an African piece of shit with Stewart Granger." Then adds, "Biggest prick I ever worked with."

"Speaking of fuckin' pricks," Stacy interjects, "Henry Hathaway, that's a fuckin' prick!" Then, adding quickly, "I mean, he's a good director, he makes good pictures. But he's a fuckin' *yeller*! And when he gets yellin' an' cussin', he makes Sherman look like he marched through Georgia pickin' posies.

"My wife did his last movie. Sweet girl, gentle as a little bird. He yelled at her all goddamn day, every day. Film's over, the poor thing practically has *combat shock*. Let me bump into that prick in a bar one of these days," Stacy says as he swigs his drink.

"Who's your wife?" Rick asks.

"Kim Darby," Stacy says.

"Holy shit," says Rick. "You're married to Kim Darby? You're talkin' about *True Grit*?"

"Yeah, I met her on the *Gunsmoke* I did last year," Stacy explains. "We're married two months tops, she lands the lead in *True Grit*."

"Fuck me swingin', you're married to a star," Rick says excitedly.

"Did you get a chance to read for that Glen Campbell part in *True Grit*?" Curt asks Jim.

"Nooooooo," Jim says dramatically. "Once Hathaway learned Kim was married, and not just married but married to some young, handsome swinging dick, I couldn't even visit the set. He didn't want my ass nowhere around."

They all laugh.

"I don't think he read anybody," Jim speculates. "They just gave it to Glen Campbell."

Rick slaps the piano in frustration. "What the fuck's the Duke's problem? He's got great cowboy roles for young guys and he keeps casting these faggot singers can't act. Ricky Nelson. Frankie Avalon. Glen Campbell. Fuckin' Fabian. Dean Martin."

Jim chimes in, "Well, Dean Martin's a little different than the rest of those guys."

"He's a goddamn fuckin' singer like the rest of 'em," Rick emphasizes.

"Yeah," Jim acknowledges, "but he *can* act."

"Yeah," Rick says, "he can act like *a fuckin' wop*!"

They all laugh at that. Rick continues, "Don't get me started 'bout Frankie fuckin' Avalon dying at the fuckin' Alamo."

More laughter. Warren Vanders adds, looking at Rick but pointing at Jim, "You know who he *was* married to, don'tcha?"

Rick and Cliff shake their heads no.

"Connie Stevens," Warren tells them.

Rick involuntarily jumps up in the air. "You were married to fucking *Connie Stevens*?"

"I was married to *and* fucking Connie Stevens."

Rick shakes his head sadly. "You greedy bastard. I had such a crush on her."

"You and all of America, pal," Jim adds.

"I kept pushin' to get her on a *Bounty Law*, but ABC wouldn't let her do NBC shows, so it never worked out. But if it hadda," Rick adds, "that coulda just as easily been *me* walkin' down that aisle."

Stacy ain't so sure about that, but he lets the statement stand unremarked on. He's used to men's jealousy over his track record with women. So he brings it back to his regrets over McCluskey: "Yeah, well, you got *McCluskey*, I got Stevens. But I don't have Stevens no more, but you'll always have *McCluskey*." Stacy bitches, "I coulda been part of a cool team in a tough-ass movie, fuckin' up Nazis. Instead, I ended up gettin' my ass kicked by that squirt Michael Anderson Jr. on *The Monroes*."

The men laugh at the Michael Anderson Jr. remark.

"But still, who am I to bellyache," Stacy says. "Yeah, I coulda been fourth guy from the left in *The Fourteen Fists of McCluskey*, but you"—pointing his brandy Alexander at Rick—"coulda been the fuckin' *Cooler King*."

Aw, not this fucking McQueen horseshit again, Rick thinks.

Cliff winces, knowing how much Rick hates this story. Rick tries to wave the story away, telling Stacy, "C'mon, man, we already went through that shit."

Warren Vanders asks Stacy what he's talking about.

Jim takes his brandy Alexander and points it at Rick again and performs for the group of men. "This fuckin' prick . . . came *this close*"—holding up two fingers on the other hand an inch apart—"to getting the McQueen role in *The Great Escape*."

Both Curt and Warren Vanders give big reactions to that revelation.

Rick holds up his own two fingers an inch apart and says, "I didn't come *this close*." Then Rick spreads both arms as wide as they go and says, "*I came this close*."

The other men laugh but contradict what they mistake as humble pie. "That close is fucking huge in my book," says Warren Vanders.

Curt Zastoupil shrugs. "Oh, he *almost* got McQueen's signature role. No big deal."

Stacy points at Curt. "*EX-ACT-LY*." Then he turns to Rick and waves his finger at the group of men. "Tell 'em about it."

Fuck me, Rick thinks, *I'm not going to tell this same fuckin' story twice in one goddamn day, especially to the same fucking guy.*

"Seriously," Rick says to the group, "there ain't nothing to tell. It's just Sportsmen's Lodge gossip."

So since Rick's being demure, Jim Stacy jumps in and tells it himself. "Apparently, McQueen almost didn't do it. So the director draws up a list. Four names. Top of the list?" Pointing at Rick: "*This fuckin' guy!*"

"He's making up that top-of-the-list part," Rick clarifies.

Warren Vanders asks, "Who were the other three?"

Jim answers for Rick, "The other three—get a load of this—the three Georges."

"Which three Georges?" Curt asks.

"Peppard, Maharis, and Chakiris," Jim tells them.

Both Curt and Warren wince, with Curt adding, "Shit, between them three faggots you woulda totally gotten it!"

"What did I tell ya?" Jim says to Rick, then to Curt, "That's what I said."

Then Maynard yells from behind the bar, "Curt, I hope

you enjoyed your little break. Now entertain the other thirty people in the room!"

Jim, Rick, Cliff, and Warren leave the piano area, and Curt sits back down on his bench and gets to work.

These eyes cry every night for you
These arms long to hold you again

The other men belly back up to the bar, where Maynard serves them another round (that's round three for Rick and Jim and tap beer number two for Cliff). Cliff pays for the round. Warren Vanders pays his tab, says goodbye to the boys, and leaves while he still can drive.

On nights like these, Cliff doesn't usually say much. It's not like he's biting his tongue, he interjects from time to time, but he knows these nights aren't about him. It's about two male actor colleagues sniffing around each other to build both an artistic and working relationship. This is *their* night.

The two remaining television actors continue to talk and drink and do what actors of their time usually do. Compare notes. Usually about directors and actors they both worked with. It turns out Stacy knows Tommy Laughlin too, from acting in Tommy's first film as a director, *The Young Sinner*. Stacy worked with the director of *Tanner*, Jerry Hopper, on a *Have Gun—Will Travel*. And both men worked with Vic Morrow. Vic did a *Bounty Law*, and Jim did an episode of Morrow's show *Combat!* They also talk about directors they like, which usually means directors who like *them* and hired *them*. Rick sings the praises of Paul Wendkos and William Witney, while Stacy champions Robert Butler.

"So how did you get so set up with CBS?" Dalton asks Stacy.

"Well, you know how it is," Stacy says. "You work for this TV director, you work for that one. Then you work for one who really digs you. Then you become one of *his guys*. If he does four episodes a year on different shows, he might plug you in one or two, if he can."

"Yeah, I had that situation with Paul Wendkos and Bill Witney," Rick adds.

"So *my guy* who thought I was *his guy*," Stacy says, "was Robert Butler. He plugged me into a few of his shows, and even the shows I didn't get 'cause they wanted a bigger name—an Andy Prine or a John Saxon—I impressed the casting directors and the producers." Stacy continues, "So word about me started to spread at CBS, then this big-deal two-part *Gunsmoke* came up. And they didn't just give it to me, I had to win it. I had to impress the network executives, the *Gunsmoke* producers, and the episode director, Dick Sarafian."

"Dick Sarafian wrote the script of my first lead role in a motion picture," Rick interjected.

"Really?" Stacy said. "What was it?"

"A hot rod picture for Republic called *Drag Race, No Stop*. Bill Witney directed it. It had a good cast, Gene Evans, John Ashley, Dick Bakalyan. I beat out Bob Conrad for the lead." Rick jokes, "Witney didn't want to dig a hole every day for the other actors to stand in so Bob could look them in the eye."

They all laugh at the Robert Conrad short joke.

Then Rick asks Stacy about the *Gunsmoke* episode. "So the network executives were butting into the casting of an episodic?"

"Well, that's the thing," Stacy explains. "They coulda just gone the big-name route and Chris George gets the role. But they didn't want a big name. CBS wanted to cast a young actor and use that episode of *Gunsmoke* to establish him with a western-watching audience and then plug him into his own show next season."

"Well," saluting Jim with his empty whiskey sour glass, Rick says, "You're a lucky goddamn son of a bitch and I hope you appreciate that."

Jim Stacy bristles a bit. "I wouldn't say I'm *lucky*. I'm fortunate. I mean it's not like I hit town and just fell off a turnip truck. I spent seven years on fuckin' *Ozzie and Harriet* saying, *Hey Ricky, want a hamburger?*"

Rick clarifies, "Whoa, whoa, whoa, I didn't say you didn't deserve it. And I didn't imply that either. I watched you today, you totally fuckin' deserve it. I'm just saying—I been you. It was me guesting on a *Tales of Wells Fargo* that got the town excited about me. And that directly led to *Bounty Law*. Anyway, my point is—this is a moment for you. And I hope you appreciate the moment better than I did."

"You didn't appreciate it then?" Jim asks.

"I did," Rick assures him. But then jabs him in the shoulder with his empty cocktail glass and says, "But not like I do now."

After Maynard sets them up with Rick's fourth whiskey sour and Jim's fourth brandy Alexander and Cliff's third beer, they start talking about sexy male actors' favorite subject, pussy.

Jim wants to know did Rick fuck Virna Lisi, and Rick wants to know did Jim fuck Hayley Mills.

Jim didn't, or if he did he's not talking. Rick didn't, but he tried. Rick tells Jim how he fucked Yvonne De Carlo and Faith Domergue when they guested on *Bounty Law*. He fucked De Carlo basically because since he was twelve he always wanted to fuck Elizabeth Taylor. And he figured Yvonne De Carlo was about as close as he was gonna ever get.

"Was it hard starting up an affair with Yvonne De Carlo?" Jim asks.

Rick lifts up his empty cocktail glass and says, "About as hard as ordering another whiskey sour." They all three laugh at Rick's line and his timing. Jim orders another round, but Cliff passes on a fourth beer. The two actors wait for Maynard to bring them their last round of cocktails.

Rick knows he has to still get home and work on his lines for tomorrow's shoot. God forbid he doesn't know his lines backward and forward when he has to play a scene with that little bitch.

She'll probably know her lines *and* his lines.

That just means this is his last drink. When he goes to bed tonight, he's going to remember in the morning *going to bed*.

But before he and his co-star say *adiós*, Rick says, "Jim?"

"Yeah?"

"You know that *Great Escape* shit you asked me about?"

"Yeah."

"I don't enjoy that story as much as everybody else seems

372

to," Rick confesses. "I mean, if I were Cesare Danova—fair enough. But my situation ain't his situation."

"Wait a minute," says a confused Stacy, "what the hell does Cesare Danova got to do with it and what's his *situation*?"

"Well," Rick explains, "once upon a time—for two minutes—William Wyler seriously considered casting Cesare Danova as Ben-Hur."

"Really? Shit, I didn't know that."

"You don't know it because, two minutes later, Wyler came to his senses and cast Charlton Heston," Rick explains further. "But you can say Cesare Danova was *almost* Ben-Hur because he *almost* was. But *his* situation wasn't *my* situation."

Jim stares at Rick, wondering what he's getting at.

The actor continues, "Look, I worked real hard on *Bounty Law*. And if that's what I'm known for, fair enough. But the thing that seems to interest everybody the most *isn't* the show I did. It's a fucking role I never played. A role I never had a Chinaman's chance of getting."

"You were on the list," Jim offers.

"The list, the fucking list!" Rick says, raising his voice in frustration. Maynard and a few other customers turn in their direction. Jim reaches over and pats Rick's hand on the bar, and says quietly, "It's okay, calm down. Take a drink."

Rick sucks some more whiskey sour out of his straw, as Jim looks at him with big eyes.

"That *list*," Rick repeats in a sarcastic whisper, "that everybody thinks is so impressive is fuckin' questionable. I mean, I never saw it. But let's just say there is a list and I'm on it and the three Georges are on it." Rick asks, "Do you realize how many crazy impossible things would hafta happen for me to get that role?"

Jim states, "I don't follow."

"First things first," Rick begins, "McQueen has gotta do the dumbest thing in his life—turn down *The Great Escape* and accept *The Victors*. You know, that thing he *didn't* do, because he's not a fuckin' idiot."

Then Rick stops and says, "But for the sake of argument, we'll say McQueen is a *fuckin' idiot*, and he turns down the flashy role in the epic movie written for him by his mentor John Sturges. Does that mean I get Hilts, the Cooler King?" Rick asks Jim.

Before Jim can answer, Rick says, "Of course not.

"If there was a list, at the time, George Peppard would have been right at the top of it," Rick insists. "I mean, there's not even a question about that. And if McQueen turned them down, they would have just turned around and offered it to Peppard. And since the role that Peppard *did* was the role in *The Victors* that McQueen turned *down*, if offered *The Great Escape*, Peppard would've *not* been an idiot and said yes immediately. And *that*, Mr. Stacy, would have been *that*," Rick concludes.

Makes sense, Jim thinks as he smiles at Rick's delivery. But little does James Stacy know, Rick ain't finished yet.

"But . . ." Rick starts up again, *"for sake of argument*, let's say before he can play the role, Peppard drives his Aston Martin off of Mulholland— No, wait a minute, that's too cliché. Peppard gets eaten by a shark, surfing in Malibu. So thus he's unavailable."

Rick sums up the situation for Stacy again, making sure he's keeping up with the train of thought. "So McQueen does the dumbest thing he's ever done in his whole life, and Peppard gets eaten by a shark.

"Now do I get it?" the actor asks the other actor.

Jim nods his head up and down.

But Rick moves his head side to side. Then, explaining to James Stacy as if he were a five-year-old child: "No, I don't get it. George Maharis gets it."

Jim Stacy starts to argue, but Rick holds his hand up to stop him before he starts. "Now, why do I say that? I'll tell you."

Rick proceeds to explain, "Look, because of that TV show of his, in '62 he was pretty popular. Not only that, two years later, Sturges cast Maharis in the lead in a thriller called *The Satan Bug*—which suggests he's partial to Maharis. I mean, he didn't cast me in the fuckin' *Satan Bug*.

"So," Rick continues, "if Steve McQueen does the dumbest thing he's ever done in his entire life, and George Peppard gets eaten by a shark, *then* . . . George Maharis is Hilts, the Cooler King."

Rick lifts up his cocktail, sips some sour booze through his straw, toasting Maharis. "But, for sake of argument, let's say, before principal photography, Maharis gets caught having sex with a man in a public toilet."

Jim Stacy bursts out laughing.

Rick continues, "So now Maharis is out, and Sturges goes back to the list. So, do I get it now?"

"Over George Chakiris, fuck yeah!" insists Stacy.

Rick shakes his head from side to side and tells Jim, "No

375

no no no no, Jim, *of course* they offer it to George Chakiris."

Stacy makes a face that indicates he disagrees, and Rick proceeds to demonstrate his point by raising his hand and counting off the reasons on his fingers:

Finger number one, "One, there is that inexplicable Oscar he's got."

Stacy nods his head, acknowledging, *Yes, that's a thing*.

Finger number two, "Two, *The Great Escape* was produced by the Mirisch Brothers *for* the Mirisch Company."

Finger number three, "George Chakiris has a *deal* with the Mirisch Company. He made the *633 Squadron* with 'em. He made *Diamond Head* with 'em. He made that goofy Aztec movie with 'em. So not only do they *like him*—he's under fucking contract with 'em!"

Seeing the logic in Rick's hypothesis, Jim Stacy nods his head yes.

Dalton sums up, "So George Chakiris gets it, and that's that."

Stacy nods his head in agreement and starts to say something, when Rick stops him with an upward-pointing index finger. "But . . . let's just say—for *sake of argument*—McQueen does the dumbest thing he's ever done in his life, Peppard gets eaten by a shark in Malibu, Maharis gets caught fuckin' a man in a public toilet . . . and it turns out the man Maharis was fuckin' . . . was *Chakiris*!"

That makes Stacy do a spit take with his cocktail.

"So bye-bye, Bernardo," Rick says with a big hand gesture. Then, hunching his shoulders, he asks Jim Stacy, "Do I get it now?"

Jim puts down his cocktail. "Of course you get it, you're the last guy on the fuckin' list!"

"That's just my point, Jim," Rick explains. "When the fuck do they hire the *last guy* on the fucking list? When you get to the last guy on the fuckin' list, you throw out the fuckin' list and start a *new fuckin' list*!"

Shit, Stacy thinks, *that is what they do.*

"So now it's not the three fuckin' Georges, it's the two fuckin' Bobs. Redford and Culp. And now they decide to make the guy British, and all of a sudden Michael Caine's got the fuckin' part. Or," Rick concludes, "they decide to say fuck it and pay Paul Newman what he's asking for. Or Tony Curtis's people call up and offer them a good deal on Tony. *Regardless*, I never stood a fuckin' chance."

Then Rick catches Cliff's eye and indicates it's time to bounce by placing his empty glass on the bar with a theatrical demonstration of finality.

"And with that, Mr. Lancer, I bid you *adieu*. I got a shit-fuck ton of lines to learn tonight, and I better learn 'em or get my eggs scrambled tomorrow by that snotty little dynamo."

Chapter Twenty-Four

Nebraska Jim

After bidding Jim Stacy and the regulars at the Drinker's Hall of Fame *adieu*, Cliff drops Rick off at his house around ten-thirty that night. Enough time for Rick to study his lines for tomorrow's work and hit the hay around midnight or twelve-thirty. As soon as Rick walks through the door, as per usual for every actor in the world, he checks in with his answering service to see if he's received any important messages. And, sure enough, there is one from the agent Marvin Schwarz.

Wow, that's fast, Rick thinks.

So he quickly dials the number the agent left, and Marvin picks up the phone on the third ring.

Marvin Schwarz answers the phone, "Marvin Schwarz."

"Hello, Mr. Schwarz," Rick says into the receiver, "it's Rick Dalton."

"Rick my boy," the agent gregariously answers, "so glad you called. I've got two words for you: *Nebraska Jim—Sergio Corbucci.*"

"*Nebraska* what? *Sergio* who?" Rick asks.

"Sergio Corbucci," Marvin repeats.

"And who's that?"

"The second-best director of spaghetti westerns in the whole wide world," Marvin informs him. "He's doing a new western. It's called *Nebraska Jim*. And, because of *me*, he's considering *you*."

"Nebraska Jim. Am I Nebraska Jim?"

"Yes, you are."

"So he's offering it to me?"

"No, he's not."

"So I don't have it?"

"What you *have* is a dinner. He just met three young actors. Thanks to me, he's now meeting four. You, Thursday after next, Sergio and his wife, Nori, at his favorite Japanese restaurant in Los Angeles."

"Who's the other three?" Rick inquires.

Marvin rattles them off: "Robert Fuller, Gary Lockwood, Ricky Nelson, and Ty Hardin."

"That's four," Rick points out.

"Oh, that's right," Marvin realizes. "Sorry about that, you're five."

"Ricky Nelson?" Rick incredulously asks. "He's considering fucking Ricky Nelson?"

"Ah, honey boy," Marvin reminds him, "Ricky Nelson was one of the stars of *Rio Bravo*. That's a helluva better movie than any one you ever made."

"Look, Mr. Sch-Sch-Schwarz," Rick stutters, "that's terrific. But can I talk straight with you?"

"Always," Marvin says.

"When it comes to this *spaghetti-western* stuff," Rick starts.

"Yeah?"

"I don't like 'em."

"You don't like 'em?"

"No I don't. In fact, I think they're awful."

"Awful?"

"Yeah."

"How many have you seen?"

"A couple."

"So, this is your *expert* opinion?"

"Look, Mr. Schwarz, I grew up watching Hopalong Cassidy and Hoot Gibson. This Italian cowboy shit just ain't my bag."

"Because they're *awful*?" the agent clarifies.

"Yeah."

"As opposed to the high-quality red-letter work of Hopalong Cassidy and Hoot Gibson?"

"C'mon, you know what I mean."

"Look, Rick," the agent says, "I don't want to be insensitive here, but your track record when it comes to motion pictures isn't so stellar that you should be looking down your nose at feature films considering hiring you for leading roles."

"I appreciate that, Mr. Schwarz," Rick concedes. "But maybe, instead of running off to Rome, it's wiser for me to stay in town and give it my best shot next pilot season. I mean, somebody's gonna get lucky; it just might be me."

"Look, kid," Marvin says, "let me tell you a story about a client of mine. Before we sent cowboys to ride horses around the sets of Cinecittà, we used to send them to Berlin. Before the fuckin' Italians got the bright idea to make westerns, the Germans got in the game." Marvin explains, "You see, there was this German novelist named Karl May. And he wrote a series of books that take place in the American Northwest during the pioneer days. Now, the fact Karl May never set foot in America didn't stop these books from becoming very popular with the German public.

"The books follow the exploits of two men. One, an Apache chief named Winnetou. And the other, his white mountain-man blood-brother, Old Shatterhand. So, in the fifties, a German film company started making German movies based on these novels. They cast a French actor named Pierre Brice to play the Indian. But as Old Shatterhand I got them to cast my he-man American client, Lex Barker. Now, before Lex went to Germany, he did a few American movies. He even played Tarzan—and was a pretty fuckin' good Tarzan, if you ask me. But he was married to Lana Turner. So no matter what he fuckin' did, he was always *Mr. Lana Turner.*

"So I get him the German picture. And he don't wanna go. A German western? What the fuck is that? A German western with a French fuckin' Indian?

"He says, 'Marvin, what the fuck are you trying to do to me? There's gotta be a limit to what an actor will do for money.' And I tell him, like I'm tellin' you, 'What's your fuckin' problem?

"'One, there's not exactly a long line of people in America who want to hire you to star in their motion pictures.

"'Two, you're not joining the fuckin' Army. You go to Germany, make a movie—five weeks, six weeks—make some good money, come back. Easy peasy. In an' out.'

"So I get 'em to go. And the rest, as they say, is *German cinema history.*

"The movie is a fuckin' *smash-ola*! And not just in Germany but all over Europe. Lex ends up playing Old Shatterhand six times! He becomes one of the most popular actors in the history of German cinema! But his movies play all over Europe. He's so popular in Italy, Fellini casts him in *La Dolce Vita*. And you know who he plays . . . *Lex Barker*! That's how big a star he is.

"After six movies, he retires from the role. They replace him with big American stars like Stewart Granger and Rod Cameron. But they don't call *them* Old Shatterhand. They call them shit like Old Skatterhand, and Old Surehand, and Old Firehand. Why? Because everybody in Germany knows Lex Barker—and *only* Lex Barker—is Old Shatterhand!"

The agent gets down to brass tacks: "Look, honey boy, you asked me could you speak straight with me. Well, now I'm gonna speak straight with you. You tried the TV-to-movies transition and it didn't work. Well, it rarely works, so welcome to the fuckin' club." Using examples that don't include Rick, Marvin says, "Yes, it worked for McQueen and it worked for Jim Garner and, most unbelievably of all, Clint Eastwood. But guys like you, Edd Byrnes, Vince Edwards, George Maharis, who spent your careers running pocket combs through your pompadours, you're all in the same boat now.

"When you weren't looking, the culture changed.

"You gotta be somebody's hippie son to star in movies nowadays. Peter Fonda, Michael Douglas, Don Siegel's kid Kristoffer Tabori, Arlo fuckin' Guthrie! Shaggy-haired androgynous types, those are the leading men of today."

Marvin pauses for effect, then says, "You still wear a

fuckin' pompadour. Fuckin' Elvis don't wear a pompadour no more! Ricky fuckin' Nelson don't wear a goddamn pompadour no more! Edd fuckin' 'Kookie' Byrnes is on TV doin' commercials for fuckin' hair spray, saying, 'The wet head is dead, long live the dry look.' Fuckin' Kookie! But not you, Rick—you're stickin' with the fuckin' pompadour!"

Rick excitedly tells him, "Well, you know this thing I shot today, I didn't wear a pompadour."

"Well, it's about fuckin' time!" Marvin says. "If you ask me you shoulda started using hair spray and a hot comb years ago."

Then Marvin switches gears. "But that's not the point. The point is, in Italy, you do what you want. You wanna suddenly get all flamboyant like Tony Curtis, have a ball. You wanna wear your hair like you did for the last twenty years, fuckin' fine. Italians don't give a shit. You know all this hippie shit all over town, all over America? Same shit happened in Rome. Difference: The Italians threw the bums out. Consequently, the youth culture didn't dominate popular culture like these hippie faggots do over here."

"*Hippie faggots,*" Rick repeats under his breath with bitterness.

Then the great Marvin Schwarz goes in for the close: "So Rick, here's the sixty-four-thousand-dollar question. Where do you wanna be this time next year? In Burbank, getting your ass kicked in by that *schvartze* on *Mod Squad*? Or in Rome . . . starring in westerns?"

Chapter Twenty-Five

The Last Chapter

Roman and Sharon Polanski are in their convertible English Roadster, speeding down the Sunset Strip. Sharon hates this car.

She hates how old it is.

She hates the noises it makes when Roman shifts gears.

She hates the shitty radio reception it gets.

But most of all she hates that it's a convertible and that Roman always insists on driving it with the top down.

Roman jokes with Warren Beatty that "Life's too short *not* to drive a convertible."

That's easy for him to say, with that pageboy hairstyle he wears. But Sharon works hard on getting her hair right. And after getting her hair done and looking fabulous, she must tie it up in a scarf?

It's a crime against beauty.

The Hollywood couple have completed their appearance on Hugh Hefner's TV show *Playboy After Dark*. It's ten o'clock as they race away from the Sunset 9000 building, where the show is taped, and whiz by Ben Frank's Coffee Shop and the Tiffany Theater, which features Andy Warhol's *Lonesome Cowboys* on its marquee.

Roman knows he shouldn't have agreed to another event the day after the party at the Playboy Mansion, and he senses her hostile silence. He's well aware she was planning to spend the night at home reading in bed. And he knows it's much more work for her to get dolled up for these TV appearances than it is for him.

Nevertheless, she did get dolled up, she did leave the house, and she did come through for him.

But now comes the cold-war resentment. Sharon has such a sunny presence that whenever she blocks out the sun, the effect is chilling.

On 93 KHJ, nighttime disc spinner Humble Harve keeps coming in and out of the Roadster's shitty speakers, as does a ridiculous tune by Diana Ross and the Supremes, *No Matter What Sign You Are, You're Gonna Be Mine You Are*. The time has come for Roman to show contrition and gratitude and poke the blond bear.

"Look, darling," he begins, "I know you didn't want to do this tonight."

The red roof of the Der Wienerschnitzel on Larrabee is visible through the windshield of the Roadster as Sharon glances over at him and nods yes.

He continues, "And I know you're sore because I didn't consult you and that was inconsiderate."

Again she shows her agreement by nodding her head.

"And I know," he continues, "you're being very good-natured about this."

Actually, she bitched about it all afternoon with Jay, but Roman doesn't know that.

Finally, the blond sphinx speaks: "Yes, all those things are true."

"You're being an angel about it," he tells her, "and I love you for that."

Oh, so that's why you love me? she thinks, and does an eye roll.

The eye roll tells him that probably wasn't the best thing he could have said.

As they drive past the London Fog on one side of the Strip and the Whisky a Go Go on the other, Roman tries to parlay with her. "So, just know I know I owe you."

Quickly, she comes back with a question. *"Owe* me what?"

"I mean, I *owe you* for doing this."

"I know. I agree. So what do you intend to do to pay me back?"

Frankly, Roman hadn't taken that statement as serious as Sharon apparently did, so he's at a bit of a loss.

"Well, I guess, I mean"—he's thinking fast—"that you can suddenly commit me to something *I* don't want to do."

Yeah, that's it, he thinks. That would be pound-for-pound reciprocation.

Giving her examples of what that could be, he says, "I mean, you come across some charity you're really serious—"

She interrupts him with two words: "Pool. Party."

"What?"

"Pool. Party."

"Pool party? Sure. When?"

"Tonight."

"Tonight?"

"Yes, *tonight.*"

"Oh, baby, I'm so tired. I'm leaving for London tomorrow. I was looking forward to going home and—"

"Wah wah wah! That's what I said last night when you committed us to this fucking thing. But where am I? I'm right here. All glammed up, doing my 'sexy little me' routine for Hugh Hefner, the television cameras, and a bunch of Hollywood dingbats."

Then she says, like an accusation, "You know I'm reading a book right now?"

He nods his head yes.

"You know I want to be in my bed reading right now?"

He nods his head yes.

"You know I don't like to put on the dog two nights in a row if I don't have to?"

He nods his head yes.

"But I did it, didn't I?"

Roman lets out a groan.

"Don't moan at me, buster," she admonishes him.

Roman tries to deflect. "You just had your hair done."

Nice try, buddy, Sharon thinks. "Is there some reason I'm unhip to that I need to have my *Playboy After Dark* hair tomorrow?"

"No." He shrugs, beaten.

"No commitments I don't know about? No personal appearances?"

"No."

"I can read my book?"

He answers with a sigh, "Yes."

"Well, then, pool party tonight means debt paid in full," then adds for effect, "if that means anything to you?"

"Okay," says Roman, letting out a defeated exhale.

"Okay, now say it with a smile on your face."

He smiles and says, "We can have a pool party."

Then she demands, "Now ask me for it."

That makes him roll his eyes. "Really? You're taking it this far?"

"Ask me for it," she insists.

Roman swallows his irritation, puts on an accommodating face, and gives Sharon what she wants: "Sharon, how would you like to throw a pool party tonight?"

Sharon squeals, claps her hands together, and says, "Roman, that's a fantastic idea!" She leans across to kiss him and says, "Let's get home. I have phone calls to make."

Rick notices a steady line of cars arriving at the Polanski residence. *They must be having a party*, he thinks. Rick Dalton stands in his driveway, dressed in the red silk kimono he bought on one of his trips to Japan, watering the roses in his garden with a hose while he runs tomorrow's dialogue with his tape recorder. A Japanese gardener once told him to water his roses at night so they fully get to drink the nourishment and not have the sun evaporate a large portion of it. He's running the lines of the scene he has with the little girl tomorrow. No way is he going to let that little monster catch him flat-footed.

Cliff had dropped him off from that bar in San Gabriel around ten-thirty.

He talked to Marvin Schwarz on the phone for about

twenty minutes. He made a German beer stein's worth of whiskey sours and started running his lines. He's run them for about an hour now—it's five minutes to midnight, and he's feeling pretty good about his grasp of the dialogue. Before he is tempted to make another beer stein full of whiskey sours, Rick's going to go to bed.

He can hear the sounds of the Polanski party echo down to his driveway. He can hear the music, the giggling, the frivolity, and the periodic splashes in the pool. The actor still has yet to meet either the director or his wife. He only spied the two of them for the first time yesterday afternoon. He looks like a little prick. But she looks sweet. Maybe one day he'll catch her going to fetch the mail.

A convertible Porsche going much too fast zooms up Cielo Drive and stops outside of the gate of the Polanski residence. Rick gives the car an irritated glance, then suddenly stops when he recognizes the driver. *Fuck me swinging, that's Steve McQueen!*

Rick calls out, "Steve!"

The driver behind the wheel of the Porsche glances over in the direction of his name being called and sees a guy dressed in a red silk Japanese kimono, holding a beer stein, a tape recorder, and a water hose. He narrows his eyes, then he recognizes the red kimono man. He tentatively answers back, "Rick?"

Dalton walks over to the car. "Hey, fella, long time no see."

McQueen answers back, "Yeah, you bet. How ya been?"

Dalton leans over and shakes hands with McQueen, "Oh, I can't complain."

Actually, Rick has nothing but complaints about his

career, his life, and the world, but he's not going to complain to Steve.

The movie star looks past him to the house. "Is that your house?"

"Yep." Rick smiles. "That's the house that *Bounty Law* built."

McQueen raises his eyebrows. "You built it?"

"No," Dalton says, "that's just an expression." *You dumb fuck.*

Steve gives him one of his trademark little smiles with his tiny gash of a mouth. "Well, good for you. You were smart with your money. I hear Will Hutchins and Ty Hardin are flat on their ass right now."

In other words, Rick thinks, *you're doing better than the other has-beens. You got a house. So says Bullitt.*

"Well, I'm not starring in *The Sand Pebbles,*" bringing up McQueen's only Oscar nomination, "but I'm making a living."

"Well, that puts you ahead of eighty percent of 'em," Mc-Queen says with a smile and a finger point.

The highest-paid movie star in the world is congratulating me on making a living as an actor. Thanks a lot.

"By the way," Dalton says, "I was rootin' for you for that Oscar nomination," referring again to *The Sand Pebbles.*

McQueen doesn't say anything to that; he just smiles.

Rick knows what that means. This little conversation is over.

But before that gate opens and McQueen and his Porsche zoom out of his life, Rick would like to connect with him. Not on the two separate realities they now exist in. But, back when the two men shared the same real estate, there was one incident that they shared that Rick *could* bring up without sounding too pathetic.

"Hey, Steve, I was wondering," Rick said, "do you remember that time—it was during the first season of my show and the second season of your show—that we played pool at Barney's Beanery?"

Actually, McQueen does remember that. "Yeah," he says, "I remember that." Going back in time: "We played three games, right?"

"Yeah," Rick says, happy Steve remembers it. "It was kind of a big deal at the time. You know, *Josh and Jake* playing pool."

McQueen gives it to him. "Well, it *was* a big deal. *Josh and Jake* playing pool? We coulda sold tickets."

Rick laughs at Steve's joke.

Thinking about it, McQueen says, "In fact, I seem to remember the whole bar watched us play the first game." McQueen points at him. "You won. And only half the bar watched the second game"—then he jerks his thumb toward himself—"which I won." And then he laughs when he remembers, "And nobody cared about the third game."

A very moved Rick nods his head yes. *He remembers.*

"But I don't remember who won the third game?" McQueen asks.

"Nobody," Rick answers. "We never finished it. You had to leave."

McQueen knows that probably means he was losing.

Then another car en route to Sharon's party pulls up behind McQueen's Porsche, bringing the reunion to an end. Both men look back at the other car, then back to each other.

"So you live there?" McQueen says, pointing at Rick's house.

"Yep," Rick says.

"Well, maybe one day I'll knock on your door and we can go down to Barney's and finish that game."

Rick knows that will never happen, but it's a nice thing to say. "That would be great." Really meaning it, Rick says, "Good to see you again, Steve."

"You too. Take care of yourself." Then Steve turns toward the call box out in front of the Polanski house and hits the button.

Sharon's voice comes out of the speaker. "Hello?"

Steve says into the box, "It's me, baby, open up."

The Polanskis' front gate opens. Steve's car, and the car behind him, drive up the driveway and disappear from view.

Rick stands there holding his beer stein, the tape recorder, and the garden hose, watching the gate in front of the Polanski residence close itself. He takes a swig of whiskey sour. Then he hears the phone inside the house ring.

Who the fuck's calling at midnight?

He trots inside the house and answers the phone attached to the wall in the kitchen.

"Hello?" he says.

The female voice on the other end of the line says, "Rick?"

"Yes?" he answers.

"Are you learning your lines?" the voice asks.

What the fuck?

He asks, "Who is this?"

"It's Trudi. You know, Mirabella from work."

A genuinely surprised Rick says, "Trudi? Trudi, do you know what time it is?"

She groans on the other end of the line. "That's a silly question. Of course I know what time it is. I don't go to bed till I know my lines cold. I don't believe in this learning-your-lines-during-the-day malarkey. Especially not on television. You don't sound like I woke you up." She asks, "Did I?"

"No, you didn't," he confesses.

"So," she challenges, "what's the problem?"

"You know the problem," he says with irritation creeping into his voice. "Does your mother know you're calling?"

Trudi guffaws on the other end of the line and tells Rick, "By ten forty-five, my mother has put away three to four glasses of chardonnay and is usually sleeping open-mouthed on the couch with the TV on, waiting for the National Anthem sign-off to happen to wake her up and send her to the bedroom."

"Trudi, you can't call me at this hour," Rick insists.

"Are you suggesting it's not appropriate?"

"It's not appropriate."

"Stop trying to change the subject and answer the question."

"What question?"

"Are you learning your lines?"

"Oh. Well—as a matter of fact, Little Miss Smartass—I am."

"Yeah, right," she says sarcastically.

"I am!" he insists.

"You're watching *Johnny Carson*," she says dismissively.

"I am not. I'm learnin' my fuckin' lines, you little bitch!"

After losing his cool and calling her a bitch, he hears her

little voice giggle on the other end of the receiver. The sound of her giggling makes him giggle.

Then in mid-giggle she asks, "Are you learning our scene?"

"Yes, I am," he tells her.

"Me too," she says, and then asks, "Wanna run lines together?"

Okay, he thinks, *this has gone way too far*. He's got to shut this little troublemaker down.

"Look, Trudi, I really don't think it's okay to be talking on the phone at midnight with your mom not knowin'," he says honestly.

With infinite patience, Trudi answers Rick, "You act like tomorrow morning I'm waking up and going to a little red schoolhouse. I'm going to *work* with *you*. And we're doing *this* scene. You're up, I'm up. You're working on the scene, I'm working on the scene. So," she suggests, "let's work on it together. Then tomorrow we show up to work, nobody knows we worked on it, and we knock 'em dead!" Then— almost like a dig—she adds, "You know, Rick, they don't just pay us to do it. They pay us to do it great."

The little squirt's making sense. I mean, she is just a acting colleague. And after the way Sam reacted to that last scene we did together, if me and her come out of the gate tomorrow loaded for bear, we would knock 'em dead.

"You off book?" he asks the little girl.

"I think I am," was her reply.

"Yeah, me too. Okay, kiddo, you start."

On the other end of the receiver, Trudi suddenly changes her voice to duplicate traumatized-kidnap-victim Mirabella's overdramatic intensity. "What do you intend to do with me?"

As he paces around his kitchen, dressed in his red silk kimono, Rick takes a swig of a whiskey sour from his beer stein and adopts his Caleb DeCoteau cowboy dialect. "You know, little lady, I ain't rightly figured that out yet. I could do a lotta things wit' ya. I could do a lotta things to ya. But I could also let ya go, your pa sees the right side of things."

Trudi, as Mirabella, asks, "What's he gotta do for you to let me go?"

Rick, as Caleb, spits out maniacally, "He can make me a rich man, that's what he can do! He can give me a basket full of money and then he can forget me. Or I'll give him a basket full of dead daughter, and he'll never forget me."

The innocent child asks the corrupt criminal, "So you'd murder me? Not because you're angry with me, or even angry with my father," Trudi takes a dramatic pause, then says, "but simply for greed?"

Caleb answers flippantly, "Greed's what makes the world go 'round, little lady."

The little lady says her name out loud: "Mirabella."

"What?" Caleb asks.

The eight-year-old child repeats her name to the outlaw leader. "My name is Mirabella. If you're gonna murder me in cold blood, I don't want you to just think of me as Murdock Lancer's little girl."

Something about the way she says that registers with the outlaw. And suddenly it becomes important for Caleb to make her understand his fairness on this matter.

"Look, you ain't got nothin' to worry about. Obviously your pa's gonna pay me my money. You're worth it and he can afford it. So when he does pay me my money, I'll release ya unharmed."

There's silence on the other side of the phone for a beat and a half. Then her voice comes back on the line, only now instead of being overly dramatic, she makes a surprisingly analytical observation.

"Interesting choice of words."

"What?" a confused Caleb asks.

Then Mirabella Lancer, sounding remarkably like Trudi Frazer, explains her observation to the land-pirate leader: "You said 'my money.' It's *my father's* money. The money he *earned*, not *stole*, raising cattle and driving them to market. But you said 'my money.' You actually think you're entitled to my father's money?"

And with that delivery, little Mirabella and little Trudi push little buttons inside of the psyche of both the outlaw and the actor, and in the middle of his kitchen—dressed in his red silk kimono—Rick Dalton as Caleb DeCoteau metamorphoses back into the snarling, megalomaniacal, murdering bandit he always was and answers her in one big explosion of breath.

"That's right, Mirabella, I am! I'm entitled to whatever I can *take*! And after I take it, I'm entitled to whatever I can keep! Your pa wants to keep me from blowin' your fool head off? He oughta pay my price!"

In other words: *a rattlesnake on a motorcycle.*

The child asks a simple question: "And my price is ten thousand dollars?"

An out-of-breath outlaw and actor replies, "Yep."

A coy little hostage remarks, "That seems rather high for little ol' me."

Sincerely, Caleb responds, "That's where you're wrong, Mirabella." Then, compelled by emotion, Rick improvises, "If I was your pa—" He stops.

"What?" the voice on the other end of the receiver demands.

Rick opens his mouth, but the words don't come out.

The child on the other end of the phone demands, "'If I were your pa' what?"

Rick blurts out, "I'd cut off my arm to get you back!"

Silence fills the room and the scene, but Rick can hear Trudi's self-satisfied smile over the phone.

Then, after a dramatic pause you could drive three trucks through, Trudi as Mirabella comes back on the line and asks, "Was that a compliment, Caleb?"

Then Trudi breaks out of character and describes stage direction. She reads, "Then Johnny comes up to the door. Knock knock."

"Who is it?" Caleb asks.

Trudi adopts a deep cowboy voice and says, "Madrid."

"C'mon in," Caleb orders.

Trudi tells Rick, "The rest of your lines are with Johnny. So I'll do Johnny's lines." With her throaty Johnny Madrid voice, Trudi asks, "What's the plan?"

Caleb tells him, "Plan is, Lancer meets us in Mexico five days from now with ten thousand dollars."

She drawls out, "That's a lotta money to carry on a long ride."

Caleb snorts, "That's Lancer's problem."

Trudi as Johnny points out, "Something happens to that money and we don't get it, that's *our* problem."

Caleb spins toward Johnny and violently says, "Something happens to that money, that's *her* problem!" With fire in his eyes, he tells Johnny Lancer, "Git it straight, boy! In five days' time, Murdock Lancer is going to pay me my ten thousand dollars! And if anything happens to my ten thousand dollars before they reach us, we will not be understanding. The name of this game ain't 'I tried.'

"Murdock Lancer puts ten thousand dollars right smack-dab in my hand—or I crush her head in with a rock!"

Rick and Caleb breathe in and out hard after that explosion. Then, after taking the well-earned dramatic pause that George Cukor denied him, Rick asks, "Now, do you got a problem with that . . . Madrid?"

Then Trudi as Johnny replies, "My only problem, Caleb, is you keep callin' me 'Madrid.'"

Caleb snorts, "That's your name, ain't it?"

Then she says, "Not no more. Now . . . the name's *Lancer. Johnny Lancer.*"

Rick goes for the imaginary pistol hanging off his hip, as Trudi on the other end of the receiver yells, "Bang bang bang!"

Rick lets out an excruciating scream as he falls to the linoleum floor of his kitchen, clutching his face as if that's where Johnny shot him.

On the other end of the phone, Trudi asks, "What was that?"

On the floor of his kitchen, Rick tells her, "I acted like I got shot in the face."

She coos an enthusiastic "Oooh, good idea." Then, after a beat, she says, excited, "Hey, man, that was a pretty frickin' good scene!"

Rick sits up from the floor and leans his back against his refrigerator. "Yeah, it was," he agrees.

His scene partner says, "We're going to *kill* this scene tomorrow!"

She's right.

"Yeah," he says, "I think we are."

A moment of silence passes between the two thespians.

Then the younger one reminds him, "Wow, Rick, isn't our job great? We're so lucky, ain't we?"

And for the first time in ten years, Rick realizes how fortunate he is and was. All the wonderful actors he's worked with through the years—Meeker, Bronson, Coburn, Morrow, McGavin, Robert Blake, Glenn Ford, Edward G. Robinson. All the different actresses he got to kiss. All the affairs he had. All the interesting people he got to work with. All the places he got to visit. All the fun stories he got to live. All the times he saw his name and picture in the papers and magazines. All the nice hotel rooms. All the fuss people made over him. All the fan mail he never read. All the times driving through Hollywood as a citizen in good standing. He looks around at the fabulous house he owns. Paid for by doing what he used to do for free when he was a little boy: *pretending to be a cowboy.*

Then he tells Trudi, "Yes we are, Trudi. We're real lucky."

His little scene partner bids him good night. "Good night, Caleb, see you tomorrow."

And a very grateful Rick Dalton says, "Good night, Mirabella, see you tomorrow."

And the next day on the Twentieth Century Fox back lot, on the set of *Lancer*, the two actors knocked 'em dead.

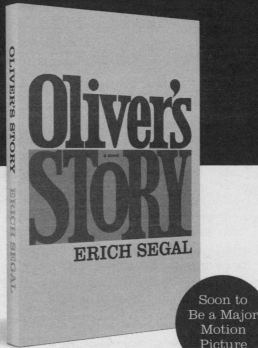

The amazing <u>true</u> <u>story</u> of
the cop who couldn't be bought

SERPICO

by Peter Maas

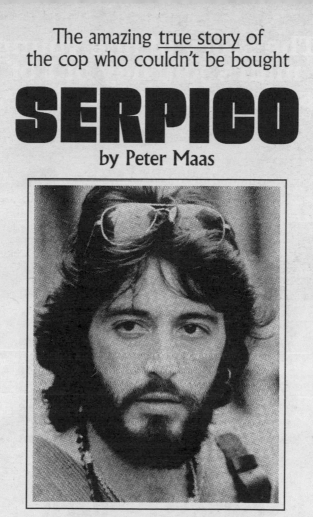

A Dino de Laurentis Picture from Paramount
Starring Al Pacino

Wherever Books Are Sold

Ordell Robbie and Louis Gara
had the perfect plan for a kidnapping
and ransom. The only thing they
didn't count on was a husband
who didn't want his wife back.

So it's time for Plan B...
and the chance to make a real killing.

The Switch

From
Elmore Leonard

the author of *SWAG*
and Mr. *MAJESTYK*

He could tame any horse in the West— until he met his match.

Out now!

$1.50
503-503

RIDE A WILD BRONC

He could tame any horse in the West—
until he met his match.

By
Marvin
H. Albert

Now
Tom Breezy
has one last
job to do—
at the
Savings
& Loan...